THREADER ORIGINS

BOOK ONE OF THE QUANTUM EMPIRICA

GERALD BRANDT

DAW BOOKS, INC.

DONALD A. WOLLHEIM, FOUNDER

1745 Broadway, New York, NY 10019

ELIZABETH R. WOLLHEIM
SHEILA E. GILBERT
PUBLISHERS

www.dawbooks.com

First Printing, January 2021
1 2 3 4 5 6 7 8 9

DAW TRADEMARK REGISTERED
U.S. PAT. AND TM. OFF. AND FOREIGN COUNTRIES
—MARCA REGISTRADA
HECHO EN U.S.A.

PRINTED IN THE U.S.A.

Jared Zane Brandt
Ryan George Brandt

My sons, who have grown to be fine young men. I'm so proud of you two.

Ye cannot live for yourselves; a thousand fibres connect you with your fellow-men, and along those fibres, as along sympathetic threads, run your actions as causes, and return to you as effects.
—Henry Melvill

ECHOES OF SILENCE

HE WAS DYING for the second time this week. The sidewalk swayed under his feet, buckling and tearing, breaking into chunks before his eyes. His gut roiled and he fell first to his knees and then to his hands. His skin stung with a sudden cold that froze the sweat on his back. His shirt hardened and cracked as the ice broke into small pieces and fell to the ground like snow. The concrete sidewalk changed to mud, morphing into frozen winter ice. Grass sprang up between his fingers. The houses disappeared in a wet smear, replaced by fields of low scrub and bogs.

No! This couldn't be happening again.

Darwin Lloyd tumbled to his side. His entire body ached with the pain of hundreds of needles. He held a trembling hand in front of his face, sure that he would see only a mass of blood and bone. Yet it remained intact. He spun it to look at the back and made a fist.

Smooth skin stretched across his knuckles, white from the pressure. They turned red when he spread his fingers out and blood flowed back into flesh. Confusion and fear plucked at the corners of his mind before panic washed it away in a mad rush. He stood, struggling to keep his balance, lurching in the sudden stillness of everything around him, and falling back down. He was afraid to breathe, afraid to run, afraid to stay still.

The concrete sidewalk reappeared, rough and solid under his hands, bringing him back to what was happening. Relief coursed through him. Maybe it was over. He lifted his head and saw ramshackle houses filling the sides of the street instead of the homes he'd grown up with. Some of these were so broken that they used their neighbors for support, leaning against each other like tired old men waiting for the end of days. The relief he'd felt only seconds before deserted him.

Everything sheared again. Tall structures rose around him, glass and steel reaching for the bright blue sky and scattered clouds.

And then it was gone.

His body exploded into a thousand pieces, each one aware of where it was. Of when. He sensed each piece fracture before they exploded into a thousand more fragments. His mind grasped for stability even as it was torn apart by the memories, the sights and smells, the tactile feedback of each part of him, spread across the vast distances of space.

Time became an abstract thing. The tip of his left pinky finger shriveled and wrinkled with age. Part of his elbow grew chubby and dimpled with the fat of a newborn baby. His earlobe disintegrated into dust.

Darwin tried to close his eyes, tried to push away the tens of thousands of sensory inputs that jabbed into his mind. Only pieces of his eyes closed, the rest continuing to feed his visual cortex, pounding it with images that made no sense.

Terror frayed at the edges and along with it, the rest of his mind. Insanity pulled at what was left, peeling away layer upon layer of his identity until all that remained was a tiny core, a sealed unit that shimmered gold, holding the essence of who he was, who he had been. Who he was yet to become.

Reality snapped back into place with the impact and finesse of a sledgehammer. He stood firmly on cement just outside his dad's house. The only thing left to remind him of what had happened was the frozen sweat on his t-shirt and shorts. He fished through his pockets for his house keys, his body on autopilot. Feeling warmth flowing down his face, he wiped at his chin. His fingers came away bloody. He shambled to the front door, the world suddenly dull and bland. Normal. Incomplete.

It had never been this bad before.

Darwin placed his keys into the bowl by the front door. His motions were slow and careful and he could already feel the headache starting to stab deep into his brain. It always happened after an episode, a sharp pain building until all he wanted to do was lie in a dark room and cry. And if the pain wasn't sufficient, the constant buzzing that accompanied it was enough to drive him crazy.

The headache intensified, focusing on a spot behind his left eye. It felt like someone had scooped it out of the socket, poured Tabasco sauce into the gaping hole, and jammed the eyeball back into place. It was still better than being torn into thousands of pieces.

And it was nowhere near as bad as waking up in a hospital after a car accident that stole your mother from you, leaving you scarred and clinging to life—even after being told the truth, that you would never see her again. The doctors had gotten rid of any physical signs of the accident, but he could still see where the scars had cut across his face, even if no one else could.

No one had been able to get rid of the emotional ones, even after years of therapy with different psychologists and psychiatrists. When you were sixteen years old and behind the wheel of a car going seventy-five miles an hour—the reason your mom was dead—those scars ran deeper than anyone knew. Her birthday was only a few days away, and that always brought the guilt to the surface, even after all these years.

The pain in his head intensified, trying to shove the memories of his mother out of its way. He stumbled to the kitchen, the constant guilt he held onto for being alive when she was dead lashing out at him, and splashed cold water on his face. The liquid came back pink. He did it again and again, his fingers trembling, until the water ran clear. He couldn't find where the blood had come from. He grabbed a bottle of Advil from the cupboard and a can of Coke from the fridge to help wash it all down. Placing the can on the counter, he bent over and pressed the ice-cold aluminum against his eye until he saw stars. It didn't help, but it gave him a distraction as he fumbled with the lid of the bottle and poured three pills into his shaking hand.

Grabbing the can off the counter, he shuffled to the living room and stared at the clock on the wall, struggling to bring it into focus. His mom had bought the monstrosity only days before the accident. The minute hand was easily seven inches long, and the hour hand pointed just past what was supposed to be a Roman numeral four. Whoever made the clock didn't know much about Roman numerals; the four was represented by four Is instead of IV. It had always bothered him. When he'd pointed it out to his mother, she'd just laughed and said she hadn't noticed. The time was four thirty-five.

He dropped into a chair and cracked open the can, throwing the pills into his mouth and gulping the carbonated liquid. A hiccup followed the quick swallow, forcing the pills back up into his throat. He swallowed again. Soft drinks always made him hiccup . . . something he had inherited from his mom. It used to drive him nuts, but since she'd died, he just took it in stride.

Mail from the day before sat in a neat pile on the coffee table, brought in by the cleaning crew who showed up every Wednesday. They knew enough to make sure the pile was two inches from the edges of the table and perfectly squared. No one worked for his dad without picking up on his eccentricities. Darwin didn't remember the OCD being a big issue before the accident, but since then, it had gotten worse, and his dad's heavy load at work was only adding to it.

He put the Coke down, using a coaster to protect the wood surface of the table, and pulled the mail pile closer, hoping to find a letter from the university. He was in his fifth year of a bachelor's degree in physics at Princeton and was waiting for the confirmation of the completion of his internship at Quantum Labs. An internship wasn't normal procedure, but with his marks and his dad's reputation, he'd convinced them to treat it as an outside course. He'd planned his final year's workload on getting that letter, and they needed it before the year started. Summer was almost over, and still no letter.

He reached for the can, missing on the first try. Closing an eye to block the blurriness, he aimed for the can again before yanking his hand back with a soft cry. A vaporous cloud wrapped the Coke, a mist that moved and circled like a drop of blood in a glass of water. Fine gossamer threads spun outward from the mist before falling gently back into the swirling mass.

He leaned in to take a closer look, trying to focus on the amorphous image. The entire can looked like it was made of individual wispy threads. Brief streaks of color flashed through it, distinct from the uniform gray of most of the strands. He watched as they wove around each other, slipping through gaps and openings, but never becoming knotted or clumped, never resting, never stopping.

The effect was hypnotic. He moved closer, confused by what he saw, yet pulled in by curiosity. The mail was still clutched in his fingers, forgotten.

He blinked.

Suddenly there were two cans, each shaped by the translucent strands. Through them, he could see the brown liquid swirling, made up of hundreds of fibers of its own, and through that, the wood grain of the table. He blinked again and the image morphed into four cans, gauzy versions of the original. Each vaporous can made up of threads that continued to twine around each other.

He reached for the cans again, hesitating, holding his breath. He couldn't tell which one was the original and which ones were the copies.

Darwin slid his fingers into the threads, not sure what to expect.

Nothing. No resistance, no change in temperature. Just . . . nothing. His fingers moved through them as if they weren't there.

Had he fallen asleep? Was he dreaming? Hallucinating? The images, despite being see-through, looked so real, so life-like.

The gossamer strands changed again and he jerked his fingers back.

A ghost-like hand picked up one can, the sheer fibers lifting into the air as the can rose. The second can wobbled as another wispy hand banged against it, the threads suddenly interacting with each other. Coke spilled from the third can's mouth as it slammed onto its side, knocked over by another hand made out of the finest silk. Darwin stared at the fourth can, concentrating on what was happening to it.

The buzzing in his head stopped with a suddenness that left him dizzy and empty.

Silence poured through him, filling the space left by the constant noise. Pain seared through his eye again, stabbing into his frontal cortex.

He fell forward, his head landing with a thud on the coffee table.

JOURNEY OF FEAR

DARWIN WOKE WITH a start. He pushed himself up and dropped back into the chair. A pool of drool lay on the pristine surface of the table, slowly spreading toward the scattered mail. He lifted the bottom of his t-shirt and wiped it away. The single can of Coke sat where he'd placed it on the coaster. He laid his trembling fingers on it, gently moving them down the smooth metal sides. One part of his mind was sure he was going insane. Another part told him he had just been hallucinating—that everything he remembered was a dream induced by the headache and pills.

His head throbbed like something inside had snapped and broken off, leaving behind a jagged, gaping wound. The pain had moved from behind his eye to the back of his skull, spreading around the sides and over the top.

At least the buzzing was gone.

The oversized clock on the wall said it was nine-thirty. What the hell? His chest tightened, and he couldn't pull in a breath. Where had the time gone?

He picked up the scattered mail with shaking hands, taking another wipe at the drying drool. His dad would be pissed if there was any mess when he got home from another late day at work. He hated if anything was out of place. Darwin took a quick peek at the clock again, gently shaking his head in disbelief. Five hours gone! He straightened the mail back into the original pile left by the maids and grabbed a towel from the kitchen to give the table another wipe down.

He left the Coke can for last.

The can was warm, with not even a hint of sweat on the outside to show it had ever been cold. He fumbled as he lifted it off the table, and he could feel the liquid inside slosh around. He waited until it stopped.

What the hell had he expected, another episode? Maybe it *was* just a dream. He'd fallen asleep and imagined the whole thing. He would almost have believed it, except for the headache left from the incident outside this afternoon.

He used the warm Coke to wash down a couple more Advil before he poured the rest down the drain and tossed the can into the recycling bin. If the headache was still there in the morning, he'd go see his doctor. It had been years since he'd been there. Basically since he had left for university. He was pretty sure he was still a patient. Maybe he'd find a psychologist.

He'd have a talk with his dad as well. Now wasn't a good time, though; there was too much going on at his work, and Darwin didn't want to put any more stress on him.

Taking one more look around to make sure nothing was out of

place, he went up the stairs to his bedroom and crawled into bed, hoping that by morning everything would be back to normal.

He wasn't going to hold his breath.

Darwin opened his eyes to the darkness of a New Jersey morning before the sun had a chance to come up. The opening riffs of Jimi Hendrix's "Purple Haze" filled the room just as his feet hit the floor. Five in the morning. He reached for his phone and turned off the alarm. He wasn't even sure why he set it anymore. The crippling episodes had started last week, and along with them had come the ability to wake up whenever he wanted to, as though part of him was attuned to time itself. He shrugged. It seemed some good always came with the bad. At least his headache was gone, and with it the buzzing. A creak outside his room told him his dad was in the hall-way. It was followed by a knock on the door.

"You coming to work with me today, or are you going to take your own car?" His dad's voice came muffled through the closed door. Another knock. "Hey, bud. You awake?"

The internship at Quantum Labs had him working with his dad. They'd been working on the QPS, the Quantum Power Source proj-ect his dad was spearheading. The machine was a power generating system, able to generate clean power that had the potential to be limitless. A huge chunk of their funding had come from the military, including Darwin's pay. Being an intern had let him get his fingers into almost every aspect of the project, though his main task had been number crunching and programming the monitoring systems for when they powered the thing up. He'd been there six months, and he figured the only person who knew more about the overall systems was his dad.

When he'd applied for the internship, he'd booked the last two weeks of the summer off. He had no friends to visit, that ship had sailed long ago, but he had wanted at least some time to relax before getting back to the grind of university. Because of it, he'd missed the preliminary evaluations of the QPS. The full test was happening today, and he wanted to be there. He wasn't going to miss it after all the work he'd done.

There was another knock on the door, louder this time. "You still coming for today's big test?"

"Yeah. Yeah, I'm up. I'll go in with you if that's okay."

"No problem, but you better move it. I'm leaving in thirty minutes."

"Yeah, I just need to shower."

"Make it quick." The floor creaked again as his dad walked away.

By the time Darwin was done, his dad was already sitting in the minivan waiting. Darwin hit the button on his phone and glanced at the screen. Damn, he had taken thirty-one minutes. His dad was a stickler for being on time; it was part of his OCD and difficult for him to control. It had been particularly tough when Darwin was a teenager. Everything was, especially after the accident, but they'd both worked hard and made it through that. Darwin set the house alarm and locked the door behind him, sprinting past his car to the van.

He pulled open the passenger door and dropped into the front seat. Even though he'd moved out of the house for university, his dad still gave him *the look*. Darwin tried to pretend it didn't bother him, smiling at his dad to cover it up, but he wasn't sure it worked. From the time of the accident to when he'd left for university, his dad hadn't let him sit in the front, saying it was safer in the back seat. Darwin didn't like it then, and he didn't like it now. His dad didn't say anything about it, though.

"I'm so glad you're coming back today. We've both worked hard to get this project off the ground. Hell, the whole team has, but having you with me . . ." He paused and cleared his throat. "This project means more to me than I've said. If it works—"

"It'll work, Dad. The preliminary tests had to have gone well, or you wouldn't be running the full ones today." It was Darwin's turn to pause as a look of irritation crossed his dad's face. "Sorry I interrupted, what were you going to say?"

"Nothing. I just . . . your mother would have been so proud of you."

Darwin felt as though his dad had wanted to say more, but he knew better than to push. He couldn't remember the last time he had even mentioned his mom.

"I know," was all he said. He'd joined the physics department at Princeton because he knew it was what she would have wanted, knew how much joy she would have gotten in seeing *her two boys* work together. It had also, surprisingly, brought him and his dad closer. He hadn't thought that was possible. Through all the surgeries and psychiatric sessions, as his school friends slowly stopped visiting, stopped caring, his dad had been there. Always willing to listen, or to talk, or to just sit in silence.

"Unfortunately, you won't be able to do much more than watch," his dad said. "Two weeks is a long time to be away from a project, and you're not an intern anymore."

Darwin nodded as his dad turned on the car radio. A shrill soprano voice belted opera over the speakers. He jammed his ear buds into place and turned up the volume on his phone, smiling as he tried to tune out the screeching. Some things would never change. He'd gotten his mom's taste in music, thank god.

Thinking of her brought in more memories. She was never far from his thoughts, but this close to her birthday it was as if the accident had happened only yesterday, and the guilt and loss surged back to the forefront. He knew his dad had blamed him for the accident. Hell, he still blamed himself. They had both healed over time, even though some pain never went away. Through it all, they had grown closer as—for him anyway—the rest of the world had faded away.

Mom had been gone seven years, and he still missed her. He couldn't remember what she looked liked—somehow the pictures on the wall beside the clock in the living room were different than what his mind conjured. Still, at night, he would sometimes wake from a dream smelling her hair from when she gave him hugs—apple blossom and vanilla—and feeling her arms around him.

She'd always given the best hugs in the world. They had made him feel safe. It was the single memory that he still carried with him every day.

The van bumped out of the driveway onto the dark street and crawled toward the expressway at a blistering twenty miles per hour. Why did he decide not to take his own car again? They picked up speed when they hit the expressway, but nowhere near the posted limit.

Several songs later, Darwin felt the van slow down and pull off the expressway. He removed the ear buds and turned off the music.

The Quantum Labs building stood across a small grassy boulevard planted with the occasional tree and a parking lot meant for visitors and upper management. Regular staff parked in the back. This early in the morning, most of the building was still dark.

The place had always given him the creeps. When he was kid, he had imagined the eight-story glass and steel structure waking up at night and lumbering on multiple stubby legs, hungry for whatever was in its path. This morning the glass reflected the rising sun, making it bleed red in small undulating waves.

It wasn't the glass that bothered him, though; it was the entrance. Massive black stones wrapped the recessed, black steel doors. No matter what time of day it was, the rock seemed to suck the light into it. This morning the rippling red blood seeped into its open maw.

Darwin held back a shudder. He was too old to be imagining kid stuff.

The Quantum Labs logo, an italicized Q with the tail formed by an uppercase L, shimmered blue above the doors. It was the only splash of color on the black. His dad pulled into a spot across from the entrance, just past the visitor parking stalls. A few of the other spots had cars in them, including the ones reserved for the owners right by the door. Out of place was a single vehicle taking up a visitor's spot. Military by the look of it. There must be meetings before the full power test.

"We're going to see history made today," his dad said. "When we push the QPS to full power, all of the world's energy problems will disappear. Poof! Just like that. Even the smallest hovel in Africa will have enough power to air-condition their backyard."

Darwin sighed. His dad had buried himself in this project for the last five years, and seemed to have fallen out of touch with the real world. "I wouldn't use that one at the press conference, Dad. I kinda doubt anyone who lives in a hovel in Africa," he made quotation marks in the air with his fingers, "has a backyard. Or an air-conditioner."

"No, I guess not. I won't be talking anyway, that will be up to the executive and whoever the military sends. I'm just the worker bee on this one."

"You're more than that. Without you, this project wouldn't have made it. There's a lot of you in every piece of software and hardware in the QPS."

His dad's steps faltered for a second before he continued to the front entrance.

Darwin forced a smile onto his face, the same thing he did every morning when he worked here, and followed his dad inside.

The reception area was airy and open, a stark contradiction to the outside of the building. The early morning sunlight, filtered through the tinted glass and mixed with the LEDs high above them, lit the space with a warm glow that contrasted with the sterile chrome and glass balcony that wrapped around the open atrium on two sides. A wide staircase curved down to connect the balcony with the main floor. The Quantum Labs logo hung from the ceiling, suspended on two thin, quivering cables. It swayed slightly in an otherwise unseen breeze.

Behind the dark wood counter that spanned the room, the only natural item in the atrium, sat two receptionists, one typing on his computer as if it were the only thing in the world that mattered, and the other looking up and smiling as they walked in. They'd probably been asked to come in early because his dad's bosses were already in.

The smiling receptionist stood as they got near. "Good morning, Mr. Lloyd. We have Darwin's guest pass ready. If he could sign in here." She held the tablet out to Darwin. "Please verify the information is correct, and then sign on the dotted line at the bottom."

He took the tablet and reached across the screen to unclip the stylus with his left hand, signing at the bottom without reading it, and passed it back. The receptionist slid a clip-on guest pass over the counter, the *QL* logo emblazoned across the top in blue metallic ink. Two weeks ago as an intern he'd had his own pass and could go almost anywhere in the building. Now he had to have an escort.

"Please wear this at all times while in the building, and return it when you leave."

She sat back down, her job done, and ignored both of them.

Darwin followed his dad to a frosted glass door under the sweeping staircase and waited while he swiped a security card through the reader. The door buzzed and he pushed it open, leading Darwin through the bright white corridors to his office.

Garth, Dad's second-in-command, was waiting for them, his tall frame leaning against the wall and a thick folder in his hands. Beside him stood Rebecca. A long curl of hair had slipped from her normally tight bun, and though Darwin had worked with her on the project, he was shocked at how red it looked under the LED lights of the hallway.

Garth's tie hung loose below the undone top button of his shirt. He looked like he hadn't slept in weeks. When he saw Darwin, he smiled and waved as Rebecca turned and walked away.

"Hi, Darwin, how ya doing? I forgot you were coming in today. The monitoring system you wrote for us is working great," Garth said.

He clapped Darwin on the back as they followed his dad into the office. Darwin forced himself to not pull away from the touch, instead using the learned smile to respond to the greeting.

Garth lost his grin, turning all business in less than a step. "Henry, I'm not sure we should run a full test today."

"Why on earth not?" His dad's voice sounded shrill and too loud for the enclosed space.

Darwin sat down, tuning the arguing men out. Arguing, even if he wasn't involved, always brought his reclusive tendencies to the forefront.

His dad's office was the same as it had always been. The L-shaped desk in the corner looked like it had never been used. Three pens lay beside the computer's keyboard, each perfectly square to the desk's edge and an inch away from its neighbor. A framed picture of his mother sat to the right of the computer's display. The round table Darwin settled down at took up another corner, the six chairs around it spaced evenly apart. Uncommonly, a stack of schematics and other documents sat on the table. It was a neat stack, perfectly centered, of course.

He picked the top document off the pile and scanned it. Computer code. It wasn't from his monitoring system, or any of the other systems he had worked on. The rest of the papers in the stack looked like they were QPS related, so he figured it must be some internal routines. He flipped the page. A long chunk of code grabbed his attention. Most of it was a random-looking block made up of four letters, and ran for pages.

```
string accession = "NT_011387";
short version = 9;
long reference_id = UNSPECIFIED;
string reference_name = "EL";
string genome = "TGTTCAGTCGGGCAGGGAGTGGGAATAGACAAGAC
                 CACAAGCAGCTTGGTGCCTCTGAAAGGGAGAGGGG
                 TGGAGGGGAGACTAGAGAGGTGGGTAGGAATACTG
                 GATTCCACTGACCACGTGCTGGATGTCATGCTTAG
                 CCCTCCTGCTCTGTGCCAGGTTAGGCACCTGGTGT
                 TTTACATATATTATATTACATTCTATTACAGACAA
                 CTCCATAGCAATCCTTTCCTCTCCATTCCATTTCT
                 CTCCACTCCATCCCATTCCATTCCACTCCCTTCAT
                 . . .
```

He drew the paper closer. He was more a mathematician/physicist than a geneticist, but he recognized a DNA sequence when he saw one.

"Yesterday's runs were clean." His dad's voice was raised again, drawing him back into the conversation. "Our four-thirty test was the best yet. We all agreed today would be the day."

Darwin sat straighter in his chair, suddenly paying more attention, the DNA sequence forgotten. Four-thirty was pretty close to yesterday's episode, just before he went into the house and fell asleep and had the weird dream about the Coke cans.

"I know, but I took another look at the readings last night." Garth opened the folder he was holding, placing it on the desk and pushing the pens out of the way. He pointed at the papers inside. "Look here, right when we went to seventy percent. The quantum force isn't as uniform as we'd predicted. We're starting to see fluctuations."

"You're not the only one who went over the data last night. Those values are still inside the calculated norms." Dad reached for his pens to straighten them out.

"They are, but each time we raise the power, the fluctuations increase. They'll be pushed right to the boundaries if we go to one hundred percent. This is uncharted territory. What if our calculations are wrong?"

"I agree they're close, but I still think we'll be fine. Those values were conservatively calculated, so if we're inside them, we still have a safety margin. You know that. Besides, if we don't run a full test today, management will be breathing down both our necks. We're over budget and months behind schedule. We have to show them something. If we don't, they may pull funding." His dad paused. "I think we'll move forward with the test."

Darwin could tell his dad was tense. He was sitting straighter in his chair and struggling not to reach for Garth's folder to straighten out the papers.

"Henry—"

"Look," his dad said. "Run through the values again. As long as we're within the one percent margin of error, we'll go ahead as planned. Anything else and we'll wait, okay?"

"Okay. It'll take some time." Garth sighed in frustration as he picked the folder up off the desk and turned to leave. "Enjoy your day, Darwin."

Darwin's dad put the pens back in order before turning around. "Make yourself comfortable. We won't run the tests until Garth has gone through all the numbers."

"You want me to help him?" Darwin asked.

"No. You don't have the clearance anymore. I had to pull some strings just to get you in for this test."

A wave of disappointment washed through him, and he pushed it away. He knew something like this would happen when he'd left, but hadn't expected how it would make him feel. He switched tracks, hoping to get his dad talking.

"Okay. Hey, Dad? What's with this DNA sequence mixed in with the QPS code?" He held up the printout and pointed at it.

"What?" His dad jumped from the chair and grabbed the document out of Darwin's hands. "That's . . . that's nothing. It's a completely different project. You shouldn't have seen it, it's highly classified. Damn cleaners." He opened a drawer in his desk and jammed the printout inside before sitting back down, touching and moving each pen multiple times to make sure they were aligned properly. He did the same thing with his keyboard and monitor.

Darwin leaned forward in his chair, his mouth hanging open. He'd never seen his dad so flustered that he didn't care where something went. Throwing the paper in a drawer and closing it was so far beyond normal that he wouldn't have believed it if he hadn't seen it, and that was probably why his dad was regressing to excessive behavior with everything else.

His dad's back was ramrod straight, making Darwin too nervous to ask any more questions. His dad gradually regained control, slowing down the furtive movements, before finally turning the monitor on.

Darwin fought the urge to approach him, to try to help in some way. Past experience had taught him it was better to leave his dad alone when he got this agitated. He would calm down eventually, and they would both pretend nothing out of the ordinary had happened.

"You can go visit the other teams, if you want. I can have our new intern walk you around. Can't have a visitor unescorted, you know."

The thought of having to interact with the people he'd worked with made his insides feel like they'd shriveled into a ball. He could do it when he had to, when it was his job, but just visiting them because he was here was out of the question.

"No, I'm okay. I'll just wait here until you're ready."

"Suit yourself."

Apparently they had both learned how to best deal with each other's issues over the last few years. Darwin pulled out his phone and plugged in his ear buds again, starting on a new playlist while his dad worked. He opened with some Ry Cooder "Vigilante Man" and Eric Clapton. It was old, but he'd fallen in love with it as much as his mom had.

He hadn't been an outgoing person before the accident, and after she'd died, he'd practically turned into a hermit. Her music had been the only thing that kept him going during the early days when he'd lain in the hospital bed staring at the light blue ceiling with its flickering fluorescent bulbs. Whoever thought a sixty hertz power supply was adequate hadn't been thinking about the refresh rate of crappy lighting.

Over the years, he'd added some new music to the list, stuff like Rag'n'Bone Man and Robert Johnson. The psychiatrists had said the music was his way of escaping, of getting away from anything that made him uncomfortable. Mainly people. Maybe that was true, but he didn't care.

He was almost through his playlist by the time his dad was ready.

Despite his best efforts, he wasn't able to get his dad's reaction out of his head, but the only thing he could think of talking about was Garth's worry over the numbers.

"What if the test fails?" Darwin asked.

His dad looked at him like he was nuts. "You went through a fair amount of the math when you worked here. Do you think it will fail?"

Darwin shrugged. He didn't have the results of the previous runs. How was he supposed to know? But now, he wanted to look through them. He followed his dad through another set of security doors and past small labs assigned to other projects before heading down into the basement. He'd had a brief stint with the quantum internet project before he'd moved to the QPS. One of the people on that project waved as he walked past. He pretended he hadn't seen it.

At the entrance to the lab, a rack of blue anti-static smocks stood ready to be used. His dad grabbed two, shoving one into Darwin's hands before putting on his own.

The lab hadn't changed much since he was last here. With the testing going live, he had somehow imagined it would be a bit different.

"I don't think the QPS was fully assembled last time you were here. It's powered up, if you want to see it. Not much to look at really. It's right through the window over there." He turned his back on Darwin, facing a large bank of monitors. "Hey, Garth, are we ready?"

Garth towered above the dozen or so people moving around the room, watching everything that was going on around him.

"Ready when you are. The fluctuations are within point two percent."

Darwin moved to the window looking into the partitioned lab space. On the other side of the clear glass sat a simple gray box about the size of a small car. Wires ran out of it in bundles, connecting in a large sheath before entering the wall with the window. They didn't come directly out his side. A single thick cable rose out of the top of the QPS and lost itself in the trusses and conduits on the ceiling. The Quantum Labs logo glowed blue on its side, seeming to jump off the dull gray of the machine. It looked smaller fully assembled than he thought it would.

"The recorders are running," said Garth.

"Okay. Bring her up to fifty percent and let's check the readings," Dad said.

The pain in Darwin's head started right away, followed by the incessant buzzing that had accompanied it for the last two weeks. The noise started low, as a simple background hum he could easily ignore, before moving into a range that filled the room and forced its way to the foreground. He reached for his pocket, realizing that in the morning rush, he'd forgotten to refill his daily stash of Advil.

"Hey, Dad, is it the QPS making that sound?"

"Hmm, what sound?" His dad stared at the numbers flashing across the displays in front of him. "It doesn't make any noise, Son. You're imagining things."

"Fifty percent and holding," said Garth.

"We knew we could do that. Let's move her up to seventy-five percent."

"Higher than yesterday?"

"That's our goal, isn't it, to finally go to one hundred?"

The buzzing in Darwin's head increased with the pain, and the voices in the lab sounded hollow and distant. For the first time, the buzz was directional. He turned to face the sound, leaning on the windowsill, and focused on the machine. There was no indication it was even working.

The glass cracked and he stumbled back.

The window shattered, throwing shards into the lab. He ducked instinctively and turned his back on the flying projectiles before twisting around to stare at the empty frame and the QPS behind it.

The machine was wrapped in a fine mist that billowed into a thick fog. The surface roiled and threads shot out before collapsing back into the cloud, coiling gently across the surface only to shoot out again like solar flares. It was the Coke can all over again, but stronger, more vivid.

He blinked and suddenly the QPS room was filled with people in blue smocks. Unlike the one his dad had handed to him, these were dirty and the cuffs had been worn down to almost nothing. Wispy threads snaked out from the machine's surface, reaching out and caressing the group, swirling around each individual in intricate patterns before they passed on to the next person. Darwin's stomach clenched and his heart pounded. He couldn't have another episode. Not here. Not now.

The image solidified into crisp detail. A woman with red hair seemingly controlled the threads moving between all the people . . . twelve of them standing in a circle around the machine. The people blurred once again. Two stood out from the rest, their dark wavy hair and gray eyes matching his memories of his mother. The threads linking them to the machine looked thicker than the others. His mind refused to believe what it saw, knowing it to be as impossible as dry water or good-tasting sushi.

"Go to full power. Keep an eye on the readings."

His dad's voice cut through the hornet's nest in his head, sounding like a distant echo of the real thing.

Darwin spun. "Stop! There are people in there." Couldn't he see for himself? Didn't he care?

The lab sheared and became two. Both labs shifted again and then there were four. Then eight. Each lab was different, juxtaposed over the others, making the differences stand out more than the similarities. The pain in his head surged.

This was different. It was as though this time, the images he was seeing were being controlled . . . guided by an invisible hand. He leaned against the window frame again, his legs suddenly weak.

The wood frame changed to metal under his fingers. Glass filled it again. Embedded in the glass was a fine mesh of wires, strengthening it. Without warning, the wall disappeared and he stumbled forward into the QPS room. The floor changed to grass, then snow, then steel before disappearing into a pit of nothing. He fell into the murky abyss, feeling the pull of a thousand hooks on his body, wanting to tear him into shreds and spread the pieces throughout the universe. His mind fractured and time slowed.

Something grabbed him, gathering the pieces, holding him together in a warm cocoon of light. Pulling him back to reality.

The world snapped back into focus. He was in the QPS room, on the other side of the wall to the lab, his back to the broken window. He wheeled around, tripping over his own feet, staring through the shattered glass. His dad's lab was constructed of the misty threads. Through them, he could see other images, the other labs.

In one image, equipment lay shattered and ruined on the floor. In another, people lay around the room, either dead or unconscious, and the displays flickered into oblivion. In the third, maybe the fourth, his dad typed feverishly at a console, deep in concentration. He had a beard, long and scraggly and unkempt, streaked with white. He looked like he hadn't slept or eaten in days.

Threads made of the finest gossamer, thin and translucent, moved in a dance that wove around everything, flowing through the empty spaces between the equipment, tying the disparate images into a living whole.

Chanting voices made him turn back to the QPS. Unlike his dad's lab behind him, there was only one image here. The blue smocks of the people were covered by cloaks of threaded light, moving and curling in patterns that never repeated. One person left the chanting circle, pulling several of the threads along with him as though they were obeying his commands. Darwin stood mesmerized as the remaining figures followed. He felt himself pulled inexorably toward them.

Ice shot through his veins and his breath froze in his lungs. Crystals of cold covered his eyes, fracturing everything he saw.

A blur stepped in front of him, and he forced his eyes closed and open again. An eternity for a task that should have taken milliseconds. Threads shifted in front of him, revealing a face. A mass of auburn hair fell forward, briefly covering soft brown eyes. He realized it was a woman. He'd seen her before, but he couldn't remember where. Her forehead was creased in confusion as she hesitantly reached out and touched his arm.

Red hot pain seared through his head, pushing daggers of fire into his mind. He fell forward, the concrete floor of the QPS room looming in his sight before the world turned black.

Darwin felt a cool hand caress his forehead, tracing one of his old scars down his cheek to his chin as if the person doing it could see through the plastic surgeon's work. The sensation of being pulled from a dark well flooded him, and the hand was removed.

"He wakes."

A soft voice. Feminine.

Memories of his mother filtered to the front of his mind, of her gentle touch when he was hurt, of the loss he'd endured when she had died, which he still felt. For a brief moment he thought he smelled vanilla. He forced his eyes open. A flash of bright light was quickly replaced by a halo of dark red hair falling toward him. He blinked, once, twice, struggling to bring everything into focus. The face above him creased into a gentle smile, the fleeting look of concern vanishing as if it had never existed.

"Hello, Darwin. Can you sit up? You hit your head pretty hard against the window frame when you fell."

He pulled back before reaching up to touch his forehead. His fingers came away bloody.

"Wait," she said. "We need to get the cut cleaned up. We can have a healer come in to take a look at it."

"A . . . a healer?"

"Yes." Her brow creased slightly. "Ah, of course, a doctor. It's been so long."

He pushed himself upright. His head swam with a sudden wave of dizziness and nausea. He forced himself to focus on the window behind the woman with red hair, trying to push through the queasiness. There was no glass in the frame, or on the floor. Everything looked blurry. Dim curls of light, the last remnants of the wisps he had seen earlier, swam through his vision before slowly fading away.

"What happened? Where's my dad?" He struggled to look through the wall of blue smocks surrounding him in a loose circle. Through the gaps he could see desks and computer equipment, but it was different. Nothing was turned on. Half of the fluorescent tubes in the ceiling were on, the others dark or broken.

He looked over the woman's shoulder and saw the top of the flat gray box. A portion of the blue *QL* logo glowed, barely visible from his angle.

"Dad?" Panic rushed in and he started to shake, his muscles twitching uncontrollably. Shifting his weight, he forced himself onto his knees. The pain in his head almost made him sit down again. Another wave of nausea rolled through him and he squatted back down on his heels, his chin lowered to his chest as he drew in long slow breaths.

On his third inhalation, reality hit like a cresting wave, driving him to his hands and knees. His breathing was no longer deep, but short shallow sips. The air tasted musty, filling his mouth and nose.

The smocks. The anti-static jackets were filthy and tattered. Just like he'd seen through the window before it exploded.

Where was his dad?

"Dad?" His voice sounded sharp, cracking at the edges as fear clutched at him. He couldn't stop the uncontrollable shaking taking over his body. *"Dad!"*

"Your father isn't here, Darwin."

Hands pulled on his shoulders until he was sitting on his heels again, holding him steady as his body continued to betray him. The woman with the dark red hair crouched down in front of him. Recognition flickered through Darwin's mind again, disappearing as fast as it came.

"There's a lot you—and we—need to know, but first we need to get you calmed down and get that cut in your forehead taken care of before it gets infected. Take a deep breath and let it out slowly. You're hyperventilating."

Black spots danced in front of his vision as he drew in another shaky breath and held it before slowly releasing it through his mouth. He did it again, and the spots faded. His body still vibrated, twitching under the skin.

"That's it, nice and slow."

After a few breaths his nausea subsided, but the panic squeezing his chest refused to let go.

"Good. Can you stand? We'll get you upstairs and fix you up. Do you think some water would help?"

She stood without waiting for him to answer and beckoned two men from the loose circle around him. They reached under Darwin's arms, pulling him roughly to his feet. The room tilted and the black spots threatened at the edge of his vision again.

"Be careful, he's our guest." Her soft voice became rougher and commanding as she looked at the two men. "Bring him upstairs. Put him in the big front office. Wait outside the door for the healer."

The two men turned Darwin around and walked him out of the lab to the stairs. Even with the almost irresistible fear that still threatened to take over, he noticed some of the equipment was missing. The large overhead displays were nothing but empty brackets on the ceiling, and at some of the desks only a pool of wires lay on the dusty tops. Just as they left the lab, he heard the woman's voice again.

"Somebody tell me what the hell just happened."

His feet caught the bottom stair up to the main level and the two men took his weight with a grunt, carrying him most of the way up. He couldn't seem to get his brain to work properly. The hallway at the top was lit, but every second fixture was off, leaving the space darker than he was used to. The men led him past his dad's office—the only thing to show it used to contain furniture was the indentations in the carpet—and through the frosted security door to the front atrium. The sudden light coming from the windows made his eyes water as he was dragged to the staircase and hauled up to the second-story balcony. They led him to a large room at the front of the building and put him inside, closing the door as they left. He heard the faint scraping and thud of a lock driving home.

One entire wall of the office was glass with an impressive view. He could see over the trees surrounding the parking lot, out to the expressway and beyond into the next industrial park.

No cars moved. A few sat in the parking lot below him and there were a couple on the expressway, the sun glinting off their windshields.

Everything looked as still as a photograph.

PROBABILITIES, POSSIBILITIES, AND THEORIES

DARWIN PULLED HIMSELF away from the window and tried the door. It was definitely locked. He banged and kicked at it, rattling the door in its frame. "Let me out! Let me see my dad."

For a while, the two men who carried him up and then stood guard just outside his door ignored him, until one of them finally broke, kicking the door so hard it almost buckled. Darwin jerked away and tripped over his own feet, landing on his back and sending more pain through his head.

He picked himself off the floor and moved to a second door in the side wall. This one opened easily and he walked into an executive washroom. No water came from the taps when he tried, and the toilet bowl was empty and dry. He left, leaving the door open behind him, and retreated to the window, lowering himself into a fancy mesh-backed chair, the kind all the high-tech firms brag about having, and swiveling to look out the floor-to-ceiling window. The sun had started to move behind the Quantum Labs building, casting a shadow across the parking lot.

The strangeness of what had happened sank its claws deeper in him. What he saw told him he was still in the Quantum Labs building, still at his dad's work, but everything else told him the opposite. It felt and smelled different. The darkened hallway lights. The empty office. The lack of any movement on what should have been a busy expressway. By the shadows outside, it was past lunchtime, and he was already mentally and physically exhausted.

The moment he let the exhaustion take control he started to vibrate again. He closed his eyes, trying to control his ragged breathing. There was no one in the lab that he recognized, and he knew almost everyone working on the QPS project. Where was his dad? Darwin couldn't see him leaving his son behind, no matter how desperate the work was. He wouldn't leave his project either, especially to strangers. Not one that he had worked so hard on, that had done everything this one had. But . . . when he had yelled about the broken window, there had been no response. What if his dad hadn't seen anything? What if all of what was happening was in his head?

He took his phone out of his pocket with an unsteady hand. There was only one contact in it, his dad's. He unlocked the device and dialed the number. Nothing happened. He tried again before realizing there was no signal. What the hell was going on? There was always service here.

The pain in his head had turned into a dull throb, culminating in the bump. He tried the door again, quietly turning the knob, hoping the two men outside wouldn't hear what he was doing. It was still locked. He slid down the wall beside the door and plugged his ear buds into his ears, old habits returning as if they had never left. They hadn't, really. As the sounds of B.B. King slid into his consciousness, he could feel some of the tension ease from his body. Still, underneath the music, the faint buzzing kept on. He kept going over what was happening, trying to boil it down to the facts he knew, that he could verify. The only ones he had were what had happened to him directly.

As soon as Garth had started the QPS, his headache kicked in and the buzzing noise had started. That tied the episodes he'd been having directly back to the QPS. But how was that possible? And what did the episodes mean? The last one, the one in the lab, had been different than the rest. Different enough for his dad to take off somewhere and leave him behind?

None of it made sense. He was going crazy trying to figure out what the hell was going on. If he wasn't there already.

By the time his music stopped, he still hadn't figured anything out. It was as if the world had turned upside down and inside out, and he was the only one that had made it through.

He checked for a signal again before turning the phone off. In the distance, he could see a cell tower. Close enough that he should have gotten at least three bars, if not more. He turned his phone on again to double check. Maybe it just needed a reset. It didn't work, still showing no service. None of this was making sense.

He didn't know how long he sat there, watching the shadows creep across the boulevard and past the trees. Eventually, he got up and moved to the mesh-backed chair, his back stiff from leaning against the wall for so long. Every time he tried to figure out what was going on, he fell deeper and deeper into a funk. He did notice what it was about the view outside that bothered him so much, more than the lack of cars or people. Everything looked wild. Untamed. The once manicured lawn surrounding the parking lot was tall and uncut. It had encroached into the parking space, leaving an uneven edge of dirt and weeds on the concrete. In places, he could still see the sharp edge of the curb through the green. Even the expressway wasn't free of the encroachment. Trees and grasses had taken hold in the small cracks, clinging to life in the harsh environment, and grown outward from there. And he was pretty sure there were more trees growing out of the roof of the office building across the gray expanse. Even some of its windows looked broken and empty. It was as if everyone had given up.

The sound of the lock sliding open behind him wrenched him from his near catatonic state. He heard the door open and shut softly. When the lock thunked home again, he turned in his chair and silently watched a man walk toward him.

"Hi, Darwin. I'm here to look at the cut on your head."

The man's voice was deep and strong, the complete opposite to the tall and skinny frame it came from. He wasn't carrying anything. Darwin wasn't sure what he expected, but at the very least one of those white first aid boxes you could find in any office building.

He reached for his head, stopping his hand before it touched. It had been so long, he'd almost forgotten about it already. He forced himself to fight his natural desire to stay silent around people he didn't know. "What am I doing here? Where's my dad?"

The man sat on the edge of the desk, looking at Darwin with a grin on his face. "I'd say you're sitting in a chair and staring out the window. I can't be sure that's what you were doing before I came in here, but it fits the probability curve."

Darwin felt his blood start to boil. Who the hell did this guy think he was, making jokes when he had been locked in this room most of the day?

"That's not what I mean." His voice rose and he took a deep breath to get it back under control. "Why am I here? Why is the door locked? Who are you people? Where is my dad? What's going on outside? Where is everyone?" As the questions tumbled from his mouth, his voice rose again. "I want answers."

The smile left the man's face. "Whoa, one question at a time. I'm not allowed to answer everything, but I'll do what I can."

"Not allowed?"

"Rebecca hasn't given permission."

"Who's Rebecca?"

"Another question? A wise man once told me you learn more by listening than by talking."

Darwin had his mouth open to ask another question, and caught himself, quickly closing it, no longer able to keep talking to a stranger. He leaned back in the chair, creating a wider gap between them. Who did this guy think he was, trying to tell him what to do? It was easy to bite down on the retort his brain had created. Instead of talking, he took the opportunity to study the man. The fact that he was tall and skinny was obvious, as was the mop of brown hair that fell over his face, but it was his eyes that caught Darwin's attention. They were a brilliant blue and seemed to hold a twinkle, as though he was just on the verge of telling a joke.

The silence in the room thickened as they stared at each other.

"My name is Michael." He paused as if expecting some response, and smiled when none came. "To answer some of your questions, I have no idea how you got here. It is beyond anything we've seen before. As for where you are, you should know. You're in the old Quantum Labs building, sitting in your father's chair."

Darwin's gaze swept around the office space. What the hell was this guy talking about? "This isn't Dad's office. His is on the main floor, near the back of the building. He always says he gets more work done if he's far away from his bosses."

Michael stood and tilted Darwin's cut toward the light. Darwin jerked back at the touch before deciding to hold still.

"Hmm." Michael's fingers probed around the bump and Darwin winced. "Hold still. The cut isn't bad. You've got a bit of a goose egg, but time will take care of that."

Darwin grabbed Michael's wrist and pulled his hand away. "What do you mean *hmm*? What's going on around here? Why haven't I seen anyone I recognize?"

Michael twisted out of Darwin's loose grip and crouched down so they were at the same height. His voice lowered to barely a whisper and the smile in his eyes turned to concern. "I can't answer your questions now. I simply don't have the information, and they may be listening." He threw a glance over his shoulder to the closed door. "Look, just don't trust them. The Qabal deal in shadows and deceit and lies. Do. Not. Trust. Them."

The last words were spoken through clenched teeth with a ferocity that took Darwin by surprise. He leaned forward to ask another question when the sound of someone at the door made Michael stand up, the smile coming back to his face.

"Who are you?" asked Darwin.

Michael pulled a small bottle of water and gauze from his pocket. So far, the only first aid equipment Darwin had seen. He wet the gauze and placed it on Darwin's forehead, squeezing water onto the dried blood. He didn't answer the question. The door opened and one of the men who had brought Darwin upstairs walked in.

"How long does it take to heal a cut?" the man asked.

Michael faced the man and a hard edge entered his voice. "When I'm done, I'll let you know."

"Well, make it quick." The man stood in the doorway watching Michael clean up the blood.

"Hold still now, Darwin. I'll just close the cut. The bump will be gone in a couple of days, and there won't be any bruising." Michael dropped his hands and his eyes lost their focus.

Darwin felt a sudden tingle around the wound. It stopped as quickly as it started.

"Here are a couple of pills. They'll help with the headache. I had to fight to get those for you, they're getting harder to find."

Darwin took the pills and dry swallowed them.

Michael threw the wet gauze, now pink with Darwin's blood, into the garbage can beside the desk and put the water back into the pocket of his blue anti-static jacket. Both men left the room without saying another word. Darwin was alone again. In the silence, he heard the lock drive home.

He touched his forehead and felt only the bump. The cut seemed to have disappeared. He pulled his hand away and stood, leaning into the window hoping to find his reflection in the glass. Outside, the shadows deepened. He thought he saw a flicker of blue at the edge of the parking lot, but when he looked at it directly it disappeared.

He raised his fingers to the cut again. Where had it gone?

Darwin twitched awake, the chair under him shifting with the sudden movement. He hadn't realized he'd fallen asleep, and a sense of dread settled on his shoulders. Had someone come in while he was out? Had he missed a chance to find out what was going on? He pulled his phone from his pocket, powered it on and looked at the time. It was just after eight thirty p.m.

The door opened and Darwin realized it was the sound of the lock moving that had woken him. He must not have been sleeping that deeply, which was a relief.

The smell of food wafting in from the open door made his stomach grumble. He followed the reflection from the door in the black window, watching his mother carry a tray toward him. He spun in his chair and the teenager holding the tray almost tripped, the look of fear and curiosity in her eyes etched into every fiber of her being.

Looking directly at her, he could see why her distorted reflection had tricked him. She had the same dark, wavy hair, and behind the fear, he could see his mother's soft gray eyes. This had happened to him before, early on in his recovery process after the accident, where he had seen his mother in the distance only to realize it wasn't her. That it would never be her. This time the resemblance was uncanny. He put on one of his forced smiles, hoping it would make her feel better. It didn't seem to work.

The door behind her stayed open, light flooding into his darkened room from the entryway behind it. He resisted the sudden urge to jump out of the chair and bolt for the door, quickly tamping it down, following the pattern of years of trying to be inconspicuous and quiet, to blend into the background as much as possible and not be noticed.

The girl placed the tray on the desk, staring at him for a moment longer before turning to rush out of the room, turning on the lights as she closed the door. It seemed to Darwin as if she had wanted to ask him a question. Once the door was closed and locked again, he examined what she had brought him.

The food looked delicious. Two slices of buttered bread with potatoes and two baked chicken legs. The carrots were fresh and cooked to the point where they still had a bit of a crunch to them. The smell set his mouth watering, and he realized he hadn't had anything to eat all day. Despite his hunger, it was the chipped mug that sat beside the plate that held his attention. He leaned in and stared at the black liquid inside it. Coffee! He pulled the cup closer and lowered his head over the steam rising from it, breathing in deeply, and let out a huge sigh. Just what the doctor ordered.

It wasn't until he tasted it that he realized it wasn't coffee. It looked and smelled like it, but the taste was way off. He drank it anyway.

In spite of the food's appearance, the taste was bland. At least it was hot, and the crappy coffee—or whatever it was—helped wash it down. A bit of salt and pepper would have gone a long way.

It had been ages since a couple of pieces of chicken and some potatoes and carrots could fill him up, but as he leaned back in his chair sipping the last of the black liquid in the coffee cup, grimacing at its flavor as it cooled down, he felt better than he had since getting to this place. He gave in to the thoughts running through his head, something he'd avoided for most of the day.

He was still at Quantum Labs—that much was obvious. But where was everybody? Just before everything went at a right angle, his dad had been running tests and the lab had been full of people. And where was his dad? Why were they being kept apart? Was it his dad's choice? He found that hard to believe, throwing the thought away as soon as it had formed. They had passed his office, and it was empty, and that Michael guy had called *this* his dad's office. What was with that? It was one more thing that didn't fit.

What exactly had happened down in the lab? The test had gone to full power and his vision had gone all funky. It was like the episodes he'd been having since he'd left work for the summer, but it had been mixed with elements from the Coke can dream. There had been multiple copies of the lab, all overlaid on top of one another. In some images it had looked empty, in others it had looked destroyed. He remembered one that was dark and stuffy, like his dreams of being buried alive after the accident.

All of it had been made up of the mist and wispy threads, and it was definitely tied to the QPS itself.

But it was the people in the images who stuck in his mind. Sometimes they were there, either doing the same thing or moved a little to the left or the right. Sometimes they were gone. Where his dad had stood was just an empty space on the floor without even a shadow to show where he had once been.

Sometimes things were just different—his dad with a full un-kempt beard, typing alone at a terminal, or rubble strewn on the floor and the sun shining through a gaping hole in the ceiling. Just thinking of the variations brought traces of the headache back.

And what were the sheer strands of light he had seen?

Darwin shook his head and turned to look out the darkened window again. His reflection showed the same guy he had seen in the mirror that morning. Maybe a little worse for wear. He gingerly touched the bump on his forehead and pressed it lightly, feeling no pain as the pressure increased. It was smaller than it had been ear-lier, but it was still there. He let his finger run down the invisible scar on his face, remembering the light touch that had done the same not too long ago.

He changed his focus to outside the reflective glass, then moved to cup his hands against the window, shielding his eyes from the light in the room, and looked through them. All he saw was black. There were no lights, no moving cars. Maybe if he turned off the lights in the office he would be able to see better. He walked to the door and flicked the light switch, turning back to the window after his eyes had adjusted to the change.

A wall of dark slate lay before him. There was nothing for him to see on the other side of the glass. Moving back to the window, he stared into the distance, straining to find something—anything—that indicated there was a city out there.

People.

That's when he noticed the stars. It was just one or two at first, and then millions of them. These were the stars he remembered as a kid, camping out by the lake with Mom and Dad beside a darkened fire pit. The memory brought back the smells of the dying fire and the sound of water lapping on the shore. He hadn't thought of their camping trips in years. He stumbled back, bumping into the mesh chair, banging it against the desk.

The movement brought a flash of blue light into focus. It was gone as fast as it had appeared. Something was out there! He leaned into the glass and squinted, looking out of the corner of his eye. There it was again, a soft blue glow that appeared at the edge of the parking lot. It was the same light he'd seen earlier today, but bigger. Much bigger. When he turned to look at it directly, it disappeared, fading back into the night.

He turned his head away from where the blue glow was and let his eyes lose focus. It shimmered back into view. It looked like a mesh, like a chain link fence that followed the edge of the parking lot, curving around the corner and disappearing around the edge of the building. The light eddied and rewove itself, changing the links, creating a living tapestry that was never the same. He tilted his head and followed the mesh into the sky. It faded into nothing somewhere above him. It was like a wall. A wire cage made of light.

A prison.

The sound of the door opening pulled Darwin away from the window, and he blinked in the sudden light, staring at his reflection in the window once more. He turned and pressed his back against the cold glass and raised his hand to his eyes.

Someone he hadn't seen before walked in wearing the same blue anti-static jacket as everyone else here. Darwin snorted, covering it up as a cough. The only point to them must have been as some sort of uniform. There didn't seem to be any other reason since the lab didn't have any equipment in it. The guy who walked in couldn't have been much older than him, though he was at least four inches shorter. His blond hair was chopped short and looked as though it had been cut with a dull knife.

"I'm Lyell." He stopped just inside the door and nodded his head in greeting. "Please, if you will come with me. Revered Mother would like to see you."

Darwin pushed off the window, feeling it flex slightly under the added pressure, and moved toward Lyell, trying to ignore the religious title and the dark road it wanted to lead him down. "Who is this Revered Mother?" Hopefully someone who would answer his questions.

"Revered Mother Henslow guides and teaches us. You met her this morning when you . . . when you came here."

Darwin stopped just short of Lyell and leaned in, using his extra height to try to intimidate the other man. He felt awkward doing it.

"I'm not going anywhere until you tell me what the hell is going on here. How about we start with *where is my dad? Why won't you let me see him?*"

Lyell didn't cower or step back. "I've been told to bring you to the Sanctum. Your questions will be answered there."

"Where are all the people who work here? Where are all the cars? All the people?" Darwin tried to sound menacing, swinging an open hand toward the windows and lowering his voice, forcing the words out. It wasn't convincing. The last question came out in a high-pitched whine. He was losing his mind.

"I can't—"

"Why the hell not?" The anger Darwin had been holding inside exploded, pushing through his reluctance to talk with people he didn't know. He was tired of waiting, of being left alone, of the whole world cascading down around him. But most of all, of feeling weak. "Tell me!"

Lyell took two steps back into the hallway and furtively looked both ways before rushing back into the room. "There isn't much time. She's expecting us. Please don't yell, just come with me and I'll answer what questions I can . . . as long as you don't draw too much attention to us."

Darwin saw the look of concern mixed with fear on Lyell's face and immediately moved away from him, feeling horrible about what he had done. It wasn't like him to confront people like that. He couldn't remember the last time he had even raised his voice. Despite that, he still mumbled, hopefully loud enough for Lyell to hear. "About time."

"If anyone sees us talking, I'll be replaced. Just keep your head and your voice down. I brought you a lab coat." Lyell pulled a dirty blue anti-static jacket from under his belt and held it out. "We guessed the size," he said, grinning. "But it looks like you already have one. Great condition too!"

Darwin didn't care what his jacket looked like. "What's going on here? Where is my dad?"

"As far as I know, still back in his lab trying to figure out what's going on." Lyell led the way out of the room, pulling at Darwin's jacket. The foyer opened up below them, with its large black entrance showing the way out.

"I was there this morning. It looked like the lab was damaged, and he wasn't there. Is he working on it now?"

"Strictly speaking, that wasn't your dad's lab. It was Henry Lloyd's lab, but—as best as we can tell—it wasn't your father's."

Darwin stopped walking, wanting to grab Lyell's arm. He didn't do it. "That doesn't make sense. Henry Lloyd *is* my dad."

"Keep walking and keep your voice down." Lyell continued on, pulling Darwin along with him. "Our Henry Lloyd died over five years ago, when they first brought the Source online at full power. He was killed trying to shut it down."

Darwin slowed down again. Lyell pulled harder and Darwin almost ran to keep up with him.

"For Christ's sake, keep moving," Lyell whispered.

"You're not making any sense. A second ago you said my dad was back in his lab. Now you're telling me he's been dead for five years?" Even saying the words opened a hole in Darwin's chest filled with pain and guilt and memories of his mom. He slammed it shut as fast as he could. It was a world he didn't want to imagine. He wasn't sure what he would do if he lost the only person who meant anything to him. He slowed his pace again, and Lyell matched it. The guy must be some form of simpleton who didn't know what the hell he was talking about. What did Lyell mean by the Source . . . the QPS? "Dad was only running at full power today, as a test. Not five years ago. And he's sure as hell not dead. I was with him just this morning."

"I said *our* Henry Lloyd. We don't have time for a history lesson now, I need to get you prepared."

"History lesson? This is my life we're talking about." Darwin paused, Lyell's words finally sinking in, and he felt a sudden chill that had nothing to do with the temperature. "Prepare me for what?" He stumbled as they took the first step down to the lobby, catching himself on the railing.

"We'll have to talk about that later. If we can. We're running out of time. Your being here is as confusing to us as it is to you. Whatever is going on, Henslow has a plan. You can be sure of that. I have no idea what she's going to do with you, but I can't imagine it's good. The Qabal are not nice people, Darwin. They use the Threads . . .

the power . . . for whatever they want. They enslave or remove every-one and everything that gets in the way of their plans."

They reached the bottom of the curving staircase. Three people stood by the front door, the blue of their jackets standing out from the black stone surrounding it. One of them was Michael, the guy who had taken care of his cut. His was the only face that didn't seem to hold some malice as they watched Darwin.

He walked quietly by Lyell's side, too confused by what he was hearing to ask any more questions. And if he was being honest with himself, terrified by it. He could feel his pulse throbbing in his neck, and his stomach felt like he was about to jump off a cliff. Things were getting weirder by the minute. Once he got to this Henslow woman, he was going to try to get some answers—she seemed to be the one in charge.

Lyell pushed open the security door to the back offices and led Darwin through.

"We're out of time. We've got to see what Henslow is up to. We don't think she knows how you got here, but if she does . . . That's more power than anyone should have. Especially the Qabal." He paused at the door to the basement and lowered his voice, the words rushing from his mouth. "We'll do everything we can to make sure you're safe, but you've got to go through with whatever she has planned. Get her to talk. If it turns bad, we'll try to get you out. Michael is waiting at the front door, just in case. You'll need one of us to get past the net."

Lyell's words did nothing to make Darwin feel better. They did just the opposite. He followed Lyell down the stairs in a daze. They reached the bottom and entered the hallway leading to the lab. The woman he had seen earlier stood there waiting for them. When they got closer, Lyell dropped to one knee and bowed his head.

"Revered Mother. As you requested, I have brought Darwin."

Henslow smiled. "Thank you, Lyell. Please join the others in the Sanctum and let them know to begin preparing. Darwin and I will be there shortly."

"Come, Darwin. Let's move away from the door while the others arrive." She grabbed his elbow and led him further down the hall to a small room and closed the door behind them. An old mop bucket stood in the corner and two chairs lined the wall. The only light came from a bare bulb on the ceiling. "There are some things you will be hearing in the Sanctum that I'd like to explain first. Please, sit down."

Darwin grabbed the first chair and sat, not allowing Henslow to get between him and the door. He hated having his back to a door at the best of times, but there was no way he was going to let someone get between him and his only possible escape route. He waited for her to make the first move, his leg bouncing in time with his heartbeat. She pulled the second chair away from the wall, closing the gap between them, and sat down. He slid his chair back to create more space.

"You don't remember me, do you?" she asked.

Darwin shook his head.

"I'm Rebecca." She paused. "Rebecca Henslow. As you've heard, most people call me Revered Mother. I am the leader of these people, both physically and spiritually. You are Darwin Lloyd, son of Henry Lloyd."

As she spoke, Rebecca pulled her hair away from her face and into a ponytail. With her face showing completely and her hair pulled back, the realization of who she was came into sharp focus.

"You're Rebecca! We worked together for a while on the QPS monitoring systems. What the hell is going on here?"

Rebecca smiled and continued as if Darwin hadn't spoken at all. "You came to us, remember? Something like this has never happened before, and we'd like to find out how you did it. All we know right now is that the Source in your world was turned on. Each Source entangles with the others. Each entanglement strengthens the whole. If people can move between worlds using the entanglement, it changes many things."

"Look, lady, you're insane. Even I can see that. Just tell me where my dad is and let me out of here."

Rebecca stood, pushing her chair away until it banged into the far wall. Darwin cringed as her face hardened and her eyes flashed steel. "How dare—" She took a deep breath, pulled the chair close, and sat down again. "Please don't interrupt." Her voice turned cold and hard. "When we are in there, we'll be asking you some questions. Once our questions are answered, we'll take care of you."

She was sitting closer now, and Darwin could feel her breath on his face. He fought the urge to shift even farther back. The closed door wouldn't have let him anyway.

"And if I don't answer the questions?"

"Although there are several potential outcomes, the Quorum will be guiding the Threads. Your choices will have already been made."

All of the frustration and doubt and rage that had been sparking in him all day roared to the surface in a white heat that burned in his chest. "My choices have already been made? Who the hell do you think you are?" He stood and reached for the door, stopping with his hand on the knob. Rebecca stayed where she was. "I want to know where the hell I am, because it sure as hell isn't Quantum Labs. You people went a long way to make it look like it, but it's not. I've been a prisoner all day, locked in that damn office upstairs, not allowed to talk to anyone. Now it's my turn. I want answers and I want them now."

"Sit. Down."

"No! Where's my dad?" Darwin gripped the doorknob so tightly, the knuckles on his hand turned white.

Rebecca's voice transformed into a hard whisper. "I said sit down. Now."

She stood and raised her hand as if she was about to slap him. Her hand separated into two images, then four, all within a split second. He flinched, catching the leg of his chair with his heel. The chair spun, and Darwin reeled into it, falling backward until he was sitting with his shoulders pressed into the door. He stared at her single hand, the multiple images gone.

Oh god, it was happening again.

"Next time I tell you to do something, Darwin, you will do it. Don't make me do it for you again." She took a deep breath. "The probabilities were slim on the easy way working, but I thought I'd give you the chance."

The door opened and Darwin almost fell back into the hallway before two men grabbed his arms and dragged him toward his dad's lab.

What the hell did she mean, *make me do it for you again?*

Darwin twisted and pulled as the men dragged him down the hall, fighting to free his arms from their grip. He lashed out with his feet, flailing them in the air until he felt an impact. The man on his right grunted and wrenched Darwin's arm until his shoulder screamed in agony. He felt it pull from its socket before it settled back into place. Even when the twisting stopped, the burning pain continued, bringing tears to his eyes. He stopped struggling, realizing the only thing he was really doing was making it harder for him to actually get away if—when—a chance came. If he appeared meek and docile, maybe they would relax a bit and he'd be able to yank his arms free.

Whatever he had to do to get out, whatever it took, he would do it. The more he told himself that, the more confidence he felt. It still took all of the lessons he'd learned in his therapy sessions—all self-taught to hide his emotions, his feelings, from the doctors—to calm himself. He forced his breathing to slow, and his racing heart followed. His pace quickened to keep up with his captors. Their grip didn't loosen, but at least he wasn't being dragged along.

He thought he had an opportunity when they reached the door to the lab. One of the men let go of his arm and he tensed. The man held the door open with his foot and grabbed Darwin's arm again before he could make a move.

His view of the door was blocked by the man's back as it opened. Had he swiped a security card to get in, like his dad had done? Darwin silently cursed himself for not paying attention before realizing it didn't matter. The damn locks were meant to keep people out, not in. When he started running, the doors would just open for him. Besides, Lyell hadn't used one to get into the office area from the lobby.

He almost stopped when the next idea hit him. The thugs gripped even tighter and pulled him along with them. Office buildings weren't prisons. Who cared if there was a lock on the door when he was upstairs? The walls were made of drywall. All he had to do was bust through to the next room and check its door, then just keep on doing that until he hit a hallway or found one he could get out of. There hadn't been any guards when Lyell had come to get him. With his anti-static jacket, he had a chance of blending in and walking out the door into the parking lot. After going through a wall or two, it wouldn't look so clean anymore. He'd spent so much time moping and sleeping he hadn't even thought about it.

The plan, such as it was, was in place. Get through whatever they were doing in the lab, and then walk out later when no one was looking. Once he was gone, he'd figure out a way to find his dad. He felt giddy with the idea.

Something Lyell had said about getting out niggled in the back of his head.

The lab was filled with a dozen or more people, creating a corridor of blue jackets leading from the door to the QPS room. Darwin noticed each jacket was slightly different, some looking as though they had been patched together from old shirts. Each one was dirty, and the room had the funky smell of unwashed bodies.

The two rows stood silent with their heads bowed. As he entered the lab, they began a soft chant that echoed in the large room, their words lost in the rhythmic melody. He thought it sounded like an odd mix of Church hymns and Toto's "Africa." Fear and paranoia almost bubbled out as a laugh.

The men holding him released their grip. The one who had twisted his arm so painfully moved behind him, pushing on the small of his back, while the other one led him through the human passageway. Just before they reached the entry to the room with the QPS, the leader fell into place with those in the line. Darwin felt a stronger push on his back, propelling him through the doorway. He lurched into the QPS room alone.

The chanting from the outer room stopped with an abruptness that sent goose bumps up his arms. Several people wearing the same blue jackets stood in front of the QPS in a rough semicircle. Behind them in the shadows stood the girl who had brought him his food, looking more like his mother than before. They all stared through him to the doorway behind his back. Even though he'd worked most of his life to be invisible to others, he felt a chill run down his back. He stepped to the side, turning to find what they were all looking at.

Rebecca strode between the rows of people, and as she passed each person, they turned toward the QPS and knelt. She moved past him as if he didn't exist, and he fought the urge to grab her arm. To stop her, to tell her this was crazy. She moved behind the QPS, facing it and everyone she had just walked past, and placed her hand on the machine. As she stopped, the group around the machine spread out, completing the circle around the QPS. The chanting started again.

Darwin risked a glance at the lab door. If he bolted now, would the people stop him, or would they be so shocked they wouldn't know what to do? He figured he would get halfway to the stairs before they dragged him down. Rebecca was the center of everyone's attention, so he had a chance. He stood rooted to the floor, indecision making him hesitate. It was strange how only a couple of minutes ago he was hauled into a closet to talk and now he was being completely ignored. It didn't make any sense. Then again, none of this did.

The religious overtones and ceremonial aspects of the whole thing were weirding him out. The best he could figure was that he'd been taken in by a cult and they had duplicated the Quantum Labs building. It made about as much sense as anything else he had come up with, which wasn't saying much. One thing he'd figured out. The blue jackets weren't a uniform, they were damn vestments.

What they had in mind for him was even tougher for him to figure out. What if it was a mass suicide, like that group up in Montana last year? Would they want him to be a part of it? Would they force it on him?

He sucked in a deep breath and held it. *Jesus Christ, get a grip.* He could feel his heart beating against his ribs and his throat tightened. He forced himself to swallow. *Calm down.* He let go of the air trapped in his lungs. Cults only killed themselves, the true believers, not outsiders. Right? The logical side of his brain struggled with how a cult could take over a building that used to house over a thousand employees.

Maybe their plan wasn't to kill themselves. Maybe they were trying to brainwash him, make him one of them. With the small amount of food and fake coffee during the day and the bump on his head, were they trying to make him susceptible, trying to weaken him to the point where he would believe anything they said or did? But why? What would be the point of it? A single thought hammered home. What if they had drugged him?

In one smooth motion, the circle around the QPS went down on their knees. He hadn't heard or seen a command, but they were all in perfect sync. Besides Rebecca, he was the only person still standing. He took a half step backward, risking another glance at the door to the hall. He still had a clear path.

Without warning, the light in the room brightened and he stopped, his weight barely on the foot he had just moved. None of the darkened fluorescents had come on and the others looked like they were at the same intensity as before. Something else had brightened the room. Something more fluid, more organic, though he had no idea how he got to that conclusion.

A flicker from the corner of his eye caught his attention. He focused on it. Nothing was there. Another flicker came from the left and he rotated. Again, nothing was there. The chanting increased and the room suddenly blossomed with wisps of light. Translucent gray threads that shifted and moved with the singing, like dye flowing into water, but more defined and directional. Every time he tried to focus on a single wisp, it disappeared and another came into view at the edge of his sight. He'd seem them before. The bump on his head throbbed in sudden pain, and the hornet's nest in his brain became more active.

The threads changed again, each becoming a distinct but faint washed-out color: pink, cyan, yellow. Too many to keep track of. The chanting stopped, and he turned back to face the machine.

Rebecca stood facing him, standing slightly apart from the twelve who formed the circle. His heart sank, knowing he had missed his opportunity to run, afraid it may have been his last. Everyone in the lab still knelt, looking at the floor in silence, while those around the QPS rose to their feet.

"I give you Darwin Lloyd, visitor from another world," Rebecca chanted.

"May you find peace," the kneeling group replied. The circle around the QPS remained silent.

Sounding more like a mad preacher at a pulpit, she continued. "Darwin Lloyd, you have done the impossible. Connecting the worlds is a task no one has done before you. Come forward and share your knowledge, so that we may grow wiser." Everyone in the other room looked at him with hope in their eyes; only those around the QPS remained focused on Rebecca.

He stumbled back against the wall beside the door, his hand grabbing the window frame. Another world? His thoughts jumped back to classes on early physics theories; names like Everett, Deutsch, and DeWitt. Theories discussed in passing and discarded before moving on to Bohr's and Heisenberg's Copenhagen interpretation. How could he share what wasn't real? "You guys are nuts." The constant fear that threatened to consume him burst, burning hot and freezing cold at the same time.

"Come to us, Darwin Lloyd, son of the creator. Be witness to the power of the Source. Watch hope become reality, thought become truth. Share your knowledge so the Quorum can better serve its people."

They *were* nuts. Rebecca, the guys standing around the QPS, those kneeling on the hard floor in the lab, every last fricken one of them. Cult was the right word. The idea of waiting until he was back in his office prison to attempt an escape didn't seem like such a good one anymore. He had to get out now, before they decided to suck his brain out with a vacuum cleaner looking for information he didn't have.

Out of the corner of his eye, the amorphous threads solidified. They still shifted and moved, weaving around each other in a tapestry of color, but they seemed more stable, more solid. Each person surrounding the QPS was connected to the next by the threads; new connections were made as the old disappeared. Thicker strands joined them to Rebecca, and as he watched, a rope as thick as his arm shot out from her toward the kneeling group, and they became united to the whole.

He flinched as the bundle flew past him, and he was filled with an inexplicable sense of loss as images of the car accident flitted though his mind. The feeling left him as quickly as it had come.

"You can See!" The whispered words from Rebecca caused a ripple in the circle, and the thread's link between them dimmed and weakened. A single wisp disconnected from the rope and weaved toward him.

He looked directly at her and the threads vanished. The buzzing in Darwin's head exploded to a volume he'd never felt before, and the pain that had been growing in his brain stabbed outward, piercing just behind his eyes. The room spun and he dropped to his knees, not feeling the impact with the floor.

"You *can* See!" Rebecca's eyes widened and Darwin thought he saw a smile cross her lips. "You, Darwin Lloyd, will be saved and brought into the fold. You will serve the Source as we do and—"

"*Darwin.*"

The shout pushed through the haze, temporarily shoving the headache into the background before it surged again. Dazed by the intensity of the pain, he lost his balance, smashing into the wall behind him.

Suddenly, it was all gone. The buzzing and the headache disappeared in a rush of silence, leaving him feeling empty and nauseous and weak. He waited for the darkness to come, almost begging for it to wipe the insanity of what was happening from his mind. It never did.

"Darwin, this way."

He searched for the source of voice. Lyell stood by the lab door, sweat running down his face, beckoning Darwin closer. Rebecca and the others lay on the cold hard floor, not moving.

"Hurry. They won't be out for long. I got lucky and took advantage of their surprise. They weren't expecting anything during the ceremony, especially from one of their own."

Darwin stumbled to his feet, bracing himself against the door jamb, and lurched toward Lyell. A single thought crawled through his muddled brain. Get out. Whatever the cost, just get out.

Lyell grabbed his arm and pulled him through the lab door into the hallway. He slammed the door shut behind him and ran to the closet, grabbing one of the chairs from its darkened interior. He wedged it under the door handle and looked apologetically at Darwin.

"Stupid, I know. But it may help for a bit."

Through the blocked door they heard Rebecca shout. "Don't let them out. The net has not been completely woven."

Lyell slid down to the floor, crossing his legs and placing his hand on his thighs. "I'll stay here and do what I can to slow them down. Michael should still be at the front entrance. He'll help you get out. Run!" He closed his eyes and turned his head to face the door to the lab. Even in the brighter light of the hallway, Darwin saw faint threads reach out to touch it.

Something slammed against the jammed door, and the sound jolted Darwin. He turned and raced up the stairs, pushing through the security entrance into the reception area, hoping to surprise the guards he had seen earlier. Michael stood alone. The two others guarding the front door lay on the floor.

"I've been working on the net, but we don't have much time. I should be able to get us past it. Come on."

Darwin didn't trust Michael any more than he trusted anyone here, but right now any way out was a good one. He followed Michael through the black stone of the entryway—the mouth of the beast—and into the cool night air at full tilt. In the darkness he could see a faint blue shimmer that hung around the building. It shifted when he looked directly at it but didn't fade into the dark. They ran across the parking lot, ducking behind a rusting car with flat tires. The incongruous image of grass growing out of the creased and cracked rubber stuck with him as he stared at the edge of the parking lot.

This close to the blue net, it looked like a sphere surrounding the building. He could see tiny individual threads weaving together, a veil that hung loosely from the sky, swaying gently as if in a breeze. Through the sphere he could see the overgrown boulevard and what was left of the empty expressway beyond it. He reached out his hand touching the woven net with his fingers. It stretched as he pushed, feeling like a rubber balloon filled with air.

"You can See it?" Michael watched as Darwin examined the sphere.

"Yes."

"That explains why Lyell made such a move. It will make getting through it more difficult. Close your eyes and take a step forward."

"But I—" Distrust flared in his chest.

"You have to just do it. We must get past the net quickly. Lyell won't be able to hold out much longer."

Darwin looked at Michael and made his decision. He closed his eyes and stepped.

The world split and split again. Threads created images. Images created probabilities. Probabilities created hope. In one image, he was at home listening to his music on his phone. In another he was back in the lab with his dad. In yet another, the sphere bounced him back toward the Qabal.

He tripped over the hidden curb and fell toward the blue weave.

THE STICKY BALANCE OF KNOWLEDGE

ROUGH HANDS GRABBED Darwin under his arms, lifting him from the ground. His toes dragged across the parking lot, leaving two lines in the thin layer of dirt and weeds that covered the asphalt. A wave of nausea threatened to consume him, and it felt like someone had driven a pickup truck into his head and was doing donuts. He lifted his chin, still in a daze, and smelled old dirt and sweat. The windows of the Quantum Labs building—wavering in a liquid wash as his eyes tried to focus—gave off a faint glow of cold light in the warm dusk of late August. As he was pulled into the black maw, he struggled to get his feet under him, managing only a couple of half steps before tripping. The men carrying him groaned as they took his weight again.

Rebecca stood waiting on the balcony overhanging the reception area, the suspended blue *QL* logo partially covering her face.

"Bring him up to me," she said.

He glared at her for a millisecond before dropping his gaze, squinting against the overhead lights that pierced his eyes, struggling to form a complete thought. He knew he should be trying harder to get away—every part of him screamed it—but his body was barely listening to the commands his brain was trying to send. He was half dragged and half carried up the staircase to face Rebecca.

The men hauled him to an office and tossed him into a chair across the desk from her. The desk was huge and gray, industrial, resembling an aircraft carrier more than anything else. Darwin concentrated on the monstrosity in front of him, focusing on the single object, attempting to fight through the turmoil in his head as his view of the metal twisted and morphed.

"Please be gentle with him. Darwin is our guest and should be treated as such." Rebecca's voice was warm and inviting, a complete contrast to the one she had used in the closet.

The two men bowed and walked backward out of the office, closing the door behind them.

"It seems we got off on the wrong foot. I apologize and take full responsibility. Sometimes my zeal comes through a little strong." She paused, waving at a side table. "I've taken the liberty of having some food and water brought in for you."

He shook his head. More to try to get the cobwebs out of it than in response to Rebecca. She must have taken it as a no, turning away from the food. He wasn't sure he'd be able to keep anything down anyway.

"Here, you really should have some water at least. It will make you feel better." She stood and poured him a glass, placing it gently in his hands. "Please, drink."

Darwin raised the glass to his lips on reflex alone and took a sip. The water was cold and refreshing as it slid down his throat. He hadn't realized how thirsty he was. He finished the glass and held it out for more. She refilled it, smiling, and handed it back to him, putting the half empty pitcher on the desk. The liquid eased the pounding in his skull.

"Good," she said as she lowered herself back into her chair. "What happened earlier in the Sanctum was unfortunate. Lyell—the man who *helped* you—was having . . . problems that seemed to manifest into anger against us. We managed to talk some sense into him, I think. I need to fill you in on some things, so we don't have another incident, and I need you to listen closely. Can you do that?"

At the mention of Lyell's name, he took another swig of the water. It took a second or two for the name to register, followed by surprise that he hadn't wondered what had happened to him. Even though his headache was rapidly receding and the buzzing had all but disappeared, his brain still wasn't working, still refused to respond.

Rebecca cleared her throat and continued. "You being able to See changes everything. We need you, and you need us. You don't know it yet, but you do. In our world, when your dad—when Henry Lloyd—turned on the QPS, the world changed. Shifted. It didn't take long for people to realize everything was different, they just didn't know what. Or why. To some, things just started falling apart. To those who could See, the Threads began appearing. Some sensed the outcome of events before they happened, could sense how random events tied together. To revisit an old trope, if a butterfly flapped its wings in Japan, people over here who could See noticed the effects. It wasn't until they realized they could alter what they saw that the world started changing.

"But I'm getting ahead of myself."

She refilled his glass of water and he took another big gulp. This time it left a faintly bitter taste on the back of his tongue.

"The people of the world were split into two groups. Those who could See the Threads, and those who could not. Those who could not became almost useless."

He rubbed his eyes, still confused. He still couldn't seem to form a clear thought. If anything, it was getting worse. Even through the numbness, he knew what she was saying didn't make sense. How could all of that happen when his dad just turned on the QPS today? And people were never useless. He focused on her face, watching her lips move.

"Some of those who could See became ruthless. They ruled over everyone around them like queens and kings, dictators, treating the less fortunate like slaves. Others, like us, tried to maintain society, tried to keep everything from disintegrating." Rebecca sighed. "We failed. The world has become fractured. Our society has broken down to its base qualities. War started, the technological people against us and those that supported us. The only way we won was by destroying the technology they depended on. Shipments of crude oil from Canada and South America stopped, and with it came the complete destruction of everything we knew. Most of us now live as we did hundreds of years ago: small communities, distrustful of outsiders. Ruled by those with power. Those who See."

Darwin finished his glass of water and put it beside the pitcher on the desk with a shaky hand. A full thought had finally formed. "Send me back home."

"We can't. We . . . we don't even know how." She leaned forward in her chair, her elbows on the gray surface of the desk. "But you might. You came here in the first place. We need you to tell us what you know."

"Why?"

"Imagine the possibilities! A chance to regain what we've lost, to trade with other worlds that haven't had the QPS turned on, to learn new things from those that have. We can't trade with Europe or other countries anymore; the distances are too great, and the skills required to build seafaring ships are still being relearned. But other worlds only a step away?" The last part of her sentence came out sounding like a question.

"And if the link can only be made here?" He noticed his headache was completely gone. He didn't even hear the faint buzzing he had lived with for the last few weeks, though it still felt like he was walking through a dense fog and his tongue had a hard time shaping the words as he spoke.

"The Qabal are known for their generosity. We would build a better world."

"And how do I know you would do that?"

Rebecca let out a slow breath and leaned back, eyeing Darwin's empty glass of water. "Those who See are a limited number. It's our duty to take care of those who are weaker and less fortunate. Without us, we would have the same scenario I described earlier: the stone age and the extinction of our species."

Something inside him wanted to shout, to scream out in anger. But even now, he could feel that voice receding behind a thick curtain. He knew he should care, that what she was saying was wrong—had to be wrong. Somehow, he couldn't muster the strength to do it. He shook his head again, trying to shake off the heavy feeling inside it.

"Enough questions for now, Darwin. You look tired. I've had a room made up for you. There's a bucket of water in the washroom to clean up a bit and flush the toilet with. Get a good night's sleep. We'll talk in the morning."

As if on command, the door opened and a man stood there waiting. Darwin tried to get to his feet, bracing himself on the arms of the chair before falling back into it. Hands grabbed his arms and lifted him up, steering him out the open door to the balcony, back to his room. He twisted back to look at Rebecca.

"Where's Michael?"

She shrugged as if it didn't matter. "He wasn't there when we found you."

His escort pulled him through the door back to his prison.

Darwin woke to daylight streaming in through the office windows. He got out of the cot—not quite sure how he or it had gotten there—and looked out over the almost empty parking lot. The sun shone in a perfect clear blue sky.

Something was wrong . . . *felt* wrong. Looking out the window, everything was messed up. There was no traffic on the overgrown expressway, no movement or noises or city life. But all that was wrong yesterday. This was something new, something different. If he could only figure out what it was. At least the headache and buzzing hadn't come back.

Yesterday . . . was it only yesterday? It felt like a lifetime had passed since he'd been in the lab with his dad. Yesterday, Lyell had told him this was his dad's office, that this version of his dad had died five years ago when the QPS had been turned on. He found it hard to believe, but if it was true . . . did that mean his mother was alive in this world? Was there another version of him walking around somewhere? The thoughts both soothed and terrified him. His mother possibly alive, with a son that both was and wasn't him. Schrödinger's cat on a larger scale. What would they do if they all met? Images of old *Star Trek* episodes where matter met anti-matter flashed in front of his eyes. It was stupid, but he couldn't help it. He forced himself to think of something else before his brain exploded, like how to get out of here and get back home.

A quiet knock on the door broke his reverie. It swung open, bringing with it the aroma of fresh coffee. A young girl carried in a covered tray and placed it on the desk. It wasn't the same girl as yesterday; this one was much younger, with dirty blond hair. She removed the cloth covering the food with shaking hands before turning and practically running for the door. She hadn't said a word.

He let the breakfast sit as he washed the sleep from his eyes using some of the water left over from the night before, before using the rest to flush the toilet one more time. The smell of coffee drifted into the tiny room and he moved back to the mesh-backed chair.

His nose had let him down. The tray held a steaming mug of whatever he had been given yesterday. He picked up the mug and took a tentative sip. It was definitely the same crap as yesterday. At least it was hot.

The bread tasted like it had just come out of the oven, warm and soft with the butter melting into the pores. He ate as if he hadn't eaten in days, jamming the bread in his mouth and licking the butter that ran down his fingers. The final sip of fake coffee slid down his throat just as there was another knock on the door. This one was harder, less timid than the previous one.

He waited for the door to open, wiping his mouth and hands on the cloth. When no one came through he answered with a firm voice. "Come in."

Rebecca stood in the doorway, smiling. It looked genuine, but he wasn't quite ready to buy into her newfound friendliness, and yet . . . there was something pushing his natural distrust for people off to the side, and he almost welcomed the presence of another person.

"Good morning, Darwin. Are you ready to start your day? It's going to be quite busy."

"I just want to go home."

"And you will, as soon as we figure out how you came across in the first place. The answer is in your head, but your being able to See makes it almost impossible to get unless you are trained in the

Threads. Without conscious control of them, your unconscious mind will fight our attempts to pull out the information. That could damage you beyond repair. We don't want to do that." She paused. "Come with me, I'd like to introduce you to your teacher."

He hesitated before he moved to the door and followed her out. He thought he saw a smile flicker across her face for a brief moment, but he couldn't quite tell.

How was he supposed to give what he didn't have? Still, if there was a chance it was going to get him home, it was worth a shot. "Teacher?"

"Yes, teacher. Today you'll start to learn how to control the Threads enough to help us get you back where you belong."

"And if it doesn't work?"

"Here we are. Bill is waiting for you," Rebecca said, opening the door. She stood off to the side and waited for him to enter. The door thudded closed behind him, leaving him alone in the dark space. She hadn't answered his question.

As his eyes adjusted to the low light, he made out a simple desk with two chairs. A shelf-lined wall was filled with boxes and things made of wire and wood and string. A small man stood behind the desk, watching him intently. It felt like he was being judged. The man's long white hair was thin and unkempt. When Darwin spotted him, he stepped further into the room.

"Ah, Darwin. It is good to finally meet you. I apologize for the lack of lights, but it is often easier for beginners to See the Threads when it is a bit dark. Please, sit down." He pulled out a chair and sat. "Did the Revered Mother give you the inhibitor?"

"What?"

"The inhibitor. It blocks the ability for you to See the Threads. The untrained and emotional human mind can only get a tenuous hold on the probabilities and possibilities before it loses control and snaps. Almost everyone who loses control requires constant care for the rest of their lives. A very few come back from that precipice, but they have no ability to See. We found the older you are when taught to use them, the more chance there is for immediate and irreversible brain damage. Since the inhibitor stops you from Seeing, it stops you from using, and there is less chance of damage."

He waved his arm through the air. "How many Threads do you See?"

Darwin squinted in the dark room. "Umm, one, I think. It's very faint, though."

"Good. As you gain more control, we'll lessen the amount of inhibitor you take."

"So you are saying you drugged me?" That would explain how he felt last night when he was talking to Rebecca.

"Well, yes." Bill looked him in the eye, a quizzical expression on his face. "Would you prefer the alternatives I just told you about?"

Darwin lowered himself into the offered chair. So that's what was different this morning. When he had looked outside, there were no Threads. Not even a flicker in the corner of his eye. When had they given him the drugs? Maybe in this morning's breakfast, or more likely in the water he drank last night. Maybe both. He knew it should bother him more, but he couldn't seem to muster the strength to do anything about it. Was that a side effect of the inhibitor, or did they slip something else in?

"The Qabal—"

Bill waved his hand, interrupting Darwin's question. "There will be no talk of the Qabal in here. I am to teach you how to safely See and use the Threads. No more, no less. Whatever philosophies you decide to wrap around the Threads make no difference to their usage, or how I will teach."

He turned and fetched a small device from the shelving on the wall. It was made of two tall rails parallel to each other with a loose stick resting on the base. Bill grabbed the stick and placed it between the rails, balancing it on its end with his finger.

"When I let go of this stick, there are basically three possibilities: the stick will fall to the left, the right, or it will balance on its tip. The rails stop any other motion, so it limits what we can See." He let go of the stick and it dropped to the left. "Now, we have a narrow stick, the probabilities of it falling are quite high, while the probability of it balancing on its tip is extremely low. Our lesson for today will be to simply predict the direction of the fall. By watching the Threads, we'll be able to See its motion before it actually happens." He picked up the stick again. "Are you ready?"

Darwin felt a small wave of resentment build and struggled to hold onto it. He wasn't sure what to do or who to believe, and interaction with others was something he always tried to avoid, even if it was one-on-one. He got ready to stand. "And if I choose not to do it?" As soon as the words were out of his mouth, the faint strand of rebellion slipped from his grasp as quickly as it had come. Even though the thought of it stopped, the emotion behind it remained. Before he could apologize, Bill spoke again.

"The Revered Mother will deal with that situation. I cannot help you there. Now, concentrate on the stick. Left or right?"

"What if one of the rails breaks? That changes the . . . the possibilities."

"True, but the *probability* of the rail breaking is extremely low. A beginner would have no hope of Seeing that Thread, and those of the rails, to manipulate them. Especially with the inhibitor." His voice became clinical as he continued. "Now, concentrate. Can you See the Threads around it?"

In the darkened room, light wispy threads began to appear

around the stick. The harder he looked at them, the clearer they became. "Yes."

"Good. I'm making the Threads stronger so you can See them. Watch the Threads. In which direction do they seem thicker? Is the thickest Thread pulling or pushing the stick in a particular direction?"

He watched the Threads as they wove around the stick. They all looked the same, thin and translucent, ethereal, like gauze pulled through liquid. He concentrated harder. The Threads partly disappeared as images flashed in their place. They were almost carbon copies of each other as the images of the stick split, and split again. Suddenly, in one, the stick fell to the right, while in another it fell to the left and in a third the stick remained upright. He raised his hand to his head, expecting the pain he'd felt earlier with his Coke can. Only a faint buzzing came through.

The images disappeared, and with it the faint background buzz.

"Are you all right?"

"Yeah . . . yeah. Last time that happened it felt like my head was going to explode, and I passed out."

"And this time?"

"Nothing, just a small buzzing in my head."

"Good! That's the inhibitor doing its job. Even the noise will disappear as you get stronger. Let's do it again. Concentrate on the Threads."

It was easier this time. The Threads appeared as insubstantial as before, and then disappeared, replaced by the images. The image of the stick tipping left seemed stronger, brighter, more real than the one falling right and definitely more substantial than the balancing stick.

"It will go left."

Bill let go of the stick and it fell to the left. "Excellent. Let's do it again."

They spent the morning predicting how the stick would fall. He was right about eighty percent of the time. Enough to beat the odds of guessing. By the time Bill called it a day, he was really beginning to hate the damn thing. A headache was building behind his eyes, and it felt like he hadn't eaten in days. Yet he was filled with an excitement and yearning to learn more. The thirst for knowledge was difficult to control.

When the door opened, he followed the men waiting for him back to his room and devoured the meal already sitting on the desk. He barely registered there was a full bucket of water in the washroom before collapsing on the cot and falling into a deep sleep.

The next day it started all over again. Darwin walked into the dimly lit room with anticipation. Even the thought of spending another day in close quarters with someone else wasn't enough to dampen the excitement. Most of it washed away when he saw the parallel bars device already waiting for him on the desk, and Bill sitting patiently behind it.

The session went for close to five hours before he was escorted back to his room, a headache smoldering in the background. A meal waited for him, and he wolfed it down before falling into his cot. That night he dreamt that Rebecca entered his room and stood by his cot, Threads moving toward his head, probing, adjusting. Beside her, his mother crouched near his feet, a knife in her clenched fist. He woke to a room that was as empty as always, with the door still locked.

The pattern with Bill continued for two more days before he'd finally had enough.

"This is stupid. How long am I supposed to look at a stick?"

"Until you get it one hundred percent right. Some students get stuck here for months. If you don't have a solid base to build off of, you'll never be able to get up to something bigger. Now, which way will the stick fall?"

Darwin stood and pushed his chair in, pacing behind the desk in the small space. Every time he changed direction he stole a glance at the parallel bars. The Threads around it swirled with no concept of time, of how long he had been pacing. Bill seemed to be taking his cue from the Threads, his finger holding the stick in place as if he had nothing better to do.

Darwin sighed and pulled his chair back out, dropping into it with resignation. He looked at the Threads, not even waiting for the images to form. "It will fall left."

Near the end of the day, he had predicted every fall with the one hundred percent accuracy Bill was looking for.

Bill picked the device up off the table and returned it to the shelf. He poked around for a while, picking up and putting back several of the constructs before apparently finding what he was looking for.

The device he came back with looked as simple as the one he had just returned to the shelf. Instead of the parallel bars, this one looked like a plus sign. Bill balanced the stick in the center of the plus and waited for Darwin to tell him which way the stick would fall.

The Threads were more complex this time. Instead of indicating only two ways, there were now four, plus the chance of the stick balancing on its end. More comfortable with what he was looking at, Darwin quickly said it would fall toward Bill.

He was wrong.

"You didn't take the time to look at all the Threads," Bill said. "And you're still agitated. Remember the exercises. Remember how emotions can lead to insanity, how a calm mind helps you with the

Threads. Breathe in and hold it for a moment. Be calm and try again."

Darwin leaned back in his chair and rubbed his eyes. It had been another long day, and he just wanted to go back to his room and sleep. Last night had been miserable. Every time he closed his eyes, he saw images of his room at home. Of the lab when the test was being done. Of his dad. Of Rebecca standing over him as Threads slithered over his body. Of his mother. He would start awake and toss and turn until sleep called again. It went on for most of the night.

"How is this helping me to get home?"

"Rebecca believes you know how you came across, that the information is in your head just waiting to be pulled out. Because you can See, but don't have control, getting that information would be almost impossible. There is a far greater chance of destroying you and permanently losing the information than there is of getting it out."

"So the more I learn the better chance I have of getting home?"

"Right. Think of your untrained mind as a fine glass. If you wet your finger and run it along the rim, the glass starts to vibrate and hum. The small amount of liquid inside begins to ripple, and there is a chance the glass will break. That's what happens when you See without knowing how to control. If you keep it up, your brain will be like the liquid, and your sanity, the container. Now, think of the glass, and take your other hand and wrap it around. The vibrations stop. The liquid stills. That is where we need you to be, but it's a process. First you need to know you have a hand, then that you have fingers. Once that is done, that you have muscles that move the fingers. Muscles that have atrophied from not being used. It takes time, constant exercise, and monitoring."

Darwin nodded. It all made a kind of sense.

"Now, which way will the stick fall?"

He studied the Threads until the images came.

. . .

The lab was filled to capacity. Darwin stood crammed with Bill near the empty window frame. Inside the QPS room were Rebecca and her twelve disciples. She called them her Quorum, which didn't make a lot of sense to Darwin. Unless there were more in the group than the ones here with her.

Darwin silently counted the number of people in the lab and stopped at twenty-two. Several smiled when they caught him looking and a couple waved. These were the people that he met in his short forays—always escorted—around the Quantum Labs building. A few had even stopped and spoken to him before continuing on with their days. Despite his hope that he would see Lyell, the young man had never crossed paths with him.

He stopped counting and stared through the empty window frame at the QPS. There were more than the twenty-two here, but with the mass of bodies, there was no way he could see them all. Only a few weeks ago, when he first came here, being in a stuffy room with this many people would have sent him running for the nearest exit. He wasn't sure what had changed, or when, but besides a mild discomfort, he was feeling okay.

The number of people in here was only a small fraction of how many were in the Quantum Labs building and part of the Qabal. Bill had told him there were several hundred, though only a few of those knew how to use Threads. These were the ones that wore the anti-static jackets.

The tension in the room had increased the moment Rebecca had walked in—last, of course, so everyone could watch her. He'd felt the tension on his skin and in the way the Threads—the ones he could See—slowed and became stiffer. He couldn't help but let it affect him, and for a moment, the old feelings came back. Bill placed his hand on Darwin's arm and whispered for him to breathe. Even after only a couple of weeks of classes, Bill's voice and whispered instructions were enough for him to relax a little and pull away from the Threads.

Rebecca took her place behind the QPS and the room got quieter. There weren't even the minute sounds of cloth rubbing against cloth, or of a foot shifting on the floor. Everyone was as still as the view out of the window in his room.

The chanting he'd heard during his first time here, when Rebecca had tried to find out how he'd moved between the worlds, started up. The same strange rhythm of church hymns and 80s pop music blended into a whole that sounded wrong to his ears and grated along his spine.

This time, when the chanting stopped, he caught the flicker in the Threads that kept the group in sync. Everyone dropped to their knees, leaving Rebecca standing behind the QPS. Darwin knelt down beside Bill.

"Praise the Source, for all it provides to us," Rebecca said.

"Blessed be the Source." Again, the reply was in perfect unison.

"May the Source guide us along the path."

"Grant us the ability to follow where it leads."

Everyone fell silent once more, staring with what he could only describe as rapture toward Rebecca and the QPS. He opened himself to the Threads the way Bill had taught him, and gasped at what he saw.

The QPS room was laced with color and light. It was . . . he struggled to find the words and settled on *alive*, though he knew it was inadequate. It was alive with Threads. The Threads were the fourteenth person in the QPS room and showed a freedom he had never seen before. The way they moved between the Quorum and Rebecca was languid and smooth. Directed, yet seeming to have a mind of their own. What would he be able to See if he didn't have any inhibitor in his system?

He shifted his focus to Rebecca, enthralled by what was happening. Every Thread in the room was so obviously under her control. He marveled at the ease she displayed with them.

Bill's touch on his arm pulled him from the display.

"Easy. Remember to control what you See. Don't get pulled in so far you forget everything you've learned," he whispered.

Darwin saw Rebecca's gaze flick toward them. Bill hadn't spoken that loud. How had she heard him? Once again, though, Bill's calming voice worked its magic and he reined in the awe that bubbled through him, limiting what he saw to only the strongest of the Threads. Occasionally, a sense of family would fill him, a sense of belonging. Images of his mother bubbled to the surface. Where the hell had they come from? Despite his silent questions, he felt as though she was here with him, guiding him. He'd never felt closer to her than he did here. Not since the accident.

The ceremony continued for at least another hour before the final Threads disappeared and people followed Rebecca out the door. She waited as everyone walked past her and stopped to say a few words. He could see that each person who went through the door was infatuated with her. It was visible in the deferential postures of their bodies and in the way they wanted to hold onto her hands for as long as they could.

There was a difference when Bill spoke to her. Although he said the same words as everyone else, he didn't have the same posture, and didn't reach out to touch her.

It was his turn next. He tried to say thank you, but all that came out was a squeak. He cleared his throat and tried again.

"Thank you, Revered Mother." It was the first time he had called her that, mimicking what the others had said before him, and somehow it felt right. Rebecca was too personal in this place. He moved on before he could embarrass himself any more. He didn't reach for her hand, following Bill's lead. If it bothered her, he didn't see it on her face. It wasn't until later when he was alone that he realized that he actually liked Rebecca and the Qabal. Another change that had crept up on him.

His standard escort of two guards picked him up just outside the lab and followed him back to his room. Now that the service was over, he had no idea what to do with himself. There were no lessons from Bill, and without that, he was lost and bored. He sat in the mesh-backed chair and stared out the window.

For the first time since his lessons had started, he pulled out his cell phone and tried to turn it on. The battery was dead. He didn't even have his music to help pass the time.

What if he tried to do some Thread stuff without Bill around? He'd never tried anything on his own; he'd always been too exhausted after his lessons. He only hesitated for a moment before leaning back and opening his Sight the way Bill had taught him.

The first thing that came into view was the blue mesh surrounding the Quantum Labs building. It wavered at the edge of the parking lot, protecting everyone inside it from scavengers and thieves. He sat forward in his chair, the thought coming as a complete shock. He didn't feel like he was a prisoner anymore. He was part of the community inside the protective barrier. It was an interesting day for revelations.

A knock on the door pulled him from examining the change anymore.

"Come in."

One of his guards walked in. "The Revered Mother would like to see you."

Darwin got out of his chair, suddenly filled with apprehension. Maybe she'd found a way to send him home.

"Darwin, please come in. Sit."

He shuffled in, leaving the guard at the door, and lowered himself slowly into the offered chair. He couldn't explain the anxiety twisting through his gut and the fine layer of sweat that covered the palms of his hands. He gave them a quick wipe on his pants and waited, trying to analyze what he was feeling.

Why did she have this effect on him? What was it about her that made him want to either run and hide or confide his deepest darkest secrets to her? The longer he sat, the more the feeling faded, replaced with a calmness that left him even more confused, until even the confusion disappeared.

"What did you think of today's services?" Her voice was serene and conversational.

"I, uh . . ."

"They can be a bit disconcerting when you're at the early stages of learning. There's so much going on, it can be overwhelming."

He stayed silent, not sure how to respond to her and waiting to find out why she had called him here in the first place. There was no way he was going to tell her how the Threads in the QPS room made him feel, how it brought memories of his mother back so vividly.

"Well." Rebecca paused as if waiting for him to say something. "I asked you to come to see what you thought of your progress with Bill. Is he pushing you too hard? Not hard enough?"

Darwin shrugged.

"Well. Good. He is quite pleased with where you are. He thinks we'll be able to find out what you know in a couple of months."

"Months?" A pit yawned open in front of him and he felt himself falling.

"Yes. We need to make—"

"Two months? I thought . . . I thought we could try sooner . . ." The calmness, overriding the background anxiety he felt, drained from him faster than he thought possible, pushed out of the way by the sinking feeling in his stomach.

"We want to make sure we don't harm you when we start looking. You need a base knowledge so you don't fight our attempt."

"I know, but . . . but I thought it would only be a week or two."

Rebecca stood and moved around the desk, sitting in the chair beside him. She rotated to face him and grabbed one of his hands. "I know it feels like a long time, but it's better for both of us. There's less chance of harming you, and a significantly higher chance of finding the information we need to send you back home."

"I need some air." He pulled his hand from Rebecca's grip and lurched to the door, filled with a sudden distrust he couldn't explain. He yanked it open, only to be blocked by the man who had brought him here. Darwin glanced back to look at Rebecca. She nodded her head and the guard stepped out of the way. Darwin moved to the railing overlooking the entryway and placed both hands on it, leaning over to look at the floor below. The receptionist desk below him lay empty and abandoned.

He breathed in through his nose, the way Bill had taught him, and out through his mouth. Two months? It was a long time to be away. He'd miss the start of the new school year. How was he supposed to catch up? He stopped a quick, panicked laugh. What a stupid thing to think of when you were trapped in another world.

He was left alone for a few minutes before Rebecca joined him at the railing. She stood beside him without speaking.

He was the first to break the silence, asking a question that had been on his mind since Michael had tried to pull him through the blue mesh. This was the first time he'd had a chance to ask it.

"Where's Lyell? I haven't seen him since my first night here. You said you talked some sense into him. Where is he?" He was afraid of what the answer would be, but at the same time so desperate to hear it.

Rebecca paused for a brief moment before responding.

"He decided not to stay here anymore. He went off to look for Michael. We gave him what supplies we could and sent him on his way."

"That's it?"

"Yes. What else did you expect? That we would punish him?"

He wasn't sure what he'd expected. The warnings from Lyell and Michael, the hints from Bill about how he didn't allow politics or philosophies into his classroom, made him imagine the worst. He gave a small, wavering smile, unsure of how to feel.

None of it made sense or fit in with what he had seen of them, and he was too tired to fight about it. He just didn't want to anymore. The wave of calmness weaved back into him, and he pushed off of the railing.

"Can I go back to my room?"

"Of course. Monty here will walk with you."

He sighed. Of course he would. He found that he just didn't care anymore.

Darwin's waking hours turned into a comfortable pattern of classes with Bill, deep blissful sleep with the occasional dream of Rebecca standing over him benevolently, trays of food delivered to his room, and the intermittent sightings of his mother that he wrote off as exhaustion and the young teenager that had brought him food once.

In the third week, he watched as Bill manipulated the Threads, pulling here or pushing there, thinning or thickening the Threads to make the stick fall where he wanted it to, though he didn't teach Darwin how to do it. By the fourth week, he had difficulty remembering any other way of living. All that mattered were the Threads and the Qabal. They had become his life. Defined who he was.

He didn't even think of questioning it.

By the time the second month rolled around, he truly felt like he belonged. Most of his meals were taken in the large cafeteria of Quantum Labs, where he'd found a group of people to sit with. People he thought of as friends, who cared about him. He left most of those meals feeling happier than he had in years. The anxiety of being around so many people had receded into the background.

He opened up to Bill. In between lessons they would talk about life, about their pasts, and in Darwin's case, what he hoped for the future.

His future plans shifted the longer he stayed with the Qabal, from wanting to go home to wanting to learn more about the Threads, to how he seemed to fit in. At times like these, Bill would stop the conversation and start a new lesson.

Darwin didn't notice.

He tried to talk to Bill about the images more than once. Each time, Bill was sympathetic, trying to convince him that Seeing anything more than the Threads would slow down his progress and make it harder to move forward. That perhaps the images were vestiges of an emotional connection and should therefore be shunned. Emotions and Threads were never to be mixed.

Darwin didn't notice when the second month slid into the third.

His walks to the classroom went unescorted. There hadn't been a guard outside his room or Bill's class in he couldn't remember how long, and the doors were no longer locked behind him. The limited free time he had away from class was spent with his new friends or practicing. The Threads were a constant part of his life, and he lived with them, breathed them in, until he couldn't imagine *being* without them. The Revered Mother continued her visits, though they had slowed down somewhat. He looked forward to them. Forward to the wisdom she had to share, to the one-on-one time.

Today, he pondered the words she had spoken during the last service. Her talk of family, of how family encompassed more than blood ties, spoke to him. He felt the same toward Bill and the Revered Mother as he had with his dad. They had more than filled the hole in his heart that had been created when he'd come over. The Qabal was family . . . not just the few that attended the services in the sanctum, but everyone in the building. Even those who couldn't See the Threads. He had more friends now than he'd had since the day he was born. His life had become richer, more complete, since he had met them. He tried to remember the last time he thought of his dad and couldn't. He knew he should have felt guilty, but when he searched, there wasn't anything there.

He remembered that the service had been subdued, muted. The Threads less vibrant and less active than he had ever seen them.

He hadn't noticed that Bill wasn't in his usual place beside him, by the empty window frame.

Today, when he opened the door to the classroom, Bill wasn't sitting behind the desk. Instead, he stood near the back of the room, where he had been the day they had first met. This time, Darwin saw him easily by the movement of the Threads.

Bill moved to the desk and sat down. None of his fancy instruments sat on the table. Darwin took his place without a word and waited. Bill smiled, though Darwin thought it had a sad edge to it.

"I have only seen one or two people learn as fast as you have, Darwin," he said. "It is really quite remarkable. The Revered Mother has informed me you no longer have the inhibitor placed in your meals. It's been missing for the last few days, though you probably didn't notice. I've been told she's been reducing the inhibitor since your first lesson, so there wasn't much to get rid of. You've already noticed, but you will See all the time now, if you're not careful. Listen to what I've taught you. Don't try to follow every Thread. Your brain will snap at the effort. As my teacher once told me, a bird can roost but on one branch."

"Am I getting any more classes?" Darwin sat still, too scared of the answer to move.

"Maybe in the future, but not now."

He suddenly felt empty and hollow. What was he supposed to do now? His life had become classes with Bill and long talks with Rebecca. He leaned back in his chair as the realization of how he felt drove home. He cared for Bill and the Revered Mother—for his life here—more than he did for his life back home.

"I couldn't have done it without your help." He stumbled over the words, not willing to say what he was thinking, what he was feeling. It was all too new to him.

"You should know a teacher is nothing without a good student, and you have been very good." Bill sighed. "I have taught you all I am allowed about Seeing Threads, but there is so much more. Only experience will allow you to master the intricacies, the possibilities, of the Threads, allowing you to manipulate them as I showed you months ago. And I'm afraid only experience will teach you about life. That is the way with everyone, but more so for you. The Qabal limit what I See. Especially when it comes to you. But what I do See . . . you have some difficult decisions to make, Darwin. And the Qabal have already started changing you. I don't need the Threads to see that. Remember, the Qabal is but one way. Do not discard the others simply because you do not understand them. A wise man first learns, and then chooses. Not the other way around."

Darwin latched on to Bill's comment about manipulating Threads, ignoring the inherent distrust of the Qabal in Bill's words. "When will I learn to do it, to manipulate Threads?"

"I don't know." Bill sighed again. "My task has been to teach you to See and to control yourself, so you don't try to follow every Thread. From here, you would normally be tested for your strengths, to find out which Threads you have more affinity for. If you can See and follow the Threads in the human body, healing would be a good path. If you can follow the Threads of a bird flying through the air, hunting and tracking may be a good path. Or war. Most pupils would go from here and apprentice with a Master for a few years." He paused, obviously thinking about his next words. "The Qabal may not let you do that."

Bill got up, walked to the wall shelves, and picked the two rails and stick device Darwin had first worked with so long ago. He brought it back to the table and balanced the stick under his finger. "I'd like you to have this, as a memento. It is the simplest test, but shows that no matter what, there is always an alternate choice, an alternate way."

Darwin sat in silence for a minute before asking, "What do you mean, the Qabal may not let me do that?"

"Nothing. I've said too much already."

"This is my life, Bill. I have the right to know." For the first time in months, he felt uncomfortable to be in the classroom.

Bill searched his face before coming to a decision. He lowered his voice and leaned forward, still balancing the stick under his finger. "The Qabal limits everyone's rights. Yours and mine." He looked over Darwin's shoulder at the closed door. "Trust the Threads. Read them. Follow them. And trust your heart. Your mind can be easily fooled, but the heart is stronger. Listen to it."

Darwin didn't know what Bill was talking about, but the words sent a shiver down his back that he couldn't control. Suddenly filled with dread, he pushed the feeling aside, choosing instead to focus on the stick under Bill's finger. The Threads wrapped around it, embracing and permeating the wood, constantly thickening and thinning, always moving. Images of the stick split from the original. But not just the three images he had seen when he started learning. This time, there were five. The months of training had focused his Sight, and the Threads held a faint hint of green, like the skin of a ripe pear. When he'd asked Bill what it was, the answer had led into a dissertation of color and Threads. It all came down to green indicating an element of time, and since Darwin was essentially predicting the future, time was a part of the Threads he saw.

"Let go of the stick."

Bill hesitated. "But why? This is child's play for you now."

"Please, let go."

Bill released the stick. It balanced on its tip for a long second, until a rail snapped and the stick fell, free from the confines created for it. Darwin fell back into his chair, an acute, piercing pain slicing through his head before disappearing as quickly as it had come. He tried to hide the sudden exhaustion that swept through him.

Bill stared at the broken instrument and then up at Darwin, a smile on his lips. "Do you know how you did that?"

Darwin paused for a long while. The last time he brought up the topic Bill had dismissed it as a distraction, something to be discarded. But he knew he couldn't lie. Not to Bill.

"I chose the image that showed it."

THE BALANCE OF LIFE AND THE COLOR OF DEATH

"**R**EVERED MOTHER." **DARWIN** bowed as Rebecca walked into his room. She hadn't visited him in a while, and her presence filled him with unbridled joy. He hadn't thought about why he felt like this in a long time.

"Please, Darwin, sit. The formalities are for when others are around. Alone, we are family. Sit."

Darwin lowered himself into the only available chair while Rebecca paced around the room.

"Bill tells me your lessons are complete," she said.

"Yes, but I feel there is so much more. I—" He almost blurted out how he had made the rail break, but Rebecca continued before he had a chance.

"There is always more to learn, Darwin, but it all needs to be paced. Too fast, and all your skills may be lost. Too slow, and time is wasted. We try to find a median that works best for every student. You need to remember that our goal was to teach you enough about the Threads so that you didn't involuntarily fight us when we tried to find out what you knew. To send you home. Are you ready to try?"

He focused on the Threads surrounding the question, finding the ones that led to the possible decision. Before he could follow them, they faded away. New Threads formed to replace them and disappeared once again.

He looked at Rebecca. "Why won't you let me See the possibilities?"

"Your knowledge of the Threads is not strong enough to follow the complexities of the question. You wouldn't understand all you would See. They may suggest a path that is not correct."

He sat in his chair, watching her pace in front of his door. How long had he been here? Two or three months? Maybe a bit more? It briefly bothered him that he couldn't remember. It bothered him more that he wasn't allowed to follow the Threads. He should be permitted to do that by now. In fact, he shouldn't need permission. How much of what Bill had said was true? Could he really trust Rebecca, or was it Bill trying to turn him from his new friends? Neither option made sense, or fit in with what he knew of this new world.

A Thread flickered to his left and disappeared before he could look at it, and the thoughts fell away. He had a choice to make.

He wasn't sure he wanted to know if his unconscious mind held the information the Revered Mother was looking for. It would mean he would have to go home. Or would it?

The Qabal had taken care of him, taught him. They had become his friends, and his family. Was he willing to give that up to go back to being alone? To be the loner? The social outcast, harassed and teased for just *being*? The years of surgery had put him behind in school, and any friends he'd had moved on. He'd worked like a

maniac to catch back up, but it hadn't helped. He had been ostra-
cized even more for it. It had made his anxieties worse, and he'd
withdrawn even further from society. The doctors had told him he
would come through everything stronger and able to face anything
the world would throw at him. They hadn't calculated how cold teen-
agers could be.

The only person who would miss him if he never went back
would be his dad. The second the thought entered his head it faded
away, and for just a moment, he lost control of the Threads and the
maelstrom almost drove him to his knees. They were gone before his
body could react, leaving him dizzy and a little nauseous. He was left
with a single thought.

"If it works, would I be able to come back, or . . . or stay here?"

Rebecca smiled and stopped her pacing. "Of course, Darwin.
You have a home here. People who care about you, about what happens to you."

He stood, straightening his back, and looked the Revered Mother
in the eyes. "There is no decision to make, Revered Mother—
Rebecca. Any way that I can help, I will."

Rebecca smiled again, and he felt his cheeks flush with happi-
ness and his heart thudded faster in his chest. He knew, more
than he'd known anything else in his life, that he'd made the right
decision.

"An excellent choice." She turned to leave and stopped at the
door, looking around the empty office once more. "Your room is a bit
spartan." She beckoned to someone standing just outside the door.
"Frank will guide you around the compound and help you fill up
some of this space. This will be your room, if you do choose to stay."
She left, still smiling, leaving Frank in the doorway.

With the Revered Mother gone, the Threads came back into full
view, and he automatically limited his Sight.

"Hey," said Frank, "I'll just be out in the hall here when you are ready to look around, okay?"

"Yeah, sure." He looked at Frank, recognizing the man from when he had been carried up the stairs after Michael had tried to get him away. Surprisingly, that revelation didn't bring on any feelings of anger or hatred. The man was doing his job, making sure Darwin was safe.

Frank closed the door and Darwin quietly reveled in the sense of belonging, of having a family. Of, finally, being home.

He looked around his room. Most of the time he'd spent here had been sleeping through the exhaustion of training with the Threads. All he had was a solid wood office desk and the mesh-backed chair. Throw in the cot with its two patched blankets and you had his room. Even with all the empty space and the big windows, it felt small and smelled stale. It was definitely time to make it more comfortable. He opened the door and stepped out. Frank waited, a questioning look on his face.

"Let's get some stuff."

"Sure," Frank said. "This way."

Darwin closed the door behind him and followed Frank to the stairs leading down to the lobby. He'd taken them many times before, going to and from Bill's or the Sanctum, but this time it felt different. It—the entire building—felt confining. The beige walls pressed in on him and the high ceiling seemed like it was sinking and compressing the room, stealing the air, making it hard to breathe. He had been inside for far too long.

"It's been months since I've been outside. Could I step out, just to get some fresh air?"

Frank didn't even hesitate. "Yeah, if you want."

Darwin kept his eye on the goal, the black stone-encased front doors. All he wanted to do now was to get outside, to breathe the unfiltered air, to have a taste of something he hadn't realized he had missed until now. The feeling had come on so strong and so suddenly, he had no ability to control it.

There were no guards in the building entryway. He couldn't remember when they had left, when they were no longer standing by the entrance, but he hadn't seen them in a long time. They hadn't been needed when he'd been flanked by two guards whenever he'd had to leave his room. By the time he'd been allowed to go to classes alone, he hadn't wanted to leave.

Bill stood at the bottom of the stairs. He lifted a hand in greeting as Darwin passed. Darwin reached out to touch Bill's shoulder, his focus on the doors that had become his goal. The drive to get outside became overwhelming and he picked up his pace. Frank followed closely on his heels. Darwin stumbled through the doors, only stopping when he reached the middle of the empty parking lot and sucked the cold air deep into his lungs.

The air tasted fresh and clean. Clouds still lay scattered across the sky, but the dark menacing ones Darwin had seen out his window earlier had moved on, leaving a wet trail in their path. He breathed in again, letting the rich moist air fill his senses. It would have been nice to walk through the tall grass, now brown with the onset of winter, that had taken over the boulevard and crept into the parking lot itself. He could still smell the moisture in it. He barely remembered the once carefully manicured lawn that had become wild, or the well-placed trees that had overgrown their allotted space, branches waving in the cool wind.

Darwin strode closer to the boulevard, over the thin layer of dirt and weeds to the curb, and reached out to touch the woven blue sphere surrounding the building. Seeing it had become commonplace, even in daylight. It was as much a part of the Quantum Labs building as the walls and the black stone entrance. Because of his training, the mesh had taken on a grayish hue, looking more steel-blue than the generic color he had first seen. The Threads of the sphere responded to his touch by gently pushing his hand away.

"Has it always been here?" he asked, not sure if his lack of ability had made it seem partial a few months ago.

"Nope."

"It was put here to keep me in." It was more of a statement than a question.

"I heard it was to keep people out. They've tried to sneak in and steal stuff. Revered Mother shares what she can, but it is never enough for them." Frank's voice hardened on the last two words.

Darwin picked a single Thread in the weave and reached for it. His finger never touched it. Instead, the Thread moved and his finger went through the mesh. He sucked in a sharp breath and continued pushing. When the rest of his hand reached the Threads, they moved again and nestled into the spaces between his fingers, pushing back and stopping his hand from going through as well.

Just over his head, a branch stuck through the weave and a single Thread had wrapped itself around it. He tugged his hand out and grabbed the branch. As he pulled and pushed it, the mesh adapted and shifted, letting the branch move, never hindering its motion, but never releasing it. Moving it sideways briefly made the gaps in the mesh larger until the other Threads compensated. It was as though the wall was a living organism.

The long grass on the other side of the woven wall shifted, and a man shot up, standing directly in front of Darwin. Some corner of his mind noted the man had attached some of the grass to his clothing, making him almost invisible until he moved. The man stepped forward, his hand reaching for Darwin, not stopping at the mesh, but sliding smoothly through and wrapping around Darwin's wrist. The man yanked, jerking Darwin toward him. He pulled back, adrenaline and panic surging through him. He pushed against the flexible mesh with his free hand. The mesh separated, and his arm fell through, stopping at his shoulder. The man pulled harder and the curtain split again, allowing Darwin's body through. His feet caught the curb and he tripped forward, landing in a heap at the man's feet, wet grass pressed into his cheek.

As he went through, something in his brain ripped away, like a bandage torn off, leaving behind an open wound that poured out memories instead of blood. The panic—the need—to get back to the other side fought with the sudden onslaught of feelings of home. Of the realization of how long he had spent behind the blue mesh. Of his dad. Memories and feelings cascaded through him as though a dam had burst. The rush fought against his impulse to get back to Rebecca.

The gap in the mesh closed as quickly as it had opened, leaving Frank on the other side. Frank threw himself against it and the Threads rearranged themselves to take the impact, stretching out as they absorbed his body weight. Darwin lunged toward him, trying to grab something, anything, that would get him back in. The action was more reflex than anything else. His hand brushed the mesh and was yanked back.

"Don't touch it. Get up, we have to move quickly."

"Let me go! Frank, help me!" Darwin scrambled closer to the weave, yanking at the grass and the tree branch to pull himself forward, desperate to get back inside. Back to his family.

His family. His dad. His classes at university. The bed he'd slept in for over a decade, surrounded by things that belonged to him. Memories of his classes with Bill and services in the Sanctum. The strange feeling that leaving the Qabal was leaving his mother fought against the old memories rising to the surface.

"I said get up."

Hands grabbed Darwin and hauled him to his feet, pulling him further from his home and the people he cared about.

"Move!"

"No!"

"My god, what have they done to you? Look at me. I said *look at me*! It's me, Michael. For Christ's sake, Darwin, look at me."

On the other side of the mesh, Frank turned and ran toward the front doors of the building, yelling to drop the shield.

Leaving Darwin behind.

"Michael?" He knew that name, struggled to pull the memory from the chaos that had taken over his mind. He shook his head to clear it. It didn't work.

Michael had helped him once. Movement caught Darwin's attention and he looked through the blue curtain, seeing a lone figure run out of the building toward them. Michael ignored it.

"That's right, Darwin. Michael. Now come on, we need to go." His words were spoken softly.

"Go?" It was as if the world had twisted. Things that should have made sense didn't. Why was it so cold outside? Summer had just ended. But no . . . he'd been here for three months. It must already be December.

The figure got close to the mesh. "Why haven't you gone yet? Do you have any idea how hard it was to get him to come outside?" Bill's voice pierced through the confusion in Darwin's head.

"Bill?"

"It's me, Darwin. You need to go with Michael. Now."

"But I . . . Revered Mother . . ."

"Dammit. They must have done something to him, given him something beyond the inhibitor. Or messed with his mind using

Threads. How could I have missed it?" Bill looked at Michael. "Can you get him away on your own?"

Darwin swayed as Michael helped him stand. "I can try."

"Bill? Don't leave, Bill. Please?"

"Damn." Bill looked over his shoulder at the gaping maw of the beast. "I'd better come with you. It looks like you're going to need all the help you can get." He stepped through the mesh as if it wasn't there. "It's going to feel good to get out of here."

Two more figures ran from the building and headed toward them.

Bill grabbed Darwin's other arm and they ran across the boulevard onto the overgrown expressway, dragging Darwin between them.

"We need to move faster."

"Come on, we'll get into the bushes over there and I'll hold them off while you prep," Bill said.

They hauled Darwin across the cracked pavement and onto the next boulevard, moving into a small clump of wild bushes and trees. Bill turned and left.

Michael sat, still holding onto Darwin, and closed his eyes.

The urge to run back had left Darwin. Instead, his head was filled with snippets of conversation, fragments of thoughts that felt more like half-formed memories that flitted through his mind. Confusion took over, making him dizzy, until even that disappeared, leaving him empty and alone. His status quo.

He watched dully as Michael pulled Threads closer to him, twisting and spinning them into a short, man-sized cylinder that pierced the air, creating what looked like a tunnel made of yellow Threads. Once it was complete, a thick Thread started forming from its center, reaching away from Quantum Labs toward some unknown goal. It grew until Darwin couldn't follow it anymore. Sweat beaded on Michael's face.

"Step inside the hole."

"Why, what is it?" The words sounded slurred, even to him.

"Bill," Michael raised his voice, "let's go."

Bill came running through the bushes and eyed the cylinder appreciatively. "Nicely done."

"Just get in."

"After Darwin."

"Just go. Make sure the destination is clear."

Bill nodded, stepped into the cylinder, and disappeared.

"Your turn, Darwin. Hurry up, I can't hold it forever."

"Where did he go?"

"South. Step through." Michael stood and shoved Darwin toward the cylinder.

Darwin tumbled inside, following Bill.

His head turned inside out, his skin burning with a cold so intense it felt like it peeled from his bones and charred to a crisp. His breath froze his lungs until he was unable to breathe.

His heart beat a rapid staccato in his chest and sweat morphed into crystals of ice, falling off his exposed skin like fine snow. Panic surged through him. He had to get out, get back to something normal.

It was over as suddenly as it had begun. An instant of time stretched to fill eternity. Darwin stood beside Bill, his mind reeling with the sudden cessation of feeling. His knees buckled and a strong arm wrapped around his waist, Bill's voice cutting through the jumble that filled his head, calm and soothing. When he finally looked up, he saw they were in the middle of suburbia. Or what used to be suburbia, anyway. The houses stood empty, their windows broken or boarded up, doors hung from hinges, and the grass grew tall enough to hide small children. To the left, an entire block looked like it had been leveled by a bomb, leaving a gaping hole in the landscape. Michael popped out of thin air beside them.

"I started collapsing the hole, but they may be right behind us," Michael said.

Bill and Michael grabbed Darwin and pushed him down the street at a run.

He pulled and twisted, trying to free himself from their grip. His brain wasn't working, alternating between complete emptiness and a cacophony of half-formed thoughts. He knew he had to get back to Dad's lab. Back to his dad. Back to Rebecca. But Bill was here, with him. Nothing was making sense.

Dad?

The thought stuck, centering him.

Bill's grip loosened and Darwin twisted free. He spun around, pulling Michael's fingers from around his arm.

Bill stood where he was, no longer trying to keep hold of Darwin. From the corner of his eye, Darwin caught sight of a deep red Thread. Without thinking, he followed it back to its source.

Rebecca and Frank stood close to where Michael had popped in. The red Thread formed in front of her, reaching toward Bill. Darwin could See tiny manipulation Threads holding it in place. The Thread pulsed, and a wave of heat flowed down its length. He followed the pulse, lost in the Thread, pulled along with it like a magnet to metal. In the blink of an eye, the pulse reached the other end of the Thread, extending it until it wound around Bill's chest. A second pulse thickened and tightened it.

A loud crack shattered the silence and Bill's face drained of all color.

Bill's hand darted toward Darwin, grabbing his shoulder in an uneasy grip. "Go. Run." His voice was strained and pinched. His gaze never left Rebecca. A series of small pulses shot down the Thread, away from Bill, fighting against the push created by her.

Darwin stood rooted in the street. Michael's pull on his arm faded into the background as he watched. He was vaguely aware of tiny Threads just outside his field of view, but he pushed them aside.

The first of Bill's pulses hit Rebecca's end of the Thread, and Darwin saw her twitch. When the second pulse hit her, the Thread became thinner and her face tightened. Beside her, Frank began to build a Thread of his own.

Rebecca thrust another pulse down her now thinner line. Darwin could See it was smaller, less controlled than her previous ones. It met Bill's only a few feet away from her, barely slowing either of them down. Bill's pulse hit Rebecca. The Thread began to unravel as she dropped to the ground, her face constricted in pain. Darwin took a half step toward her when Bill screamed.

Her pulse had hit him square in the chest just before the Thread dissipated into nothing. His blue smock had ripped open, revealing a scrawny white chest. The skin had split and shattered ribs thrust obscenely through the opening. Bill fell to his side, his head hitting the concrete with a sickening thud.

Darwin felt the yank on his arm again.

"We need to go. Don't waste what Bill gave us."

Darwin turned and ran blindly after Michael. His last view of Rebecca was of Frank kneeling over her still form.

Part of him hoped she was dead.

MOTHER NATURE HAS TAKEN OVER

THE IMAGE OF Bill's shattered body lying in the street seared through Darwin. He ran with Michael, stumbling over curbs and cracks in the concrete, every crevice overgrown with vegetation, not seeing where he was going and not caring. Houses slipped past them. Their empty windows, some with tattered remnants of curtains hanging from the barren frames, stared into his soul and saw nothing but darkness and pain. Tears blurred his vision and ran down his face, dropping to the ground to be run over and forgotten.

Bill was . . . had been the friend he'd never had, the mentor. He was attentive, appreciative when Darwin did well, sharing his joy, and stern when he needed to be. He was always there. The only stable thing in the world Darwin had found himself in.

Besides Rebecca.

And she had killed him. In a single instant, she had robbed

Darwin of both of his anchors in this new world he had been shoved into.

Darwin's foot caught on the edge of a crumbling piece of fencing and he almost fell. Michael's strong grip kept him on his feet, constantly moving forward. They stepped over the rotting wooden stump, running toward the houses.

"We need to get off the streets," Michael panted, his breath misting in the air.

They sprinted between two bungalows, the shade a cool respite despite the frigid temperatures. Michael stopped and leaned against the white stucco of one of the houses. Darwin put his forehead against the rough wall. He gulped the air, trying to force more into his burning lungs. He turned, sliding down the wall, wanting, needing, to sit. To rest for just a minute. Rough stucco pulled at his blue anti-static jacket and scratched his back. He barely felt it. Michael pulled on his arm again, forcing him to rise to his feet.

"Come on. We can't rest yet. They followed us through the hole, so they know where we are. There's nothing stopping them from creating another one and sending more people after us."

"Why don't you make another one? Get us out of here?"

"I can't. It just takes too much energy. I don't have the concentration for another one. Seeing Threads is the easy part. Manipulating them is tough. Come on, we need to keep moving." Michael dragged Darwin between more houses and through backyards before heading down a back lane.

For the next hour, Darwin's world was a blending of houses and streets, some of it looking like it had been on the losing end of a war. At some point they left suburbia, walking across a cloverleaf intersection, staying off the fractured concrete and in the long grass and bushes at the sides when they could, before heading back into the jumble of never-ending houses and overgrown yards. The setting sun shone directly in their faces when Michael finally called for a rest.

"I think this is good enough. We can't run through the dark, and we need to rest or there won't be anything left in us tomorrow," said Michael.

Darwin fell to his knees. He felt as though he had been running on empty for too long. For months.

"Get up." Michael offered his hand. "Let's at least get under some shelter before the sun goes down. We'll stay in one of the houses tonight and start again in the morning."

Darwin lifted his aching body off the ground, ignoring Michael's outstretched hand. They walked through the broken back door of a dark gray two-story house, its paint cracked and peeling off in sheets. He barely noticed the dust and the animal tracks before collapsing under the table in what was left of the kitchen. He was out almost instantly.

Morning came too quickly. He opened his eyes, spying the spider webs that hung thickly where the legs met the tabletop. He was pretty sure there was movement, though it must have been his imagination. Nothing could possibly be living in the cold that permeated the house. He shivered in his blue anti-static jacket, wrapping it tighter around him and wishing he had something warmer to wear. He rolled out from under the table, his body protesting even the smallest move. Every muscle reminded him of yesterday's mad rush in a single instant. He hadn't exercised in months, and yesterday had pushed him to his limits, and well past them. He groaned as he forced himself to his hands and knees before using the table to lift himself to his feet.

He wrapped his arms around his waist, hugging himself to keep warm, the cold driving aside the pain. He knew it would only be worse tomorrow. He could still feel, or imagine he felt, the strange wrenching and tearing sensation he'd experienced in his head when he was pulled through the blue mesh. It was like a dam had burst and all the water that had been held back poured through the gaping hole. With the release came thoughts of home and his dad. Good thoughts. Thoughts he hadn't had in a long time. Had Rebecca done something to him? How much of the last three months had been real, and how much had been created by her manipulating him, using the Threads or that damn inhibitor against him?

What was it that she'd said that first time they had talked? *Don't make me do that for you again.*

Thirst cut through his thoughts, and he looked for something to drink. The kitchen was big and open with brown water-stained walls and splotches of black mold bleeding from the corners. He instinctively threw an arm over his mouth and nose. Two counters created an L against the walls, with dusty gray granite on top and a sink in the corner with yet another broken window in the wall. A brisk wind blew through the empty frame, chilling him to his core. Ignoring it, he walked past the stove and turned the taps on. Besides a short, faint hiss of air, nothing came out.

"You won't find any running water."

Darwin turned and stared at Michael. He looked like Darwin felt. His clothes were covered in dirt and grime and his eyes were shadowed in deep black circles. Darwin's own clothes were in the same condition, and the blue anti-static smock was torn in a few places. He had no idea how that had happened. Michael returned the stare.

"I got some water from the hot water tank in the basement. It's a bit stale, but it is clean. Food will have to wait until we get to a cache." Michael's voice sounded cheery, though it was obviously forced. "I thought getting away from there would be a bit more organized. That we would have time to grab my stuff before we left. I should have known better."

Darwin practically snatched the water out of Michael's hand and drained the cup. "Where are we? Can I get more water?"

"Definitely west of Philadelphia," Michael said as he poured another glass from a canteen. "My best guess is somewhere in or near Marple. I was hoping to at least get to Lancaster, but I didn't have time to get us that far. Hopefully we'll get there this morning. I have a cache there, which includes food and some warmer clothes for you. We'll have to wait until then before we get to eat. You can look around the house for some clothes, but I imagine it will be slim pickings."

"What about Bill?" Saying his name filled Darwin with conflicting emotions. Bill had been such a big part of his life for months, and yet he barely even knew him. The signs that he had been against the Qabal and Rebecca had always been there, but to be actively working against her? How could he have missed that?

His thoughts must have shown on his face. Michael's voice lost its forced cheerfulness, and he sighed. "There is nothing we can do for him. We can't go back. The Qabal know exactly where he is and will most likely be waiting. If they left him there, there won't be much to go back to anyway. You've seen what we ran through yesterday. Mother Nature has taken over, and she knows how to attend to the dead."

Dead. The word struck at Darwin like a direct blow and he stumbled back into the counter, placing a hand behind him to stop from sliding to the filthy floor. Of course he was dead, but hearing it spoken out loud made it so concrete, so final.

Michael took a step toward him and then paused, leaving the kitchen table and its nests of spiders between them. "I . . . I'm sorry, Darwin. He spoke highly of you." He turned and left the kitchen.

. . .

They didn't make it to Lancaster that morning. Michael sat in a small circle he'd created in the overgrown backyard, trying to build what Darwin thought of as a tunnel. He watched from the kitchen window as the Threads pulled together before fizzling out and disappearing. Michael was exhausted by the time it was done. He stumbled from the backyard and back into the house, muttering "not my forte" under his breath. Darwin found him a few minutes later on the filthy, stained beige carpet in the living room, fast asleep and still covered in sweat from the effort of trying to create one of his tunnels.

Darwin sat on the floor by the doorway watching Michael's chest rise and fall in a steady rhythm. What was he supposed to do now? Just hang around until the guy woke up? Take off and run to the Qabal? The thought stuck in his head.

The Qabal had given him something he'd never had before, something he didn't realize he even wanted. A sense of belonging, of being part of a group that accepted him for who he was. A place where he wasn't shunned because he didn't fit in.

Only yesterday he'd told Rebecca he wanted to stay. Only yesterday he couldn't have imagined *wanting* to go back home. There he'd be just another student at university, never having the right friends, the right clothes, the right personality. He hadn't even thought of his dad. Not really. It was as if the man who had helped him through the toughest time in his life didn't even exist. All that had changed when he'd been pulled through the steel-blue mesh. What had they done to him to make him forget the only person in his life that meant something?

Inside the blue-walled prison, everyone liked him. They all said hello in the hallways, welcomed him into the Sanctum services, sat with him at lunch. Now he saw it for what it was. A sham designed to fool him into doing whatever they wanted.

The image of Bill's twisted, tortured body rose to the surface. In his head, he watched again as the blood pooled around Bill's broken chest. A feeling of helplessness filled him from his head down to the soles of his feet. This time he let the tears fall.

The Qabal had killed him. *Rebecca* had killed him. The woman he'd trusted. In the blink of an eye, Bill went from a living being to an empty dead shell, broken as easily as Darwin had broken the rail on that stupid device. He rubbed his eyes with the backs of his hands, wiping the tears away. In the end, even Bill hadn't told him the whole truth.

It was Bill who had pushed him to run with Michael. It was Rebecca who had pushed him to be part of the Qabal, to agree to having his mind probed for information he wasn't even sure he had.

He jumped to his feet. It was enough. Enough of being told what to do by other people, of being controlled. He wasn't going back to the Qabal, wouldn't give Rebecca the chance to brainwash him again, or whatever it was that she had done to him.

How could he trust her to keep her word, to let him go back even if he did have the information they needed to create the link between the two worlds? That she wouldn't use the link and her power with the Threads to wreak havoc on his world?

Anyone who could get rid of someone like Bill so easily, take a life without a second thought, could get rid of him as well, and probably would. Especially if they thought he had joined Michael. Then there was Lyell, and he suddenly knew the man who had helped him didn't just leave the Qabal. Rebecca wouldn't have let that happen. He was as dead as Bill was.

And Michael. Should he follow him to wherever he led? Bill had thought he should, but in the end, Bill had *lied* to him, making him as bad as Rebecca. Maybe worse, because Darwin had thought of him as a true friend and confidant. What was it that Bill had said? That he'd had enough? The implication was that he didn't want to be there in the first place, that he wasn't Qabal. His double agent cover bullshit hurt almost as much as losing him did.

One thing was sure, he trusted Michael about as much as he trusted Rebecca, and that was enough to make the decision. He was better off alone. It had always been that way, and always would be.

He could try to find his mom. Lyell had said his dad had died, but was she still alive or had the wars Rebecca talked about taken her? If she was alive, would she want to see another version of her son? As much as every part of who he was yearned to look for her, a small part of his brain kept telling him it was a bad idea. He was the stranger here. Despite the quiet voice, he knew he was heading home.

He glanced at Michael, still fast asleep on the floor with a faint sheen of sweat on his face. He grabbed Michael's bag and emptied it on the kitchen table. There was no food, so Michael had been telling the truth about that. There were a couple of canteens of water. One felt full and Darwin put his head through the strap, resting it on his shoulder. Even full, there wasn't enough water to last more than a day. He'd have to get more as he went on or he would end up a babbling dehydrated idiot.

He grabbed a big hunting knife as well and wove the sheath through his belt. He wasn't sure what he would use it for, he had never hunted in his life, but its weight on his hip was weirdly comforting.

His search of the house had given him an extra-large man's button-up shirt and a pair of dress socks with holes in the heels. He wore them both anyway. Any little bit helped against the cold.

He closed the door on his way out, hoping it would keep some of the animals that had made the tracks on the floor at bay.

Things were as they should be, as they always had been. He was on his own.

Darwin looked at the sun and headed what he thought was north-east. Michael had said they were just west of Philadelphia, and that meant home was in this direction. It would bring him closer to the Qabal, but it was a risk he was willing to take. Just the hint that his mom was alive, that he had the chance to see her, to hold her, was worth the risk. His heart had won the battle over his brain.

He had no idea how long it would take to get there, and winter was settling in, but he'd find warmer clothes along the way. He'd make it. He'd read somewhere the average person walked just over three miles per hour. He had no idea how far Philadelphia was from his home. It was over two hours by car, but what it was on foot was something else.

Once he got home, whether his mom was there or not, his next plan would be to find someone who could send him back to his world, or could teach him how to do it himself. Maybe she would come with him, and they would be a family again. He laughed quietly as he left the yard. So simple.

He traveled most of the morning before realizing he'd have to change his priorities. The water he'd taken from Michael was already running low and he couldn't remember the last time he'd felt so hungry. His lethargic pace, set by the aching muscles created by yesterday's mad dash away from Rebecca and her Qabal, slowed him even more. His body was craving anything that could keep it fueled.

That changed his first order of business to finding some place to get more food and water, and something to carry it all in. He figured he'd made it far enough from the house he'd left Michael in that it would be next to impossible to find him.

Every house he passed looked like the one he had left, broken and ransacked. Paint peeling in sheets from the outside walls, leaving whatever was underneath it exposed to the elements. Maybe if he could find something more commercial, he would have a chance. He left the streets lined with empty and collapsing homes and followed what he hoped was a main road to a place with small businesses. Any place with restaurants or small neighborhood stores.

The first store he came across, a small corner Indian grocery called Patel Foods, had obviously seen better days. The bars had been ripped from the windows and doors, and broken glass lay scattered on the floor and empty shelves, a large brick nestled amongst the shattered shards. Even the sign had been smashed, though he didn't know if it had been intentional or just Mother Nature doing what she always had—reclaiming what was rightfully hers anyway.

Darwin moved through the store and examined the empty shelves. He was too late, and by the looks of things, years too late. Dust lay on the shelves in an even layer, indicating that nothing had sat on them for years. There wasn't even the track of mice or rats to indicate anything lived here at all. Taking one more chance, he got on his hands and knees, brushing glass away from in front of him as he went, and peered under the shelves. Hoping something was left behind by the looters who had obviously been through here.

A lone tin of cat food with a pull-tab top lay wedged deep in a corner. He stretched as far as he could, pushing his shoulder into the metal shelf until it hurt. His fingers were still inches away from the can. He pulled out Michael's hunting knife, using the extended reach to sweep the can closer, and grabbed it out. No-name Beef Supreme with real chunks of meat. Even the label was a generic yellow with plain black text. The can was halfway back to the shelf before he changed his mind and shoved it deep into his front pocket.

He wasn't going to eat it yet, but he was at the point where he knew he had to think about it.

There was nothing else left in the tiny space.

He left the store, his thoughts on the single tin of cat food. How hungry would he need to be before he opened it? The fact he'd even kept the can was indication he was pretty close already.

A deep growl drew him from his reverie. Ahead on the broken road stood a German Shepherd, its tail straight and tense with its ears pulled back along its skull, staring at him. Its face told a story of battles won and lost, scarred and misshapen, lips curled to reveal long white teeth. Matted fur covered its body. No one had taken care of this dog in a long time. Another low growl started in its chest and Darwin took a trembling step backward. The dog took a forceful matching step forward.

Fear shot through him, and his stomach churned, forcing what little was in it into his throat. He swallowed and slipped the hunting knife from its sheath, gripping it tight, sweat making the leather-wrapped grip slick.

The last few months of training with Bill fell away as though they had never happened, and Threads pushed into his view, each one clamoring for his attention, begging for it. The dog took another step forward and deep red Threads shot out from it toward Darwin. Pain drove into his head like a rusty nail.

He struggled to regain control, but it wasn't working. His mind tried to follow every Thread at once, crowding into every corner of his brain. Blackness narrowed his vision and threatened to close off the world completely. He dropped the knife, falling to his knees and grabbing at his head, pressing the heels of his hands into his eyes.

Another low growl came from his left. He raised his head, trying to push through the blinding pain, and stared blankly at the massive beast. The dog stood only a few yards away, its eyes level with his. It took a second before he realized it wasn't the Shepherd.

He closed his eyes, blocking the starving animal from his view, and concentrated on the exercises Bill had taught him, forcing the fear—the emotions—away. He groped wildly around before finding the knife and forcing himself to stand, pushing through the Threads that threatened to drown him.

New Threads forced their way into his view. He could hear Bill's voice in the background telling him to breathe, to concentrate. Darwin opened his eyes and looked at the dogs surrounding him. He could see seven of them now, spread out in a rough circle. Two were blocking his retreat back into the store. The pack had taken a step back when Darwin stood, but had not moved since.

He saw the Thread just before the attack. It shot out from the German Shepherd to the other dogs in the pack, then seven strands flew toward him all at once. They rushed forward before he knew what had happened.

Reacting instinctively, he pushed hard on the Shepherd's Thread, not knowing if it would even work. The dog yelped and faltered and Darwin was hit on all sides by the pack. Teeth grabbed at his leg and his world slowed to a crawl.

The German Shepherd attacked the other dogs, unused to being the last one to the prey.

He felt his jeans resist the pressure of a dog's teeth squeezing his calf.

Two dogs left the attack, turning to face the threat from the Shepherd.

His jeans gave way in a sudden release, and sharp teeth punctured his skin, sending searing pain lancing through his calf.

Two more dogs backed away, looking uncertainly between Darwin and the Shepherd.

Blood flowed from Darwin's veins, soaking through his pants and rushing into the dog's hungry jaws.

Darwin slid to the ground and a mangy mutt rushed in, its bared teeth reaching for his throat.

He rolled to the side and his world began to fade as he felt a sharp tug at his shoulder. Another yelp pierced the air and the darkness dragged him under.

Darwin floundered awake in a darkened room, memory and pain rushing in to fill the place left empty by sleep. The bed he lay on smelled of dust and old age and when he moved he could feel a cloud rise and re-settle on his face.

From a closed door on the opposite wall, voices sounded like they were arguing. He shut his eyes, pushing through the urge to sneeze, to hear what they were saying.

". . . Darwin Lloyd . . ."

". . . superficial . . ."

". . . leave him here . . ."

". . . Enton . . ."

". . . No . . ."

There was a brief moment of silence followed by, "He's awake." The voice sounded excited, and Darwin heard a faint slap. The door opened and two men walked into the room. Silhouetted in the light streaming through the door, they looked like twins.

Both men wore dark pants and shirts and had short-cropped hair. They weren't wearing the Qabal blue smocks, but Darwin wasn't sure that meant anything away from Qabal headquarters.

He glanced quickly to the window, dismissing it as an escape route. Maybe if he rushed them fast enough he would be able to squeeze through the door and get out.

"I wouldn't do it," said the one on the left.

"Yeah, not a good idea. The window isn't either. We're on the second floor," said the other.

"He could do it, though."

"Yeah, maybe. There are the bushes right underneath. They might break his fall."

"Nah, too close to the building. You're right, it is a bad idea."

Darwin raised himself to a sitting position in bed, realizing for the first time a thin sheet had been pulled over him. They had talked about both of his ideas to escape. Either they had done this before, or they were reading the Threads to See what he was planning to do. That meant they were either Qabal or with Michael's group. Or another group he didn't know about. Either way, this didn't feel like a place he wanted to be

"We cleaned out the bites on your leg and wrapped it. You won't need a healer; the damage was fairly superficial. Bled like a bugger though. You'll need new pants." He bent over and picked up a pant leg, torn at the calf and cut just above the knee.

The one on the left spoke up again. "The shoulder was just a scratch. We stopped that dog before he could do any serious damage. So, how did you get here?"

Darwin just continued to watch them.

"Last we heard, the Qabal still had you. If you got away from them you should have been with Michael."

Well, that made that clear. They weren't Qabal, but they were with Michael and his group. On one hand, Darwin felt relieved. He was pretty sure if they hadn't found him, he'd be pieces of meat in a dog's belly. On the other hand, he was back where he didn't want to be. What did it take to get away from these guys?

"I guess the dogs got his tongue as well. We kind of forgot to check that."

The one on the right laughed and elbowed his friend in the stomach. "Good one!" He looked back at Darwin and got serious. "Now, Carlos here has first watch. Until we figure out what's going on, you are basically a prisoner. One of us will be watching," he made a double quotation mark in the air with both hands, "all the time. Even when you go to the bathroom."

"Hey, that's your job, not mine," said Carlos.

The door closed on their arguing. Darwin could See steel-blue Threads form and cover the glass-filled window and the door.

He collapsed back onto the bed, the new cloud of dust finally releasing the sneeze that had been threatening since he'd woken up, and fell into a fitful sleep, his calf throbbing in time with his heartbeat.

The phone on his desk rang, and Darwin pulled himself from the equations and simulations running on his screen. He was only halfway back into the real world when he picked up the phone.

"Hello?"

"Darwin, come down to the lab. We're having an issue calibrating the quantum receptors and I'd like you to look at it."

"Andy knows more about that than I do, or Rebecca." He was already looking back at his screen. His math was off, and some of the results he was looking at weren't making any sense.

"Andy isn't in today. His kids are sick and he stayed home to be with them." His dad's voice sounded angry, which meant he was so deep into a problem he didn't have the extra capacity to be polite. "You worked with him on this. Pick up the calibration schematics from my office on the way down."

The line went dead.

Darwin took one more look at the screen and rubbed his eyes. It would take hours to get back into the problem, but when your boss called, you jumped. Especially when it was your dad. He pushed himself to his feet and left the cube he'd been assigned, heading for the stairs that would take him to his dad's office.

He walked into the lab ten minutes later, pulling the anti-static smock over his shoulders while trying to keep a grip on the rolled-up schematics. His dad was in the QPS room, sitting cross-legged on the floor beside Garth. Both men looked up at him when he walked in, but only Garth smiled.

Rebecca walked past him, her back rigid and a frown on her face.

"Bring over the schematics and help us figure out where we went wrong. Andy picked a hell of a day to take off."

"I thought you said his kids were sick."

Darwin's dad sighed. "I did. I'm not mad at him, it's just . . . we're so close."

Darwin unrolled the schematics onto the floor and kneeled beside the QPS. "What's the problem?"

"All the readings are off. Not by much, mind you, but enough to make most of our calculations invalid. We've swapped out the board already, and the problems stay, so we're not sure what's going on," said Garth.

His dad got to his feet, knees cracking as he straightened them. "Garth and I have been over this thing a dozen times. Maybe a fresh set of eyes will help."

Darwin moved to where his dad had been and pulled the test equipment closer. "Okay. I'm pretty familiar with the anti-oscillation circuit. Why don't we start there?"

It took them over half an hour to find the issue. Garth double-checked all the readings while Darwin narrowed down the trouble circuit. His dad was leaning over them just as the readings flipped.

"That's it! Where the hell is that?"

Darwin reset the tester and took another reading. "Something in the photonic sensor board. Let's see if I can narrow it down."

"We've replaced that damn thing twice already. What is it, a manufacturing problem? We're paying those guys way too much for shoddy work." His dad started pacing the floor again.

Darwin pulled the sensor wiring harness and checked the major system points. Everything looked good. He plugged the harness back in, and the readings faltered.

"It's the wire harness to the data collector, or the data collector itself."

"Let's replace the harness, Garth. See where that gets us," his dad said. He turned to Darwin. "You must get your patience from your mother, Darwin. We'd only been working on it for fifteen minutes before I was ready to throw everything away and start again. Good job!" He squeezed Darwin's shoulder before leaving the room.

Darwin stared at his dad's back. The reference to his mom's patience took him by surprise and filled him with a sense of accomplishment. It didn't matter how old you were, it seemed you always needed to hear stuff like that from your parent.

He passed Rebecca again on the way out.

"Was it the data collector?" she asked.

"Yeah, or the harness. Why?"

"I told them that's what it was before they even called you down here. It seems a man has to find the solution before it's believed. I'm sick and tired of being treated as if I don't know what I'm talking about just because I'm a woman."

"I wish you would have said something to me," Darwin said. "I would have loved to have gotten out of there sooner, and I would have told them who'd come up with the solution."

Rebecca gave him a small smile and turned back to the computer in front of her.

. . .

Darwin woke to the sound of rain splattering against the bedroom window in a slow steady rhythm. The soft sound had kept him in a half-asleep state where dreams of his dad warped his reality and made him feel like he hadn't slept at all.

The dream made him think about his mom, about how many times he thought he'd seen her over the years since the accident, and how the frequency had increased at the Qabal headquarters. Had Rebecca been manipulating him through that as well, using the girl that looked like his mother to make him feel even more at home, make him more compliant?

Though the light from the window was dim, he took time to examine his surroundings as best he could. The window coverings were simple blinds, blue by the look of it, though that could have been reflected light from the fine mesh covering the glass. The blinds swayed with every gust of rain, which helped explain the temperature in the room.

The bed was small, a single with a plain square headboard that looked more like a piece of plywood than anything manufactured. Everything shouted low cost. If this was a regular place these guys hung out, it wasn't in an expensive part of town, but it looked to be in decent condition. He shivered in the cold that seeped through the walls and snuck in the loose-fitting window.

Rising from the bed, he grabbed the top sheet and wrapped it around himself. Every part of him still ached, most of it probably from the run with Michael, but he was sure the dog attack had contributed its fair share. As well as having most of his pants chopped off, his shirt was missing, and he saw scratch marks covering his exposed shoulder from the dog's attack.

His first step made his calf pound, but after he moved around the room for a short while, the feeling subsided to a dull ache, blending in with the rest of the soreness.

The door opened and Carlos walked into the room.

"About time you were up. We need to get moving. We'll talk later."

"I need some clothes."

Carlos looked over his shoulder and yelled, "Hey, Wally. He talks today! Looks like I owe ya."

There was a muffled response from somewhere in the house.

"You'll have to borrow from one of us until we get back to Safe-Haven. We're not stopping so you can go shopping. As for the rain," he glanced out the window, "we have a spare garbage bag we can cut holes in for your arms and head." A grin spread over his face.

Darwin chose to ignore it. "I won't be able to walk fast."

"And there won't be much walking, so you'll be fine. We'll be in SafeHaven in four days, if all goes well. From there, Enton can figure out what to do with you. Now head downstairs and let us get some cleaning done."

Carlos stepped back into the hallway as Darwin limped past him. The interior of the house felt a bit warmer than the bedroom, a small reminder that the sun still carried some heat. All that seemed to have abruptly ended this morning with the clouds and the rain.

Darwin leaned against the railing as he headed down the stairs to the main floor, almost hopping instead of walking. Most of the stiffness seemed to have left his leg already, and it didn't feel that bad, but he figured he might as well play it up. If they thought his leg was worse than it actually was, they might lower their guard and he'd be able to slip away. As long as he could stay away from the dog packs, he would probably be okay. He reached for the knife on his hip. It was gone.

Wally sat on the floor in the middle of the living room. To

Darwin it looked like he was meditating, but when Darwin walked in, he glanced up.

"Wait at the bottom of the stairs. I need to finish cleaning."

Darwin waited, still keeping most of his weight off the bitten leg. Apparently, "cleaning" meant sitting and waiting. He opened himself up to the Threads to See if anything was happening there. It surprised him that he had blocked them without even thinking about it. Bill would have been proud. He shoved away the thought. Bill was dead and there was no point in always bringing him up.

"Look, but don't touch," said Wally.

Darwin used the banister to lower himself onto the bottom stair. The sudden bending of his knee relaxed his calf, making it hurt again. He straightened it out along the steps. How had Wally known he'd started Seeing? He hadn't done anything except look, and even then only superficially.

Now that he was looking, the room was a maelstrom of Threads. There were so many he couldn't even follow them. Generic Threads of gray were covered in tiny strands of green, moving the gray ones around the room. Without thinking about it, he slowed a Thread, trying to figure out what was happening.

"I said don't touch," snapped Wally.

He pulled back immediately, embarrassed by what he had done, and the quick flash of anger at being yelled at turned to guilt that he had been caught. He sat and watched, but still couldn't figure out what was going on. Not all of the Threads seemed to be present or real, but in a different way than when he saw how a stick would fall in the future. He opened himself to the images Bill had called ridiculous, and they slammed into him.

An image of a mouse running across the floor and then skittering back in panic the way it had come dissolved. Half-visible green Threads rebuilt the movement, continuing the mouse's path around the living room, until it linked back to where the original mouse had stopped.

A fly buzzed in through an open door, landing on the floor to explore the debris. A foot came down beside it and the fly took off. He watched the foot reverse its course until it faded into nothing.

Wally was remaking history. Things that had happened in the past were being altered to make it look like no one had been here. Concentrating harder, Darwin could See it wasn't that the past was being replaced, but that the *view* of what had occurred was changed. Whatever had scared the mouse, probably Wally or Carlos, was slowly being altered from the truth.

Darwin's head began to pulse and he pulled back, closing off his view of the images and the Threads. He knew he had overextended again and was paying the price.

Not knowing how else to describe what he had Seen, Darwin said, "You're changing the past. Hiding that we were here."

Wally opened his eyes and looked at Darwin. "Superficially. The past doesn't change, but a quick look at the Threads will show nothing out of the ordinary. If someone decides to look deeper, all this work falls apart. But if you're searching a hundred houses for us, chances are you won't be looking too deep." He closed his eyes and continued.

It seemed there was more to the Threads than Darwin knew.

WHEN ALL GOES FLAT

DARWIN ENDED UP getting an extra pair of jeans from Wally, and after they had argued for a while, a plain black t-shirt from Carlos. He was as happy about giving it up as Wally had been about the jeans, though when he handed it over he gave Darwin a wink.

The pants were too long and Darwin had to roll them up, making a donut-shaped cuff at his ankles. He looked like a dork, but it was way better than walking around in torn pants and a bed sheet.

The rain outside had stopped and turned into a fine mist that hovered in the air. Darwin fought against wearing the garbage bag raincoat, but Carlos and Wally both insisted.

"The mist will soak you through to the bone in no time flat," Wally had said with a straight face, "and we'll be walking a bit, to keep some separation between where we sleep and where we hole. We don't want it to be easy to detect where we stay."

He finally caved. His mom had always told him to pick his battles. If you tried to fight all of them, you were bound to lose the important ones. His hand automatically moved to where he kept his phone, and he patted the empty pocket. He missed his music, and the connection it gave him to his memories.

They almost fell on the floor laughing when he put the garbage bag on.

Externally, Darwin ignored them as best he could. Inside, he collapsed into a tiny ball, his stomach churning. It was his fault he was here with them. He was the one who wasn't paying attention when he came out of the store. He tried to convince himself that he didn't know them, he didn't like them, and what they did or said didn't matter. He threw up the barriers he'd perfected after the accident to keep everyone as far away from him as possible, locking himself in his safe place. It had never really worked.

Despite trying to push everything away, his mind continued to churn through what had happened, reviewing his actions and what he could have done differently to avoid the situation. By the time they moved outside, he'd managed to convince himself that this was different. It was as though the three of them were part of the joke, instead of him being the brunt of it.

Wally had been right, though—the mist soaked through his exposed pant legs immediately. But it was the icy cold rivulets that ran from his hair and down his back that bothered him the most. He thought he would have almost been better off without the damn bag. At least then he might not feel the cold stream running between his shoulder blades.

Once they walked a few blocks from the house, picking their way through the backyard and the collapsed garage to the back lane choked with stunted trees and prickly bushes, Wally sat under a tree while Carlos stood close by with his back to them, watching the nearby houses. Darwin didn't need to See the Threads himself to know Carlos was looking with more than just his eyes. He was more interested in what Wally was doing anyway. He let the Threads enter his vision.

The patterns being woven by Wally looked similar to those created by Michael the other day. Darwin watched as the Threads pulled together and a short tunnel began to take shape. When it was fully formed, with a thick Thread reaching toward the distance, Wally stood and gestured for Darwin to enter it. This time he didn't hesitate. Stinging cold bit through his wet clothes and hair as soon as he entered the tunnel, and his breath was sucked from his body in a sudden rush. When he emerged out of the other side a split second later, he fell to the ground, shaking fragments of ice from his hair and pant legs.

Wally stepped through, almost tripping over him. "Geez, dude. At least move out of the way."

Darwin rolled from the tunnel's exit, looking around. "Where are we?"

"East of Sunnen Lake, Missouri."

He wasn't sure why he'd asked, since the information didn't really help him.

The trees here were thick enough to choke out any undergrowth that had tried to take root, and were still changing color. A few had dropped their leaves, creating a carpet of soft reds, oranges, and yellows on the forest floor, and the earthy scent of fall was in the air.

It took a couple of minutes for Carlos to come through, and to Darwin's untrained eyes, the tunnel was beginning to look like it was deteriorating. Threads were peeling off and fading away.

"You keep waiting much longer and you're not going to make it out one day," said Wally.

Carlos grinned. "If you did a better job, I wouldn't have to stay so long to clean up."

"Yeah, right. You're just trying to make sure I feel guilty when it does happen."

"What happens if he steps through late?" asked Darwin, interrupting their banter.

"As the hole deteriorates, your particles lose entanglement and get spread across the galaxy. Whatever makes it to the other side is what you're left with, and there's always some of you on the originating side as well. It's not pretty, and a horrible way to die," said Carlos.

"Hole? I thought it kinda looked like a tunnel."

"The way the Threads get pulled together, it can look that way," said Wally. "Some people even create them as if that's what they are. Really, it's more like a door. You step through it and you're somewhere else. The door closes when you're halfway through, and—"

"The reality is something else," interrupted Carlos. "It's quantum physics and quantum teleportation on a huge scale. Kinda scary if you think about it too much, so I don't."

"So . . . so you can go anywhere you want?"

"Nah, it's not that easy. We'd have people on the moon if we could do that, or at the very least be able to trade with other countries. You need to have been to the place you're holing to at least once, sometimes more. Having been there makes the process easier for everyone. And the range is based on the individual's strength with the Threads as well. Holing is a pretty advanced skill. Not many can do it. It takes a lot out of you."

Darwin had seen that firsthand when Michael had failed to create a hole the day after he'd been taken—rescued—from the Qabal. Hadn't Michael also said he had no real clue where they were? How was that possible if you had to have been to a place you were holing to? He was probably lying to scare Darwin into not leaving. Michael had obviously not realized how strong the urge to go it alone was in him.

"It's a lot easier to disrupt a hole than it is to create one," Wally said. "That's why we make such an effort to clean up after ourselves, especially in Qabal territory. One low-level guy could kill anyone going through. Without even trying. Even just observing a weak hole can destroy it."

"Quit your yakking," said Carlos. "We're here till tomorrow, so set up camp. I won't be happy until we're someplace warmer. My Mexican blood is too damn thin for this cold. Keep an eye on question boy while I get our stuff." He walked a short way before turning back. "And even though he looks mighty manly in that garbage bag, have him take it off. In case you didn't notice, it's all blue sky up there."

Darwin sat with his back to a tree, the plastic bag under his butt, while Wally and Carlos rummaged through the underbrush and pulled out tents and tarps. He'd trampled down whatever had managed to grow below the thick canopy, and settled in for the long haul. Weatherproofed sleeping bags came down from one of the trees, and some food from another. He guessed since you had to have been somewhere before you could hole to it, you may as well have stuff ready for when you got there.

By the time the camp was set up, the sun shone directly overhead and the day had warmed up considerably. Even Carlos had removed a layer, though he was still bundled up more than Darwin. The dappled sunlight on the forest floor was mesmerizing, lulling Darwin into a dream-like state. He fell asleep leaning against the tree, his chin hitting his chest with a soft thump, far from the cold and wet of Philadelphia.

Carlos woke him from a sleep so deep, it took him what felt like minutes to focus his eyes and let his surroundings in. A small fire flickered a few feet away and a pot simmered in hot embers.

Wally scooped steaming brown beans onto a plate and threw on a handful of canned carrots before holding it out. "Come on. Get some food in your stomach before you fall asleep again. Tomorrow will be an easier day, but you'll still need your strength."

He'd barely gotten the plate in his hands before Carlos sidled closer.

"So, what can you tell me about your dad?"

Darwin lowered his spoon full of beans. "What?"

"Your dad. He's the one that started all of this, you know. I was his military contact for the QPS project. Since this" he waved his hands through the air "happened, I've been studying him. I've been to Princeton and found a copy of his old yearbook . . . I didn't think they'd need it anymore. You look a lot like him, you know. I've even been to your home, that two-story in New Jersey, before the Qabal got so strong. I was hoping to get some of your dad's papers, but someone else got there ahead of me. Left the place in a mess. I straightened it up before I left, though. It didn't feel right to leave it that way, you know."

Darwin stared at him, beans and sauce dripping from his spoon onto the edge of his plate. He snapped his mouth shut and waited. Carlos leaned forward, closing the gap between them even more, looking ready to ask more questions.

"It's been a long day, Carlos. Give the guy a break," Wally said.

Carlos leaned back and grabbed an empty plate, his gaze breaking contact with Darwin as if he was suddenly embarrassed by his outburst. "Sorry," he mumbled under his breath.

"Eat and get some sleep. The tent on the left is yours. We'll clean up and get things ready for tomorrow."

Darwin finished his plate as fast as he could and stepped behind a tree to relieve himself before almost running to his tent when he was done. He'd spent more than enough time with other people over the last few days, and to top it off, Carlos definitely knew how to make someone feel uncomfortable. He considered himself lucky that one of them hadn't followed him when he took a leak. Then again, where the hell would he run to? He had no real idea of where they were.

The next three days were a repeat, though the type of forest changed from deciduous to coniferous. Carlos and Wally alternated who did the holing—Darwin surprised himself with how easily he'd picked up the terminology—and who did the cleaning, though they weren't as careful about that as they had been in the house. Occasionally, Carlos would ask a question about Darwin's dad—how was it growing up with him, was his OCD worse at home than it was at work—but it didn't reach the level of intensity he'd felt the first night.

They never stopped in a city, or even close to one, from what Darwin could tell. When he asked why, Carlos had simply replied, "Scavengers." Darwin thought part of the reason might have been because they knew he was a city boy, and he wouldn't know how to survive alone in the wild.

Despite that, he'd thought of trying to get away. He was always the first one they sent through a hole, and in the few moments it took for one of the others to follow, he probably could have hidden somewhere, or even destroyed the hole.

The last thought actually scared him. Could he destroy it knowing someone was coming through? Knowing that they would most likely end up dead? Even though he was essentially their prisoner, it wasn't something he really wanted to consider.

They had ended up in the mountains today. Dry brown peaks

spread out to the horizon until they faded from view. Darwin heard Carlos and Wally talking, and caught the phrase "almost home."

Even though they had swapped the holing task every day, he could see they were getting more exhausted as the trip went on. By the time they reached the mountains both men had dark circles under their eyes and it took longer to make camp. Darwin helped as much as he could, but he always felt in the way as the two men worked. He was the third wheel in a team that had obviously been together for a long time. Yet, even though it had only been four days, he felt comfortable around them.

They were pushing hard to get home and he guessed he was the reason why.

Carlos's head poked into Darwin's tent, pulling him from nightmares of being ripped apart by dogs that threw pieces of his body through holes that disintegrated even before they had fully formed. He swam through the final remnants of sleep and opened his eyes. The first thing he saw was the faint steel-blue Threads still wrapping the outside of his tent. Carlos and Wally continued to put them around Darwin every night, as if he would be able to survive in the middle of nowhere. Seeing the Threads around him had become second nature. The next thing he saw was Carlos's silhouette outlined against the blue.

"Get up. Quiet. Fast. Now!" Carlos's voice was a fierce whisper.

"Wha—"

"Quiet. Now."

Carlos's head disappeared, and the blue Threads parted gently as Darwin crawled out, still rubbing the sleep from his eyes. He considered expanding his Sight to scope out the area around them, but Carlos was waiting for him, grabbing his arm as soon as he was free of the tent. He was dragged, none too gently, to a small gully just behind where they'd set up their camp. Wally was already there, sitting quietly at the bottom. His forehead shone in the waning moonlight with a glaze of sweat.

Carlos pushed Darwin low to the ground and leaned in close.

"You touch a Thread, and we all die," he whispered.

The words sliced into Darwin's still sleepy brain. It stirred more excitement than fear. He almost asked if he could look, but Carlos had already turned his back and sat down beside Wally.

So he did it without asking. After all, looking wasn't touching.

He rode the Threads in the gully for a few minutes—making sure to listen to Carlos's warning about touching them—trying to decipher what Wally was doing without being caught. One Thread grabbed his attention and he focused on it more. He felt the Threads dim, and a soft outside force dampened them even more.

Darwin opened his eyes to find Carlos studying him.

"How long have you been watching?" Carlos whispered.

"Since you dragged me in here."

"Geez. You don't listen very well, do you? What part of we're all dead didn't you understand?"

Darwin just shrugged in response.

Carlos stared at him for a moment longer before his eyes closed and he sighed. "You'll try again as soon as I let go, won't you?"

He didn't even respond this time.

"Since I got you out of your tent, eh?" He sighed again, obviously coming to a decision. "Okay. If I can't stop you, at least I can make sure you're not detected. Start again, but gently, and not as directly as before. Do you understand?"

"Not really."

"Don't focus on the Threads. Know that they are there, but don't try to follow or monitor them. Watching a Thread changes its state, and chances are, these guys are good enough to See it. Wally's busy obscuring—hiding us from their view—so I'll watch you, and cover you up when you make a mistake. Just work slowly. No sudden actions. This is not where I planned on dying."

"What guys?"

"Your friends," he said. "Qabal. About twenty-five hundred feet north, near the scrub line."

Darwin decided to let the comment pass. He hadn't had any friends in a long time, despite what Bill and Rebecca had tried to do to him. He had trusted them both. The key word being *had*. His confusion about the Qabal and what they represented had started to change with the wrench he felt going through the mesh, and had become clearer as the days passed. Confusion had turned into dislike, and dislike to anger and distrust. They'd brainwashed him. They were no friends of his. No one was. He wouldn't make the same mistake again.

He pulled himself out of his thoughts and focused back on the problem. Half a mile seemed a long way away to worry about a bunch of guys, even if they were Qabal. Darwin closed his eyes and let the Threads in, careful not to touch any of them. He'd never tried to See a Thread that wasn't in direct line of his sight before. Hell, he didn't even know it could be done. He slowed his breath and watched.

The Threads in the gully appeared first. His Sight immediately wanted to focus on Wally, to See what he was doing, but a gentle nudge from Carlos stopped him. The three sat in an odd bubble of Threads that had no pattern, a pale green interwoven with muted turquoise. As he extended his Sight beyond the bubble he could feel Carlos tense. He pushed through anyway and looked back. The only thing he saw was more of the scrub and dirt that they had built their campsite on. He couldn't distinguish where they were hiding from the surrounding area. Even the gully was partially obscured.

He opened his Sight more and a single image flooded into his head before he felt Carlos clamp down on him again.

What had appeared to be random Threads from below now looked like the rest of the landscape. A bug crawled on the ground, and changed direction to bypass them.

He drew in a deep breath and held it for a moment before releasing it slowly through his mouth. As he let his Sight unfocus even further, more Threads came into view. He took another breath and relaxed, looking into the middle distance. His peripheral vision took over.

Threads popped into existence and disappeared again, constantly weaving through the area. He could see their tents set on the level ground not far away, distinct from the Threads of their surroundings. And the number of Threads! He'd never Seen so many before. His mind balked at the massive expanse of . . . of *everything* around him. He felt on the edge of control. An abyss yawned before him, threatening to swallow him whole. A steady hand touched his knee, and he forced his breathing back under control. He could feel Carlos pulling him back, controlling—even a little—of what he saw. As the discipline Bill taught him came back, he sensed Carlos letting go again.

He pushed his Sight further out, past the gully, concentrating on the tents, and drew in a sharp breath. Both tents still had people in them. Carlos and Wally's had two, while his, still wrapped in the blue mesh, had one. At least that's what the Threads told him. This was different than predicting the Thread or image that would create the reality, this was the Threads *changing* reality. Creating the perception of something that wasn't there.

He was tempted to find out if the images would show him the same thing, but Carlos hadn't liked it last time he'd done that. Out here, near the tents, he knew the risk of exposure had to be even greater than in the gully where they were protected by Wally.

Movement in the distance caught his attention, and he shifted his Sight to look at it, making sure to not focus directly on what he was Seeing. From the distant scrub line, a crimson Thread moved, weaving slowly along the ground. His impression was of a small animal, foraging for its meal, but it seemed to have more purpose than that. Yet, if he focused somewhere else, the Thread almost disappeared into the background noise. He stayed near the tents, suddenly too scared to venture closer to where the Qabal hid.

The Thread moved closer to his tent, slowly meandering around its base. Though the Thread never changed, he began to get the impression of weight. It still looked and acted like a small predator, but it felt like a small car, then a truck, and finally like a jumbo jet.

Without warning, the Thread shot hundreds of feet into the air and came back down directly over the top of Darwin's tent. It had lost all pretense of being an animal as it thickened and picked up speed. A single column of air sped in front of it, pushed downward toward his tent with a force Darwin could scarcely believe. The impact of the Thread against his blue-encased prison was completely silent, and his tent flattened to the ground, a thin nylon smear on the brown turf.

If he had still been in there . . .

Beside him, Wally let out a soft sigh, and the impression of someone in the tent went out as fast as the column of air had crushed it.

Carlos clamped down on his Sight just as he felt himself lose control, yanking him back to the gully as fast as he could. The shock of the tent, flattened like a bug, washed through him.

If Carlos hadn't gotten him out, he'd be dead.

. . .

Darwin wasn't sure how long he sat in the bottom of the gully. He was vaguely aware of Wally still working the Threads beside him, but time seemed to have simultaneously stretched and compressed. It could have been seconds or hours later before Wally groaned and stood up, stretching his back and legs, announcing, most likely for Darwin's benefit, that the Qabal had moved off. All Darwin felt was numb.

Carlos helped him to his feet and walked him out of the gully. Darwin blinked in the glare of the sun just beginning to peek over the mountains. The tents remained where they had set them up. Carlos and Wally's stood as pristine as when they had left it. Darwin looked down at his; the nylon material followed the contours of the ground it had been set up on like it had been painted there. There wasn't even a lump from the sleeping bag.

"It looks like if the Qabal can't have you, they don't want anyone else to, either. They want you dead," said Wally.

"How did they know I was here?" Darwin's voice came out squeaky and he swallowed to cover up the fear that threatened to take over.

"That's the question, isn't it? Striking this close to SafeHaven takes guts. Something I didn't think they had. They threw a fair amount of manpower here last night."

"But I—"

"But nothing," Wally snapped, his natural, easy humor gone in an instant. "It's time for you to wake up. You're not supposed to be here. They want to know how you did it, how you came across. They trained you so they could use you. That's it. Get the information on how to cross between worlds out of your head and throw what's left of you away like a broken toy."

"I . . . I didn't know," said Darwin. "I trusted them. Trusted Bill."

He blurted out the last words without thinking, the pain of Bill's deception hurting more than Rebecca's. More than it should have. Bill had never professed his love for the Qabal. He'd done the opposite. So why did it hurt so much? Maybe because he'd let—hell, helped—the Qabal's plan go forward.

He turned away from Carlos and Wally, rubbing the unexpected tears with a furtive wipe of his hand, and looked at his flattened tent. He had been willing to help them, the Qabal and Rebecca, considered them family. What an idiot he had been.

A gentle hand fell on his shoulder. "They were brainwashing you with drugs and Threads. If Bill knew that, he wouldn't have let it continue. He would have stopped it and gotten you out sooner. You have to believe that."

Wally's voice was soft and caring, and the last thing Darwin wanted. More people trying to be his friend. He twisted out from Wally's hand just as Carlos spoke.

"Come on, we have got to get going." There was no tenderness in his voice, just an urgent need to move.

When Darwin turned around, he saw Carlos had their tent all the way down. He bent over to pick up a corner of his flattened mess.

"Leave it. We would if you were in it." Wally's voice was subdued, as if he could read Darwin's mind. He stared at Darwin's feet. "I hope those running shoes of yours are comfortable. We've got miles to walk today, and it won't be easy travel. I'm exhausted from this morning, and Carlos is still resting from holing yesterday. We need to find a new hole point. The Qabal obviously know about this one. I never liked it much anyway. Too exposed. We'll stop to eat after we get a couple of miles behind us."

Darwin watched until they were done, staying as far away from his own tent as he could. He followed them back into the gully, his mind a complete blank.

THE DANCE MASTER

DARWIN, WALLY, AND Carlos walked through dawn and most of the day. As promised, they stopped for a quick breakfast before continuing the torturous journey. On a normal day, Darwin wouldn't have had any issues, but his three months of sedentary life with the Qabal coupled with his throbbing calf turned the day into a prolonged nightmare. Every step was either up or down hill. Sometimes they even had to scramble across rock faces using their hands for support. At one point, he was so scared of the potential fall that it took Wally and Carlos half an hour to coax him across a span of only six feet.

As the day progressed, the culmination of the dog attack, the thin mountain air, and the tension he'd carried with him since the attack concentrated in his muscles. He hurt. Every part of him ached and he fought through the exhaustion to keep up. When they stopped, looking around an area for its holing potential, he would slump to the ground while either Carlos or Wally would find a reason to not like it, and struggle back to his feet, plodding along behind them as they moved on. By the time they found something they both liked, he was beaten both physically and mentally. Even his bones hurt. When they stopped again, he simply lay on the ground struggling to breathe while Wally set up the single tent and Carlos prepared an easy meal of cold peas and carrots from a can.

He ate sparingly and drank water when he was told to. The third time he almost dropped his plate Carlos pulled him to his feet and walked him to the tent.

"Get some sleep," he said. "Wally and I are both keeping watch tonight. We'll wake you up in time for breakfast."

He fell on top of the sleeping bags and slept through until morning.

Carlos woke him up early, placing a handful of dry crackers and a cup of water in his hands. He choked down the food with the tepid water while the two men packed up and hid everything near the base of a small cliff. Yesterday's walk still weighed heavily, though he was sure it was more due to the mental strain of the last few days and someone wanting to kill him than the actual exercise. The thin air couldn't have helped either. He wasn't that out of shape. Despite that, all he wanted to do was lay still until his body had a chance to heal and to pull in a full breath.

After their meager breakfast, Carlos created a hole, pulling in yellow Threads that reminded Darwin of the color of fresh corn. For the first time, Darwin wasn't sent through before anyone else. He stepped through after Wally, and almost tumbled back. After days of holing into woods or onto mountains, the painted walls of a small room took him by surprise.

Four people stood facing the hole, and from the way they were greeting Wally, they were all old friends. When Carlos stepped through, he walked around Darwin and joined them.

Darwin took the opportunity to look around. The room was bigger than he first thought. Most of it was behind the hole they'd just come through. The far wall was filled with racks and shelves, each stacked with an assortment of outdoor gear. This place was cleaner than the house they'd stayed in, but it had the look of being heavily used. He finished his quick scan and refocused on the group that had greeted them.

The four were dressed pretty much the same as Wally and Carlos. Worn but good condition jeans and dark, muted-color t-shirts and jackets. Two of them, a tall blond man with a few extra pounds around his waist and a shorter woman, wore backpacks. Her dark hair was tied up in a bun, and her t-shirt hugged her slim form. She caught Darwin looking, and gave him a quick smile and a once-over. He quickly glanced down, his cheeks turning warmer.

"Who's your friend?" Her voice was harsh and raspy, and Darwin saw the top of a scar at the base of her throat.

"Ah," said Carlos, some of his humor that had gone missing over the last day coming back. "That would be our very own Darwin Lloyd. Fresh from the clutches of the Qabal. Darwin, this is Mellisa. The other three would be Toby, Brian, and Manuel. There will be a test later, so keep sharp."

Darwin struggled to fight his natural desire to melt into the background and grinned sheepishly. "Hi." Inside, he wanted nothing more than to be alone, although he knew the first thing he would do would be to go over the events of the last few days, second-guessing his decisions at every step until he drove himself crazy.

He'd noticed that since the attack, Wally and Carlos had treated him more like a companion than a prisoner. Maybe almost being turned into a wet smear by the Qabal had changed their minds about

him. Even before that, being with them was different than being
with the Qabal, prisoner or not.

In hindsight, everyone with the Qabal was always so serious,
almost suspicious of each other. Especially when Rebecca was
around. All of the smiles and camaraderie had felt forced. Carlos and
Wally were the complete opposite. A point driven home by the four
that met them here.

Carlos continued. "Speaking of the Qabal, we were hit yesterday,
up in the mountains."

All four turned to look at Carlos. "That close?" Manuel asked.

"Yup. Darwin and I were fast asleep. I had just holed, so Wally
was on watch and . . ."

Mellisa gave Carlos's cheek a quick kiss and grabbed Darwin's
arm. Instinct almost made him pull it away. He stopped himself. If
she noticed, he couldn't tell.

"Come on, I'll show you around SafeHaven while these two em-
bellish their story. I'll read it in the report before Toby and I head out
again." She turned and stuck her tongue out at Carlos. He just
grinned in return and winked at Darwin. Darwin couldn't help but
smile back.

"Welcome to SafeHaven, California. It's actually a pretty nice
place to be," Mellisa said. "It used to be called Alpine, until Enton
and some of his crew got here. They found the place abandoned, and
over time built a piece of it into this." She led him through a door and
onto a busy street.

He knew the Qabal had more people, but he'd never seen so
many at one time as he did here. He took an involuntary step backward. After so many days with just Carlos and Wally, it was a bit too
much for him. Mellisa must have noticed his hesitation.

"It's a bit busy here, but once we get further down Columbine, it
will thin out. You want to wait inside, or . . ."

Darwin shook his head. "No, it's fine."

"Okay." Mellisa continued her description of the place as though there had been no interruption. "SafeHaven is a training ground for Threaders. That is what we call ourselves, anyway. This is where we learn to use the Threads, and how much we can safely handle without going insane. Everybody Sees differently. Some, like us," Mellisa pointed over her shoulder with her thumb, back at the doorway they had walked through, "are scouts and watchers. We can hole, clean up, and be defensive if we need to. Some become healers or teachers—"

"And some learn to fight," said Darwin.

"Yeah. Unfortunately, we need that too, thanks to the Qabal." She touched the scar on her throat.

"What happened?" Darwin mentally kicked himself as soon as the question came from his mouth. She probably enjoyed talking about her defects as little as he did about his.

She didn't skip a beat before answering.

"I met a Qabal troop on a recon mission three years ago. My partner didn't make it. She created a hole for us, and never stepped through." She touched her throat again. "The healers managed to give me this."

"I'm sorry."

"Don't worry about it. I don't. The sooner you figure out what the Qabal are, the better off you are."

"I think I'm getting there."

"Good. Now come on, I'll show you the important places." She pulled Darwin down the street. "This is pretty much all living space, though you'll find some places like where you holed into." They went through a T-intersection with some large pine trees on the corner. Mellisa pointed right. "This sidewalk will take you to the old Community Association building. That's where we eat. Mealtimes are fixed, just listen for the bell and walk in, you'll get a pretty decent meal. Over here is the . . ."

Mellisa took the morning to show Darwin where everything was. SafeHaven wasn't a big place. They had only taken over a tiny portion of the original neighborhood—an outskirt suburbia type of place with a couple hundred houses and only two roads in—building walls around the neighborhood they controlled. When he asked if there was anyone else living nearby, he was told no. Everyone had moved into SafeHaven or one of the smaller communities down in San Diego.

SafeHaven was obviously well organized. People patrolled the walls in pairs, and it looked like everyone had some sort of job to do. He even saw what he thought was a classroom sitting in the shade of a building, and watched a teacher as she wrote on a large white-board. The one thing that stood out to him was the lack of neglect that he had seen outside Quantum Labs and during his run with Michael. There wasn't any vegetation taking over the yards and roads, and the houses were well maintained, if a bit worn. The small spots of grass in the front lawns were all brown, but without running water, that was to be expected.

Before she left him to hunt down Carlos, Mellisa said someone would show him where to bunk down before night came. She also warned him about leaving. "We're kind of in the middle of nowhere here, and we close the gates at night. If you leave the compound, make sure you're back inside before the sun goes down."

Before she left, he finally got up the nerve to ask the question that had been bothering him most of the morning. "Why do you have the wall?"

"We're willing to give food and shelter to anyone who needs it, but for some people, that doesn't matter. They can only think of taking and stealing. Nothing like that has happened in a few years, but we stay vigilant. It looks like we may need it against the Qabal now. With Carlos and Wally having seen them so close . . ." She shook her head, letting him complete the sentence for her.

Only think of taking and stealing. He'd heard that sentiment before, and it didn't make him feel any better about being here. Was he a guest, or was he still a prisoner? Was the warning about the locked gates meant to keep him inside? He couldn't quite figure out what was going on.

He spent the rest of the day walking the perimeter of SafeHaven and some of its smaller areas, avoiding any place that looked crowded. No one tried to stop him or asked what he was doing.

The slow pace he kept helped loosen his stiff muscles, though he rested in the shade whenever he had a chance, even falling asleep a couple of times. At one point, he asked someone for water and got an old plastic bottle with a screw top handed to him. He carried it with him for the rest of the day. When the dinner bell rang, he found his way back to the mess hall. The place wasn't big enough to feed everyone who lived here at the same time, but no one seemed to mind when he joined the tail end of the line leading into the large building.

The meal wasn't as good as what the Qabal had fed him, but it was filling and better than what Carlos and Wally had given him on the way here. Strangely enough, even the background sound of people talking and eating felt reassuring. Despite that, he found a spot at an empty table near the door. It was always easier to put up with crowds when he was close to a way out.

No one sat with him while he ate, and he didn't see Wally,

Carlos, or Mellisa walk in. They'd have to walk past him to get to the door. Maybe it was better that way. The less he knew people—the less he cared—the less chance there was of him being fooled again.

Supper consisted of not quite fresh bread slathered in butter and a hearty serving of what he thought was pumpkin soup. It was tough to tell, but the color matched and it tasted pretty good. As the food settled in his stomach he decided he would stay here as long as he could . . . at least until he could figure out a way to get back home.

He hadn't looked beyond the walls during his walk, but from the palm trees and other plants he'd seen, never mind the dead brown grass that covered a lot of the front lawns, he didn't think they grew a lot of food locally. That meant SafeHaven traded with other communities, and trade meant communication, which meant he had potential access to a wider network of people here. People who might know how to send him home.

Someone came by and cleared away his plates as the room started emptying out. The vast majority of the people seemed to be heading in the same direction. Since he hadn't been told where to sleep yet, he followed them, winding through the street to a dead-end cul-de-sac. The people streamed between the houses and through the backyard, following a drainage ditch down a slope. Below him, a circular stage had been built and benches had been cut into the rocky slope.

The amphitheater started to fill up. He figured it would be able to hold at least five hundred people, maybe more. Couples sat close to each other, families quieted their kids, and some, like him, sat alone. Everything looked so normal, so routine. He was filled with a sudden feeling of loss so intense he could almost smell home. It wasn't the setting that had done it, or even the families that sat grouped together. This came from inside, and the loneliness it brought with it blurred his vision with tears.

He wiped them away as the crowd fell silent and seven people walked onto the stage. They were all dressed the same, light brown shirts and pants, loose at the wrists and ankles and tied with a golden sash at the waist. Their ages varied. The youngest, a girl, looked like she was only nine years old, while the oldest looked older than his dad, older than Bill.

With their entrance, his homesickness became physical. His stomach felt hollow and his chest tightened and burned. He blinked to force back the fresh batch of hot tears that fell down his cheeks without warning. He realized he'd been so focused on getting home that he hadn't thought about his dad in a long time, and the sense of loss threatened to overcome him. It wasn't easy losing the only person he had a connection with, the only person he could talk to. Who would listen. He'd been here so long. Did his dad think he was dead? Had an empty casket been lowered into the ground beside his mother's, his name engraved on a new headstone? He didn't want his dad to hurt that way. He knew that kind of pain . . . how it tore you apart every day, made you feel somehow less than what you had been. Made you remember things long since forgotten. Made the world an unbearable place to be.

At that exact moment, the oldest in the troupe—Darwin thought of her as the leader—stopped scanning the crowd and looked straight at him. She began to move, never taking her eyes off of him. As if he was the trigger for the start of the show. It unnerved him, yet he couldn't tear his gaze away.

The dance was simple at first, the troupe moving along the stage in slow languid motion, looping between each other but never directly interacting. The movements looked like a martial art, but they were smoother and suppler. Definitely slower. It took Darwin a few minutes of absolute boredom to realize the audience was enthralled by the performance, moving in time with the dancers and occasionally gasping out loud. It was as if they were watching a different show.

What if they were? In theory, everyone here could See, in some form or another. What if the Threads were part of the dance? Darwin opened his Sight, and gasped.

The Dancers weaved amongst each other, sometimes running and jumping, sometimes barely moving at all. The Threads, multicolored and shifting between vibrant hues and muted wisps, wove between them, creating a tapestry of color and making the individual dancers a single cohesive unit. Where the leader went, the patterns changed and the colors shifted. One half of the stage was a brilliant version of the Aurora Borealis he remembered from camping as a kid. The other half looked like a tartan, shifting and changing its pattern in sync with the aurora. In the middle the leader blended the two into a curtain of color that she threw over the audience until a huge Bald Eagle made of Threads flew from it, its beating wings shifting the patterns once again. Darwin had never Seen Threads like this before. Not even Rebecca had done anything close to what he was Seeing.

"They do not See."

"What?" The voice shocked Darwin from the artistry being created before his eyes. An old man had sat down beside him. When he had done so, Darwin couldn't say. He had been pulled too deeply into the performance.

"The dancers, they do not See," the old man repeated. "It is said they *feel*, and the intensity of the emotions changes the color and strength of the Threads."

Darwin turned back to the dancers. They stood in a rough circle now, with the leader at its center, and as she spun and danced, Threads arced between her and the rest of the troupe, creating the images Bill had told him would only slow down his learning. He watched, mesmerized at the immeasurable beauty on display in front of him. The old man beside him was completely forgotten.

It was over before Darwin realized. The troupe of seven stood sweating in the center of the stage and bowed once before leaving. Threads flickered off their bodies like flames, slowly dissipating as they controlled their breathing—their emotions. The old man beside him waited until Darwin looked at him again. He held out his hand.

"I'm Enton. I think you and I should talk."

Darwin and Enton stayed seated as the audience moved out of the amphitheater, their voices carrying in the curves of the ground, merging into a dull drone. Enton said hello to those who passed close by, calling each one by name. He didn't say anything else to Darwin, and when Darwin got up to leave, he simply placed his hand on Darwin's shoulder and continued to acknowledge those who walked past them.

The last to leave were the Dancers, now out of their performance clothes and into well-worn blue jeans and t-shirts. The lead woman came up to them. She nodded at Darwin and looked at Enton, smiling.

Enton introduced the Dance Master.

"Where do this one's talents lie?" she asked.

"We don't know yet, Baila," said Enton. "He just came to us today."

"A bit old to be recently discovered."

"His circumstances are quite unique."

"Hmm. It's a shame he's so old. Even with the Sight, I would have been able to teach him to dance. He has the ability to become a Master, this one. Perhaps he still does."

"Thank you, Baila. I'll keep that in mind."

She turned to Darwin, and he was immediately drawn into her almost black eyes, unable to break contact. "I and my students believe emotions are key to the Threads, and emotions run deep in you. Learn to trust them, to control them, so they don't control you. If you do so, the Threads will do your bidding. If you do not, you will fail."

The Dance Master left with her troupe behind her, leaving Darwin confused. What the hell had just happened, and what did she mean?

"Apparently, you've managed to impress several people during your short time here. Bill was quite overwhelmed, though Michael not so much."

At the mention of their names, Darwin flinched, the pain of Bill's loss still too fresh, and he turned away.

"Yes," Enton said, tightening his grip on Darwin's shoulder as if reading his mind. "Bill will be missed by all. He was one of our best teachers, and a dear friend. When he volunteered to infiltrate the Qabal, he knew the choices he was making. We were fortunate he was there to guide you. You, on the other hand, have no idea what your choices are, and when you make a decision, no idea of the consequences. A person's life is made of choices. Some are easy, some are difficult, and each one molds you into what you are today and what you will become tomorrow."

Darwin pulled his shoulder out of Enton's grasp with a sharp jerk, uncomfortable with the intimate contact. "So you'll be making decisions for me?" His voice was harsh, and the anger that had become so familiar after his mother died rose to the surface. He didn't know if it was because of Enton trying to take control or because of Bill's betrayal.

"No. We are not the Qabal. Your choices will be your own. We will simply give you the information you need—or help you find it yourself if you wish—to make an informed decision. Having you here is an anomaly no one had even thought of. The many-worlds interpretation of quantum mechanics had been discarded long ago. Traveling between the worlds, between the decision trees if you will, is quite remarkable. Can you imagine the branches, the complexity, if every decision made by humans alone created a new world, a new path? What if the choices made by animals or fish did the same thing? The mind boggles at—"

Enton must have seen the look in Darwin's eyes, and he abruptly stopped, apologizing.

"I'm sorry. I tend to ramble at times." He changed the subject. "I heard about what the Qabal did to your tent last night. It seems they don't like you."

"That's an understatement." For the first time, it occurred to him that maybe it wasn't the Qabal who did it. Maybe it was some of Enton's people. Maybe they were trying to convince him they were better than the Qabal, trying to guide his choices. Everyone had been surprised the Qabal had struck so close to SafeHaven. Were they trying to control him, just using a different method than the Qabal had?

Enton just smiled. "It's late, and an old man like me needs his sleep. I'm sure you have many questions. We'll get together in the morning. Just ask anyone you meet; they'll tell you where to find me. You've been assigned a room in the house behind the mess hall. Get some sleep." Enton turned to go, then paused to look back over his shoulder. "And welcome to SafeHaven."

"So I'm just supposed to trust you? I get brought across the country, most of it as a prisoner, and suddenly everything is fine?"

"That will be your choice to make," said Enton without turning around.

. . .

Darwin was woken up by a bell ringing outside his window. It took a few seconds for it to sink in that it was the call for breakfast. He hadn't set his internal alarm clock to wake him up, and had obviously slept in. Either that or they had breakfast pretty damn early here. He stood and opened the curtains to bright sunlight. He figured that answered the question. He'd slept in. He pulled on his shoes and left the room to find a table.

As soon as he left the house, he felt the chill in the air. His breath misted and he pulled the cold air deep into his lungs. He still hadn't gotten anything more to wear than his t-shirt, and the slight breeze cut through the thin material. This wasn't quite the warmer south he'd expected. He ran across the open area to the mess hall.

The place was fuller than it had been last night. The odor of people was overridden by mixed smells of porridge and toast and eggs. He'd never seen so many people so eager to start their day. It made finding a quiet place to eat alone impossible. In the end, he decided to brave the cold and took his food out to the street and sat down in the sun, leaning against the building. He wolfed the eggs and buttered bread down as fast as he could, missing even the weird-tasting coffee substitute the Qabal had served, and was almost finished when someone sat down beside him.

Mellisa's raspy voice spoke before he even knew she was there.

"Good morning," she said.

"Hey."

"Nice day to have breakfast alone, out here."

If she was being sarcastic, he couldn't tell. "I don't know anyone, and I . . . I don't feel comfortable in crowds."

"Because of the accident?"

Darwin stared at her. "How . . . how do you know about that?"

"Carlos told me."

"I never told him. I don't tell anyone."

Mellisa shifted uncomfortably on the curb. "When they were looking at your wounds from the dog attack they saw the scars. Even buried beneath the surface, a trained healer can See them. You were hurt pretty bad." She raised her hand to her throat.

If anyone else had said that, had noticed that he was different on the inside, he would have been hurt. Maybe it didn't because she was damaged as well. You could barely see the scar on her throat, but the voice was a dead giveaway.

"I know how you feel," she said. "It took me a long time before I could just be myself again."

"It must be different here, then," he said, fighting the urge to run his finger along the invisible lines on his face.

"Different?"

"It *has* been a long time, and I still don't fit in. At home or here."

"You've just gotten here. Give it time. We're not bad people, just ones trying to live and laugh and love. You should try it sometime."

He didn't answer her. What was it that Enton had hinted at yesterday? He didn't belong here. He finished off his plate before changing the topic. Mellisa didn't try to fill the short silence.

"I'm supposed to meet with Enton today," he said.

"Oh?"

"Yeah. I saw him last night. Is he always so weird?"

Mellisa laughed, the sound coming out low and gravelly. "I thought he was a bit strange when I first met him as well. He loves to go off on these tangents. Sometimes you need to rein him in and get him back on track."

"Kind of like Carlos."

She gave another short laugh. "He wanted to know about your dad, didn't he?"

"Yeah. It was weird."

Mellisa laughed again. "It sounds like he talked about your old house. It was a huge highlight for him. I guess everyone has their thing. Did he tell you he knew your dad before the change? Carlos was the military liaison and he was there that day to watch the demonstration." She changed the subject abruptly, as if she'd said too much. "What did you and Enton talk about?"

"Nothing really. Just that I was supposed to see him this morning. Do you know where he is?"

"Chances are he's just about to begin his walkabout to see how everything is going. Your best bet is to catch up with him in an hour or so. You'll find him in that building over there." She pointed to a house with a faded blue door on the corner of the street.

Darwin stood to put his dishes back. Mellisa followed suit, placing her hand on his forearm.

"We aren't the Qabal, Darwin. We're family here. We take care of one another. Take the time to learn that. Give us a chance to show you before you decide to write us off. Please."

She took his dirty plates from him and left him standing in the street.

Darwin spent the time waiting for Enton in the room they'd assigned to him. There was no real heat in the building, but it was definitely warmer than it was outside. He left his room twice to check the place Mellisa had said Enton would be. The door was never locked, but Enton wasn't there yet. The second time, Darwin considered just staying and waiting, but he wasn't sure what the protocol was, so he went back to his room. At least the sun was shining through the window and warming the place up a bit.

When he went next, Enton was sitting behind a desk reading

from a stack of papers filled with handwritten notes. He smiled as Darwin walked in.

"Darwin, good morning! I hope you had some breakfast already." He didn't wait for an answer before continuing. "Don't you have something warmer to wear? I'll have to have a chat with Wally and Carlos about how they treat people. Come on, let's go to stores and see if we can't find something you like. This paperwork is pretty boring anyway."

"Umm. Good morning." Darwin wasn't sure if Enton even wanted an answer, but it was nice to be able to get a word in. He followed the older man back out the door and onto the street, turning away from the mess hall.

The storeroom was similar to the room they'd holed into when Darwin first arrived, but a hell of a lot bigger. Someone had knocked down the wall in one of the houses, creating a large open space filled with racks and shelves of clothing. He went straight for some thick winter coats before Enton stopped him.

"Those are probably a little heavy for what you want. We're in a bit of a warm spell, so it will probably get over seventy-five degrees today. You just need something for when the sun goes down."

He picked out an insulated windbreaker, a dark blue that wouldn't stand out, and they left the building, once again turning away from the mess hall. Darwin was the first one to break the unexpected silence.

"How do I get home?" As soon as the words were out, he knew he'd sounded rude. Before he could correct himself, Enton answered as if he hadn't heard Darwin's tone.

"I really have no idea. We don't know how you came here in the first place. If we knew that, maybe we could work backward from there, but who knows. Threads don't behave the way we always think they should."

"Rebecca said that maybe there was someone out there who knew how to get me home." He couldn't keep the hope out of his voice.

"Maybe, but I doubt it. I don't know how much the Qabal told you, but the world is a different place than it used to be. In your world, the Threads have just started. You still have phones and computers and ships and airplanes. We have none of that. The knowledge is still there, but there's no oil or gas or electricity to keep things going. The shipyard in San Diego is trying to build new ships, but the skills required to make them haven't been used in over a century. It takes time to relearn. If some group had the ability to travel to other worlds, I'd think they would be able to travel *in* our world as well. That hasn't happened. We've grown to live in small enclaves, separate groups that trade with one another."

"I don't get it. Why did everything fall apart like that? It's not like the Threads stopped everything from working, is it?"

Enton sighed. "No, but it may as well have. There was a lot of fighting. In some places all-out war, but mainly small skirmishes. Those that couldn't See the Threads were scared of what we could do. They didn't understand. When you're that scared of something, it's human nature to try and destroy it. Both sides lost a lot of good people. Threaders destroyed almost everything non-Threaders needed like communications hubs, oil refineries, shipping yards, and airports. They didn't think about how devastating that would be. Non-Threaders just tried to destroy us. The end result is what you see . . . smaller groups trying to survive, trying to rebuild what's been lost as best they can."

That explained the devastation he'd seen when he'd first been pulled from the Qabal's grasp. How many more places had been razed to the ground by the war?

"How many died?" He hated the question as soon as it came out of his mouth.

"We're not sure. I can say that I lost more than half of the people I knew. I don't know if you can extrapolate that out, but I'd say it's pretty close."

Darwin stopped talking, keeping pace with Enton as they walked through SafeHaven. More than half of the population gone? The numbers were astronomical, and his dad had just started the same chain of events in his world. How many families would be broken—destroyed—by what his dad had started? What *he* had helped start? A new reason to get home nestled into his brain. He had to shut down the QPS.

They continued on in silence as Darwin mulled over every-thing. How long had it taken before the fighting had started? If he went back now, would it be too late? Would it matter? If he could shut down the QPS everything would go back to the way it was. Wouldn't it?

"Rebecca . . . the Qabal thought they could get the information out of me. That's why Bill taught me how to use the Threads, so they could get in there and not do any damage."

"Huh. Interesting. They thought you had the knowledge but didn't know it?"

"Yeah, something like that."

They'd reached the eastern wall of SafeHaven and left through a small gate, moving south to catch more of the sun's warmth.

"Come then, sit. Show me what Bill taught you."

"Will you try to pick my brain as well?"

"That's not our decision to make, Darwin. It's yours. At the very least, we can find out how much you know about the Threads, and plan some more training for you, if that's what you want."

They spent the next few hours going over the last three months of his life. Enton somehow created a similacrum of the Thread patterns Darwin had Seen using Bill's devices, and Darwin predicted the results he saw. By the time they were done, the sun beat down on them, and Enton's promised temperatures were close to being met.

"Good. Bill did a great job, but then it was against his nature to do otherwise. Let's try something else." He placed his thumb and forefinger around the stem of a dandelion that had opened, taking advantage of the southern exposure. "I will pluck this dandelion. Doing so will set off events that have absolutely no correlation with the plant itself. On the other hand, there is a chance nothing will happen because of my actions. Look at the Threads and tell me what you See. There is the possibility of many Threads resulting from this. Don't try to follow them all, only the strongest ones. Remember, a bird can roost upon only one branch at a time."

Those words pulled Darwin back to Bill's small, dark room in the Quantum Labs building as if he had never left. As if Bill was still alive. Did Enton and Bill have the same teacher, or was Enton the teacher Bill had spoken of?

Enton reached out and touched his shoulder, pulling him back to the small field in SafeHaven. "Concentrate."

He looked at the Threads coming from the dandelion. The one showing it being plucked was the strongest, and he followed it. He had never done something like this before, following a Thread beyond its initial state to See what happened next. Without any effort on his part, the Threads split and the images started appearing. Those that stayed in the same place—by the wall—overlapped; others seemed to show places he had not seen before, places he had never been to.

The strongest image showed the weed being raised to Enton's nose and then being crumpled in a fist. Others showed the plant being discarded, stepped on, thrown into the air to be forgotten.

Against Enton's instructions, he focused on the weaker images. In one, a rock skipped across a pond before sinking into its murky depths. In another, an owl flew through a darkening sky, intent on its first kill of the night.

A third image jumped into focus, hardening into a perfectly still picture with colors so intense it felt like he was there. Before him stood a person with their back to him. The person was in front of a cairn made of rocks and chunks of concrete in a small opening in the woods. The trees still held yellowed leaves, and the smaller plants had withered and browned. A crooked cross had been fashioned out of sticks and wedged into the rocks. He knew who was under that pile. Knew with every part of himself. Knew it was Enton.

A hand shook his shoulder followed by a soft voice. "Only the most immediate and strongest Threads. Don't go down the rabbit hole. Few ever come back."

He shook his head, closing his eyes, and breathed deeply. The images disappeared and the original Threads came back into focus.

"Please don't," he said. "Just leave it where it is."

"Is that the action you See me taking?"

"No . . . I . . . I just don't want you to do it." How could he tell the man that he had Seen his grave?

"That's not an option here. I will rip this flower from the plant. I'm only asking you what you See me doing after that."

Darwin shook his head, trying to push the image of the grave out of his mind. Instead, it grew until he was sure what he saw was the truth.

"If you do that, you'll die." He blurted the words out in a mad rush, placing his hand over Enton's. "Please, don't."

"What did you See?" Enton's voice was still gentle, almost a whisper. It was as if he knew what Darwin had Seen and was looking for confirmation.

Darwin told him, describing the scene with every detail.

"Beginners often follow Threads to the wrong conclusion, Darwin. What you saw may not even be related to whether I pluck this dandelion or not." He moved his hand away from the plant anyway. "But why risk it, eh? What did you See happening before you followed the Threads so deeply?"

"You smelled it, then crushed it in your hand."

"That was the plan, so you saw true based on the original knowledge you had. You did well. Bill was always a good teacher." Enton drew in a breath. "If you like, we can help bring back any memories you may have tucked away. The process is not pleasant, but may help you find your way home. We can also teach you more. Your skills are strong, but incomplete, and we can help. Don't answer now. Think about it. Let me know tomorrow." He stood, leaning against the wall for support. "I forget I'm too old to sit on the ground for that long." He took a step, heading back to the gate they had come through.

His right foot dragged across the dandelion, separating the bright yellow flower from the plant and partially covering it in dirt.

Darwin sat up in bed with a jolt, his heart pounding in his throat. Something had woken him from a deep sleep. He held his breath, all vestiges of sleep vanishing as he listened to the silence of the night and the thumping in his chest.

A scream filled the air, high-pitched and panicked. He flinched, the visceral reaction kicking in before thought. He jumped from his bed, pushing against the coarse sheets that wrapped around his legs, and yanked on his pants and shoes.

Another shriek tore through the night before he reached the door of his room. Feet drummed just outside, echoing down the hallway, and he paused before pulling open the door, waiting for them to recede, letting the panic that grabbed hold of him reduce from its mad rush. He drew a steadying breath and stepped into the dark, empty hall. A third scream ripped through the night air, ending too abruptly. He ran down the hall toward the rectangle of gray that led outside. The faint smell of smoke met him as he stopped just outside the door.

Deep red Threads raced across the night sky toward the northern section of SafeHaven. A mass of people surged around the corner in the opposite direction, running down the street in front of him. He stumbled back into the open doorway as they rushed past.

A mother carried a baby in one arm and dragged a small child behind her with the other. Both kids were crying, scared and not knowing what was happening. Older children grabbed onto their parents, their knuckles white and faces filled with fear as they were pushed by the crowd behind them, barely staying on their feet.

The Threads thickened, racing just above the horde of people, rushing in the direction they had come from. Darwin stepped back into the crowd, fighting to hold his position against the tide. Part of him screamed to just let go. To move with the masses, to get away from whatever was behind them. Another part made him stand his ground. Only a few days ago, he'd watched as the Qabal had tried to kill him. Before that, he'd stood only feet away from Bill as he had died. Bill had put his life on the line to give Darwin the chance to get away. In the end, he wasn't sure what made him push against the crowd, whether it was because he wanted to live up to Bill's standards, or because he felt he owed Bill something in return. Maybe it was as simple as thinking there was something he could do.

He drove against the torrent of bodies, hugging the buildings until the crowd thinned and disappeared. The street dead-ended and he turned left, the crowd receding as he jogged toward the flames that flickered in the night, casting the space between the houses into dark shadow. As he came around a corner he saw a girl standing alone in the middle of the street dressed in nothing but a nightgown. White streaks stood out on her dirty face like fresh paint, showing the tracks of her tears. A man rushed up behind her, blood on his face and clothes. He scooped her up, barely breaking his stride, and ran past Darwin, following the earlier mob. The look in his eyes was one of barely controlled terror, and the girl clung to him, her small muscles taut under her skin.

Sounds of fighting came from in front of him, and he slowed before he reached the next corner. Smoke billowed out from the street ahead, thick and black, shrouding the night with its acrid smell. He faltered. What the hell was he thinking? SafeHaven was a city of Thread users, and by the sounds of it, people who knew how to fight. What did he think he could do here? Help? He continued on, entering the thin smoke at the edge of the cloud. He didn't know what he could offer, but he wouldn't turn his back on anyone who needed help.

A small figure stumbled from a doorway just ahead, falling to her knees and crawling away from him. In one arm, she held what looked like a small bundle of clothes close to her chest. Even in the dark, he recognized her as the youngest girl from the dance troupe. The bundle in her arms let out a choked cry and squirmed, almost falling from her grasp. She held the baby tighter as he pushed through the smoke toward them and she struggled to her feet.

As he ran, the air began to clear and another figure strode out of the dark in front of the dancer. He was tall, at least six feet if not more, and muscular. In the dark, his skin looked taut and gray. Darwin skidded to a halt. The man was wrapped in a mist of fine red and steel-blue Threads, creating a violet hue around his body. A weapon and a prisoner at the same time.

The dancer looked tiny against him. She lurched to a stop,

tripping over her feet again, twisting her body as she fell, placing it between the ground and the child she was holding. Her head hit the street, and Darwin could almost feel the thud from where he stood. The child rolled a few feet away and lay still. Neither of them made a sound.

The man bent down, holding his hand out as if to help her. Instead, he drove his fingers into her throat and clenched. Tendrils of smoke rose from the point of contact. The dancer spasmed once. Darwin stood rooted in the street. His body drained of all heat, frozen in time as he watched her life end. The man moved toward the baby, and Darwin's terror galvanized into action.

He sprinted without thinking, trying desperately to close the gap between them. His body slammed into the man. It felt like hitting a wall. He stumbled back in a daze, the entire left side of his body numb and hot from the impact. The man swung the child, aiming for Darwin. With the clarity of someone just waking from a nightmare, Darwin saw it was a young boy, barely old enough to eat solid food. The boy's heel clipped him across his chin, and in the same move, the man released his grip, slamming the boy's body into the side of a building.

Darwin fell backward, scrambling on his hands and feet as he stared up into the man's face.

What he saw wasn't a man, it was a monster. Skin stretched tightly over its face like a white sheet. Where its eyes should have been were two indents, darker shadows on the waxen skin. Its nose was two small vertical slits in the middle of the blank face, and it had no mouth. The creature took a step toward him.

Darwin rolled over and raised himself to his knees, adrenaline pushing him to his limits, forcing away the numbness. He jammed a foot forward and shoved off it as he rose, launching himself away from the monster, stumbling on the edge of control. A hand clutched at his shirt, grabbing the material in strong fingers. Darwin arched his back, pulling out of its grasp.

Another faceless monster emerged from the smoke-filled street, and Darwin veered toward the buildings. Ahead of him a door swung on its hinges, smoke rolling out of the entry before being sucked up into the night sky.

He dashed for it. He could feel the breath from the beasts that followed him. A hand grabbed for his arm, fingers pushing through the thin material of his shirt to touch his skin. Heat seared into his arm and his mind went blank. Images flashed through him. A man bouncing a baby on his knee. A woman smiling as she stood over them. Nets falling from the trees, followed by sheets of agony. Then darkness and uncontrollable pain.

Darwin jerked away and the images stopped. He felt hollow, empty, as though something had been taken from him. The loss followed him as he ran into the smoking doorway.

His first breath pulled stinging smoke into his lungs and he fell forward, landing on carpet that burned the palms of his hands as he slid forward. Tears flushed his eyes and he coughed, sucking in the cleaner air near the floor. Before he could see again, before he could properly breathe, he lurched deeper into the burning structure. Anything to get away from those abominations.

He felt the floor shake, and for a panicked second he thought the building was going to collapse and bury him alive. Another shake, chased by another. Footsteps. The damn things were in there with him, following him to finish him off.

He crawled forward into the pitch-black room as fast as he could, not caring how much noise he made, how easy he was to find. His only thought was to get as far away from those things as he could. His head slammed into a wall and stars swirled across his eyes. His arms and legs kept moving with a mind of their own, and his head slammed into the wall again before he turned right, following the flat surface, hunting for a doorway. The sounds of footsteps echoed behind him. He scrabbled for another few feet before his head hit another wall.

He turned his back into the corner, pushing against it as if hoping the walls would absorb him and he would be able to pass right through.

The footsteps stopped, replaced by the crackling sound of fire consuming the building. Smoke curled just above his head and the wall behind him seared him with intense heat.

Darwin held his breath. Could they have left? Did they lose him in the dark and the smoke? He strained to look through the blackness, struggling to see. He tried to focus on the Threads but couldn't See any. A deeper fear grabbed him. He was blind.

Darker shadows flitted across the room, drawing closer and veering off. His eyes tricked by the blackness. He heard the soft sound of cloth rubbing against something, the noise amplified in his ears. A rough hand grabbed his arm, pulling him to his feet. Darwin swung, his fist hitting something that felt like rough leather, giving slightly before his hand stopped. The grip on his arm tightened and he was jerked toward where he thought the door should be. The pungent smoke stung his eyes and he took an involuntary breath, gagging once again. Tears flowed freely down his cheeks, making him think of the girl on the street. *A strange thing to think of just before you're going to die*, he thought.

The hand released him, pushing him out the door into the street. He fell to his knees again, drawing in huge gulps of the fresh air. Tears still fell, creating small craters in the footprints covering the dusty street.

Something grabbed the back of his shirt and pulled him up. Darwin spun around to face the monster, hoping that at least his death would be quick.

Michael stared back at him.

"Move." Michael pushed him in the direction the crowds had run. "Everyone is in the amphitheater. You're no good to us here." Michael pushed again and then turned and ran back into the smoke-filled street the monsters had come from.

Darwin stood in the midst of the destruction listening to the receding sounds of the fighting. Some of the buildings around him threw flames high into the air, casting twisting shadows of hate on the street. As he turned to head back, he saw the boy's body, lying where it had been thrown. He walked slowly to the baby's side and bent over the inert form, reaching out to touch the boy's face, still warm in the cool night air. The arm and shoulder on the left side looked out of place, probably broken or dislocated. Burn marks in the shape of human fingers wrapped the small arm. He couldn't see any other damage. As he pulled his hand away, the boy moaned and his eyes fluttered open.

He was still alive! Darwin gently placed his hands under the small form and picked him up. The boy's mouth opened, and he screamed, screwing his face into a tight grimace, the pain from his shoulder overriding everything else. Darwin stood, shifting the boy's weight to take pressure off the injury, and began the walk to the amphitheater.

MERCY OF ANGELS

THE AMPHITHEATER REMINDED Darwin of pictures he'd seen of World War Two refugee camps. People crowded the area, dressed in whatever they had on their backs when they'd run. They sat or stood in small groups, looking lost and confused, speaking in hushed tones. Occasionally the din of hundreds of people was shattered by shouts or screams. Darwin carried the boy through the ring of Threaders protecting the space and stood in the mass of humanity.

He looked down at the frail figure in his arms, the dirty face looking almost peaceful in sleep, or passed out, his chest rising and falling in a ragged rhythm. The arm resting across his chest still lay at an awkward angle, but the boy seemed beyond caring about it. Darwin brushed the boy's dirty face with his thumb, wiping away the tears that hadn't had a chance to dry.

He stepped further into the crowd, trying to find a path to the stage. From where he stood, he could see people lying on it and being tended to by others. The natural acoustics of the amphitheater made every sound clear, even over the noise of the crowd: the soft consoling voices of the caregivers, punctuated by the sharp cries of those hurt.

He spotted Wally through the crowd and pushed his way over. Sullen faces turned to look at him, until they saw the young boy in his arms, and then they separated, giving him room to move.

"Wally," Darwin yelled, trying to raise his voice above the crowd's.

Wally spun around, scanning the faces in front of him. He passed over Darwin and looked like he was going to turn away before he spotted the boy Darwin carried. Darwin watched as Wally moved easily through the crowd, people separating just before he reached them, and closing back together shortly after he passed. Instinctively, Darwin tried to watch the Threads. It felt like he'd had a fresh batch of inhibitor put in him; what he saw was faint and few. When Wally reached them, he looked down at the boy.

"He's hurt," Darwin said.

"I can see that. The healers are on the stage. Follow me." Wally turned and moved away, the crowd opening for him again. Darwin rushed to follow before the gap behind Wally closed.

The stage was a quiet zone compared to the confusion of the people on the slopes. Patients lay on the floor in orderly rows, some staring at the stars in the night sky, others with their eyes closed. As new people were brought in, the less injured were quietly moved off the stage to make room. Through all of this, several men and women walked, helping those who required it before moving on to the next person. One of them stopped in front of Darwin and Wally.

"Just the boy?"

Darwin nodded. He was bruised and the burn on his arm hurt,

but it was nothing compared to the injuries already here. At the other end of the stage he watched as a blanket was pulled over the face of a young man who looked like he should have been going to high school.

Once he saw that, others filled his view, scattered amongst the living. Bodies with their faces covered were being moved from where they lay to the far end of the stage. From there, a group of men and women carried them farther down the slope.

He felt the weight of the boy being lifted from his arms, and his attention focused back on the healer in front of him. A woman. He noticed the blood on her clothes and, in the back of his mind, wondered if it was hers or someone else's. He turned, following Wally off the stage.

"What were those things?"

Wally pivoted and looked Darwin in the eyes. Whatever he was looking for, he apparently found it. "Skends."

Darwin's blank look must have prompted him to continue.

"We call them Skends. We first saw them last year on the east coast, fighting for the Qabal. We lost some good teams before we figured out how to defeat them. We think they were human once, just like you and me. But they've been . . . modified." Wally used his fingers to put quotation marks around the word "modified." "We have no idea how, or what has been done to them, but whatever it is, it's not a good thing. They're taller and stronger than most men, and we don't think they feel pain. Everything they touch is scorched—metal, wood, people."

"Don't think?"

"We don't know. We've never managed to capture one alive." He shuddered. "I'm not sure we want to." He glanced at Darwin's burned shirt and arm. "One of them touched you?"

Darwin nodded.

"You won't be able to use Threads for a while. Skends have the ability to dampen what you can See. Makes them a bitch to fight."

"How did they get in?"

"Past the defenses? I wish I knew. None of the alarms went off, and we always have five or six scouts monitoring them, plus another crew watching the Threads. A group of Skends and their handlers holing into the area shouldn't have been tough to See . . . unless they were brought in one by one over a long period. Something on the order of months. And then they would have to be walked in from pretty far away." Wally stopped talking and rubbed a hand over his forehead, leaving a streak of dirt. "That's a scary thought. There could be even more out there. I've got to find Enton and let him know, though he's probably already thought of it."

Before Wally could turn to leave, Darwin asked one more question. He thought he already knew the answer, and it filled him with a cold dread.

"If they've been here for months, then why? Why now?"

Wally looked Darwin in the eyes again. "You, Darwin. *You* are the reason. The Qabal want you, and if what they've done—what they're doing—is any indication, they want you dead. Enton seems to think you're worth all of this." Wally sighed and waved his hands around him before turning, leaving Darwin standing alone in the crowd.

The world slowed to a crawl. People moved around and past him, fading into the background. The noises dimmed in his ears, even though he saw them talking.

His fault.

All of the people hurt. All of the people dead. All of it was because of him. The shock hit him full force, like a car crashing into a concrete wall. A feeling he barely remembered but that still came to him at night when he slept. He felt the skin on his face tighten, and his insides clenched into a ball. His breath came in short gasps, lungs refusing to expand to take in more air. The world blurred and his legs felt like rubber. His knees slammed into the ground. His stomach heaved, but nothing came out. It heaved again and bile filled his mouth, dripping onto the dirt.

His fault.

A pair of hands reached under his arms and lifted him slowly to his feet. The look of concern on the stranger's face drove his guilt deeper, and he pushed away, stumbling downhill into the crowd, sure that they could see the regret and shame written all over his face. Bodies pressed against him, and the stale air clung to him. Every breath taken by the people packed into the small space seemed to suck another one out of his lungs. He had to get out. He had to have space to breathe again. He pressed against the stage, squeezing along its perimeter until he stumbled into the shadows behind it.

He leaned his head against a tree in the darkness of the night and sucked in lungfuls of the cooling air. The rough bark scraped against his forehead as he turned to his side and looked up. The night sky over SafeHaven glowed orange against the smoke that rose to the north. He tried to take some consolation from knowing only a part of the community had been hit. It could have been so much worse.

It didn't work.

As his eyes grew accustomed to the darkness, the area behind the tree came into focus. Dozens of white sheets filled the open space, each one draped over a body. How many people had died tonight? How many children had lost a mother or father? How many parents had lost a child? How many girls would never dance again? The thoughts and questions raced through his brain like the fire that had raced through the streets.

His fault.

He had to get out. There was no point in him being here. What if the Qabal tried to attack again? Would everyone turn on him, point to him as the outsider, the reason they had lost family and friends? Homes?

Hell, he shouldn't be *here* at all, he should be sitting in a classroom starting his last year of university, the loner who just showed up and got his work done. He should be preregistering for his master's next year, for the next phase of his education.

It was all fucked up anyway. Here or there.

He walked past the bodies, refusing to look at them, his arms pressed against his roiling stomach, and shuffled down the hill behind the stage, following the gully in the dark, not caring where he was going.

Time blurred and faded. Minutes stretched into hours as Darwin struggled through the dark and rugged terrain. The light from Safe-Haven's fires had long since disappeared behind the hills he had climbed. The waning moon barely gave off enough glow to see his own hand before his face, yet he continued on. Guilt lodged deep in his gut with talons as sharp as steel, refusing to let go. Wally's words echoed in his head, driving his guilt deeper into his soul.

By the time he realized he was lost, it was too late to backtrack . . . not that he would have been able to. Instead he pushed on, trying to keep heading in the same direction by looking at the stars near the horizon. He had no idea if he was looking at a constellation or just a random grouping, but it didn't matter. As long as the same pattern was in front of him, he was pretty sure he was heading in a straight line. The stars and the cold were his only company. In his mad rush from his room, he'd left the jacket Enton had given him draped over a chair.

Yet he was far from alone. Besides the sounds of him forcing his way through thick underbrush and tripping over exposed rocks, he could hear the rustle of animals in the tall grasses. Occasionally, something louder echoed in the night and he'd freeze midstride, holding his breath until whatever it was had moved off. He didn't notice when the wilderness turned into an overgrown gravel road, or that he'd stopped following the stars and turned to follow the barely visible path.

Shortly after, the gravel ended at a cracked concrete ribbon just wide enough for a single vehicle. The morning sun rose at his back, casting a long shadow in front of him. The heat of it warmed him until his shirt stuck to his skin with a slick layer of sweat. It wasn't that late in the day, but the intensity from the low-lying sun hinted at the heat the day would bring. A little over an hour after finding the narrow road, he climbed a small hill to a twinned highway. Keeping the rising sun to his back, he turned west, leaving SafeHaven behind him.

Houses with broken windows and wide-open doors sat on top of the small hills on either side of the road, their paint long gone, and the exposed wood faded. Exhausted from hiking most of the night, he turned and, leaving the road, forced his way through the overgrown hedges and grass, sometimes crawling to make it through. He walked into the cooler interior of the first house in his path.

"Hello?"

His voice bounced through the empty structure. To his right, a staircase led to the second floor. He hesitated before climbing the steps, knowing it would be hotter, but hoping it would be safer than the main floor. His mind made up, he trudged his way up the stairs and collapsed on the floor of the first room he found.

He woke to the bright sun pouring through the windows into his eyes. Rolling away from the light, he used the door to help him stand, the hallway a black chasm in front of him. His lips felt dry and the back of his throat was sore from the arid air. Already knowing what the result would be, he followed the walls into the bathroom and turned the taps. Nothing came out. Even the back of the toilet had been opened and drained of water.

He went down the stairs, looking for the basement door. Michael had gotten water from the hot water tank; maybe there was some left here. He stumbled down the basement stairs, catching himself on the wall, and maneuvered through the dim space by the light shining through small windows. All he found was an on-demand system with no tank.

The other five houses he tried were the same, whether they had a tank or not. Each one as dry as the previous. He could feel his lips starting to crack.

He stumbled from the last house and fought his way back through the brush to the road. Turning to face the setting sun, he continued to walk away from SafeHaven. Heat rose from the crumbling concrete, enveloping him in a stifling cocoon. Someone had told him it was unusually warm; he couldn't remember who. The thought disappeared as quickly as it had come.

Occasionally, a small breeze would wick away his outer layer of sweat, and for just a moment he would feel cool again. He had no idea what time it was, but even his muddled mind knew he'd been gone for most of the day plus at least half a night. It had to have been at least eighteen hours since he'd had anything to drink. With the hard hiking last night and the heat of the sun during the day, he knew he was in trouble.

His memory became a smear of concrete roads and intersections, the dead stop lights and street signs casting longer and longer shadows. Cramps shot through his legs, forcing him to sit until they passed and he could continue on. Hours later, dusk found him shambling along yet another long stretch of road, surrounded by the empty shells of strip malls. He crawled through the broken window of a market looking for water, for anything he could drink. He had stopped sweating long ago.

Shards of glass cut into his palms and knees, but he crawled on, not feeling the pain, not caring. A strip of metal that once held the glass in place jutted out from the wall. It sliced through his jeans and cut into his thigh. He sat numbly inside the store, watching the blood seep from the cut. One part of his brain told him he needed to do something about it, but he had no idea what. Thirst cut through his stupor again, and he rolled back to his knees. The shelves were like the houses, empty. Nothing was left. He needed something, anything. Wet. Water. He lay on the cool tile floor. *Just a few minutes,* he thought. *I just need a bit of a rest.*

Darwin bolted upright, remnants of a nightmare burning into the back of his eyes. He ran his tongue over his lips, feeling the crusty splits in them. They didn't hurt. The only thing that really did was the burn mark on his arm. It radiated heat that coursed through his body in waves. Through the thick fog in his head, a single thought forced its way through. He was going to die here. Die in a dead city. Darwin chuckled and it turned into a dry rasping hack. He didn't even know where he was.

He forced himself to stand, using the empty shelves as temporary stops along the way. His legs trembled, threatening to drop him back to the floor in a heap of quivering flesh and bone. He took another shaky breath, leaning against an empty cash register for balance before shuffling out into the cool, dark night. The still air caressed his skin, removing some of the feverish heat.

At some point he found himself back on his hands and knees in the middle of the road. He couldn't remember if he had fallen, or just decided to rest a bit. Or if it even mattered. How long had he been here? His tongue felt dry and swollen in his mouth. He tried to swallow, but there was nothing left.

Concrete rushed up to meet him as his arms gave out.

Sounds cut through the murkiness surrounding Darwin, pushing cobwebs from his brain. Voices. Soft and quiet. He struggled to pull himself awake, reaching through the gauze-like layers of sleep, and opened his eyes to nothing but darkness. Two hands pushed him gently back down by his shoulders and he felt a cold wet cloth touch his forehead. The world faded again.

When he next woke up, his eyes opened in a dimly lit room. He rubbed away the dry mucus that clung to his eyelids like glue and looked around without lifting his head. Curtains hung from a window at the foot of his bed, blocking the light from outside, filtering it to a pale yellow. He turned his head. The rough pillow scraped his cheek, feeling like it took a couple of layers of skin with it.

Pillow? Bed? His eyes focused on a doorway in the far wall as his mind struggled to work through how he had gotten here. He remembered leaving SafeHaven, walking most of the night and the next day, crawling through scrub brush and weeds to get to a house. And then . . . nothing. He was sure some time had passed, but it was all a blank.

The memory of SafeHaven brought with it the sudden rush of fear. The Skends! They had found him there. Would they find him here? Were there mothers and fathers and children who would be hurt because he had been brought here? He had to leave.

The doorway was covered with a curtain matching the one in the window, red flowers on a yellow cloth faded almost to white. It swayed in a gentle breeze coming from the other room. He could hear quiet murmurs through the curtain as he raised himself on his elbows.

He felt like he had been run over by a truck, and then the driver had decided to back up and do it all over again. He let out a soft moan as he fell back to the bed. It didn't matter how much he wanted to leave; he wasn't going anywhere.

The curtain across the door pushed open and a young woman walked in. Darwin breathed deep to smother the pain, but only succeeded in starting it anew as his rib cage expanded to hold the air. He let it out slowly and gazed, unfocused, at the ceiling.

"Shh. Lay back and rest."

The woman lifted a glass of water from the side table and put a hand behind his head, lifting gently.

"Drink some of this. You put your body through hell out there. I did what I could, but now it needs water and rest."

"Where—" The sound was more of a croak.

"Questions later, water first." She held the cup to his mouth and poured slowly.

It was the sweetest thing he'd ever tasted. Before he'd had his fill, she lowered his head to the pillow and put the half-empty cup back on the side table. His eyes were already closing before the glass reached the tabletop.

His dreams exploded with dark images. Skends strode through streets running thick with darkened blood. The broken bodies of children lay stacked in the gutters. Rebecca rode on a Skend's shoulders, laughing as her horde gathered more kids and drained the lifeblood from them. He tried to run, tried to reach the children to pull them out of her way, but his feet refused to obey his commands and he stared wide-eyed as the carnage continued. As she passed him, her laugh turned into a snarl and her face morphed into his mother's, full of hate and anger and blame as she glared into his eyes. Her body twisted and broke, mimicking what he had seen of her after the accident. A silent scream tore from his soul. He wanted to close his eyes, close his mind, to dispel the images before him, but they too refused to listen.

Just before he woke, an angel with dark hair and soft brown eyes walked down the streets touching the broken bodies, her feet leaving no trace of her passage in the drying blood. At each touch, the child's eyes opened and they smiled before their bodies disappeared in a swirl of soft white Threads. One, a young boy no older than two, with his arm bent grotesquely around his torso, ran up to Darwin, wrapping a thin arm and legs around him. Tears flowed down his cheeks, staining Darwin's shirt.

He woke up in a cold sweat. Damp sheets grabbed at him and he struggled out of them as he dug himself from the nightmare. A jug of warm water and a glass sat on the side table, and he drained half of it, gasping for breath between chugs. The image of his mother remained.

A faint rectangle of light showed where the window was in the darkened room, the curtains faded into a translucent white by the pale moonlight. He stood, leaning briefly against the bed before his legs stabilized under him. His clothes had been removed and he shivered as the sweat cooled on his bare skin. He stepped to the window, moving the curtain aside, and stared onto the moonlit street, half expecting to see fire and Skends. A lamppost stood sentry by the curb, its lamp holding no light. Across the four lanes of pristine asphalt stood more houses, their unbroken windows reflecting the glow from the moon. Though the night looked peaceful, he couldn't shake the images of SafeHaven out of his head. He had no idea where he was, but that didn't stop the Skends from attacking before. What if they could find him? What if they were already on their way here?

Leaving the window behind, he grabbed the damp sheet from the bed and wrapped it around himself before heading for the doorway. His clothes had to be somewhere around here. He pushed aside the curtain and stood in the entry, listening for sounds from the quiet house before moving into the next room. A couch and chair lined one wall, facing a small fireplace painted white. To his left was a dining room, though it was difficult to see in the dim, filtered light. The windows here had thicker curtains, and the moonlight barely pushed through the material. A single shaft of light cut across the floor, created where the curtains failed to meet.

He turned and shuffled back to bed, suddenly exhausted from his foray into the house. He barely had the strength to make it back, never mind getting dressed and walking through the night. He still had no clue where he was, but the people who lived here had taken the time to nurse him back to health. He didn't think they would do that if they had any plans to hurt him, or if they thought he'd bring the Qabal down on them. He lay down and was asleep almost before his head touched the pillow.

No dreams interrupted his sleep.

Darwin woke to sunlight streaming in through the window, the curtains pushed back. All he could see out of it was a patch of pale blue. Beside the filled water jug on the side table, a pile of clothes lay neatly folded. He could see they weren't his, but it was obvious they were meant for him.

Closing his eyes, he let the Threads come into view, mentally kicking himself for not trying to use them last night. The only excuse he had was he must have been more tired than he had thought. It took him a moment to realize he could use them again. Apparently the Skend's touch was only temporary.

Threads drifted through the room, soft and white. He had Seen Threads like this before but couldn't remember where. They moved through the wall and doorway into the living room he had seen yesterday, and he followed them with his Sight.

As the Threads moved through the living room, the muted sounds of whispering voices stopped. Darwin pulled back and pushed himself to a sitting position in bed, waiting for his visitor.

A gentle knock came from the doorway, and *she* walked in. This was the angel from his nightmares last night. She couldn't have been much older than he was, and as in his dreams, her long dark hair hung freely, framing her face in a halo of backlight from the window. As she walked closer, he could see her eyes were a deep brown, almost black, and filled with understanding and compassion and strength. He suddenly felt naked and exposed, and he pulled the bed sheet higher up his chest.

"You are looking better this afternoon," she said.

Afternoon? Darwin glanced out the window again. The sunlight was bright and harsh.

"You have been asleep for quite some time."

"How long?" Darwin's voice came out hoarse and scratchy. He cleared his throat and tried again. "How long?"

"Just over three days. If we had found you a couple of hours later than we did, I think it would have been too late. Walking around during the day with no water isn't a very wise thing to do, even at this time of the year. Throw in this weird heat wave we're getting, and it's a recipe for disaster."

Darwin noted her voice, though still soft, held a bit of an edge to it as she chided him. "I hadn't planned to be walking around," he said.

"I could see that." The edge had left her voice and a hint of laughter could be heard in it. "There is fresh water in the pitcher.

Drink as much of it as you can, then get dressed and meet me in the living room. You are a bit late for lunch, but I think I can warm up some leftovers and get some food into you."

The thought of food made his stomach rumble, and he realized that he was starving. His angel laughed at the sound, a gentle laugh that lit up her whole face, and turned to leave.

"By the sounds of it, I'd better hurry with the lunch," she said.

By the time he had finished a few glasses of water and gotten dressed, he could smell the food coming from behind the curtained doorway. The clothes didn't fit too badly. The jeans, though the same size as his old ones, felt loose and baggy. The shirt, black with a faded and pixelated image of the *Enterprise* from the old *Star Trek* TV show on it, fit perfectly. When he stepped into the living room, he saw the table had been set with a single place setting, just a plate and a spoon, tortillas, a bowl of steaming beans, and what looked like chicken in another bowl. Beside it was a large pitcher filled with water. His angel—he'd have to find out her name—sat across from the food. He fell into the chair, and the smell of the beans made his stomach rumble again. He reached for a tortilla and a soft touch on his arm stopped him.

"More to drink first, then a little bit of food. Your body is still feeling the effects of severe dehydration and will for a couple more days. Put on some extra salt as well, you need it. After that," she tilted her head toward the bedroom door, "back to bed."

Darwin dutifully poured a glass of water and took two gulps before reaching for the food again. He wrapped the soft tortilla around the chicken and beans and took a giant bite, grabbing for his water before he had a chance to swallow. The cracks in his lips were on fire, and his tongue felt like he'd laid it on a red-hot stove. The water did little to hold the fire at bay.

"Jesus, that's hot," he gasped.

His statement was met with another gentle laugh. "I didn't think you were from around here," she said. "It is the beans. That's as mild as we make it, unless you want baby mash." She pushed the pitcher closer to him. "I suggest you just suck it up and drink more water."

Darwin unrolled his tortilla and scraped most of the beans onto the plate, replacing them with another chunk of chicken. Either the second bite was better, or he had burnt away so many of his taste buds it just didn't matter anymore. He made his second tortilla with just the chicken. The gnawing hunger subsided halfway through to a dull pang, and he started asking questions.

"Where am I?"

"San Diego, near the old Chollas Reservoir."

She tilted her head, focusing her beautiful eyes on him. It felt as though she was looking into his soul, if he believed in stuff like that.

"Where did you come from?" she asked.

"New Jersey."

"That's quite a walk. Did you do the whole thing without food or water?"

"No, I . . ." He stopped, realizing she was joking with him again. "No. It's a long story."

"I'm sure it is. I may even know some of it. You had a burn on your arm, in the shape of fingers. There aren't too many things in this world that can do that kind of damage."

Darwin's hand went automatically to his arm where the Skend had touched him.

"There's only one place I know of where Skends have been recently. My mom and brother are there now, helping the survivors. If one got close enough to you to do that, you're one lucky guy." She paused. "A lot of people left SafeHaven that day."

The image of the eyeless and mouthless face rose unbidden into his mind, and he shuddered, putting the rest of the tortilla on the plate. Suddenly, he was more tired than hungry.

She placed her hand on his arm, the warmth of her fingers spreading through him. "We can talk again later. Why don't you get back to bed and get some more rest?" Her fingers slipped from his arm and he immediately missed her touch.

He stood without answering, picking up his plate to bring to the kitchen.

"Just leave it, I'll take care of it."

He put the plate down and stumbled back to his room, stopping as he reached the curtained doorway. He turned back and leaned against the doorframe.

"I didn't get your name."

"Teresa," she said, without looking up from the table. She said her name with a slight rolling of the "r" and as if it had an "a" after it instead of an "e."

"Thank you, Teresa."

"Go to bed, rest." The corners of her mouth rose in a slight smile.

He turned to walk into his room before changing his mind. All of the water he'd drunk had brought on another need. "Is there a bathroom I could use first?"

THE WORLD IS A MUCH SMALLER PLACE

DARWIN SLEPT THROUGH the rest of the afternoon and night, waking the next morning to the sounds of pots banging in the kitchen and the smell of coffee. God, it felt like forever since he'd had a good cup of coffee. Chances were this was just more of the roasted barley fake stuff the Qabal had served.

Sometime in the night someone had thrown a thin blanket over him; he still lay on top of the ones he'd fallen asleep on. He tossed the blanket off and walked into the living room. There was no one there. He thought of following the noises into the kitchen, but the sight of the open doorway leading outside made him change his mind.

He stepped out onto a covered porch. Green paint peeled from the railings and the beige exterior walls looked worn and tired. The porch itself was small, with barely enough room for a single chair, and raised off the ground by a handful of steps. Across the road was a similar building at ground level, its red clay roof tiles missing in spots. Over the closed double doors Darwin could see faded print: District Office, and a sign on the small dead lawn read Lincoln Military Housing.

The doors opened and Teresa walked out, holding a clipboard and pen in her hand. She wore a summer dress, plain white with two straps over her shoulders. Darwin stared, mesmerized by the gentle curve of her collarbone in the sunlight. His angel was beautiful. When she looked up and saw him, she smiled and walked over.

Her smile lit up the world for him. He felt his face stretch into a wide grin, threatening to pull apart the freshly healed cracks in his lips, and struggled to regain some composure.

"You look better than yesterday," Teresa said as she walked up the stairs.

He grinned again as he followed her back into the house. "Thanks. I had help. Someone took excellent care of me."

"You'll still have to take it easy today. Lots of rest and water."

The aroma of coffee hit him again and he started toward the kitchen. "Is that real coffee? It smells great."

"We haven't seen coffee in years. This is acorn coffee. It's not bad, but nowhere near the real stuff. You can get me one while you're in there."

Darwin walked back into the living room carrying two steaming mugs. Teresa put her clipboard down and reached for one.

"You were pretty close to gone when we found you. Another couple of hours and it might have all been over," she said.

"Yeah." Darwin sat and leaned back in his chair. He looked into his cup, watching the steam swirl off the hot liquid. It reminded him of the white Threads his angel had used in his nightmare. "I couldn't stay there. I . . . I can't stay here either."

He took a sip of his coffee and grimaced, putting the cup down. "I should really leave right now. I guess I'll need some water to take with me."

"And where would you go, boy from New Jersey?" She said it with no malice in her voice.

"Darwin. Darwin Lloyd."

Teresa's voice softened. "So where would you go, Darwin? We are already into December. The days are pretty warm, but the nights can get awful cold. Besides, you wouldn't be able to make it very far with the water you could carry, and some of the communities out there aren't as nice as we are."

"I don't know." His voice was a whisper.

"No, you don't, do you? Well, while the rest of my family are in SafeHaven helping with the wounded, I am the healer here, and I don't think you're ready to go anywhere yet. You will have a room here for the next few days at least. After that, you will have to talk to one of the elders."

"You don't understand—"

"I do," Teresa interrupted. "SafeHaven isn't that far from here, really. Especially if you can hole from one place to the other. Enton has already been here to check on you and left behind a couple of teams of Watchers. He doesn't usually make the same mistake twice. Skends won't make it anywhere near here without us knowing about it."

At the mention of SafeHaven and Enton, Darwin felt an unexpected wave of relief. At least the entire town hadn't been destroyed by the monsters. He didn't think he would have been able to live with that.

"I told Enton you needed a few more days before I could let you go. He will wait. No one bothers my patients until I say they're ready."

Darwin's insides tightened, feeling like he'd been dealt a blow to the gut. A patient. Of course, that's what he was after all, just a patient to Teresa, nothing more. He couldn't help but let a little bite come into his voice.

"So you made me healthy so Enton could take me back?"

"Of course not." She placed her empty cup on the table and rose. "You needed help. I, and the people of my community, gave you that help. If you want to leave before Enton comes back, you're free to do so." Darwin watched as she walked to the open doorway and stepped outside, her silhouette outlined by the bright sun before she walked down the stairs.

He sat in silence, finishing the concoction they called coffee. It wasn't bad if you didn't think about it too much. *No matter how life changes, parts of it always stay the same,* he thought. Meet a pretty girl, and if she smiled at him, he was head over heels before he knew it. Stupid.

The hot drink had taken the edge off his hunger, so he stepped back out onto the porch and looked down the street. To the right, he saw a large house painted in the same yellowy beige, but with white trim instead of green. To the left, the street turned into a small cul-de-sac, and he could hear the sounds of children playing. The noise made up his mind for him and he left the porch, turning to follow the cheerful squeals.

The cul-de-sac ended at a small playground, situated just behind a rusted red metal monstrosity. He had no idea what it was meant to be, some sort of art piece was his guess. He stood at the playground's fence and watched the kids from a distance. They played without a care in the world, laughing, pushing, climbing, grabbing handfuls of the sand beside the play structure and throwing it onto the slide before climbing up and sliding down, pushing most of the sand onto the soft black pads under the play structure. They were innocent, carefree. Just like the kids in SafeHaven killed by the Skends. Was he going to bring the same threat down on them? Could he live with it? Enton wasn't able to stop the attack before, so what made him think he could do it if it happened again?

He turned and strode back to his room, his mind made up. He'd get what food and water he could carry, if they would let him, and be on his way. He didn't want, or need, another SafeHaven on his conscience.

Darwin stopped short, his hand still holding the curtain to his room open before he moved slowly in. Enton sat on his bed, waiting.

"Hello, Darwin," he said. "You left before we had a chance to talk."

"Yeah."

"Any particular reason? I thought we had almost become friends."

Darwin shrugged his shoulders, embarrassed by Enton's words. He wasn't quite sure why, but the picture of the rocky grave he had Seen in the images in SafeHaven rose to the surface.

"Okay. I'll get right to the point then. I'd like you to come back." Enton paused as if waiting for an answer. "I think you could become very good at using the Threads. There's no better place to learn than SafeHaven."

"SafeHaven?" asked Darwin. "That's made up of two words, isn't it? Safe and Haven? It doesn't seem to be much of either of those, does it? How many people were killed or hurt by those—those things? How many more will have to die before you decide to just give me over to them, or worse?"

Enton stood and gazed out the window. For a brief moment, he reminded Darwin of Bill.

"We haven't made a very good impression on you, have we?"

Enton sighed. "You are right, though. SafeHaven has never been attacked before. The fact that there were Skends so close to us is . . . disconcerting. We should have Seen them. I think your being there simply changed the timing of their attack, not the fact that they were going to. People would have died with or without you there. In fact, your being there may have saved lives. Because of the attack on you in the mountains, we kept a lot of our scouts back, so we had more people able to protect us."

Darwin continued to stand, not saying anything.

"What is it you want, Darwin?"

"I want to go home." The words tumbled out of Darwin's mouth without volition. He could feel the walls he had put in place, the barriers to his emotions, beginning to break. Tears filled his eyes. He turned his back on Enton and his shoulders sagged. "I just want to go home."

A hand came down gently on his shoulder. "I know, son."

Darwin shoved the hand away. "I'm not your son. My dad is . . . my dad is somewhere, and I plan on getting back to him."

"And how do you plan on doing that? Go back to the Qabal? They're the ones who sent those things after you. They're the ones who brainwashed you, trained you just enough so you wouldn't fight them when they drilled into your head for information."

"It was Bill who did that."

Enton paused, as if letting that fact sink in for the first time. "Yes, it was. But he also gave you more than you needed. I heard what you did at your last lesson. An extraordinary feat for someone who hadn't been shown how to do it. Bill did what he had to do. The Qabal only want more power, and you were the pathway to that end. Now that you are no longer with them, they would rather see you dead than for you to pass your knowledge on to someone else."

"But I don't know anything. I told them I had no clue how I got here."

"Rebecca didn't believe that." Enton sighed again and sat back on the bed. "You have the potential to control Threads that many have never Seen before. She didn't know that when she asked Bill to train you, but she's a fool if she didn't see it at all. And she's no fool. Maybe she thought if the Qabal could control that power . . ." Enton paused, emulating Darwin's shrug. "But until you learn to use the Threads, to control them, you're as weak and vulnerable as a newborn."

"Could I control them enough to go back home?"

"I don't know. No one has been able to cross worlds besides you. That I know of."

Darwin turned and looked into Enton's eyes. "That you know of?"

"It is a big world, Darwin, and we lost the ability to communicate with most of it a long time ago. For all I know, no one is left in Europe or Australia. Or anywhere. Or there could be people in Bolivia that have done it. We just don't know."

The curtain was thrust aside and Teresa stood there panting. "Qabal. Lots of them. We need to get out of here."

"Qabal? Are you sure?" Enton rose from the bed and pushed past Darwin as he headed for the front door.

"Of course—"

"Damn. How did I not See them? That's twice they've pulled the wool over my eyes. How did you See them? Where are my Watchers?"

"I didn't," Teresa replied, "our lookouts saw them. You guys rely on the Threads so much, you've forgotten how to use your own damn eyes. They're out by the old mall."

"Show me."

Darwin followed as Teresa led Enton out the door. Enton stopped and turned back as they walked through the living room.

"Stay here."

Darwin stopped in his tracks. "What?"

"Stay here. Once I see what's happening, I'll come back." Enton continued out the front door, catching up to Teresa just outside.

Darwin felt himself come to a slow boil. What the hell was that about? He hadn't done anything in SafeHaven when they'd been attacked, and he wasn't about to make the same mistake here. He didn't know anyone who lived here besides Teresa, but there was no way he was going to let anyone get hurt through his inaction again.

By the time he reached the front door, Enton and Teresa had jogged to the end of the street, moving against the flow of people walking in the opposite direction. In contrast to what he had seen in SafeHaven, everyone here seemed calm. There was none of the mad, panicked rush. These people were apparently prepared to leave, to move on at any time. Each person had a backpack, even the smaller children, though sticking out of the top of one was the head of a teddy bear, its glass eyes staring back into the crowd.

He picked a path between the buildings and the moving people and ran against the stream, trying to catch up to Enton and Teresa. Turning the corner they'd gone around, he automatically scanned the street sign as he ran past. Fauna Drive. To his left he saw Enton disappear between two houses where the road ahead curved. He ran faster, already feeling the effects of the dehydration. It shouldn't be that hard to catch up to an old man.

Between the houses stood an empty children's slide, the plastic worn smooth by use. Just beyond that was an eight-foot-tall chain link fence. Teresa held a section of link aside, allowing Enton to crawl through. She smiled as Darwin got close, and he almost stopped, taken aback by how beautiful she was. Once Enton was through, she stayed, holding the chain link for him.

"Thanks."

"Any time," she said.

When Darwin was through, he held the fence for her.

"I told you to stay back there and wait for me," Enton said.

"And I told you I wasn't your son. You have no right to tell me what to do."

Enton shook his head in exasperation. "You have no clue. This is the Qabal we're talking about. These people want you dead, and I'm trying to stop that from happening."

Darwin straightened his back and stared at Enton. "Yeah, and I'm not going to stand around and wait for them to try. Like you said, it's *me* they're trying to kill. If I don't have a right to be involved, who does?"

"Okay, guys," Teresa said, "if you want to see them, then we should move now. You can argue all you want later." She pushed on through the remnants of a second fence line, following a dirt path overshadowed by tall, white-barked trees. "We'll go past the reservoir to the road. There's a bit of a hill covered by scrub. We should get a half-decent view of the mall from there."

They jogged past an old public washroom adjacent to a small parking lot. To the right, just beyond the parking lot and through some trees, Darwin saw the glint of sunshine off of water. Past the washrooms, the landscape changed to brown and gray scrub. They continued to jog, following the dirt path past an old sign warning them to watch for snakes as it meandered past the scraggly growth. He struggled to breathe but wasn't about to say anything.

It didn't take long to reach the top of the small knoll, and as they crawled the last few feet, staying below the height of the plants, he could tell the view was pretty crappy. In front of them was a large four-way intersection, and just past that the dull slate of a huge parking lot. Beyond the empty parking lot, he could barely make out people milling around in small groups.

"My god!" Enton muttered. "Even now, I can't See them. How are they hiding themselves from my Sight?"

"Like I said, you guys have forgotten how to just use your eyes. You rely too much on the Threads," said Teresa.

Despite her comment, Darwin took a deep breath and allowed the Threads to come into view. He had no idea what he was looking for, or what he was doing, but he knew he was able to follow the Threads. He'd done it back in the mountains with Wally and Carlos. He found one moving in the right direction and rode it in.

From what he could See, everything felt normal. Then again, he didn't really know what *normal* was. The Threads moved randomly, weaving a pattern that he couldn't quite understand. Slowly, he followed them further out, riding the Threads without manipulating them. If the Thread he was on drifted off course, he moved gently to the next one, and the next, until he found one that took him closer to the people below.

Darwin closed his eyes, concentrating on the Threads instead of relying on vision. For a split second, he thought about Teresa's admonishment. But he'd already used his eyes. Now he wanted to know what he could See. He opened his senses to the Threads more, pulling on the theories Bill had taught him long ago. Without warning, things were different. He could *feel* the asphalt under him. But that was impossible, he was lying on his stomach in the dirt. His mouth filled with a bitter taste, and a dark oily smell hit his nose. As the Thread moved, the texture of the concrete changed for just a second, smoother and . . . it tasted blue. It was like his synapses were misfiring, changing color to taste, texture to smell. He had the distinct impression of old paint. This was different. He'd gotten used to the Threads and the images, but this was disconcerting.

The Thread he was riding angled off, a curve to the right followed by another one to the left, returning to its original path. It was a short ripple, languid, feeling like the Threads' natural movement. But something was off. Something didn't ring true. He had no idea what made him think that. Leaving the Thread, he moved to other ones until he found one that would bring him back to the oddity. The Thread rippled again, but this time he got the distinct taste of blood in his mouth and the smell of a dark heavy cloth pulled against his face. The cloth tasted old and dirty.

Blood and cloth? A body? Darwin opened his eyes. He couldn't see much from here, but the people seemed clearer and closer.

He rode the Thread back to the intersection, passing through a wave of intense heat, and closed his Sight, suddenly dizzy. His stomach roiled and he pulled himself back into a crouch, breathing roughly through his mouth.

"That was amazingly well done. Even I couldn't follow you," Enton said.

Teresa knelt beside him, one arm across his shoulders and a hand holding his drooping head. "Are you all right?"

Enton pushed through, opening a flask and holding it to Darwin's mouth. "He's obviously not used to using Threads. He's got some basic skills but doesn't have the stamina for it yet." He raised the flask to Darwin's lips. "Drink."

Darwin leaned back and took a swig. Fiery liquid burned down his throat and he gagged, wiping the tears from his eyes.

"Good. You need to be more careful. Until you get more training, you're liable to go insane doing what you just did. Bill must have told you an untrained mind can lose the path entirely if it's not too careful. Hell, a trained mind can. I've seen it happen."

"Here they come." Teresa's voice had gotten small and thin.

Darwin got his voice back and looked at the parking lot. He couldn't see them, but he knew they were there. "They have Skends."

As Darwin spoke, groups of people and Skends streamed out of the old Sam's Club building, heading toward the hill they were on.

"We need to get out of here, now," Enton said. He pulled Darwin to his feet, catching him as his legs buckled. "Come on, girl, help me. I am too damn old to do this by myself."

The Skends moved inhumanly fast, crossing the parking lot and intersection and starting to move up the hill.

Teresa put her hand under Darwin's arm and helped Enton so they supported Darwin's weight together. He tried to move his legs under his body, but they barely listened to him. The two of them dragged him yards down the hill before he got some control back.

"We're not going to make it at this rate. I'm going to have to hole us out of here. You take Darwin through, I'll follow you."

"I can't," said Teresa. "My family—"

"Your mother and brother are still in SafeHaven. You'll never see them again if we don't move. I'll bring us back when things are settled."

To Darwin, the hole seemed to appear instantly. He shook his head, trying to clear the cobwebs that thickened and slowed his thoughts. Where was the delay, the preparation he saw when Wally or Carlos created holes?

The sounds of brush and scrub being trampled crested the hill behind them.

"Quickly now, get him through. I'll start dismantling the hole so it will be gone by the time they get here."

"But what about the—"

Enton interrupted again. "I am not daft, girl. I'll be right behind you."

Darwin felt a push on his back and Teresa's hand tightened under
his arm. He teetered into the hole. The cold came in a sudden rush,
biting into his skin and searing his lungs. When the warmth came
back, the hand under his arm let go and he fell to the ground, his
head resting on Teresa's shoulder. The biting cold had cleared his
head at least. He rolled over as quickly as he could to watch the hole.
He knew there wasn't much he could do if one of the Qabal, or worse
a Skend, came through. But somehow, knowing seemed to make it
better.

The hole started closing, destabilizing to the point he could
barely See the Thread that reached back through it. Enton popped
out, his eyes wide, the whites filled with a pattern of fine red lines.
His face had drained of color, and the hole closed behind him.

Not all of him had come through.

"I . . . I may have cut . . . cut that one a bit close." Enton's voice
sounded disjointed and faint. His eyes fluttered shut and his breathing deepened.

Teresa sat up, shaking tiny shards of ice from her hair. "Is it always like that?"

Darwin looked at her. "Yes. Help me with Enton."

"Enton? Why? What . . . ? Oh."

Her gaze moved down to his legs, and Darwin could see the realization of what had happened displayed on her face. Enton was
missing half of his left foot and all of his right. The cold had frozen
the wounds, sealing the blood vessels instantly. There wasn't a single
drop of blood on Enton or his clothes.

"Christ." Teresa paused. "I don't have the training to deal with hole injuries." She paused again. "I need to seal the cuts before they thaw, or he'll bleed out before I can even try to help him."

"Whatever you need to do, I think it's going to have to wait," said Darwin, thinking of how quickly Rebecca and Frank had followed them. "I don't know if it's possible to follow holes after they're closed, but if it is, we're sitting ducks." Darwin stood and his body swayed on shaky legs. He bent down to grab one of Enton's arms. "Come on, grab the other one."

"You're not going to make it; you look like can barely stand."

"I have to. If they come through . . . the farther away we are, the better. So let's *move!*"

At his shouted command, Teresa jumped and grabbed Enton's other arm. They both pulled, dragging Enton down the weed-choked street and around a corner.

"Do you know where we are?" Teresa asked.

He looked around. Widely spaced houses stood on either side of the curbless street. Wherever they were, the place didn't look like it had seen a human being in years. Wilderness had taken over the yards and houses, encroaching on the street in waves. In another year or two, there wouldn't be much trace of humanity left. Still, the whole feel of the place screamed small town and the air had a cold edge to it. He could feel winter in it. The leaves on the trees had changed from green to a bright yellow, though most of them still clung desperately to the branches. They had definitely moved north. None of that gave him the answer to her question.

"No, but he does," he said, tilting his head toward Enton. "Let's get him into one of the houses. Find a place to rest. If the Qabal were going to come, I think they would have done it by now."

They headed toward the closest house and walked through the

open door, laying Enton on the dirty hardwood floor of the living room.

"Let's get him on the couch," said Teresa, looking back at his feet. Blood flowed from the stump from dragging him across the street, and the heel of his left foot was scraped. Somewhere along their path, Enton had lost what was left of his shoe.

"I need some water and clean towels," Teresa said.

Darwin reached for Enton's flask. "It's not water, but it may help sterilize the cuts while I'm looking. I'll see if I can find something in the kitchen."

He found some tea towels in a kitchen cupboard and grabbed a couple from the middle of the pile, where the dust and dirt hadn't gotten to them yet. The mice had, and feces and nests of dead grass and other debris fell to the floor. Hanging on a hook over the sink was another towel.

"There's no clean towels," he said, walking back into the living room.

Teresa had rolled the bottom of Enton's pants up. She gripped his shirt just above and below the shoulder and pulled, straining to rip the material apart. It finally gave and she poured the contents of the flask over it. Enton didn't wake up when she carefully began to clean the dirt from the cuts. "I'll need some water. If you could find a way to boil it, it would be better."

Darwin moved toward the front door. "I'll see what I can find." What he really wanted was to be alone for a while. He could feel his defenses collapsing under the stress, and he didn't want anyone around when it happened.

Teresa, bent over Enton's feet, didn't reply.

He decided to turn left leaving the front door. They had come from the other direction when they'd holed in, and there didn't seem to be too much that way. With some luck, he'd find a small store or gas station that hadn't been completely ransacked. He hoped these small towns didn't have the frenzy and panic of the big cities. Maybe there would be something left he could use.

It didn't take him long. The street dead-ended on Front Street, marked by a bright green sign covered in withered vines. Wherever they'd ended up, the plants loved it. It almost felt like he was in a jungle. A small grocery store sat on the corner with two cars still parked at an angle in front of it. Except for the flat tires, they looked surprisingly ready to go. The store windows were intact, and the door was closed. Taking that to be a good sign, he leaned against the wood siding and looked through the glass.

He waited a few minutes, scanning the dark interior. The place looked empty, just like the rest of the town he'd passed through. He tried the door. It was unlocked, and when he walked in, a tiny brass bell tinkled overhead. As his eyes adjusted to the dim light, he saw the shelves weren't bare and breathed a sigh of relief. Maybe it was small-town courtesy that stopped people from taking everything. Whatever it was, Darwin didn't have that problem. He grabbed a couple of bags from behind the open cash register and walked through the store filling them.

He only made it through half of the tiny space before he felt the walls caving in and he collapsed to the floor near empty wire racks that once held potato chips and other junk food. The tears fell hot and fast and a chasm opened in his chest, filled with memories of what his life should have been like. The drudgery of classes filled with nameless faces and professors droning at the front. Being able to talk to his dad about anything. He'd know what to say that would send Darwin back on a solid path, back to being able to deal with life.

He didn't have that now, and he missed the connection so badly the pain was almost physical.

Trying to pull himself together, he collected the items that had fallen out of the bag, jamming them back in with barely controlled anger. Enough of this bullshit. His dad wasn't here—would never be here—and it was up to him to pull himself together. He was supposed to be an adult. And he wasn't alone, was he? Enton had saved both him and Teresa and was paying the price for it. He hadn't needed to do that, he could have saved himself, but he didn't. Enton wasn't quite a friend, but he wasn't somebody to be pushed away either.

And then there was Teresa. She was in the same position he was, far from home and mostly alone. She had taken care of him, so maybe it was his turn to take care of her. He laughed out loud. For one, she could more than likely take care of herself just fine without him. And two, how had he gone from someone who wanted nothing more than to be left alone, to someone who was suddenly willing to help people he barely knew? He didn't want to follow that line of questioning too far. It felt surprisingly good to help them. It was something he hadn't felt in a long time.

He made up his mind. If Teresa was willing to accept his help, he'd do what he could to get her home. In the back of his mind, his old demons stirred, interjecting the thought that SafeHaven seemed to be his best chance to get himself home, so they were both heading in the same direction anyway. He stood on shaky legs and went back to searching the shelves.

By the time he was done, one bag was filled with canned and boxed food. It was so heavy, he thought the thing would split, and triple bagged it just in case. He had no way of opening or cooking some of the items, but that would be a bridge he'd cross when he got to it. The other bag held drinks. He'd found a couple of large bottles of water. The rest were soft drinks. On the way out, he grabbed a jar of instant coffee and a bottle of Advil. The coffee was for him and

Teresa, and the Advil was for Enton. He didn't think it would help much, but even a little relief was better than none.

Like most small-town grocery stores, there was a section for liquor. It was the only section that was empty. He was disappointed. He could have used a stiff drink or two.

Enton was still out when he got back to the house. His body was drenched in sweat. Darwin rested the bags on the living room table, his arms aching from carrying them. Teresa had wrapped both of Enton's feet in towels. They weren't the ones he had seen in the kitchen. Blood seeped through one of them. He heard noise coming from the back of the house and walked toward it, entering the small kitchen.

He had been in such a rush to find towels for Teresa earlier that he hadn't noticed how old the place was. The only modern convenience seemed to be the fridge. Even the stove looked like it had been built sometime in the last century, baby blue and clunky looking, with the oven beside the two burner elements rather than below them. The whole thing sat on four spindly legs. It must not have been working when the owners had left, since beside it on the counter was a camping two-burner propane cooktop.

"I found some bottled water and food." He lifted the coffee out of the bag. "And some coffee, if we're boiling water anyway."

"Did you find anything to eat?"

Darwin emptied the plastic bags on the countertop. "Canned beans, some canned soups, rice and pasta. Pretty basic, but I think we got lucky with the store."

"It all looks good to me. Do you know how to cook?"

"Yeah, a bit."

"Good. How about you cook some rice and heat up a can of beans. When it's all done, we'll mix them together. It won't be fancy, but it should taste all right. I'll be with Enton. Oh, and I think we'll stay on the main floor. The original owners of the house are upstairs.

There's not much left of them, but we can at least let them rest in peace."

Teresa left the room before he could say anything. He glanced up the stairs to the second floor and shuddered. Staying downstairs sounded like a good idea.

Cooking rice and beans was easy. It seemed being left at home alone after his mom died, while his dad worked, had some benefits. He started Teresa's water first. When it was on, he found a mug and filled it twice with water, pouring it into another pot, and set it to boil as well. The beans could wait until the rice was cooking.

When Teresa's water boiled, he brought it out to her, and quickly retreated to the safety of the kitchen when he saw what was left of Enton's feet. The tender skin and sealed cuts had been ripped open as they'd dragged him from the hole site, and the raw wounds were still dripping blood. Teresa sat by Enton's side, her eyes closed and a vertical crease on her forehead.

The rice water was boiling, and Darwin turned down the heat, poured in a mug of rice, and put the lid on top. He knew they were in trouble. Enton needed a doctor or a healer, whatever they called it here. Teresa was a healer, but even she had said she was still in training, and that she didn't know how to deal with this.

The rice was done in twenty minutes, and he fished through the drawers, found a can opener, and just opened the can of beans and threw them in cold. By the time they were mixed, they would be warm enough to eat. He carried two cups of coffee into the living room before going back for the rice and beans. Just pouring the water over the instant flakes made his mouth water. Anything was better than the barley or acorn stuff he'd been drinking, and a nice shot of caffeine wouldn't hurt either.

When he went back into the living room, Teresa was already lifting one of the coffee cups to her nose.

"I haven't smelled coffee in years."

She breathed in deep and took a sip, closing her eyes as she smiled. Darwin's heart beat a little faster.

Enton woke up as they both sat on the love seat in the corner, shoveling food into their mouths between sips of hot black coffee. Teresa was beside him instantly, her food all but forgotten.

"Here, have some water." She lifted his head and brought a cup to his mouth. He took a couple of sips and sagged back down.

"I may have cut that one too close," Enton whispered.

"Just a bit, but don't worry about it now. You have a fever and need to rest. Just lay still, and I'll take care of you."

Enton did as he was told, and in seconds was back asleep. She sat back down beside Darwin and put her bowl into her lap.

"We're in trouble, aren't we?" Darwin asked.

"Yeah. Even if his fever breaks, we have no way to move him. He is too heavy for us, unless you can hole right from here." She looked at him, half expectant, half hopeful.

"If I knew how, you would already be back home."

Teresa leaned her head on his shoulder and a rush of heat infused his body.

"Don't worry," she said, "we will figure something out."

LIKE A SPIDER IN ITS WEB

THREE DAYS LATER Enton's fever still hadn't broken. He'd started tossing so much in his sleep, Darwin and Teresa had moved him back down to the floor, wedging the couch and love seat cushions beside him to keep him from rolling around. He lay there now, moaning, his head lolling back and forth.

Darwin had found a river at the back of the property. The water looked clean, but they boiled it anyway, saving what was left of the bottled water he'd found in the store for emergencies. The propane had run out the day before and Darwin had scoured the deserted town looking for more. There was none to be found, so everything was done over a fire behind the house instead. On his last trip out, he came back pushing a large, empty wheelbarrow that barely fit through the front door.

"We need to move. Find a bigger city or some people willing to help us," Darwin said.

"How are we supposed to do that? We can't move Enton."

Darwin pointed at the wheelbarrow. "We fill the barrow with blankets and put him in it. I should be able to push it fairly well, I think."

"We really shouldn't move him."

"We don't have much choice. No one knows where we are, and we're running out of food." The nights had gotten colder as well, and he didn't want to face a winter where they were.

Teresa sighed and looked at Enton. "Do you think it will work?"

"It has to. We can't leave him, and we can't stay here."

It took them four tries to lift Enton into the blanket-lined wheelbarrow the next morning. Teresa grabbed his legs and Darwin reached under his arms, heaving Enton's dead weight. Darwin placed two boards he'd pried off the backyard fence under Enton's legs, tying them together so they stuck out the front of the wheelbarrow like antennae. It didn't look comfortable, but at least his feet wouldn't be dragging on the ground.

Enton's feet—Darwin couldn't think of them as anything else even with the damage—had gotten worse. Teresa had told him she'd cleaned out the wounds perfectly, and when she used the Threads, they looked clean to her. It wasn't working, so there had to be something she was missing.

He didn't think what was happening was due to the dragging anyway. Enton's feet started turning black where the hole had sliced them, not at the cuts and scrapes they had given him dragging him into the house. If Darwin watched, he could almost see the black creep up Enton's legs, following the blood veins. It had already crept a quarter of the way up his calves, and they'd swollen to almost twice their size. He didn't think Enton was going make it.

It was something he and Teresa never talked about.

It took both of them to lift the wheelbarrow over the transom and down the short flight of stairs to the cracked sidewalk. From there, Darwin put a pair of thick work socks on his hands and took over, pushing the wheelbarrow down toward Front Street. At the store, they tucked whatever was left on the shelves in beside Enton. Even the cans of dog food.

They'd figured out where they were. Kind of. The name of the town was Gaston. What state or county it was in, they had no clue, which meant they had no idea of how far they had to walk, or for how long.

They had talked about it earlier, quietly in the dark while Enton moaned in his fever-induced sleep. Without knowing where they were, their best bet would be to head south. An extended search through the nearby houses didn't reveal the proper clothes for the bitter cold of winter. They barely found enough just to keep warm now, and they'd gotten lucky with the temperatures so far. That wouldn't last. Together, they agreed to stick to the only southbound road out of town until they found a bigger one, and then follow that. Eventually they would reach somewhere they knew, even if just by name, and could plan the rest of the trip home.

Home. There was no home for him, Darwin thought, no place to return to that he could call his own. No family that would welcome him. He pushed the thought from his head. There was no point in wallowing in self-pity; it wasn't going to get him anywhere. He'd had his moment in the store on their first day here. That was enough.

Once they got Enton somewhere safe, and somewhere there was someone who could actually heal him, Darwin would make sure Teresa got back to her family. After that . . . he didn't know. All he knew for sure was that if SafeHaven couldn't figure out how to send him back to his world, he would leave. It seemed that wherever he was, people ended up getting hurt, or worse. That was the last thing he wanted for his angel.

Even in the wheelbarrow Enton was heavy. Darwin locked his shoulders and elbows and concentrated on putting one foot in front of the other. The vegetation had taken over the highway, with the trees arching overhead creating a canopy that blocked out most of the sky. They maneuvered the wheelbarrow over cracked and broken concrete and saplings that had grown there. Travel was slow, and sometimes it took them both to get Enton to the next block of almost flat ground. They stopped a lot to rest, and each time he reached for the wheelbarrow handles again, he could feel the blisters on his hands stretching. The socks helped, but he just wasn't used to this kind of work. Walking to and from his dorm room, sitting in a class-room with a bunch of other students, even his jogging didn't build up the kind of muscles or calluses he needed for this. At least the constant concentration needed to keep the wheelbarrow balanced stopped him from thinking too far ahead.

He managed around four hours before he couldn't do any more. Teresa took over and did a couple extra before they had to stop for the night. They moved off the road as best as they could, into a copse of trees. Though they weren't sure where the road ended and the wilderness began.

Teresa checked on Enton, tucking in the blankets around him before shrugging off her backpack and rummaging through it. "What do you want for supper? We have roasted chicken, prime rib, and lasagna."

"The lasagna sounds great." He could hear the forced cheerful-ness in her voice but couldn't match it. His arms were sore, and his hands were covered in broken blisters.

"Okay, toss me the can opener." She grabbed a can from their meager supplies. "It looks like our lasagna today will be green and long." She showed him the can.

"Green beans?"

"Nope. Lasagna. Dripping in tomato sauce and loaded with spicy ground beef and fresh pasta."

Darwin made a face. Green beans had never been one of his favorites. He lumped them in the same group as zucchini and eggplant. Disgusting. "I may not like lasagna after this."

"Want to bet?" Teresa looked at him, her face set into a wide smile that made her eyes glow.

"No!" He started laughing; the stress of everything that had happened since he was pulled from his world swept through him. If he wasn't laughing, he'd probably be crying instead, worse than what had happened in the store back in Gaston. He didn't want to do that in front of Teresa. He knew it was stupid macho bullshit, but she was so strong and holding up so well, he had to try to do the same. She posed with the can of green beans and licked her lips. He fell, clutching his sides, and laughed harder. The tears came anyway, streaming down his face. But these were tears of laughter. The more he laughed, the more the Qabal slipped away. The Skends slid into the past with them.

Gasping for breath, he looked up. Teresa sat on the ground holding the can like a baby and quietly crying. Oh crap, what had he done now? He sat up, roughly rubbing the tears away.

"Hey . . . is everything okay?"

She wiped at her cheeks with the back of her hand and made a face. "No, it's not all right. I hadn't expected to be here, you know? Taking care of a hurt old man. Wondering if the Skends hit Safe-Haven as well . . . if my mom and brother are all right." She hesitated, lost in her own thoughts before shaking her head as if to clear it. "Walking god knows where with a complete stranger."

Darwin's chest tightened. "Not a complete stranger anymore. We have been together a few days." He tried to smile.

"You know what I mean." She waved her hand through the air, dismissing his attempt at being funny. "I'm supposed to be in Chollas Heights, learning how to use my talent to help sick and injured people, not watch them get worse."

"If you were there right now," Darwin said with an edge in his voice, "you would probably be dead, not helping anyone."

She turned her back on him, rummaging through her backpack again.

Well, if I didn't screw up before, I sure as hell did now, he thought.

"If you two are done bickering, I could use something to drink."

They both turned around to face Enton. His face was still flushed, but his eyes were clear and alert. Teresa ran past Darwin and knelt at Enton's side.

"Here, have some of this," she said, holding a canteen and getting her arm under his head. "Not too much."

Enton took two sips and leaned back, the effort obviously draining him.

"You haven't been learning to heal for too long, have you?" Enton asked, looking at Teresa.

"No. I just started when I turned eighteen, a little over two years ago."

"Too bad, you might have been able to save me."

Darwin rushed in. "Save you? You're awake, you must be getting better."

"No, I'm not. I figure I have maybe a couple of days at the most. Mis-timing a hole is almost always fatal, unless you have a very experienced healer around."

Fatal? Shit. The anxiety he'd managed to hold at bay rushed to the forefront. "Why did you stay so long?"

"The Qabal holed some Skends right next to me. I had to stop them from coming through with us."

"You could have holed and stopped them on this end."

Enton sighed. "Maybe. I made a decision. It may have been the wrong one, or it might have been the right one. No one will ever know, and second-guessing a decision you can't change does no one any good."

"But if—"

"Stop it," Teresa interrupted. "He needs rest and more water, not an interrogation."

Enton raised a hand and placed it on her arm. The look of concentration on his face when he did it drove home how bad things were for him. "It's all right. He's just scared and not sure what to do. I would be the same in his, and your, place." He shifted in the wheelbarrow, and Darwin moved forward to stabilize it as Enton's face twisted with the effort it took. "Now listen up. I'm not going to be here for long. Darwin, I've tried to follow your Threads, tried to See the images of your future, but everything is so cloudy, so convoluted. I don't know what will happen, or what you will do, but I can feel that you are important to our universe, as well as your own. I believe the Qabal knew that. They took a chance by trying to turn you to their side. Now that that has failed, they just want to get rid of you."

"Important? I'm just a guy from Jersey. I can barely use the Threads. I sure as hell can't use them to take care of you or Teresa out here. What makes me so important?"

"You are strong, Darwin. Stronger than anyone I have ever met. With the right training, I think you could be the best Threader I've ever seen. And I wouldn't worry too much about Teresa, she can take care of herself."

Darwin barely heard the last comment. Two things had settled into his tired brain. Only one seemed to matter right now. "You See images too?"

Enton smiled, ignoring the question, and his voice got softer. "You already know more than you realize. That trick you did when you searched the parking lot took a lot of finesse and a lot of control. I can't think of a single master who could have done it as easily, and they have had years of training. Teach yourself. Remember what the Dance Master said to you, follow your intuition, your emotions. The Threads will guide you, if you let them."

"I can't do that. I . . . I don't know how."

"You'll figure it out." Enton's body relaxed into the wheelbarrow. "I'm so tired. Let me sleep." His voice got quieter again and Darwin and Teresa leaned in to hear his words. "You can start by working together and maybe setting up a protective grid around us. Just try, you can . . ."

Darwin pulled back. Enton had fallen back to sleep, his face more flushed than before and sweat beading on his forehead.

They hadn't asked where he'd holed them to.

Teresa used some of their precious water to wet a cloth and lay it on Enton's forehead. It seemed to help. His breathing became easier and some of the flush left his cheeks.

She lifted his pant legs. The black creeping up his veins had gone above the knee. They couldn't see more than that without cutting the pant leg open. Darwin felt a sudden sweat trickle down his back even though he was cold.

"He's right, isn't he?" asked Darwin. "He's not going to make it."

"No," Teresa whispered. "I don't think so."

He stood and took a tentative step back, watching her fuss over Enton for a few more minutes. Without Enton, they were in deep trouble. Somewhere in the back of his mind he'd always thought that Enton would get them out of here, would help him find a way to get back home. Now he'd been told he had to learn to Thread. On his own. It was like walking into a physics exam without knowing any math. Teresa stopped her fussing and turned back to him.

"Shouldn't you be trying to build that grid?" Her voice was hard.

"I don't even know where to start."

"Sure you do. Just sit down and start. Standing there isn't doing it."

Sit down and start. She made it sound so simple. But where to start? He walked back to where he and Teresa had their argument. Their first argument, he thought, and immediately felt heat rising up his cheeks. What was it about her that made him feel like he was still a teenager?

He lowered himself next to her pack and leaned against it. The cans and boxes dug into his back and he shifted to find a better position. It didn't help.

Enton had told him to follow his intuition and emotions. The pain of what was happening to him must have affected his thought process. Even Darwin knew that bringing emotions into the equation was a fast track to insanity. It was one of the first things Bill had taught him.

Follow his intuition. How was he supposed to do that? He drew in a deep breath and closed his eyes, focusing on the Threads around him.

He had never tried to create Threads from nothing before. He didn't know if it was possible, or where to start. Or if it was even the *way* to start.

Okay, could he convert an existing Thread into a "prison" one? The blue Threads around the Qabal building and his tent were fresh in his memory; maybe he could recreate one. He followed a single

Thread, the way Bill had taught him long ago. It felt like years, but it had only been a few months. It slowed in front of him and hovered, as if uncertain of its path.

He moved the Thread closer, shocked that it actually responded to his request, and reached out to touch it. He felt nothing, which was to be expected. If you could physically feel every Thread, it would make life pretty complicated. The blue Threads he remembered were flexible, but strong. They'd wrapped around a tree branch and restrained it while still letting it move freely with the wind.

He poked beside the Thread and at the same time moved it to intercept his finger. They intersected right where he thought they would, but that still wasn't right. If the blue Threads at the Qabal building were being controlled by a person, they would have known he was escaping without Frank running back to tell them. That meant him moving the Thread to intercept was completely wrong. That, and his Thread wasn't blue. There was still something he was missing.

Pain started creeping in from Darwin's right temple to just above his eye, feeling as though someone had taken a dull knife and jammed it in through his ear. He managed to ignore it for a while, but he knew he wouldn't be able to keep this level of concentration up for much longer. At least not without becoming almost incapacitated like at Chollas. There was no way he was going to get any blue Threads to protect them tonight. Hell, he didn't even know if he was on the right path.

He stopped and sat thinking for a while, feeling the headache recede a bit. Experience told him it wouldn't go away until he got a good night's sleep. As soon as he stopped, the doubt crept back in. What was Enton thinking? He shook his head. There was no point in the self-doubt. He could either do it, or not. He had to at least try.

Back at the Qabal headquarters and in his tent on the way to

SafeHaven, he could See the blue Threads pretty easily, even before he had any training. If he created a shield around them, wouldn't any Threader from a mile around be able to See it? They would stand out like a geeky kid on a football field. If the Qabal were around and saw it, it would be game over. If anyone who could See was around.

Maybe he was thinking about this all wrong. What if he just monitored the existing Threads to See if they were being manipulated or maybe even touched? Just being aware of the Threads was way easier than trying to See or follow any one in particular. It was basically what he'd done with Bill's devices. It wasn't what Enton had asked him to do, but it was worth a shot. It couldn't have anything to do with the images. As far as he knew, they were the only two who could See them. He would question Enton on the images the next time he came out of his fever-induced stupor. If he had that chance.

"Teresa, could you come here?"

Teresa left Enton's side. "Yeah, what can I do for you?"

"Could you walk in front of me, about three feet away?"

"Sure, why?"

"Just testing something."

He opened himself up and let all the Threads in the area brush his senses. As Teresa walked in front of him, the overall pattern of the Threads changed. The change was faint, but there was definitely something there.

"Could you walk in a circle around me?"

Teresa moved, and as she did, he could feel a ripple in the Threads. Even with his eyes closed, he could detect where she was.

"Do it again, but change the radius of the circle, please?" He followed her again. "Are you about seven feet away, just about there?" He pointed.

"You're pointing right at me."

He felt like a spider sitting at the center of its web. Every vibration, every telltale sign of something entering his world sent a tiny signal back to him, a vibration in the web—the Threads. The interesting part was, it hardly used any of his strength. He just had to remain receptive, but not active. He did feel his arm affect the Threads when he pointed at Teresa, so he'd have to stay fairly still himself.

"Okay." He opened his eyes, still trying to stay aware of the Threads. "I don't think I can build a protective grid like Enton wanted, but I can tell when someone gets close to us. My best guess is I have about a one hundred-foot radius. That will have to do until I get better, or some training."

"What about when you sleep?"

Her words sent a chill through him. "I hadn't thought of that. Crap." What kind of idiot didn't think about sleeping? What the hell was he supposed to do now? "Look, why don't you take the first watch now, while it's still light out. I'll sleep, and when it gets dark, you wake me up and I'll watch through until dawn, then wake you up and I'll get a couple more hours."

"You'll stay awake all night?" asked Teresa.

He could hear the skepticism in her voice. He wasn't sure he could do it either. "I kind of have to, don't I?" He could tell the false bravado didn't work on her, but he also knew they didn't have any other choice.

They shared the cold can of green beans, saving the liquid in the can once the beans were gone. Enton wasn't able to eat, but if they dripped something into his mouth, he swallowed reflexively. It wasn't much but it would have to do.

He was still hungry after, and he was pretty sure Teresa was as well, but without knowing how far they needed to go, it was better to ration their food, though they'd need more than a can a day to be able to continue walking. He kicked himself for not asking Enton where he had holed them to. He told himself there just hadn't been enough time, but it was really just another mistake he'd have to live with.

After the meager supper, he rolled into a couple of the blankets and quickly fell asleep. It seemed like he had just closed his eyes when Teresa woke him up.

It got cold that night. Darwin sat shivering in the dark, wrapped in one of the blankets he had slept in. He had given the rest to Teresa and Enton. They lay together on the cold ground, sharing each other's warmth. Even watching the Threads, he jumped at every unexpected sound and saw shadows moving at the edge of his vision.

They had talked about starting a fire, but decided it was too much of a risk. The smell might have brought in animals and the light would be too visible. Right now, Darwin was regretting the decision. He moved to collect some wood, accidentally letting the blanket that wrapped him slip open. The cold rushed in, and he moved back to where he was sitting, deciding, once again, against the fire. The lesser of two evils. He blew on his fingers and pulled the blanket tighter. If it got much colder, they wouldn't have a choice.

The Threads wove around him, a soft gray that shimmered slightly in the pale light from the moon. He could feel them moving around and through their campsite. A hawk swooped out of the sky on silent wings, following a faint red Thread to its prey. Did it See the Thread, or was it all instinct? Did animals See and use the Threads the same way humans did? He thought back to the dog attack, remembered the Threads just before the attack, and wasn't sure of the answer.

He guessed it was around midnight when the wind picked up. It didn't affect the Threads' movements, but the branches swaying and moving through them did, changing their pattern in random ways, sending signals through Darwin's web. Suddenly, he could feel each branch, each leaf. His senses were overloaded, and it all became white noise.

There was no way this was going to be effective. If he stayed up all night with a wind like this, a whole army of Qabal and Skends could walk right through their campsite and he wouldn't even notice. It was like the boy crying wolf. When do you actually believe what you're being told? He decided that tonight he would have to risk it; he would try to follow the patterns of the wind and the branches and block them from his senses. Tomorrow he could experiment to See if there was a difference when a person—when something living—touched a Thread and when it was something inanimate like a tree. Was a Skend a living thing?

He didn't know when he fell asleep, waking with a start, the blanket slipping from his shoulders, and he stared into the early morning gloom. An icy mist hovered in the air and his breath came out in a giant fog. He yanked the blanket back into place and tried to control the tremors sweeping through his body as it fought the cold, forcing himself to sit as still as he could and feel the Threads. Nothing seemed to be moving. The wind had died down, and the pre-dawn was quiet and still.

How could he have let himself fall asleep? How long had he been out? No more than a couple of hours was his best guess. It was his job to protect Teresa and Enton while they slept, and he'd failed miserably. Another failure he could add to the growing list.

He felt a twitch in the Threads, something that broke the pattern he had been watching for most of the night, and a chill ran down his spine that had nothing to do with the cold. Even in the wind last night, he'd learned a pattern that had remained essentially the same, if you took away the differences created by the branches.

A task he hadn't quite been able to do. This twitch was new, and he knew with certainty it was what had woken him up.

He held his breath, deepening his concentration, and followed the Threads.

It felt easier here than in Chollas; they almost seemed to welcome his touch and accept him as a passenger. He felt invited as they shifted again, and he jumped to one leading in the right direction. His senses moved along the ground, over the top of Teresa and Enton's sleeping forms, and back toward the road they had been following yesterday. When he swept over Teresa, the air felt like honey, and he paused, feeling a bit like a Peeping Tom. Moving over Enton's form brought back memories of the film *Labyrinth,* when Sarah and Hoggle had walked through the Bog of Eternal Stench. He shuddered and moved on. The air got warmer as he drifted closer to what was left of the blacktop highway, still retaining some of the heat from yesterday's sun.

The Threads twitched again and then fell back into their regular patterns. Whatever was out there was moving. He expanded his senses again, ready to jump Threads when the next one changed its pattern. He suddenly tasted coarse fur in his mouth. The warmth hit him stronger, and he could feel a wildness rub along his cheek. He gently nudged the Thread closer to the ground, and the sensations changed. Now he tasted dirt and he tried to spit it out. There was something hard as well. It *smelled* pointy, but not really sharp. The thing moved, disturbing his Thread again. It lifted from the ground and settled back down into the overgrown gravel by the side of the road. A deer! Darwin smiled to himself. What he had felt was a deer walking along the road. He let go of the Thread and was once again back in the campsite, monitoring the general pattern of the Threads. He'd done it! He'd followed a Thread, and without physically seeing, he knew what was out there.

Yet it wasn't enough. He remembered Carlos and Wally while they were traveling to SafeHaven. As far as he knew, they had both slept through the night. Yet the attack when they were in the mountains showed they had watched the area around the campsite. And they did it a lot farther out than he had. How did they do that? How had he just woken up? He sighed, wishing Bill had taught him more stuff. He was floundering in a sea of possibilities with no one to guide him. He would have to do all he could to train himself, then.

By the time the sun broke through the trees and the mist had started clearing, he still hadn't figured out how he had woken up when the deer had entered his area. He would have to experiment when Teresa was awake. But not now. Exhaustion saturated him and a new headache was needling its way up to the front of his head. He struggled to his feet, pushing the cold from his joints, and went to wake Teresa.

She woke up instantly, the look of alarm on her face changing to a smile that warmed her eyes. Darwin resisted the urge to touch her smile, to feel the warmth between his hands. He smiled back and sat down beside her, almost forgetting the chill in the air before pulling his blanket around him.

"You look tired," she said.

"I am. I fell asleep a bit this morning," he said, feeling better telling her the truth. "But I managed to stay up most of the night. I think if I get a couple of hours, it will help."

"Okay. I'll wake you when it's time." Teresa got to her feet and handed him one of her blankets. "The sun will be up soon, and it should get warmer. You use it and get a good sleep."

Darwin took the blanket with a thank you, glad she didn't harp on him for not being able to stay awake. He lay down and pulled the warm blankets over him. Sleep came quickly.

. . .

When Teresa woke him up, she looked as bone-tired as he felt, and though there was still a slight chill in the air, she had removed her jacket and her face was flushed. Darwin jumped up, concern pushing all vestiges of sleep away, and scanned their impromptu campsite to see what was wrong. He reached for the Threads without thinking. The first thing he noticed was that Enton was nowhere to be seen.

"Where's Enton?" For a brief moment he believed the fever had broken and Enton was just standing behind a tree.

"He didn't make it." Teresa's voice cracked.

"Didn't make it? Where is he?"

Teresa placed her hand on his arm and he shook it off, consumed by an irrational anger that built up from the soles of his feet.

"I covered him up," she said. "He's under a pile of rocks, just through there."

Darwin followed her pointing finger. A trail of trampled grass led through the trees to a little opening beyond. He didn't—couldn't—move, his feet frozen to the cold ground until Teresa pulled him down the path she had created, and they came to the cairn at the edge of the overgrown field. She moved out of his way, but he refused to pass her. In front of him was a perfect snapshot of the image he had Seen back in SafeHaven. Teresa stood with her back to him, staring at the pile of rocks Enton's body lay under. What used to be fields, but were now overgrown with shrubs and weeds, spread out to the distance and a small cross made of branches tied together by grass blended in with the background brown. Another lost life fell on his shoulders. Was it him that had brought Enton here, to this point? Was it because he had Seen this image, brought it to life?

He wasn't strong enough to do this.

"I'm sorry." Teresa turned back to him and leaned her head on his shoulder.

"I . . . I didn't really know him."

"Does that matter?" she asked.

He stood in the shadow of the trees staring at the cairn, barely recognizing that Teresa hadn't moved. She was right, it didn't matter. It felt like a piece of him was suddenly missing, a piece he didn't even know existed until it was gone. Despite Enton's words yesterday, he had still held onto the hope that somehow Enton would get them back, maybe even get him home. All that and more was gone now.

"He sat beside me when the Dancers came to SafeHaven. He was just another old guy in the crowd. We met again the next day, and he tested me. I . . . I saw this. Enton dead, the cairn, the fields. You, though I didn't see your face." He wiped his cheek with the back of his hand. "I told him what I saw. He brushed it off as though it didn't mean anything. That night, the Skends attacked, and I left."

He turned his back to the pile of rocks and took the trail back to their campsite, the anger that had dimmed when he saw the cairn flaming into a raw heat. "Come on, we had better get moving."

They packed up in silence, each lost in their own thoughts, and started down the road, the wheelbarrow left behind to become a rusty relic. The sun barely broke through the trees, leaving them in shadows. They slowed in the occasional spots of sunshine to soak up as much of the heat as they could before moving on.

Half an hour later, Teresa broke the silence.

"What are we going to do? I mean, Enton knew where we were. He was the only one who really knew how to use the Threads."

Darwin didn't answer. He hadn't let go of his rage, and it had wormed its way through every part of him. Was she trying to make him feel weak and stupid? It was pretty obvious he didn't know what the hell he was doing, but then, neither did she. Who did she think she was to put him down like that? It was because she blamed him for being out here. And she was right. A sharp retort had formed on the tip of his tongue when she spoke again.

"I'm scared. I don't want to be out here. I don't know what to do."

He heard a slight tremor in her voice and the rage fell instantly silent. He wasn't mad at her, or even at Enton. He was mad at himself for being inadequate. For the deaths that fell on him like lead weights, making every step forward more difficult than the last. Here he was just about to bite her head off for putting him down, when all she wanted was for him to step up. He was so used to being an outsider, so used to being alone. He slowed his pace and walked beside her, putting his arm around her pack, and pulled her close.

"I don't know what to do either," he sighed. "I guess we just keep on going, keep heading south to get away from the cold weather. Eventually we'll figure out where we are, and then we can make a plan to get you back home."

Teresa was silent for a while. "What about you?" she asked.

"My home is a long way from here, though I think Enton might have said it's not really that far at all." He let her go and picked up his pace a bit, forcing some cheer into his voice that he didn't feel. "Come on. Another couple of hours and we'll stop for a bite to eat."

Two days later, they sat huddled beside what was left of a cold, empty farmhouse, the first shelter they had found. Everything before it had been destroyed by what looked like a massive carpet-bombing attack. Even the highway had disappeared into a landscape of craters and shattered vehicles. They'd opened a can of creamed corn that had partially frozen overnight. It was like sucking down frosty mucus.

Darwin added a new item to his green bean, zucchini, and eggplant list. They packed up their makeshift campsite in the overgrown front yard they'd slept in. The house itself had almost burned to the ground, apparently years ago. Black charred timbers held up a partially collapsed roof and a tree had rooted itself firmly in the middle of it. They hadn't wanted to spend the night in it, even though it was the only protection from the bitter wind that had sprung up yesterday afternoon. He didn't think the structure would stand for another winter. Frost coated what was left of the roof, and lay on the tips of the tall grass and weeds that had infiltrated the house's footprint. The breeze created the illusion of a silvery liquid sea.

They were both well rested. Over the last couple of days, Darwin had tested and discovered he could monitor the Threads while he was asleep. He wasn't sure how it worked, but if something entered his area, he woke up. The more practice he got, the larger his area became. He guessed he was close to five hundred yards out now. Enough to find a place to hide if someone came close.

They'd averaged four or five hours of walking a day, getting maybe ten miles in during that time depending on the condition of the road and how much bush they had to weave through. It was less than they had done starting out pushing Enton's wheelbarrow, but it was progress that gave them enough energy to start the next day. They stopped to share a small bite of food when the heat of the day got to its worst, moving when it got cold again. It surprised him how warm it could actually get at this time of year.

The nights, though, had gotten worse, with temperatures falling dramatically. Teresa had insisted they huddle together under their blankets to conserve body heat. Despite his feelings toward her, the closeness made him uncomfortable, but common sense told him it was the only way to make it through. Over the last two nights, he found himself looking forward to it, enjoying their whispered conversations and shared warmth before finally drifting off to sleep.

Darwin pulled on his pack. Even lifting it seemed more difficult than yesterday.

"You're not putting rocks in here while I sleep, are you?"

Teresa laughed. "Nah, just most of what I used to carry in my pack."

He looked over and saw she was struggling as much as he was. They'd each been eating around a can of whatever they had every day, but it wasn't enough. "I think maybe we should be eating more. I know we don't have much, but if we can't carry what we do have, then it's useless to us anyway."

"We need it to last."

"I know, but—"

"Let's talk about it at lunch." She finished shouldering the pack and walked down the overrun driveway. He watched her for a while before jogging to catch up. What was with her attitude?

Their feet had blistered and the packs weighed them down at every step, feeling like they were double the weight they had been when they'd left Gaston. Even though the nights were cold, the sun shone down during the day with an intensity that surprised him. They both had red sun- and wind-burnt faces, and their water was down to less than half of what they'd started with.

Ten minutes after starting their day, a sign told them they had entered Lafayette. They still had no idea what state they were in. The only Lafayette Darwin could think of was in Louisiana, and the traces of snow that had lined the ditches on the two-lane highway told him they were nowhere near there. The place was bigger than Gaston, but still had a small-town feel. A few blocks in, Teresa made them stop.

"We need to find another store."

"I don't know if we can carry more food. We're both getting tired and weak. This place looks bigger than Gaston. They've probably all been raided."

"Whether we can carry it or not is beside the point. We need more food."

He knew she was right, but the thought of carrying more weight tired him even more.

They spent a total of two hours in Lafayette, coming up empty-handed in the food department. When Teresa split from him in the stores, he pretended to be busy looking elsewhere. He had no idea if she found what she was looking for, and the topic was never brought up again.

They didn't hit another town for days, continuing to walk during the coldest parts of the morning and afternoon, and resting when it was warm. If they found a farmhouse when it was time to stop, they huddled inside it, too scared to build a fire. It was still better than sleeping in the ditches or fields.

The house they'd found the previous night was a good one. All of its windows were still intact and there was a well outside. When they dropped the bucket, it broke through the thin layer of ice forming across the top. They'd even risked a small fire the night before, hidden behind the two-story structure, bringing the water to a boil and pouring it into their empty bottles, enjoying as much of the heat as they could.

The next morning, only a few hours after they left the farm, the view changed. Overgrown fields gave way to houses, and soon they were walking down a wide deserted street that surprisingly was still mostly intact, a high concrete wall on their left and what used to be well-maintained houses on their right. Somewhere along the road, they had either missed the sign for the city, or it had been taken down.

This place definitely had the feel of a much bigger city. Darwin crouched down in the bushes on the side of the street opposite the wall and waited for Teresa to join him.

"We need to keep sharp. Last time I was in a bigger city—well, before San Diego—I was attacked by a pack of dogs. Who knows what else could be in here."

"I live in San Diego, remember?"

"All I am saying is people may not be the only problem. We've been lucky so far, I think. You told me yourself that some of the communities wouldn't be as friendly as yours. I'll watch the Threads the best I can, but I've never done it while moving, and you'll need to catch the things I miss. Someone I know once said to use my eyes and not rely solely on the Threads. You're our eyes."

Teresa flashed a brief smile. "I can do that."

They stayed closed to the treeline and continued into the city.

Despite his monitoring, he almost missed the smell of rough, textured cloth and the taste of bad breath. He reached out to Teresa, grabbing her arm and pulling her to a stop.

"What is—"

He held up a hand to keep her quiet. He followed the Threads, trying to find the source of the disturbance, but couldn't locate where he'd felt the person. A Goodwill Donation Center stood on the street corner to his right and he tightened his grip on Teresa's arm.

"Come on," he whispered, moving his grip to her hand and pulling her after him.

She followed him without any complaint.

He pulled her into the shade between the building and a mass of overgrown hedge and hunkered down behind them. They didn't have much cover, but with the contrast between bright sun and the darker shade, he was hoping anyone looking would miss them and keep moving on. Teresa had just squatted down on her heels beside him when a group came around the corner by the overpass they'd been heading for. They pressed deeper into the foliage.

There were five of them, walking in a loose circle. As they got closer he could tell their clothes had seen better days; they didn't fit and the pants had holes in the knees. He doubted it was a fashion statement. It was like they got them from a secondhand store. His heart thudded in his chest and his blood froze in his veins. What if that's what they were doing now? He took a quick glance behind him at the broken windows of the Goodwill, but couldn't tell if there was anything still inside.

The five sauntered down the middle of the street, four of them constantly scanning the buildings, two looking left and two looking right. The leader, dressed in all black and taller than the others with long greasy black hair hanging from a bald pate, kept his attention forward. It looked like he was ignoring the others, but if one of them stepped in his path or got too close, he moved around them with no hesitation. A Threader? If he was, and the group was violent, Darwin knew his hiding spot was useless and he wouldn't last a minute against them.

Risking detection, he touched a Thread that was moving in the general direction of the group and rode it closer, just like he had at Chollas when the Qabal had shown up. He figured he was about four feet away when the greasy-haired one stopped in his tracks and slowly turned in a circle, the rest of the group following his lead. Darwin dropped the Thread and watched with his eyes.

After doing a complete circle, with the four peering into every shadow, the group whispered amongst themselves before moving on again, turning down a side street by the car wash on the next block. Teresa let out a huge breath and Darwin followed suit.

She leaned in and breathed in his ear. "Is it safe, are they gone?"

Darwin shrugged. "I don't know. I don't want to follow them. I tried to get closer when they walked past, but it was like the taller one suddenly noticed me. That was when they stopped and looked around."

"Do you think they know we're here?" Another soft whisper in his ear. He could feel her hair brushing against his cheek.

"I think he knows something is here, just not what or where." Darwin paused, still looking at the street corner the group had disappeared around. "I don't think they're Threaders, or they would have tried to find us." He paused. "I'm tempted to head back the way we came, but they may be waiting behind the car wash. We should move on, try to stay near the buildings. When we get close to the street, run across it as fast as we can until we reach the cover of the beer store."

"There is no place to hide there."

"No, but we should be able to use the shadows. And look just past it, on the other side of the big intersection by the overpass. You can hide in those trees."

"What about you?"

"I'll be right behind you."

"Do you want to wait a few minutes? Make sure they don't come back out of there?"

He thought about it for a bit before answering. "Yeah, good idea. I don't want to stay here too long, though. It feels exposed."

They waited and watched for five minutes before he put his hand on her knee, feeling a tingle run up his arm. "Okay, let's do it."

When she stood and moved to the corner of the building, he immediately missed the heat from her body, the tickling of her hair on his cheek as she whispered to him. It wasn't the first time he'd fallen hard for a girl, but somehow, this felt different. There seemed to be a connection between them that went beyond their shared experiences. Or maybe it was the experiences that made what he felt so real.

He watched her as she stood peeking around the corner and mentally chastised himself. Days of walking alone on the highway and sleeping wherever they could, and she only got close to him when they were in trouble or at night for warmth. He shook his head. This was no time to lose it over Teresa. He told himself to get his head together, to get over it, and followed her to the corner.

The beer store was maybe thirty to forty feet away across the intersection. They would be fully exposed when they ran. Was it a risk they wanted to take? He looked down both streets—twice in the direction the group had turned—and made a decision, nudging Teresa forward. She ran without hesitating and without looking back. He kept looking down the streets, seeing no motion, no sign of anyone watching. When she settled into the shade of the beer store, she almost disappeared from view. Only a slight smudge from her shirt could be seen, but it could have been anything. At least she'd grabbed a darker color when they'd left Gaston. Darwin took one more look down the streets, sucked in a deep breath, and bolted after her.

There was barely enough room in the shadows for both of them, but they huddled together, holding their breath, and waited for any reaction to the mad dash. Nothing moved, and he started to breathe a bit easier. He glanced over his shoulder to look at the clump of trees by the overpass. A sidewalk cut through them, leading up to the overpass road, but it looked like it would provide enough cover to hide them while they caught their breath and decided what to do next.

The intersection they had to cross was bigger than the last one: two lanes in each direction and a turning lane instead of a small side street. And they had to cross the beer store parking lot before they got there. Darwin briefly considered staying where they were, but the trees offered much better protection. Enough to be worth the risk. But it wasn't just his decision to make. A whispered conversation with Teresa confirmed what they were going to do.

His heart hammered in his chest, and he was sure he could hear Teresa's over his own. He took one last look behind them.

"Are you ready?"

She just nodded in reply.

"Go!"

This time he didn't wait until she crossed before following her. He took off just after she did, and she slowly widened the gap as they ran. By the time they reached the cover of the trees, he was winded by the mad dash. It was only about a hundred feet, maybe, but running full tilt was different than the walking they'd been doing. It was different than the jogging he used to do at home. Teresa seemed to recover faster than he did and was breathing normally and watching the street while he was still bent over sucking in huge gobs of air. He knew it was shallow, but he hoped she would blame it on the lack of food.

"I think we made it," Teresa whispered.

"You think so?"

Darwin jumped at the voice, straightening and turning in one rushed motion.

THINGS ARE GETTING SQUIRRELY

"**W**ELCOME TO SALEM, you little shits."

This close, the long black hair looked like it was glued to the man's bald head with grease, and his breath almost pushed Darwin backward.

His first instinct was to run, but he couldn't; there was no way he would leave Teresa behind. He turned the flight response into an attack one, and bent his knees, preparing to launch himself at the man.

"I wouldn't." The man waved his hand and his four companions stepped out from behind the trees.

Darwin knew they were too tired and hungry to face four of them. Teresa moved up behind him and he felt her hand slip into his. Her grip tightened and he almost winced, but he returned the squeeze, trying to give her the same strength she was giving him. He fought the urge to step back when the man moved closer.

"Well, you have a pretty one with you, don't you?" The man reached for Teresa's hair and she jerked back as Darwin raised his arm to block the touch.

"We're just passing through," Teresa said.

The man laughed, revealing half-rotten teeth. That explained the breath, anyway. "I'm sure you were." He spoke to the four men without looking at them. "Tie 'em together. Make sure they can walk, though. We'll take 'em back to camp with us."

One of the men stepped forward, just to the left of Darwin. He was shorter than the greasy-haired man, with long skinny arms and a smirk on his face that made Darwin's blood boil.

"You're sure, Rob? What if they're Threaders? We don't want their kind at camp."

Rob answered without taking his attention off of Darwin. "If they was Threaders, don't you think they'd have used 'em by now? Nah, they are just a couple of bodies we can use." At the last words he looked at Teresa.

"But back there you said—"

"I know what I said," Rob interrupted with a bite in his voice. "Could be they have what you call latent abilities, like me. We can deal with that. Now shut yer trap and tie 'em up like I told you to." He spoke the last words with a sharp edge, though he kept his voice at the same volume. There wasn't any doubt that it was a command.

The short man stepped in front of Darwin and pulled two coils of wire from his back pocket, his grin getting wider. He uncoiled them into long strands. What looked like rust flaked off and settled to the ground.

"We use these to catch squirrels," he said. "Sometimes when they fight, we find them with their legs or heads sliced clean off. It makes a hell of a mess with all that blood and stuff." His grin disappeared and he grabbed Darwin and Teresa's clasped hands, wrapping a length of wire around both their wrists, tying them together. "I wouldn't recommend you try and pull this off, you wouldn't want the same to happen to you." He bent down to wrap another wire around their ankles, binding them together as though they were in a three-legged race.

Darwin felt the thin wire bite into his pants and he fought the urge to pull away.

As soon as they were tied Rob stopped looking at Darwin and addressed the other three men. "Me an' Ben will lead. You three stay behind 'em and keep yer eyes sharp." He turned without waiting for a response and led the way out of the trees and under the overpass.

Darwin and Teresa tried to hobble after him and nearly fell.

"I'll count," Teresa said. "On one, we move our tied together legs, on two the other one. Ready? One . . . two . . . one . . . two . . ."

At each step, the wire around their wrists tightened, eventually feeling like it cut into skin. Darwin was pretty sure he felt blood trickle down the back of his hand, but he didn't want to look, too afraid of what he would see. Instead he used his spare hand to hold his and Teresa's arms together, just above the wrist. It made walking a bit more difficult, but it kept their arms relatively in sync and the wire stopped biting in as much.

"One . . . two . . . one . . . two . . ." Teresa did her best to keep up the pattern.

He had no idea how she could sound so calm. His mind was racing, flitting between thoughts of escaping and increasingly bad scenarios of what the group would do with them. When Teresa missed a count and they stumbled, his thoughts bubbled over into words.

"You have to slow down. We can't keep up," he called out, unable to hide the edge of anger in his voice.

Rob paused and looked around. The smile on his face didn't reach his eyes, but Darwin could tell he was enjoying their pain. "Too bad," he said, and continued walking.

By the time they cleared the underpass, Darwin could smell water and the temperature had dropped a couple of degrees. Just ahead, concrete barriers placed to stop cars from driving off the road crossed their path. A few steps later, he could see the shimmer of the sun reflecting on the river below. Rob turned left in front of the barriers and followed the road before hopping over them at the first group of trees and jogging down a steep hill to what used to be a parking lot. The only thing that differentiated it from the small park beside it was its flatness and the occasional glimpse of gray through the tall grass.

Darwin and Teresa stopped at the barrier while Rob and Ben walked further into the parking lot. How the heck were they supposed to get over this? The barrier came above their knees even with the crumbled top, and the slope on the other side was severe enough that there was no way they would be able to keep their balance.

He felt a shove on his shoulder and stumbled, his feet hitting the wide bottom portion of the concrete barrier. By the time his knees hit the top, he could feel Teresa pulling against him, trying to keep them both upright. His body folded over the short wall. Instinct forced him to put his hands out in front of him, trying to stop his momentum. He jerked Teresa forward, the wire biting deep into his wrist, and they both fell, teetering over the top before toppling and rolling down the hill in a pile of arms and legs and trap wire.

They tumbled to a stop at the bottom on the hard asphalt of the parking lot. He felt like he had been run over by a steamroller. Every part of him hurt to the point he was sure something had broken. As he lay there, the world slowly coming back into focus, he heard a soft moan from beside him.

He forced his eyes wider, squinting at the bright blue sky above him, and turned to look at Teresa. She had twisted in the somersault down the short hill and lay on top of their arms, her head near his shoulder and face down on a rough piece of exposed cement. Her shirt had torn across her shoulder and back, and blood seeped into the tattered fabric. His pain faded into the background as concern for her took over.

He raised his head and nudged her with his free hand. She moaned again. "You okay?" He waited for a while before he nudged her harder. "Teresa, are you okay?"

She moaned in reply.

"Come on, answer me. Teresa!"

"Damn, that hurt." Her voice was muffled by the concrete.

He lowered his head with a sigh and closed his eyes again. "Anything broken?" He felt her head shift by his shoulder.

"I don't know."

"Can you get off my arm? I can't feel it."

Teresa struggled to roll over and gasped in pain as the wire around their legs twisted and tightened before letting her leg rotate enough for her to lie on her back.

Blood rushed into Darwin's arm, and with it a bright stab of pain. His wrist felt warm and wet. A wave of dizziness passed through him, and his stomach roiled.

The wire around their wrists had cut through the skin. He thought if he looked closely enough he might even be able to see bone. He couldn't help but look, and his gut churned again. His brief inspection showed the wire embedded just above the back of his hand. Thank god they had been holding hands when the wire was wrapped around. If the insides of their wrists had been exposed . . . Darwin swallowed harshly, fighting the nausea that churned his stomach. He never did like the sight of blood. His or anyone else's.

A boot prodded him roughly. "Get up."

He opened his eyes again and glared at the man standing over him. The boot kicked him in the side and Darwin sucked in a sharp breath. It felt like someone had jabbed a knife in his ribs and twisted. Tears streamed from the corners of his eyes and fell onto the dry grass.

The boot moved again but stopped short when Rob's voice cut through the air. "Watch what yer doin'. He ain't no good to us if he can't work. What happened?"

"They fell coming down the hill."

Darwin gasped between the waves of pain. "Bullshit. You pushed us over the barrier."

The boot pressed into his ribs and the knife twisted again. Darwin let out a small cry.

"Leave him be." Teresa pushed up onto her elbow and stared at the man standing over them. Another boot came from behind her and pushed her shoulders back down to the ground.

"You'll find it best if you keep yer mouth shut," said Rob. "Until you're told not to," he said with a leer in his voice.

"Get 'em up and have Dale look at 'em." Rob turned and headed back toward the small park across the lot. The men left behind muttered to themselves and bent down to help Darwin and Teresa up.

"Count of three then lift. One . . . two . . . three . . ." Two of them heaved and lifted Darwin and Teresa to their feet. Teresa twisted out of the overly familiar grasp of the man helping her, and almost fell again. She caught herself and leaned against Darwin for support as he moved between them. Pain seared through his ribs with every breath he took, but it wasn't enough to push away the rage building inside of him. How dare they treat her that way.

Blood ran from the wire embedded in their wrists to drip from their knuckles on to the ground.

"Move."

Still leaning against each other, they shuffled in the direction Rob had taken. Each step shot flares of fire through their wrists where the wire was tied.

Just ahead, under the yellow canopy of trees already losing their leaves, a few tents had been set up. In the center of them stood a tall, screened sunroom tent with a few picnic tables inside it. Darwin could hear Rob talking loudly about his two captives. He leaned in closer to Teresa.

"You okay?" he whispered.

"I think so. The wire's bad. There's nothing I can do until we get it out. It's going to get ugly if it isn't taken care of right away. The one on our legs is okay. I don't think it cut through our pants."

"Nothing broken?"

"No, thank god. I'm not good at healing broken bones yet. I . . . I didn't think of looking at you, I was too worried about the wire. You okay?"

"My ribs are bad, where he kicked me. I think they might be busted." Darwin felt Teresa get pushed forward and turned his head to look behind him.

"You two quit your yapping and keep moving," the man said.

It was the same one who pushed them down the hill. "You get off pushing around people who can't protect themselves?" Darwin snapped without thinking, but as soon as the words were out of his mouth, as soon as the anger and resentment had an outlet, he felt better. The man's attention had moved from Teresa to him, and as far as he was concerned, that was all good.

"I said quit talking and keep moving." The man shoved Darwin forward, creating a fresh surge of pain across his ribs.

They hobbled across the parking lot and stepped up the curb to the grassy park, almost falling over again. A tall woman with thick, hot pink, plastic-framed glasses came rushing toward them, eyeing the tied-up pair with distaste. Her clothes were disheveled and dirty, and she looked old enough to be Darwin's grandmother.

"I thought Rob was joking when he said he'd done this to you," she said. "That man is an idiot. Untie them immediately and bring them to my tent."

"Rob said to—"

She turned her gaze on the man who had spoken and her voice took on a steel edge. "I don't care what Rob said. You will do as you are told, Jacob, or next time you come to see me, I'll be pretty damn busy doing something else."

The two stood and stared at each other for a few seconds before Jacob moved to untie the wire Ben had wrapped around them. He did their legs first, and as the wire came loose, Darwin could feel the rush of warmth flowing back into his foot with the increased blood flow.

When Jacob moved toward their arms, Darwin could feel Teresa tense up and pull away slightly. He moved his free hand to Teresa's cheek and made her look at him.

"It's better if it's out, right?"

Teresa just nodded.

"Okay. Then let's get it done."

Jacob grabbed their arms and jerked them toward him. His hand hadn't even touched the wire before the old woman stopped him.

"Never mind," she said, "I'll do it. You're doing even more damage to them, being so rough."

"They're prisoners," Jacob said. "What's wrong with the way I'm treating them?"

"Prisoners? They must have attacked five grown men to put so much fear into you."

"No. We just—"

"You just what? You just want to be a prick and act all superior?" She pointed a thumb over her shoulder. "Why don't you guys join Rob and talk about all your manly exploits? Maybe you can tell everyone how good it feels to scare the bejesus out of strangers."

"Rob told me to—"

"Yeah, we covered that already. Now I'm telling you. Does it look like these two are going anywhere soon? They'll just as likely bleed out when the wire is removed. They're not leaving."

Jacob looked at the men with him and shrugged. They walked past the woman and moved toward the sunroom tent.

"Come on, follow me. The name's Dale."

"You're a healer?" asked Teresa.

"Yup. And so are you."

Darwin felt Teresa hesitate in her step.

"Don't act so surprised, girl. We know our own kind. You're far enough along in your training to understand that, would be my guess." When Teresa didn't answer, Dale stopped and turned to face them. "What's your name, girl?"

"Teresa."

"Well, Teresa, welcome to Salem. This is Rob's crew. While we're away from home, what Rob says happens. No questions asked."

"Then why did Jacob listen to you?" asked Darwin.

"I'm a healer, boy. Without me, people get hurt and they don't get better." She looked at Teresa again. "Being a healer ain't so bad. At least you won't be put to work in the fields or kitchens." She paused. "Or worse." Dale turned and continued walking.

"What about Darwin?"

Dale continued as if she hadn't heard. When they reached the circle of tents, she disappeared inside one while they stood and waited. Darwin thought of running, but how far would they get before the rest of Rob's crew chased them down? There was no way that would end well.

"What the hell is going on 'ere?" Rob stormed up to them with Jacob in tow just as Dale emerged from the tent with an empty bowl and some towels. Jacob could barely contain the smirk on his face.

"Good. Just in time. Rob, get some hot water in here," Dale said, holding the bowl out to him.

He looked at the bowl, a scowl on his face. "I said I wanted these two tied up. What gives you the right to tell 'em different?" he said, jerking his thumb in Jacob's direction.

Dale stood calmly as Rob ranted, obviously waiting for him to finish. When he was done, she said, "These two aren't going anywhere. Somewhere along the way here they got pretty busted up. And using trap wire isn't tying them up, it's torture, and it's wrong."

"I give the orders around here, woman."

"Yes, you do. And I do the healing. These two aren't going to be any use to us if that damned wire gets them infected. What if the guy's got a broken rib? What if it doesn't heal right? Do you think he'll be any good in the fields?"

Rob hesitated for a second. "I want 'em tied up."

"Fine. You can tie them up after I'm finished with them. And use something that doesn't damage them. Nico won't be happy if he's got a couple more mouths to feed that can't support themselves."

At Nico's name, Rob took a step back and glowered at Dale. "If they ain't gonna support themselves, Nico ain't gonna see 'em. Jacob," he spoke without taking his gaze off of Dale, "you stay 'ere. Ben'll bring some rope. I want 'em tied to the trees as soon as she's done. Got that?" When Jacob didn't answer right away, Rob turned and swung out his arm, backhanding Jacob across the face. "I said, you got that?"

Jacob stumbled backward, the quick look of hatred that crossed his face replaced with subservience. "Yes," he said, rubbing the four finger-sized welts that covered his cheek.

Rob stared at Dale a bit longer before turning and walking back to the sunroom tent without saying another word.

"You shouldn't rile him like that, Dale," said Jacob. "One day he won't care what you are, he'll just take you out."

"It's not going to happen anytime soon." She held out the empty bowl to him. "Now get me some hot water."

"I am not leaving until Ben shows up. Rob will kill me if I leave them again."

"Fine, watch them. I'll get the water." As Dale walked away, she stopped and turned back. "If I see any more damage to them, you'll pay the price for it." She started walking again without waiting for a response.

"How long have you apprenticed as a healer?" asked Dale, sitting across the weathered picnic table from them.

"Almost two years. My . . . my mom was teaching me." She fell silent and watched as Dale put a clean towel in the steaming bowl of water.

"So you've covered the numbing of pain?"

"Yeah. I haven't had a lot of practice or done it without supervision."

"Well, you get to practice on your friend. I'm going to get the wire out, and it's going to hurt. The blood is already starting to clot a bit, which means the wire might be a tad stuck. I'll numb your arm after you do his. Let's see what you can do." Dale took the towel out of the water and wrung it out lightly. "Start now, before I place the towel on. Sometimes it's easier when you can see what you are working on."

Teresa sucked in her breath and stared at Darwin's wrist. The sharp pain dulled to a light throb instantly and he looked down, involuntarily opening his Sight. Vaporous white Threads moved around his wrist and entered his skin.

"Good," said Dale, "now spread out, further up the arm and hand. When the wire tugs, it'll be pulling skin and meat from the general area of the wound."

The pattern of the Threads changed, thinning out to cover more of his arm, and the light throb almost disappeared. He kept watching, intrigued by what he was Seeing, making sure not to touch any of the Threads.

"Good. Now hold it there while I do yours."

Threads formed around Teresa's wrist. To Darwin, they appeared as thin and insubstantial as the ones Teresa had used, but the pattern was different. These Threads sank into her skin at regular intervals, some of them moving and shifting once they had entered, but most holding still. Just like when Teresa did it, once the wire cut was completely covered, new Threads formed to cover a wider spot.

"Do you See how I did mine?"

Teresa nodded as sweat broke out on her forehead. Darwin saw the pattern of Threads tighten on his wrist, matching what Dale had done, and his arm went numb from his elbow down to his fingertips.

"Much better. Now hold it." Dale reached for the towel. It still dripped water as she brought it closer. "Keep holding it while the towel blocks your direct view. Remember how the pattern feels and keep it there."

Dale wrapped the towel around their wrists. Her Thread pattern on Teresa didn't change, but the ones on his arm did. He sucked in a quick, sharp breath as the pressure of the towel cut through Teresa's Threads. The pain disappeared almost as fast as it came.

"Sorry."

He just nodded. More Threads formed around both of them, gently wrapping the warm towel. Darwin felt some pressure, but the pain didn't come back.

"Good," said Dale, "now keep holding it while you monitor the clotted blood over the wound. Can you feel it? Slightly hard but still flexible? The blood hasn't had time to form into a scab yet. Watch how the top of it gets softened by the water, and then duplicate the process deeper in the cut. The water will come of its own accord, as long as you open the path."

More white Threads moved into the towel and touched his arm, but he didn't feel it as much as he Saw it. Teresa's grip on the pain-killing Threads remained strong as the new Threads moved to soften the clotting blood. A duplicate effort was happening on Teresa's wrist, but he could See it was more controlled, more precise, and Dale was working much faster.

"Have you reached the wire yet?" Dale asked.

"I don't know."

"You will. The Threads will push back, almost as if you knocked a stick against a steel post. If the push back is softer, gentler, then you've reached bone. You shouldn't; the wire hasn't cut into the bone; it's just sitting on top of it."

His stomach took a flip and his cheeks drained white. Dale noticed right away.

"Are you going to hold it together, boy?"

He straightened his back. "Darwin. The name is Darwin. I'll be fine."

"You're looking at your wrist an awful lot. You're not a healer. Can you See?"

From out the corner of his eye, he saw Jacob, who had been sitting on the grass with his back to a tree, lean forward, obviously listening more intently. He didn't like to lie, but these people had taken them in as prisoners, and maybe some things were best kept a secret.

"No. Maybe I'm just kind of hoping so much."

"Mmmm. At your age, you would already know. You should know that. No point in trying anymore."

Darwin relaxed when Jacob leaned back against the tree and watched the Threads in and around his wrist again. He could See when Teresa hit the wire and pulled back a little.

"I'm there," Teresa said.

"Okay, let's take a look." Dale looked at his wrist without losing control of her own Threads. "Good. Now work around the wire a bit, make sure it's loose. Don't push so hard that you soften the bone, though."

The Threads wrapped around the wire and moved along it in both directions. He wasn't sure if he saw or felt the wire release, and his stomach twitched again.

"Got it."

Dale started unwrapping the towel, gently lifting the last bit from Teresa's cut. Darwin stared at the blood-soaked towel and this time his stomach threatened to do a double somersault. There was a lot of blood, and he couldn't tell what was his and what was Teresa's.

Dale pulled a pair of wire cutters from her kit and placed the tip between their arms, the wire wedged in between its sharp edges. She squeezed and the wire snapped, springing apart, coming halfway out of Darwin's cut. Blood started seeping out of the open wound right away.

"Can you slow the blood?" Dale asked.

Teresa nodded tersely and a frown cut through the sweat. The seeping slowed down and almost stopped.

The wire moved again. Dale had grabbed it between her fingertips and was gently pulling it from Teresa's wrist. As it came out, the cut slid shut, leaving an angry red slit just above the back of Teresa's hand. The white Threads moved in patterns too complex for him to follow.

As Dale pulled, the wire's coiled tension pushed it back into his wrist, and he swallowed hard to control the sudden increase in his nausea. He still felt no pain. She held onto the separated end she pulled from Teresa's arm and moved her left hand to the other end of the cut wire. As she pulled it out of him, the cut didn't close itself like Teresa's had.

"Start closing the wound, Teresa. The sooner it's closed the better it will heal."

"I can't. There's something . . . something different . . . wrong, but I can't tell what it is."

Dale grabbed the towel and wrapped it tightly around his wrist. As soon as she was done, she concentrated back on Teresa.

The Threads were still white, but they appeared much thinner than before. Dale pulled them through Teresa's skin as though she was stitching a shirt, but deeper. It was like she was suturing the wound deep, by the bone, and working her way back up to the already closed skin. When she was done, all that was left on Teresa's arm was a fine white line with tanned, dark skin puckered around the edges.

"So, what is the problem over here?" asked Dale, moving her attention to him.

"I don't know. Something's not right. It . . . it kind of feels like an infection, but I can't See anything."

"Pull out so I can take a look, then," said Dale.

Searing pain crashed into his wrist like a wave smashing against a cliff face. He hadn't realized how much work Teresa was doing until she pulled her Threads from him. He doubled over, laying his chest on his knees as he tried to draw in slow and steady breaths. The pain in his ribs doubled as he did, and he struggled to push himself upright. His arm went numb almost as fast as the pain had come, its sudden absence as disconcerting as its arrival.

"When you're pulling out of an open wound like that, take your time. It is a simple matter of deadening some of the nerves in the cut as you're doing it, just to make sure your patient doesn't keel over, like this one almost did."

Teresa put her arm around his waist and gave him a gentle squeeze. "Sorry, it won't happen again." She looked into his eyes. "Are you okay?"

"Yeah. I'll be better when it's finished, though." The fresh pain in his ribs had brought tears to his eyes. He wiped them away, deciding he didn't need to See what they were doing anymore, and focused on the picnic table instead.

Teresa watched as Dale probed the slice with the Threads, but she didn't move her arm from around him.

"There's the problem."

"What?"

Dale looked at Teresa. "Come on and take a look, just don't do anything."

Teresa nodded and bent over his arm. "I can tell something isn't right, but I can't See what."

"Let me guide you."

Teresa sucked in a breath and nodded, never taking her focus from the slice.

"Look here, and here," said Dale.

"I don't See anything, just blood."

"Right but take a closer look."

Teresa moved her arm from around Darwin's waist and placed her hands on his arm, just above and below the cut. She bent lower, looking at something deep inside.

"It looks just like blood."

"It is blood. It's just not *his* blood," said Dale.

Darwin blanched again. He could taste bile in the back of his throat.

"I . . . I think, maybe. This one feels . . . tastes wilder. It is not like the rest."

"That's because it's squirrel's blood from the damn trap wire."

Darwin leaned over and spewed what was left of their hastily eaten breakfast onto the ground beside him. Neither woman looked at him. Jacob snickered from the tree.

"That took a while," said Dale. "For a second, I thought you were going to make it all the way through."

He spat some of the remaining chunks from his mouth and grimaced.

Teresa ignored them both. "So how do we get it out?"

"Same as with an infection. Just find the bad pieces and push them out of his body." Dale stood and stretched her back. Darwin could hear the pops. "I'll give you ten minutes while I look at the other damage you two have, starting with those ribs, then I'll see how good a job you did."

Darwin stared at the thin white line on the back of his wrist. Matching scars. Not exactly what he had in mind. A warm hand touched his shoulder before moving to his wrist.

"How are you doing?" Teresa's voice was soft, and she traced the fine white line with her finger.

"Okay, I guess." The truth was, he felt pretty stupid for throwing up.

After Dale and Teresa had fixed him up, Jacob had forced him to haul water from the river and wash the ground clean. All he had succeeded in doing was creating a puddle of mud with chunks of corn floating in it.

Dale had talked to Rob about Teresa, and he'd decided not to tie her up as long as Dale kept a close eye on her. He said she wasn't going anywhere with her boyfriend tied up anyway. Instead of using the tree, they pulled the picnic table over the mud puddle and tied his legs around one of the inner supports. Then they looped the rope through the top slats and tied his hands down. He had to lower his head to the tabletop just to scratch his nose.

In the brief pieces of time they were left alone, he tried to convince Teresa to leave, to slip away while no one was watching and just run. Every time she refused, he felt the anger rise up in him like a tide and he had to bite it back down. She was a grown woman and could do what she wanted. But he hated that she would be one of Rob's slaves, and he hated even more the feeling of relief he had when she stayed.

Dale sat at one end of the table, her face buried in a book, *Midnight at the Well of Souls* by Jack L. Chalker. Darwin had the series on his bookshelf at home, the pages old and tattered. They were a gift from his mother, a series she had loved when she was younger. She had read them to him at bedtime when he was younger, and he'd read them at least every year since she had died.

Teresa put a cup of water in front of him and gave one to Dale before she sat beside him. "You're sure?"

"I said yes," he snarled. He hung his head, feeling guilty. "Look . . . I'm . . . I'm sorry. I'm not at my best today." He glanced at her and saw concern written all over her face, almost calling her his angel. How long ago was it when he first thought of her as that? It felt like a year but couldn't have been more than a few weeks. Could it?

"None of us are," she said.

He shifted his position and looked in Teresa's eyes. "I'm really sorry. If I wasn't here—if I wasn't somehow transported here, none of this would have happened. SafeHaven would still be whole. You would still be in San Diego learning and healing."

"It is not your fault, Darwin." Teresa moved her hand from his scar to his hand, wrapping her fingers under his palm. "None of this is. It wasn't your choice to come over, and it was the Qabal that sent the Skends. It's them, not you."

He nodded, not quite believing her, but desperately wanting to. Dale stood suddenly, the book closed and forgotten on the table in front of her. She sat down across from them.

"What were you two just talking about?"

Teresa answered without turning to face her. "Nothing."

"Nothing my ass. You are talking about the Qabal and Skends. What about them?"

This time Darwin turned to face her. "Nothing. We're just talking."

Dale looked over her shoulder at Jacob. He still sat under the tree, fast asleep in the dappled shade. The afternoon had turned warm. Darwin wasn't sure if the temperature was normal for this time of year, but he was glad for it.

She leaned in closer to Darwin. "You had better tell me everything. And now. If you don't, I'm going straight to Rob, and I guarantee he'll get everything out of you, and you'll be a patient of mine again."

Darwin glanced over at Teresa and she gave an almost imperceptible nod. He sighed and turned to Dale. "Okay," he said. "I'm not
from around here."

"Yeah, we kinda figured that out already. Neither is she."

"No, I mean . . . *I* am not from *here*. I'm not from this universe.
I have no idea how I got here, but the Qabal think I do. Now that I'm
not under their control anymore, they're trying to kill me. All I want
to do is go home . . ." His voice trailed off.

At his last words, Teresa pulled her hand from his and placed it
in her lap. He immediately missed the warmth, the contact.

"How are they trying to kill you?" Dale asked, apparently only
caring about the Qabal and not where he'd come from.

"Well, they tried at their headquarters, but I managed to get
away, with some help."

Once the story started, Darwin found he couldn't stop. All of it
came out, from the brainwashing to Bill's help and his death. His
trek to SafeHaven, and everything that happened after it. He skirted
around his Threading skill, though Dale had already probably
guessed. By the time he was done both Teresa and Dale sat in
stunned silence.

"Damn." Dale paused, slowly shaking her head. "How did the
Skends find you in San Diego?"

"I don't know. Enton showed up to take me back to SafeHaven,
and there they were."

"If they're following you, we're in a lot of trouble. I need to talk
to Rob." Dale stood up.

"But you said—"

"I know what I said. This is too big. If the Skends are following
you, we don't have a chance. Shit." Dale turned and stared at Jacob,
still sleeping under the tree. She sighed and looked at Teresa.
"There's a knife in the top pouch of my backpack. It will cut through

the rope pretty easy. Rob isn't going to let you come with us, which means he would rather kill you. Run. It may give you a bit of a chance. And hurry up, I'm not giving you much time." Dale jogged toward the sunroom tent, leaving them alone with a sleeping Jacob.

Teresa stood and sprinted over to the tent while he kept watch. Jacob didn't even move when the tent zipper opened. She came back with a small knife and bent under the table, cutting his legs free. By the time she was standing again, Darwin was ready to leave. With his hands still tied, trailing the rope from his legs behind him, he pushed Teresa until they were behind Dale's tent.

Just a few yards away the road rose into a bridge, the underside of it cast in a deep shadowy gloom. They ran into the darkness, bent over at the waist, until they emerged from the other side, pausing long enough to finish cutting the rope, picking up the pieces so Rob wouldn't know what direction they took.

FOR FOOLS RUSH IN

SECOND BRIDGE RAN parallel to the first, leaving a small gap of sunshine on the brown grass in between. Darwin and Teresa dashed through the light and back into the shadow. He slowed to a stop, keeping his grip on Teresa, and glanced back. No one was following them. Yet.

Ahead of them a storage facility surrounded by a chain link fence blocked their way. In one direction, the fence stopped just short of the river. In the other, it carried right through to the street. Both distances were too far to run if Rob started looking for them. Darwin looked around desperately, trying to find a quick way out. He ended up pointing to where the bridge met the ground.

"Come on, we'll hide in here."

Teresa pulled back, keeping her hand firmly in his. "We need to get away."

"We're not going to get around that chain link fence fast enough. Our only chance is to hide. Hopefully they won't expect us this close. They'll think we've run away as far as we can. *Come on.*" He pulled her hand again and she followed him. Before they got there, Teresa yanked on the pieces of rope he was holding. He stopped and let her cut the rest off. She threw the pieces toward the river. When she was done, they dashed to where the bottom of the bridge met the ground, crawling on their hands and knees into the dark recess. He could tell she was still hesitant as the smell of wet earth and moldy leaves surrounded them, and the temperature dropped.

"Rob will be able to sense us here. He did it before. This is such a bad idea." The words rushed out of Teresa's mouth in a tumble.

"I think I can block him. He didn't seem that strong. Sensitive, but not strong. Plus, he doesn't know I'm a Threader, he may not be looking that closely."

"Dale knows."

"She won't tell him." He didn't know how he was sure, but as the words came out, he knew it was true.

He pushed her ahead of him, deeper into the darkness, forcing her to lie on the cold, wet ground. He pulled leaves and debris toward them, piling it up, hoping the dark would stop Rob from seeing them. When he lay down, placing his back to her, he threw more garbage on top of them until the smell of mildew and mold almost made him gag.

"And if you can't?" The question came out forced and whispered.

He reached behind him and put his hand on her thigh. "I will." He heard her sigh in response.

They lay there together, trying to breathe as quietly as possible. When the first shouts came from the camp, doubt stabbed through him. Would there have been enough time to run around the fence and keep on going? What if he couldn't block Rob, or they had another Threader, or someone crawled into the narrow space to look? He moved his hand off of Teresa and began to concentrate. It was too late to change their minds, and he might have just gotten them both killed.

The Threads in the area came into sharp focus, and he pushed and prodded them, watching their response. The ones closest to him, close to the moist earth and rotten leaves, felt heavier than the rest. They were thick and sluggish, and he thought he felt a slight resistance when he tried to move them. He opened his mind further. They tasted dark. His tongue felt covered in slimy mud and small chunks of dirt and leaves. His nose tickled with the crawling of sowbugs and earwigs. His skin felt clammy in the cold, dank air.

He changed the Threads coming from him and Teresa to match what he felt and tasted.

But he knew it wasn't enough. He could still smell the cloth texture of his and Teresa's clothes, feel the scent of her over that of the leaves, taste the fear that they were both struggling to contain. He closed his eyes and slowed his breath, letting the quality of their dark corner wash over him until there was nothing else, taking the Threads of their hiding spot until they were part of him, part of who he was. The mold on the leaves took on a life of its own. He could sense the slow decomposition taking place. Under them, the dirt teemed with life, turning the debris into nutrients for the soil. Nutrients that would never be used by plant life in his small black corner of the world.

The Threads split into images: the dark corner he had seen before Teresa crawled in, their bodies pulled out and leaking blood into the ground, a faded Darwin standing over Teresa's body. More images flashed through his mind, and he pushed them away, concentrating on the single image of the empty space.

As he focused on what he saw, he wove the pattern around them tighter. Where pieces of them rose to the surface, he moved the Threads lower and broke them into strands that were indistinguishable from the others. His world slowed, and he became the small angle between the rusted iron of the bridge above them and the dirt teeming with life below. His hands became the moldy leaves. His being became the black cold earth, and time ceased to exist.

Hands pulled at him and the dirt under him shifted. He fought to stay where he was, who he was. Dirt, bugs, compost.

"Come on, Darwin. Move. I can't lose you now."

He felt his body being dragged from the haven he had built for them, not by the physical feeling of being moved, but through the disruption of life around him. Fungi rolled between him and the dirt. Sowbugs scrambled to move out of the way, running helter-skelter into any covered cranny they could find. One squished under his hip and he could feel its life draining from the wet smear that remained.

Warmth and light struck his face, pushing away the Threads he had so carefully created. He pulled at them, forcing them back into the protection they both needed. Something hit his cheek, sharp and hard. Again. And again. The sting settled into a dull throb and his face flushed with heat as blood rushed into it.

"Wake up! Damn you, Darwin, wake up."

Soft white Threads floated into his view, probing into his body, moving through his haze and around his brain. They pulled back suddenly, and he felt a hot drop of liquid touch his throbbing cheek and roll down to his ear, finally stopping as it met resistance from a strand of hair. The liquid smelled salty and familiar, but this was different. It felt like . . . Teresa.

The name nestled in his head. Teresa. His angel. He remembered the curve of her cheek in the sun, the feel of her hand in his, how her eyes seemed to look directly into his soul, making him want to be a better man. His lips moved, and breath flowed from his lungs through his vocal cords. "Teresa?" The barest whisper. He sucked in a deeper breath and forced it out again. "Teresa? My angel?" It sounded like a shout to his ears.

"Yes. Yes, I'm here. We're safe now. Come back."

A soft hand wiped dirt from his cheek and then came back, resting on his face. Another hand touched his other cheek, cradling his head in their warmth.

"We're safe, Darwin. Wake up."

He listened to the voice. Her voice. They were hiding. He had created a safe place for them. Someplace they couldn't be detected. She said they were safe. The memory suddenly came into sharp focus. He'd created a cover for them, made their place invisible to . . . to Rob. They had been prisoners.

"Safe?" His voice came out raspy.

Another hot tear fell on him and one of the hands moved to wipe it away. "Yes, safe."

He took a deep breath, washing away the musty smell he had held in place. He pushed at the sluggish Threads, releasing them from his hold. Some resisted while others fled back to the dark gap under the bridge. The ground under him felt warm. The dirt was still there, but there was a layer between him and it. Something different, no longer compost and bugs. It had less life to it.

He pushed harder and new Threads came into view. The hands moved from his face and a shaft of sunlight landed on his closed eyes. He fought the urge to scramble back to somewhere dark and safe, like an earwig exposed to sudden light. He opened his eyes, blinking rapidly.

The sunlight was cut off, forcing Darwin to focus his eyes closer.

Light filtered through dark hair, creating a halo around the face of his angel. She smiled.

"It's good to have you back."

"Back?"

"I . . . I thought I lost you. The first day . . ." Teresa moved and the sunlight hit him again. "We'll talk about it later." Her voice had turned crisper, more professional. "First, we need to get some water into us. Do you think you can stand?"

"Of course, why wouldn't I?" Darwin raised himself onto his elbows and pushed to his feet. The world spun, and before he realized what was happening, he was back on the ground breathing in the scent of the brown grass.

"That's why," Teresa answered. She reached out for him. "Let's try that again. Maybe we can make it to the picnic tables."

He stood again, this time with Teresa under his shoulder to help keep his balance. Together they walked back to where the tents had been set up, the square impressions still on the flattened grass. The picnic table they finally rested at had a piece of rope tied to one of the central supports.

He looked around the deserted area, squinting in the bright sun. "When did they leave?"

"Two days ago."

He nodded and was about to ask another question before what she had said sank in. He stared at her. "Two days?"

Teresa just nodded.

"How . . . how long?"

"About three days total."

He wiped the back of his hand across his forehead. It came away smeared with dirt and rotten leaves. "Maybe you should tell me now." Teresa's stare examined him, and he could feel her assessing whether he was strong enough. "Just tell me, please?"

She sighed. "It was closer to dusk than I thought when we got away. Rob and Jacob and the other two came out pretty quick to look for us. They all ran right past, didn't even look under the bridges. They came back maybe an hour later. I could barely see through the blind you had built, but I'm pretty sure they came back without Jacob, and I haven't seen him since they left. I don't know what they did to him. A few minutes later, the group was back with flashlights. I have no idea where they found batteries; we haven't had any in San Diego for a couple of years. Anyway, they all came back. All except Rob. He just kind of walked around in wider circles from the picnic table. He spent a lot of time under the bridges, telling everyone to search while he just stood back. He walked right over to us in the dark. He even called someone over with a light to look. I . . . I swear he looked me right in the eyes, but they both acted like they didn't see a thing. I didn't understand how they could have missed us.

"Even after everyone left, Rob stuck around. I think he stayed under the bridge most of the night. He must have noticed something. I guess I fell asleep at some point. When I woke up, the campsite was down and everyone was walking away. I saw Dale put a backpack in the long grass behind the tree by her tent just before the whole group left.

"You didn't move, though. I wanted to get up, but I was too scared to. You wouldn't talk to me when I tried. I thought maybe you knew they were still around, even though I couldn't see them. Maybe Rob had stayed behind, hoping we would come back or something. I don't know. Maybe the backpack was a ruse.

"I started getting worried, and then the Skends showed up. There were three or four of them, I think. I only saw one really good. They just kind of stood there and waited. A couple of minutes later the others showed up. Definitely Qabal, by the look of those idiotic blue jackets they wear. They poked around the campsite for a while and then took off in the same direction Rob and his crew went. They didn't even come near us.

"I was too scared to do anything until I had to pee so bad, I couldn't have stayed where I was even if I wanted to. I washed up in the river a bit and came back, and that's when . . . that's when I noticed you were . . . I don't know how to describe it. You just weren't *there*. Our hiding spot was empty. I ran around looking for you, calling for you.

"I came back and started digging through the leaves. That's when I found you. You were still there. You were there all the time. I . . . I cleared the pile from around you, but you didn't respond. You started disappearing again. The leaves and dirt just built back up over you.

"I tried to use my training, to See if I could find some sort of injury or bring you out of your . . . your state. That's when you completely disappeared. I knew you were right in front of me, but the place we hid just became another dirty hole. I freaked out. I started screaming and pulling out whatever was in there. I finally grabbed your arm and dragged you out here. You . . . you wouldn't wake up." Her shoulders started shaking.

Darwin slid down the bench and moved closer to her. He raised his arm to put around her and ended up just patting her on the back. Teresa leaned in, resting her head on his shoulder. Her tears flowed and he could feel his shirt soaking them up. He did put his arm around her then, pulling her into a full hug as the sobs took over.

When she was done, they just sat there for a while. He kept his grip on her. He wasn't going to let her go until she was ready.

"You must think me such a wimp." Her voice came muffled through his wet shirt.

"I don't," he said. "I don't know what I would have done, if I could have kept my cool as long as you did. I don't think I'm that strong."

She pulled away and he let his arms drop. The cool air washed away the heat between them, and a small piece of him wished she were still crying.

"Thanks." She stood and walked through the flattened grass where Dale's tent had been, toward the tree behind it.

"Come on," she said, wiping her eyes, "let's see what Dale left for us."

He watched her walk away and shook his head. She was the strongest woman he had ever met.

The pack was his, filled with spare clothes and canned goods. Teresa's was missing, so they had lost half of their food. After they did a quick inventory, she shoved some of his clean clothes into his hands and pushed him toward the river, wrinkling her nose. She stayed at the picnic tables. He got the hint, stripping and cleaning up the best he could in the freezing water. He threw his old clothes into the bushes by the riverbank.

They didn't stay there that night. Crossing the river using the old overpass, they chose to continue heading south. According to Teresa, Rob and his group, followed by the Skends, had headed northeast, maybe following where Rob thought they had run, maybe just heading back to the bigger group Dale had hinted at.

He wished them luck. No one deserved what the Skends and the Qabal could do. Not even Rob.

They finally figured out where they were, at least. Oregon. By Darwin's best estimate, it would take them over three months to walk to San Diego, if they were lucky. More if they avoided the bigger cities, and recent experience told them it was a pretty good idea.

He didn't know if the Skends had left anything intact in San Diego, but they would deal with that when they got there. They followed Commercial Road out of Salem until they hit Interstate 5, the long empty road ahead of them.

.   .   .

The days turned into a monotony of cold nights and dreary days. Each night they stopped at another empty farmhouse or dilapidated barn, opened a cold can of food, and ate in silence. After the paltry dinner, they would huddle together under their thin blankets and try to sleep, only to wake up early the next morning to eat and start the process over again. Nighttime was the best for Darwin. It was when he could hold Teresa and listen to her soft breath as she slept.

It was too dark to see her, but he didn't need the light to know what she looked like, to remember the shape of her nose or the strength of her chin. In the morning they would talk for a bit, figuring out how far they had come, how much they would walk that day, before they left the relative warmth of each other.

The houses they stayed at were usually stripped bare and falling apart, but they searched anyway. Any scrap of food or drop of water was saved, placed into the small rusted Radio Flyer wagon they'd picked up from another abandoned yard.

Every night Darwin practiced working with the Threads. Before Salem, he had tried everything that he could think of. Now he approached the process with trepidation. What if he overstepped his control again? What if he made a mistake, and this time, Teresa wouldn't be able to bring him back? And yet, things were different. Despite his fears, the Threads were brighter and more responsive to his touch, the images came easier and held more detail.

He kept a constant watch on the Threads. The skill he had learned the night Enton died became easier with use, and his new-found strength expanded his radius until he was no longer surprised by how Carlos and Wally had detected Qabal a half a mile away, though most of the time he only monitored a smaller circle around them.

It saved them once. They were plodding down the middle of the southbound interstate following a path created by animals when he felt the Threads shift. They ran to the overgrown ditch, dragging the cart behind them, and hid, waiting almost a full five minutes before a group of six men and women walked past in the opposite direction. He had no idea if they were friendly or not, but the risk of finding out was too big to take.

·They passed small communities along the way, smoke rising from chimneys and the occasional screech of children playing. They avoided them as best they could, pulling the wagon through stubbled fields and furrowed soil. The memory of Salem and Rob kept them as far away from humanity as they could get. It was a skill Darwin had perfected over the years.

It took almost four weeks to get to California, bypassing any bigger cities and scavenging for anything edible along the way. They crossed the border in the late afternoon, reading the sign with a glimmer of hope. State borders usually had rest stops close by, and that might mean fresh water and maybe something to eat. If there wasn't any large population group around, they figured their chances were pretty good.

They pushed on, agreeing to stop there for the night. Half an hour later they sank into the sun reflecting off the wall of a small building. It wasn't a rest stop, but it would do.

"We're not going to make it, are we?" asked Teresa.

"As long as we can keep getting water from the farms, we should be okay. Maybe we should have followed the coast, it would have been warmer. More places to find water, maybe."

"And more places to find people."

"Yeah. They can't all be bad, though. You weren't," he pointed out.

"Do you really want to take the chance?"

He knew she was right. Past experience had taught them that

lesson. But he also knew that at some point, they might not have a choice. He pushed himself to his feet and held out a hand for her. "Come on, let's check if there's any water left here, and find a place to sleep. Maybe we'll find some food!" Their supply was dwindling dangerously low.

"You still need to practice."

"Not tonight, I'm too tired."

It took them over an hour to search the several small buildings in the complex, starting with those closest to the highway. They were careful to not leave an obvious trail in the overgrown space. The liquor store—apparently the only reason for the small clump of buildings—had been destroyed, the windows smashed and walls torn down. The only thing that still looked intact was a sun-faded pirate statue, one foot resting on an overturned keg, and a small sign that read All Star Liquor.

Their search of the property led to a small bathroom tucked in one of the back buildings. The place had obviously not seen a person in years. Layers of dirt and animal droppings covered the floor and the boxes of food stashed there. On the shelves were tightly wrapped sleeping bags and blankets that had seen better days. Mice or rats had eaten through the wrapping and nested in the soft filling of the sleeping bags.

To Darwin, it looked like a stash set up for holing, a place Threaders could rest before their next hole. It also looked like no one had used this site in a very long time. They grabbed the three cases of bottled water stacked on the floor and put them into the Radio Flyer before deciding it was safe to spend the night. With the condition of the stash, there wasn't much chance of some holers stumbling in on them.

They chose the house in the corner of the property, clearing the floor of mouse crap and dirt the best they could. It had been ransacked, but the windows were intact. It was better than most places they'd stayed. Teresa opened two cans of beans, smiling as she handed one to him.

"A full can to celebrate reaching California. It's no name brand, we finished the good stuff off a couple of days ago," she said.

He took the spoon offered to him and started eating, remembering that he used to care about the brand. It was more food than he'd had in a while.

"After this, you practice."

"Yes, Mom," he said, knowing she was right.

"Don't you dare. If you start thinking of me as your mother, I'm taking a different route home."

He saw a blush start to rise on her cheeks before she turned away. He felt his own face follow suit. "Don't worry, that's not going to happen." Teresa was as far from the images of his mother that still haunted his dreams as you could get.

They ate the rest of their cold beans in an uncomfortable silence. When he was finished, he threw the empty can out the door into a clump of bushes and sat back on the floor beside Teresa. He slowly built up his defenses, knowing where the conversation was going to go.

"You don't talk about your mom too much," he said.

Her spoon hesitated partway to her mouth. "Neither do you."

"Mine died, a long time ago. We . . . we were in a car crash. I made it, and she didn't. I thought of looking for her in this world, but I don't know how—or if—that would work out." It was more than he'd wanted to say. He didn't tell her it was his fault, that he had been driving.

She placed her hand on his arm, rubbing it slowly. "I'm sorry."

Darwin gave his stock answer, already feeling the guilt rise to the surface. "Don't be. Like I said, it was a long time ago."

"My mom taught me everything I know about healing. She's very good at it, you know. Everyone back at Chollas says they're lucky to have her and my brother. He's older than I am, and already a full healer. He wanted to stay behind, to send me to SafeHaven instead. He said the experience would be phenomenal. Mom insisted he go with her, that she needed another full healer." Her voice hitched, and she drew a deep breath before carrying on. "What if . . . what if the Skends hit SafeHaven again? What if they didn't make it?" Silent tears fell down her face.

"SafeHaven was probably the best place to be if it happened. They have a bunch of great fighters. They know how to deal with Skends. Besides, those monsters were coming after me, and they seem to know where I am. Remember Salem? They caught up to us there. Your mom and brother are fine. They're probably more worried about where you are than any stupid Skends."

"You're probably right. No! You *are* right. We'll get back home, and I'll introduce you to them. They'll like you." She lifted her hand from his arm and rubbed away the tears. "Now, go practice."

Darwin fought the sudden urge to lean in and kiss her, pushing himself away instead and standing. He found a corner and sat with his legs crossed.

The spider web of Threads he monitored constantly popped into sharper focus. He pushed them into the background again and began following the other Threads around him. He always started his practice sessions by relaxing and getting a solid view of the area. Riding the Threads that flowed through the room and across the rest of the property helped him focus. He was back at the highway they'd just left, smelling the residual heat rising from its surface and tasting the faded paint of the white and yellow lines, before he dropped off and followed an intersecting Thread back.

The talk of SafeHaven made him think about Enton, and the memories that came were pleasant. In a way, Enton and Bill were similar to him, and memories of one easily moved to memories of the other, creating a pattern and recognition between the two. Both were older, both were smart and knew how to use the Threads. Both were teachers. Both were dead because of him.

The pain of losing Bill burned through him again, and with it, the loss of Enton. He relived the day Bill had died, standing helpless as Rebecca's Thread tore into him, felt Michael's grip on his arm pulling him away while Rebecca lay on the ground. He still felt the tearing in his head when Michael had pulled him through the blue net around the Qabal building.

He hoped she was as dead as Bill, but he doubted it. If she was alive, he had no doubt they would meet again one day.

He wondered what had happened to Michael, to Carlos and Wally, Mellisa. She was the one who had been so nice to him when he first showed up in SafeHaven. Before the Skends attacked. He had liked Carlos too. He could still remember his sense of humor, sharp and sarcastic. Carlos always had a quick smile. Were they hurt when the Skends showed up in San Diego? Were they even alive? What were they doing without Enton there to guide them?

Filled with concern, he struggled to remember more. If they didn't make it, it was his responsibility to keep their memories alive. It was important, at least for him. They had all helped him escape the clutches of the Qabal, physically or mentally. He owed them. Carlos's face was round, not fat, but circular. There were wrinkles at the corners of his eyes from laughing and smiling and spending so much time in the sun. His short hair always stood straight up.

Where would he be right now, if he was still alive? Darwin tried to picture him in San Diego, but it didn't feel right. Carlos would be in SafeHaven, trying to rebuild and keep the school alive. Maybe even taking over from where Enton had left off. He could almost see him now, poring over the list of damaged houses, checking off what work was done and what was left.

The image of Carlos working grew sharper, images replacing Threads. Darwin could see him looking up with a puzzled expression. Carlos stood, throwing his chair to the floor behind him.

"Darwin? Darwin! Where are you?" Carlos gestured wildly and Mellisa came into view. "Locate him."

Darwin felt more than saw Threads touch his face before taking off through the wall.

"Carlos?" The image wavered, and suddenly it was as though he was looking through a murky pool of water. He could see Carlos send a questioning look to Mellisa. She shook her head.

"Darwin, concentrate. Keep doing what you're doing. We can't lose this link."

"But . . . what's happening?" As Darwin spoke, the image sharpened again.

"Damned if I know, but keep doing it. Tell me where you are."

"We're . . . we just crossed into California. We're at the rest stop on Interstate 5. It's called the State Line, I think. I—"

"Darwin, who are you talking to?" Teresa asked.

Her words shattered the image.

"Darwin?"

"I . . . I don't know. I was . . ." He turned to look at her. "I was talking to Carlos in SafeHaven. It was like we were in the same room together."

"Did you tell him where we are? Are they coming to get us?" The look on Teresa's face was filled with hope.

"I told them. I don't know if they're coming—" Alarms started going off in Darwin's head. His constant background monitoring of the Threads jumped to the foreground. The familiar taste of cloth slid across his tongue. He threw up the shields he had been practicing, hoping it would hide them, and jumped to his feet.

"What?"

"Someone's here."

"It's them. It's got to be them." Teresa ran to the door and threw it open. A steel-blue Thread jumped across her path at chest level and stopped her in her tracks.

"What did you do that for?"

Darwin jumped to his feet and pulled her back in the room, shutting the door behind her. Never mind what, it was the how that bothered him more. He had no idea.

"Let me go." Teresa twisted in Darwin's grip and he released her.

"What if it's not Carlos?" he asked.

"Who else could it be?" She moved toward the door again.

"Anyone else. It could just be a coincidence. It could be that the Qabal saw what I did. We need to hide until we know."

He could see the realization dawn on her, the anger on her face replaced with recognition of what she had almost done.

"We can't stay in here," she said. "There's not enough room to move, just in case." She scrambled for the cart.

"Leave it. We need to move now." Darwin raced for the side window and threw it open, pushing the screen to the ground outside. He helped Teresa out before jumping and landing beside her.

Together they ducked and ran through the deepening gloom to a row of stunted trees ten feet away.

Back at the house they could hear a door open, and a shaft of light fell from the window. Voices carried in the still night air.

"Are they here?"

"No, but this is the right place. I recognize the color of the walls."

A shadow cut through the light, followed by a figure leaning out the window.

"Darwin? Darwin, it's us."

It was Carlos's voice. He was here, and they were going to be all right. Relief flooded through Darwin faster than he could lower his shields. His breath rushed from his lungs and he sucked in another, coughing on the mix of adrenaline and relief. He stood, holding Teresa's hand, and stepped from the trees. "Over here," he said.

"Well, don't just stand there, come on back in." The door was open when they reached it, and Mellisa rushed forward and gave Darwin a sweaty hug, almost lifting him off his feet before her grip gave way. She must have been the one to hole here. He dropped Teresa's hand and returned the hug.

Carlos waited his turn. When Mellisa let go, he stepped up and shook Darwin's hand solemnly. "We weren't sure we'd see you again. Welcome back."

Darwin grinned. "Thanks!" He dropped Carlos's hand. "Umm, this is Teresa. She was with us when the Skends hit San Diego."

"Nice to finally meet you, Teresa. Your mom will be thrilled we found you. We have a lot to discuss, all of us. Let's get home first, though." He turned back to Darwin.

"Enton . . ." Darwin couldn't put his thoughts into words.

"We know. We found what was left of him in San Diego." He turned away, ending the conversation abruptly.

Carlos created a hole and they stepped through, ending up somewhere in a forest. When they all got through, he closed it and opened another one to SafeHaven. It wasn't lost on Darwin that Carlos had created two holes back to back. He wondered if Mellisa had done the same to get to them.

They ended up in the same building Darwin had first seen the last time he'd been holed to SafeHaven. Carlos stepped through as the hole closed and leaned against the wall, breathing and sweating heavily.

Mellisa stepped in, taking Darwin and Teresa to be looked at by healers, and finally for a long hot bath. By the time they were done, they'd already been in SafeHaven for a couple of hours and exhaustion sucked at their bones.

THE LETTER

DARWIN AND TERESA were led to a two-story house farther down the street from where Darwin had stayed last time he was here. By the time they got there, they were both dragging their feet and practically tripping over them to keep up, the exhaustion of the past weeks finally allowed to show itself. Teresa was shown to her room first. She hesitated, watching Darwin being shown to his room just down the hall.

Even though he was indoors, and the building had windows to keep out the chill of the night, he kept his clothes on, too tired to care. He took off his shoes before falling between the sheets, pulling them up to his neck and closing his eyes.

Sleep refused to come.

For the first time in over a month he was warm and safe and dry, and though he still monitored the Threads, he'd pushed them far enough into the background that he barely noticed people around SafeHaven.

He was also very much alone. His thoughts flitted between memories of the long walk and the cold nights. He missed Teresa beside him, missed the gentle sound of her breathing as he drifted off to sleep. Missed their conversations.

A creak outside his door pulled him from the in-between world of sleep and wakefulness. He lay still as his door opened and a shaft of light fell across his closed eyes. Without conscious thought, he followed the Threads to figure out who it was, relaxing as soon as he found out.

Teresa closed the door behind her, her bare feet padding across the floor. Without a word, she crawled in under the covers with him, and his senses filled with her presence. The smell of her clean clothes was different than it had been on the road, but to the Threads, she was the same as she had been when they'd huddled together for warmth. To-night it was for the comfort of the familiar and the continuation of the companionship they'd needed to live. He sent Threads out into the night, creating a shield around them, and finally fell asleep.

He woke with his heart pounding and every muscle in his body tense, ready for a fight or a mad dash to safety. Dozens of Threads had shifted all at once. By the time he remembered where he was, Teresa was sitting up, staring groggily around the room. She placed her hand on his chest until his racing heart settled down, and then left without a word. The room felt empty without her in it.

He wished he could just tell her how he felt, but he knew it would end the same way as every other time he'd tried, a pitying look and a firm no. He pulled on his shoes and followed her out.

Breakfast in the mess hall was simple, but Darwin couldn't ever remember having a better one. From the way Teresa was eating she obviously felt the same way. The fake coffee was hot and liquid gold, sliding down Darwin's throat and warming him to his toes. He hadn't realized just how much he'd missed it. They'd just finished wiping their plates clean with a slice of oven-fresh bread when Carlos walked in and asked them to join him.

They put their plates in the giant wash bins and followed him out to the street.

"I do this every morning," Carlos said. "Walk around, see how the repairs are coming along, what else needs to be done. But more than that, I meet the people."

The several people they passed along the way smiled and nodded or said hello.

"Enton did it, when he was here. I could never figure out why, until I started doing the same thing. I know pretty much every face in SafeHaven, and a fair number of names. I know the work that needs to be done and what is getting done. It helps. Keeps me in touch with why I am doing all of this. Why he did it."

They walked in silence for most of way, watching the people and looking at the damage done by the Skends. Almost all of the houses burned on the night of the attack were being worked on. Crews replaced damaged wood with new, and the sounds of pounding hammers filled the morning air. Those houses that could be salvaged had piles of material beside them. The others stood empty, husks of what used to be someone's home. Darwin stopped in his tracks, staring at one of the husks.

It was the house he had tried to hide in. He could still feel the heat of the flames, the sound of the Skend moving through them, getting closer, wanting nothing more than to kill him.

"I can't be here," Darwin said.

Carlos sighed and walked to the building, breaking off a piece of charred wood with his hand. "The family who lived here are on the next street. They all made it out safe."

"That's not what I mean. I can't *stay* here. I am the reason the Skends came. I'm the reason SafeHaven was burned down and people died. The reason Teresa's home was attacked. How many people died that night? How many parents won't ever see their children again, or kids their mom or dad?"

"You are the reason? I guess the Qabal knew you would be here years ago? That's how long we think it took them to bring Skends close enough to SafeHaven to attack it. There were never any warnings. No alarms went off. The Threads showed nothing unless you compared what we saw the day before the attack to what we would have seen a few years back. No one does—can do—that.

"This attack was planned well before you came over. You may have changed the timing, but that's it. You may have even helped us. With you here we had double shifts on watch, and a couple of extra teams stayed home instead of going out. Without them here, things could have been much worse."

"Enton would still be here," Darwin said. "Teresa would still have a home."

"Teresa still has a home. We had enough warning to get everybody out. Enton gave us some extra breathing room as well."

"If I'm here, they'll be back."

"Maybe. The good news is they don't know you're here. They know you escaped with Enton, and they know he's dead—"

"How—"

"Like I said last night, we all saw what was left of him on this side of the hole. He barely had a chance with a healer trained for hole injuries, never mind an apprentice," Carlos said, glancing at Teresa. "You both saw what happened to him. Hole injuries are almost always fatal."

"If I'm here, they'll be back," Darwin repeated. "They found me in Salem."

Carlos stopped and searched Darwin's face before throwing the charred hunk of wood back into the empty building.

They finished the rest of walk through the damaged part of Safe-Haven in silence, ending up near the mess hall again. Carlos gestured to a small building off to the side and they followed him through the door. Mellisa stood from behind a desk when they entered and gave Darwin a small smile.

"Are you two feeling better?" she asked in her raspy voice.

Teresa stepped up beside Darwin and reached for his hand. "Much better, thanks."

"So, what happens now?" Darwin asked.

"First we talk about last night, then we figure out what to do."

"Last night?"

"You were in this room last night, sitting right there in the corner. Scared the shit out of me."

"You mean when we were talking?"

"Yeah. I've never Seen anything like it." Carlos pointed to two chairs in front of the desk and sat down behind it.

"I don't understand," said Darwin.

"If we need to talk to each other, we need to be in the same room as each other, just like we are now. We can't talk over distances like you did last night, let alone project our image somewhere else. I don't think even Enton could do it, and if he did, he didn't show us. The best we can do is hole letters or people."

Darwin sat in his chair and stared at Carlos.

"We need to know what you did and how you did it. You know what it's like keeping an eye on the Qabal. Teams have to hole back and forth across the country. By the time we get the news, it's already old. Being able to talk across large distances would be a huge advantage for us."

"I don't know—"

"Just think if Enton could have sent a message from San Diego to here. Even though we managed to get everyone out, it was close. He might even still be with us."

Anger and pain surged through Darwin. How often would he be reminded of what he had caused, of how many had died because of him? "Dammit. I don't know. It just happened. I have no clue what I'm doing—" He stopped short, realizing he'd shouted the words.

Teresa placed her hand on his arm. "Maybe we can try to recreate what you did that night. Why don't we go back to your room where it's quiet, and you can sit in the corner and get ready to practice again, like when we were at the border."

Teresa's touch calmed him down, and he looked at her, grinning sheepishly and feeling stupid. He nodded.

As they walked down the street back to their rooms, Darwin went over the previous evening in his mind. What had he done? He remembered not wanting to practice, and he had been so tired.

"So . . ." Teresa's voice broke through his thoughts. "You know Mellisa . . . and Carlos . . . them . . . pretty well?"

"Not really. Carlos and Wally brought me across most of the country to SafeHaven. Mellisa I met when I got here. I think her and Carlos are together, but I don't know. Why?"

"Oh! Oh . . . no reason, just asking. They just seemed to go out of their way to get you back here."

Darwin stopped walking and Teresa turned to look at him.

"Do you think they want me for something?" he asked.

"I don't know. It's just . . . I don't know. They seem so friendly, so willing to help. It just feels weird, that's all. Maybe I'm still thinking about what happened in Salem too much."

"Your mom came here to help when they needed it. Does that

change anything? All I know is that I trust them more than I trusted the Qabal."

Teresa ignored his question, asking one of her own. "Why?"

Darwin thought for a minute before answering. "Being with the Qabal was different. They . . . the people there all seemed to be afraid of something, or someone. Everyone guarded what they said, like if they said the wrong thing, they would get in trouble. Here everyone seems happier. They're not afraid to say what they think, and those in charge listen." He paused again. "Someone like you would never have hung around with the Qabal."

Teresa leaned forward and kissed him on the cheek. "Thank you." She grabbed his hand and pulled him toward his room. "We had better get started, or they'll think you failed."

Darwin bumbled after her, unable to keep the grin off his face and the heat from spreading through his body.

The room had gotten warm in the morning sun and Teresa moved to open the window. A fresh breeze blew in as he settled himself in the corner, bringing with it the faint stink of burned buildings. It was different than a campfire smell, rancid and full of chemicals. It left a bitter taste in his mouth.

Besides being tired and cranky, what else had he done or felt last night? He remembered preparing to practice some Thread work, and then his mind had wandered. He had started thinking about Carlos, remembering what he looked like, imagining what he would be doing, the Threads forgotten.

He tried it again. The details of Carlos's face formed in his mind, and he could See the Threads in front of him shift as the details became clearer.

Next was what would Carlos be doing right now. That was easy, he was in his office, waiting for Darwin's image to magically appear. He concentrated on the details, and the Threads shifted again.

He was sweating now. The breeze from the window made him shiver when it hit his damp skin, and he wished Teresa would close it again. He put more detail in the image of Carlos in his office, and the Threads shifted for a third time. He thought he saw a pattern and pushed the Threads some more.

His head exploded in pain and he fell sideways to the floor with a sharp yelp before the blackness took over.

Darwin came to lying on the floor. Teresa was on her knees beside him, her forehead scrunched in concentration. He could See soft white Threads moving around his head.

"Hi," he said.

"Hey. How are you feeling?"

"I don't know. The pain seems to be gone, but I'm a bit dizzy." He pushed himself upright and leaned back into the corner.

"I'm going to get one of their healers. You wait here, I'll be right back." Teresa moved to stand up and Darwin reached for her hand, keeping her where she was.

"No, wait. I need to try again. I think I know what I did wrong." Maybe if he concentrated on the actual task, and ignored the Threads, it would work.

"That's not a good idea. I've never seen what happens when someone pushes the Threads too far, but I've heard about it. They go insane, like a whole portion of their brain is fried. I don't think anyone has come back from that."

"That's not going to happen to me."

"And how do you know that? You suddenly have magical powers? You can See into the future?"

Darwin grinned. "Yeah, kinda."

"This isn't funny."

He wiped the grin off his face. "I know," he sighed. "Carlos and Mellisa may be my only way of getting back home. I need the QPS, and I can't get past Rebecca and the Qabal without their help. I'll do whatever I can to help Carlos, so he'll want to help me."

Teresa sat back, pulling her hand out of his grasp, and moved farther away. "Right. That's the goal, isn't it? To get back home?"

He felt a sharp stab of guilt. He knew what she was thinking: after all they had been through together, he was still willing to leave her behind as if she didn't matter. It couldn't be farther from the truth. He wasn't going to say anything out loud, but he couldn't deny to himself that he'd fallen for Teresa, and the thought of leaving her behind was something he just wasn't prepared to deal with. He didn't know how. Instead, he fell back to his default.

"Even if I can't go back, I still have to try. Maybe I can figure out how to turn off the QPS. I don't want my world to become what this one has, a handful of small groups barely staying alive."

"So, we're primitives who are barely smart enough to speak our own minds? And you're the one who is going to enlighten us and bring us out of these dark times?"

"That's not what I—"

"Not what you meant?" Teresa stared at him and then stood. "Whatever." She turned and left the room, the door slamming behind her.

It felt like his heart ripped out of his chest. What the hell was he supposed to do? Couldn't she see what was going on? He wanted to stay, with all of his heart, but he couldn't get rid of the image that had been haunting him since he'd escaped the Qabal . . . his dad struggling to move on with his life, visiting two graves instead of one. Darwin had been gone so long, they had to think he was dead. He couldn't be the cause of that much pain in another person. In his dad. Darwin felt the all-too-familiar anger rising. Even though he knew it was a defense mechanism, he couldn't stop it. His default. She hadn't done anything to deserve it, but it flowed through him anyway.

Enough of this bullshit. *Pull yourself together.* He sat upright again, keeping his back in the corner, pushing Teresa and the ache that permeated his soul out of his mind as best he could. Once again he thought about Carlos, concentrating on the details of his face. When he had a complete picture, he moved on to where Carlos was and what he would be doing. He did his best to ignore the Threads swirling in front of him, letting the eddies shift without him watching them. The Threads popped into images.

He could See Carlos sitting behind his desk, grinning from ear to ear. Dust motes sifted through the shaft of sunlight from the window before disappearing into the relative darkness of the room.

"Welcome back to my office," he said.

"It . . . it's working? I have no idea how I did it."

"Damn right it is. I'm going to send Mellisa over to See what you're doing. She'll examine the Threads as we talk, and then ask you to stop and start the connection again. This is bloody awesome!" His grin got wider.

Darwin's field of view was narrow, like he was looking down a short tunnel. He heard a door open in Carlos's office and turned to look. Teresa walked in, staring at the image of Darwin. He gave a quick smile and raised his hand to wave. She turned and left, closing the door behind her. Carlos gave him a quizzical look but didn't say anything. He watched Mellisa walk into view and follow Teresa out.

A few minutes later Mellisa knocked gently on the door and entered his room. He barely heard her. She sat on the floor in front of him, a ghost in his vision, and watched. After a while she touched his arm, pulling him from Carlos's office, and asked him to start again. She interrupted him five times, asking him to start from scratch again, and each time the task became easier. He told her about the images, about how Enton had Seen them too, and how Bill had thought they were a waste of time.

On the fifth and final try, the images came into sharp focus quicker. There wasn't any pain.

He fell asleep where he sat, exhausted and sweaty, and didn't wake up until the next morning, tucked into the bed, starving and alone. He got up, searching for Teresa and some food.

She wasn't in her room when he knocked on her door, or at breakfast. He wolfed down an omelet with peppers and onions and went looking for Carlos, finding him talking to a construction worker in front of one of the damaged houses.

"Good morning! Good to see you up and about."

"Morning. Have you seen Teresa?"

Carlos held up his hand and finished his conversation with the construction worker before turning back to Darwin. They began walking back to Carlos's office before Darwin got an answer.

"I'm sorry, Darwin. She left last night. A group was heading back to San Diego, and she joined them. She said she wanted to see her family."

Darwin stopped in his tracks, a hole opening in his chest. She'd left him.

Carlos put his hand on Darwin's shoulder, looked into his eyes, and spoke, his voice soft. "I'm really sorry. She made sure you were comfortable in bed, wrote you a note, and left."

"A note?"

"Yeah, somewhere in your room."

Darwin turned and ran back to his room. The letter was stuck under his pillow.

Darwin,

We've been through a lot together in the last few weeks, and I think, I hope, we have gotten to know each other fairly well.

One thing I've come to realize is, despite my feelings for you, you don't belong here. Your home is somewhere beyond where I can imagine, and somewhere beyond where I can go.

I will miss you, more than I can put into words, but our journey has come to an end. I've gone home to my family. I'll finish my apprenticeship and figure out what to do from there.

I hope you find what you are looking for, and I hope you get back home to your Dad.

Love always,
Teresa.

A tear dripped off his nose, falling onto the letter. He wiped it off, smearing the neat handwriting, before folding the note with shaking fingers, putting it in his back pocket, and lying on the bed.

THE ENEMY OF MY ENEMY

DARWIN LAY IN his room most of the morning, watching the sun cast its light through the window as it crawled across the floor. When the streak of warmth reached his feet, he stood and moved to look outside. The street below was busy, sounds of construction and people pulsing through the dirty glass, but he barely heard them and stumbled back to the bed.

He had lost her. The only girl who had returned his feelings, and he had pushed her as far away as he could, letting the world—a universe—come between them. It was for the best, wasn't it? He couldn't . . . wouldn't stay here, and bringing her back with him would have been impossible, not with her mom and brother here. He knew what it was like being separated from family.

He shouldn't have let her get so close to him. He shouldn't have fallen so hard.

His shoulders dropped as he leaned against the wall for support, suddenly dizzy. If it was the right thing to do, then why the hell did it hurt so much? It felt as though his heart had been torn out of his chest and shredded, and he had no idea how to fix it . . . wasn't sure he wanted to.

With that thought stuck in his head, he pulled the folded note from his back pocket and stared at it, his hands cupped to minimize the vibrations running though him. He put it back in his pocket and picked up his almost empty backpack before opening the door.

Mellisa sat in the hallway, her back resting against the opposite wall. How long had she been there? She looked at the backpack and then up to his face. "Planning on going somewhere?"

"Yeah, maybe." Darwin strode past her, heading for the stairs. He could hear her coming to her feet and jogging to catch up to him.

"Where do you plan on going?"

"East."

"East? Can you be any more specific? There is a lot of country to the east. Most of it, in fact."

He didn't return her smile.

"I'm going home."

"That's definitely east, and then some."

They reached the top of the stairs and he forced his way in front of her, taking the steps two at a time all the way to the bottom.

"You are in a hurry," she said.

He didn't respond.

"Listen." Mellisa grabbed his arm, pulling him to a stop just inside the door to the street. "This isn't something you can do alone. You know that. Rebecca and her Qabal will slaughter you, or worse, capture you and get whatever information you may have. Most likely destroying your brain in the process."

He pulled his arm away and continued walking out the door, not caring what the consequences were.

Mellisa called out to him. "We can help you. We can help each other. At least talk to Carlos before you take off."

He kept on going without looking back. He knew he couldn't do it alone. If he knew it, then why was he so hell-bent on getting out and leaving everyone behind? The answer was simple, really. Anytime he got close to someone, they were either killed or left him. Either way the result was the same. Even the level of guilt felt similar. He was better off alone. He'd done pretty well up to this point. Except that he'd never been alone. His step faltered. But dammit, she was right. He would be like a mouse fighting with a cat. A game. Rebecca might even play with him for a while before she killed him, but he doubted it.

Darwin sighed, stopping in the middle of the street. She was right, and they both knew it. He would just have to make sure he didn't get too close to them. Hell, he already was, but that could be changed. He would make it change.

Carlos was in his office, the first place that Darwin looked. He knocked on the door and walked in.

"Mellisa thinks she may have figured out how you project your image and talk with us. She says it has something to do with the images you described to her. The Threads are too complex to follow, but the imagery may be easier. It looks like you also need to know where the person you want to talk to is, maybe even know what they are doing. We're looking for some Threaders that See images. Apparently, it's rare."

Darwin fell into the chair in front of Carlos's desk, ignoring what he had just said. "I need to go back."

"Back?"

"To New Jersey. To the Qabal."

Carlos leaned into his chair, rocking it on the two back legs, and watched Darwin.

"I need to get home, and as far as I can see, Rebecca is the only one who might know how. She saw the Threads when I came through. Maybe she's got it all wrong. I don't have the information she's looking for. She does."

"And how do you plan to do that?"

Darwin drew in a breath and held it before releasing it slowly. "I don't know. I do know I can't stay here. I don't belong here, and the Skends will come back. We both know that."

"We can fight them. You could stay, if you wanted to."

No, he couldn't. He had gone down that path already. He got to his feet. "Are you willing to help me or not?"

"I know Teresa leaving hurt you, we've all been—"

"Yes or no, Carlos. That is all I need."

Carlos leaned forward, rubbing the stubble on his face with his hands. "We started drawing up some plans to attack the Qabal. They've been fighting us for years. Maybe it's time to bring the fight to them. I just don't know if we're ready."

The door burst open and Mellisa rushed in, slightly out of breath. Carlos stood, and she looked at both of them, finally stopping at Darwin and looking directly into his eyes. She reached out to touch his arm. "Teresa is missing. The people she was traveling with were found dead this morning with Skend burns."

Darwin stumbled back into a chair, searching Mellisa's face for a sign that she was lying. He didn't see any. Why would he?

"There are indications of a struggle, and no tracks leading away from the attack site. We think the Qabal have her."

His body went numb, his brain racing. They had her. Rebecca had her. He slumped forward, resting his elbows on his knees. There wasn't a choice anymore. He was going back to New Jersey whether Carlos helped him or not.

He felt an arm around his shoulder and tensed, pulling away and standing. "I'm going to get her. Will you help me or not?"

"It'll take weeks to—"

"We don't have weeks. Yes or no?" He picked his backpack up from the floor and turned toward the door. Mellisa stood in his way, her gaze fixed on Carlos. She gave an almost imperceptible nod, and he heard Carlos sigh.

"If you're dead set on leaving, we can get you as close to the Source as we can. I don't know how much help we'll be; we need to leave Threaders behind to protect SafeHaven. And we can't do this alone, either."

Mellisa turned at a shout from the street. Wally was pulling a young man behind him and calling for Carlos.

"The Qabal were here," he panted. "They holed in front of this guy and left almost right away. Tell them what you were told."

It was obvious the guy was scared. He was shaking where he stood, and his voice vibrated when he spoke. "I . . . I'd just negotiated shipments of wheat from our farm, and they showed up. I'm not a Threader, I'm just a farmer. I didn't know what—"

"What did they say?" Darwin interrupted.

"They said they have someone named Teresa, and if a guy by the name of Darwin doesn't turn himself in, they'll kill her. They said they'd be waiting where he first appeared." The words tumbled from his mouth almost too fast to understand. "Can I go now?"

Wally nodded his head, and the man ran back down the street.

Darwin clenched his fists. He wasn't about to have anyone else's blood on his hands. Especially not Teresa's.

"Do you believe them?" Carlos asked.

"That they'll let her go if I turn myself in? No, but I don't have a choice, do I? At least I have a chance to get her out if I'm closer to her. I need to get back to New Jersey."

Carlos studied Darwin thoughtfully before responding. "That settles it then, doesn't it? It's normally five days to hole there, with rests. All our regular sites are being watched, so they'll know if we use them, and we'll be limited in what we can do. Five days isn't much, but we've been planning for a long time. We'll need to accelerate our plans. I think we can get a sizable force before we reach them. We just need to find a secure route so they don't see us."

"I need to get there faster. And they'll know if I'm not on my way."

"Yeah, they will. They seem to know almost everything else. Sit down, we need to hash this out."

He dropped into the chair once again and listened. By the time they were done, the underlying shape of the plan had been made.

Basically, one of the new Threaders would head out with Wally and another tracker and take a well-known route to the Qabal. The Threader would be about Darwin's age and shape. With the right clothes, he would be able to pass as Darwin from a distance. Carlos figured they would need six days to get everyone ready and get close, so Wally would have to delay a day somehow.

In the meantime, Carlos and Darwin and a few others would head north and pick up the main forces before moving east. They had a couple of strong holers and would pick up more from their allies in order to shave a day off of their travel, putting them in New Jersey just ahead of Wally. The timing would be tight.

Once they were close, they could use the cover of night and a few good Threaders to hide their approach and try to get Teresa out. As far as Carlos was concerned, the more Qabal that were destroyed, the better.

Darwin hated the extra delay for Wally; every delay put Teresa in more danger. But in the end, he agreed it would be easier to get in if the Qabal thought he was still a day away. They would be unprepared. That's what they hoped for, anyway.

Wally and his partner left with the decoy Darwin that evening, holing to the plateau in the mountain where Darwin had been attacked on his way to SafeHaven. Neither Wally nor his partner could See images, so there would be no communication with them, and Darwin keenly felt the immediate lack of information. If their plan was discovered, Teresa would be dead long before they got close to her.

Darwin, Carlos, Mellisa, and a group of fifteen others left an hour later, their first hole to the north. When Darwin stepped from the hole, small shards of ice falling from him, he almost bumped into the sign.

Salem, Oregon, Population 161,000.

Darwin's entire body went cold. "What the hell are we doing here?"

"Picking up people who will help us fight the Qabal, what else?"

Darwin searched Carlos's face for any deceit but couldn't find anything. He rubbed the fine white scar at his wrist. "Teresa and I were here, after Enton died. I don't trust this place or the people."

"Why not? We've traded with Nico for years. The potatoes they send us keep SafeHaven running in the winter, and the fruits and vegetables are canned every year. They are one of our major suppliers. They've always been nice enough, though maybe a bit cautious with outsiders at first."

At the mention of Nico, Darwin went back to studying the Salem sign. He had heard the name before, and it had to do with Salem. Suddenly he had it. When the healer had threatened Rob, she'd mentioned Nico, and Rob didn't like that at all. "Do you know of a Rob who works with Nico?" he asked.

"Yeah, sure. I've met him. A bit of an odd fellow. Bald spot with long, black, greasy hair. Likes to be alone. Seems to have some latent sensitivity to the Threads—he knows when a Threader is working—but that's about all. Why?"

A shiver ran through him that had nothing to do with the temperature change. "That's him. Rob captured Teresa and me as slaves, to work in their fields or something. Before they found out Teresa was a healer, I thought they had other plans for her . . . closer to prostitution. These aren't good people."

By this time, Mellisa had walked through the hole and joined them. "I never liked them," she said. "Rob always creeped me out, and Nico seemed extremely selective about where we went."

Carlos cleared his throat. "I don't know about slaves, but they've got a lot of people working the fields. Most of what we do here is through traders, but every time we've made direct contact I didn't see any signs of slavery. Poor people, yes, but there isn't anything we can do about that. Are you sure we're talking about the same guys here?"

"All I know is a guy named Rob wrapped trap wire around our wrists and legs. We were his prisoners, and he didn't care if he hurt us. If it wasn't for Dale, we'd still be there."

Mellisa looked at Carlos at the mention of Dale. "It sounds like them."

"How does a slimeball like Rob get in charge like that anyway?" asked Darwin.

"If he's the guy I'm thinking of, he's Nico's brother or something like that."

"Look," Carlos said. "We don't have a lot of time. If we did, I'd go look for other allies. But we can't be picky. The enemy of our enemy is our friend. It's an old line, but it's true. We need them.

We'll have to deal with the mess later." He grabbed Darwin by the shoulders. "The Qabal is our first priority. We need to keep that in mind."

"The Qabal is yours. Teresa is mine."

"Right now, they're the same thing. Work with me on this one. We both need all the help we can get."

"You don't know what—"

"What it was like? No. But we *need* them. You have to keep your emotions in check on this one. Can you do that?"

"I don't know."

"Well, you better figure it out. We stay here tonight and walk in first thing in the morning. I need to know I can trust you, Darwin. That you won't do anything stupid."

Darwin pressed his lips together, biting back the retort rising from his gut, and nodded. He hated every part of what Rob had done to them, but he'd partner with the devil if it helped him get Teresa out of Rebecca's clutches. He nodded.

"Good." Carlos paused as if considering his next words. "Neither of us is going to be getting much sleep tonight. I can't let you walk into the trap the Qabal have set without some preparation. Tonight you get a crash course on how to protect yourself, defensively and offensively." He turned and walked to where tents were already being set up. "Come on, let's eat before we get going."

They started small, with Carlos creating the tiniest blue Thread Darwin had ever Seen.

"Protection or containment Threads are the easiest. If you can pick up these, then we can move forward. If you can't, then we'll have to figure out something else. This blue one is part of the testing we do to see if your skill set lies in this area. Some can't do it, some can't even See it, but it's where we'll start."

"I can See it. I even created one once, though I don't know how, and its color was different than this one. When you guys came to us at the border, I stopped Teresa from running out to see you. I was afraid it might be the Qabal."

"Interesting. So we know you can do it. Differentiating the shades is important as well. It's my job to show you how. It's easier to think of it as a containment system, rather than protection. Protection implies an attack, and that can bring out involuntary reactions—like fear—that could hinder your ability and move the Thread color into the reds."

"I'm confused. Bill said emotions were a pretty direct path to insanity, but the Dance Master said emotions were the key to using Threads, and Enton said to use intuition and emotions to train myself."

"Enton said that? Not in my experience, or my teacher's. Bill knew what he was talking about, he was one of our best."

"But he was wrong about the images. He told me they were useless, but we know it's needed for that communication stuff I did."

Carlos sighed. "Maybe, but the only way I know how to teach you is the way I was taught, so we'll have to go with that. Now, back to the Thread. Think of it as containment. If you want to stop leaves from blowing into your tent, the best thing would be a screen, so pull the Threads in and build a screen. The Threads will respond and start turning blue. If you want to stop a person, think of steel rods or prison bars. If you want to stop a fist, think of a shield or a wall. The shade of blue will be different for each one, and you need to *know* how a leaf would respond to hitting a net, or a fist a wall to get it right. Let's start simple. This Thread," he raised his hand, "wouldn't stop anything. But if you believe it will, the Thread will still form. Think about stopping a grain of sand or a dandelion seed, deflect it off its course."

It took Darwin over an hour to create his first blue Thread. It sat wavering in the palm of his hand, moving automatically to intercept the flakes of dirt and dead grass Carlos threw at it. It wasn't quite the right shade, but it worked. At one point, Carlos had asked him if was sure he'd created a blue Thread once before. Apparently, it didn't usually take as long to get to this point. The breakthrough came when Darwin let the images come. He was learning that he needed them.

From that point, the lessons continued at a blinding pace, and he kept up with Carlos easily. Two hours in, and he was stopping Carlos's shoe thrown at full speed. He was getting the hang of it, but it still took him time. If something came too fast, he couldn't build his Threads quickly enough.

Carlos repeated the process for the attack Threads. Even though Darwin picked them up quicker, he still had problems with how long it took him.

"I think we should take a small break," Carlos said a few hours later.

"Not yet. I'm on a roll. I want to know more."

"Well, I need a break. It took a while, but now you're picking this stuff up like you already knew it. I'm exhausted, and it can't be good for you to learn so fast."

"Why not?"

"What? I don't know. Are you getting any headaches yet?"

Darwin sat up straighter. He hadn't been getting even the feeling of a headache coming on. In fact, he felt invigorated and alive, like he had when Bill had put him through his paces. "No, I'm fine. I haven't felt this good in a long time."

Carlos sighed and stood, arching his back to stretch it out. "Okay. I'll see if Mellisa can take over for a while. I need to be good for tomorrow. Wait here, I'll go get her." He wandered over to the fire still crackling by the tents.

Darwin held back a shiver and sat alone in the dark, though he knew it would never truly be dark for him again. Bill's initial training, and the experience under the bridge, had woken him to the Threads like never before. Carlos's training had only added to that, even in the few short hours they'd practiced together. The sun was down and the sky was black, but through it moved the Threads, each one showing him the world in a new way.

They showed Mellisa moving between the tents toward him. The Threads around her wove a pattern that spoke of strength and grace. With every step, they moved so her foot was placed perfectly on the uneven ground. Her balance remained as she stood briefly on an exposed root in the dark and continued toward where he sat. There was a beauty in it that Darwin hadn't Seen with his eyes.

"It seems you've exhausted Carlos," she said, her gravelly voice becoming part of the rhythm of the Threads.

"Yeah. It just . . . it just seems I can't get enough. Is that bad?" he asked again.

"As long as you can handle it, no. It *is* tiring for your teachers, though. Come on, we'll see how far we can get before I fall asleep in front of you. Now, enough chit chat and show me what you've learned."

Mellisa looked impressed by what he showed her, blue Threads to protect himself, the same ones used to create the prisons he had been in. Unlike the one he'd thrown across the door at the rest stop, he knew how he'd created these. Red ones that reached for leaves and ripped holes in them or snapped twigs in half. One that created a hole in the ground over three inches deep.

"Nicely done, and the Threads were controlled. Now, I'm going to throw some Threads at you. They won't do much, just feel like a sharp pinch or a hot spot. I want you to block them as they come."

The night continued until Mellisa was exhausted as well. This time, Darwin was glad the session had come to an end. He'd fought off a headache during the last couple of tests, and his clothes stuck to his damp skin in the cold night air, chilling him to the core. After Mellisa had gone to Carlos's tent, he stood by the fire with one of the sentries, letting the heat from the flames dry his clothes and bring some warmth back into his fingers.

Darwin woke to the sound of voices outside his tent. The sun had risen, burning away the frost from the morning, and warming the air in his tent. He rolled out of his sleeping bag and pulled on his clothes. They were cold, but dry. One thing he had learned when his family went camping was not to wear his clothes to sleep, unless he had to. By morning they would be damp with sweat and chill him right down to the bone.

He zipped open the door and joined the group around the fire pit. They poured him a hot cup of what everyone called coffee and continued talking. He listened with half an ear until the talk turned to the people they had come here to recruit.

Sometime this morning, someone from Nico's group had walked into the camp, and they were now sitting with Carlos and Mellisa by the road, deep in conversation. Darwin was taking the last sip of his still hot coffee when they finished and Mellisa walked up.

"Okay, guys, let's get the tents down and the site cleaned up. Time to move into town. Tonight we hole somewhere new and start over again."

By the time he'd cleaned his mug, someone had already packed up his sleeping bag and taken down his tent. He helped put out the fire then moved with the group to the road, sucking in a deep breath to calm his jangling nerves, and followed them. It was time to face his demons, and he still wasn't sure he could do it.

Carlos slowed down, dropping from the front of the group until he came beside Darwin. "Are you going to be all right?" he asked.

"Yeah, sure."

"If it's a problem, I can leave you here with someone. We'll pick you back up before we hole to our new site."

"I said it's okay," Darwin responded, immediately sorry for his tone. "I'm sorry. It isn't going to be easy if we see Rob."

"What can I do to help?"

"Rob doesn't know I'm a Threader." It was the first time he had consciously used the term to describe himself, and he felt pretentious. "I'd like to keep it that way. I don't trust him and I don't like him. I think the feeling is mutual. If he tries something, I want to have a bit of a card up my sleeve."

"Okay, but if he's part of the group joining us, he'll see you training tonight."

"I'll deal with that if it happens."

"If that's the way you want it, I'll tell the others." Carlos picked up his pace again, stopping at every member of their group to say a few words, before rejoining Mellisa at the front.

Darwin felt the morning sun on his face as the group walked through Salem. In the time since they'd been here, the temperature had dropped, and the sun felt good. They had entered Salem from the south, though he had no idea how far from the river where he had been held prisoner. It didn't really matter, but he searched for anything familiar anyway. As the houses crowded around them his skin started to crawl. He rubbed the scar on his wrist again, still feeling the wire cut in and nestle close to the bone.

They walked for another twenty minutes down a street named Lockhaven Drive, turning off at River Road until they came to the McNary Golf Club. A ramshackle gate had been placed across the entrance, and it opened as they got closer. It closed behind them with the clang of a prison cell and the tension in Darwin's neck and shoulders doubled. He twitched at the sudden flashback to the Qabal headquarters, pushing the feeling aside before it could take over. He was heading back there, so he either had to get used to it, or get over it.

The parking lot had been turned into a ghetto. Shacks made from pieces of shattered drywall and scraps of wood or broken pieces of plastic scavenged from what was left of Salem vied for a spot on the rough asphalt. It looked like a recent rain had destroyed portions of the structures and tattered remains lay strewn near the curbs. The smell that rose around him was enough to make him gag. He fought the reflex and followed the group. As they walked down the street created by the encampment, people stopped talking and looked at their feet. The noises picked up again once they had passed. Somewhere behind them a child cried and was quickly shushed. It felt like they were walking in a bubble that kept the outside world at bay.

Darwin saw Mellisa stop and wait for him to catch up. The Threads circling her had lost some of their grace, creating a pocket of turmoil that followed her. They walked behind the group together, staring at the poverty around them.

"Is it always like this?" Darwin asked.

"I don't know. I've never been inside the compound before. I've always dealt with the traders that came to SafeHaven. It was Carlos or Enton that came." She paused. "I can see why."

As they walked, Darwin's opinion of both men dropped. There was no excuse for tolerating any of this.

They left the slum and were greeted by a small patch of lawn, still slightly green in the crisp winter air. A flagpole stood behind a low sign. Darwin didn't recognize the flag, and it looked handstitched as it hung limply in the still air. Behind it lay the clubhouse, its windows intact and paint still vibrant. Combined with the lawn, it stood in harsh contrast to the parking lot and the people who struggled to live there.

A tall blond man strode out from the front doors and extended a hand to Carlos. Together they walked back inside. The rest of the group was led to the back of the building to wait on an outdoor patio. Beyond the small trimmed hedge around the patio he could see pieces of the golf course, the greens cut and flags still in the holes.

Carlos came back in half an hour with a smile on his face. "They're willing to stick with the agreement they made with Enton. We won't be getting as many Threaders as we wanted, but it'll help. They can spare eleven, including two healers and a couple of good holers. It will be tougher for us to cover up our movements, but with some luck we'll get one or two good at obscuring at our next stop. They said they'll send provisions and people to help cart it all around as well."

"Slaves?" Darwin blurted the word before he even realized. He took a quick look around, and thankfully they were alone, though he almost wished someone from Nico's group had heard him. Carlos threw him a dirty look.

"They'll be here right away, let's get ready to hole."

Carlos barely finished talking before a group walked around the corner. Darwin saw Dale first, and she gave him a quick second glance before Rob came into view.

Rob stopped in front of the group from SafeHaven, looking at each one in turn. He showed no sign of recognition when he looked at Darwin, skipping past him as quickly as he had the rest. Darwin began to wonder if he was forewarned, or if he really didn't remember. Was what Rob did to him and Teresa so low on the scale that he simply didn't care enough to recognize a face?

Dale obviously had, and she was ignoring him along with the rest of the SafeHaven team. Maybe she was just protecting herself. He couldn't blame her.

Rob raised his voice. "All right, everyone. Pack up. We leave in one minute." He turned his back on them and Carlos and strode back to his own crew. Darwin sidled up to Carlos.

"I don't like that he has more people than we do."

"I'll take anyone we can get. They barely escaped Skends a while back. They want the Qabal gone as much as we do."

"Yeah, so they can become the next Qabal."

Carlos gave Darwin another dirty look and walked to where Rob stood. Darwin watched the men until two holes were made, and people started walking through.

Darwin exited the hole into an overgrown grass field and cleared the space for the next arrival. In the distance a rusted train stretched across the horizon. Between it and them sat a graveyard. The headstones were simple crosses—sticks tied together mostly, with a couple looking like they had been carved out of a bigger piece of wood. Darwin tore his gaze away from the rows of graves.

"Where are we now?" he asked.

Mellisa's gravelly voice answered. "Marcyes Park, Forsyth, Montana. Does knowing make you feel better?"

He couldn't pick up any spite in her voice, so he answered honestly. "A bit. It's not really the specifics that matter, so much as the progress. We were in Oregon, now we're in Montana. We're closer to where we need to be."

She gazed back into the holes as people came through, whispering almost too softly for him to hear. "I hope so."

The rest of the crew came through and milled around the small park, trampling the grass flat. Darwin helped set up tents, keeping busy, but from the corner of his eye, he could see the Salem

Threaders standing around while the people they brought along set up the tents. At one point, Rob wanted some food that wasn't unpacked yet, and he lashed out, striking a young man to the ground. Rob took a quick look around to see if anyone was watching, and they locked stares for a brief moment. Darwin turned away before the anger rising in him boiled over and threatened the entire plan. He still needed them to help get Teresa. But that didn't mean he would trust them.

Once the tents were set up, a woman approached from the town, winding a path through the graveyard and past the Salem Threaders directly to Carlos. They shook hands, and a smile broke the stern look on her face. They spoke for a few minutes before Rob barged in, and Darwin watched the mood change almost instantly.

"It looks like she knows Carlos and Rob." Mellisa's voice broke his concentration and he glanced at her.

"It does, doesn't it?"

The woman walked a pace away and pointed at Rob. Carlos moved toward her.

"I'd love to be a fly on that wall," said Darwin.

"You and me both."

The woman stormed off and Carlos spun on Rob. They could hear Rob yelling, but couldn't make out the words. Darwin saw Rob's Threaders move toward the argument, and elbowed Mellisa. "This doesn't look good."

She turned without a word and gathered the SafeHaven group together. As one, they moved to back Carlos. Darwin held back. Any of the SafeHaven group were stronger than he was in battle, and if it all worked out, he still preferred Rob not knowing about him.

He jerked when a hand touched his shoulder, and spun around, ready to call on the Threads he'd only learned to use the previous night, before he recognized who it was. Dale stood beside one of the tents, carefully hidden from Rob's line of sight. She glanced at the ongoing argument and beckoned Darwin toward her. He hesitated, remembering the incident in Salem. She'd given him and Teresa a chance then, and took another risk leaving behind the backpack. His mind made up, he followed her.

"What are you doing here?" she whispered.

"You know I came from SafeHaven. Teresa and I managed to get back. We were only there one night before the Qabal took her." Damn, he didn't want to let that out. What was it about Dale that made him talk?

"They have the healer you were with? Why?" She paused for a moment, obviously changing her mind. "Never mind. You had to know if you came back to Salem you were taking a risk. Those damn Skends took three of us before we got away, and Rob blames you."

"He didn't even recognize me."

"Not yet, but how long do you think it will take?"

"Who cares? We're supposed to be *united* now, working as a team."

"Rob cares, that's who. He's always been a mean son-of-a-bitch, and he'll do anything to get revenge on somebody he thinks did him wrong." Dale waved her hand to stop Darwin from interrupting. "Imagined or real, and those Skends were pretty damn real."

"He wouldn't dare do anything, not with so many people around."

"You don't know him. You won't know anything is wrong until he has a knife to your throat."

Darwin shrugged. "He won't ever get that close."

The arguing had stopped and Darwin stepped out from behind the tent. The Threaders had moved back to whatever they had been doing, and Rob stood where he had been. Carlos was following the stern lady's path. Rob glanced at Darwin and he could see recognition flicker on Rob's face. It was replaced with a look so evil that Darwin shivered. Rob pivoted and marched back to his group.

Darwin went back to helping set up camp before Mellisa interrupted him.

"Come on, time for class again."

He followed her. "What was the argument about?"

"Sandra, the woman from the city, recognized Rob. Apparently she's taken in a lot of travelers. Some of them made it out of Salem with stories. Some of them are buried here. It's going to take a lot of work for Carlos to convince her to join if Rob and his crew are with us."

They left the hastily set up camp and walked through the graveyard up to the rusted train. There must have been over a thousand gravesites. They climbed over the coupler where the cars met. Once on the other side, Darwin looked back. They were safely hidden from view.

"That's a lot of dead people," he said.

Mellisa looked at him with a serious expression on her face. "I'm surprised you haven't seen more of them. This is a small one. War kills a lot of people, Darwin, and it's never pretty."

He changed the topic. "Do you think Carlos can do it?"

"Do what?"

"Get Sandra to help?"

"I don't know." They crossed a street in silence and stopped behind the first house they found. The temperature had continued to drop, but Mellisa didn't seem to notice. It was her turn to change the subject. "Who were you talking to?"

It took him a minute to realize what she was referring to. "Oh. Dale. One of Rob's people, in theory anyway. She healed Teresa and me after we'd been captured and helped us get away."

"Do you trust her?"

"Yeah, I do," he said, surprised at his own words. "She told me Rob would kill me if he recognized who I was, and I think he just did. They were attacked by Skends, and he blames me." He didn't say he agreed.

"I wouldn't trust any of them. We'll have someone keep a lookout for you at all times. If he tries anything, if any of them try anything, we'll know about it."

"Thanks. I kind of want him to try, you know? I want him to feel how he made me and Teresa feel. I want him to know what it's like to be helpless and scared and—" He stopped, shocked at the rush of heat that infused his body. And at the hatred that suddenly consumed him.

"I think he already does. It's why he became what he is."

He thought about it for a while, giving himself time to relax. "That's not an excuse."

"No, it never is. But if we remember, it stops us from becoming that."

He looked back the way they had come, lost in thought. Was that what he was becoming? A vindictive person out for revenge? Someone who enjoyed taking advantage of people who couldn't protect themselves? He shook his head. He would never become like Rob. He wouldn't allow it. He turned back to Mellisa, suddenly glad for her words and her friendship. "Thank you."

They entered a small house, the roof sagging and the walls cracked. She sat down cross-legged on the dusty linoleum of the kitchen, motioning for him to join her. "Come on," she said. "Let's start."

The lesson went longer than Carlos's had, and she monitored him at every step, correcting him when he made a mistake. After five hours she had him stop, tired and sweating in the cool afternoon. His speed had increased to the point where the Threads responded almost instantly.

"That's good for now. If you can keep your head under pressure, I think you would be able to keep up with most of the crew we brought with us." She stretched her legs out. "I don't know how you learn so fast. I never could. It would take me weeks just to pick up a nuance you See without even trying, and all of my students were the same."

Darwin shrugged. "I don't know either. I usually let the images come, and it just all makes a kind of sense. It feels right when I do it right, and wrong when I don't."

"You are a freak of nature, my friend. And I mean that in a good way."

He smiled, his face flushing red. "Thanks, I guess. And thanks for all of this." He waved his hand back toward the park. "I don't know what I would do without you and Carlos. It's . . . it's not usually how I work, you know? I don't like being around people. They make me uncomfortable. Nervous. I've been alone a long time, except for my dad. This is all . . ." His voice trailed off.

Mellisa gave him a quick hug. "I don't know if I'd be able to cope with what you've been through. Anything we can do to help, you know we will."

"Yeah, I know." As soon as the words came out of his mouth, he knew they were true. Despite his moods and the trouble he had brought to SafeHaven, he truly believed her. "Come on, I think I smell food cooking. Let's head back, I'm starving."

The scene at the camp was . . . interesting. Carlos had somehow managed to bring back the stern-looking woman, Sandra. He sat in a group of five, with Rob and Dale, Sandra and a short man. As soon as Carlos saw Mellisa, he beckoned her over.

She sighed. "No rest for the weary."

"Or the wicked." Darwin watched her walk over, feeling Rob's stare bore into him. At some point things were going to come to a head. He found himself no longer looking forward to it.

The talk around the camp felt relaxed, and some of the Salem crew were actually mingling with the SafeHaven group. He hadn't expected that. The Threaders were, for the most part, welcoming if a bit guarded. The Salem slaves—the thought made his stomach turn—kept mostly to themselves. The faint smell of brewing coffee hit him full force. He could tell this was real coffee, and he went to hunt it down.

If the people from Forsyth could supply ten or fifteen people, that would bring them up to around forty. That wasn't even close to enough. Bill had told him there were hundreds of Qabal. How many of those were Threaders? Just the ones he saw during Rebecca's ceremonies, or were there more? If they couldn't add to their numbers in a big way, they would be heading into a war they wouldn't be able to win. Even if the Qabal did have only the twenty or thirty he saw in the lab, it was the Skends that worried him. How many of those abominations had they made?

After seeing them in action, he was afraid to face even one. What if they had twenty, or thirty? Or more? Hundreds? Would he be able to stand up to them? Would any of them? Certainly not for long.

He tried to shake away the feeling of dread that had seeped into his bones and continued to follow the smell. If things went the way he was planning, he wouldn't have to fight much. A small group should be able to sneak in and get out without being seen, if they were lucky. Especially if they did it while everyone was occupied on the front lines.

It all sounded so easy. Too easy.

He found the coffee steaming at the edge of a small fire near the

Salem tents. There were other SafeHaven people there, no one he knew, but the smell drew him in anyway. He stepped past a couple. "Excuse me, could I get a coffee?"

A mug was pressed into his hands almost before the words were out of his mouth. He looked down at the woman who served him. She was old and weather-beaten. Deep lines creased her dark tanned face and her back hunched in a perpetual stoop.

"Thank you."

She bobbed her head, never looking directly at his face. She held a bowl of sugar up to him. He hadn't seen sugar since he'd been here.

"No, thanks. I take it black." He paused. "What's your name?"

The old lady just bobbed her head again. A younger man stepped up beside her. He, too, never raised his face to look at Darwin.

"Sorry, sir. Her name's Missy, sir. She can't talk, sir."

Without thinking, Darwin asked why.

"She's got no tongue, sir. They said she gossiped about the higher-ups when she was young, sir, so they cut out her tongue." He said it with no emotion in his voice, as though afraid to express it. Or worse, as if it was just the way the world was, and there wasn't any point in being upset.

"They what?" Darwin's voice was the opposite. His body trembled, and he couldn't hide the fury that burned through him. "They did what?"

"Sorry, sir," the young man said, speaking louder. "They cut out her tongue for gossiping, sir. There was no harm done, she was treated, sir."

Darwin felt a tug on his sleeve. One of the SafeHaven people tugged again. "Come on, we should go."

Darwin spun around, noticing everyone else from SafeHaven had already left.

"Come on. Now is not the time. We need them."

Darwin looked into the earnest face in front of him. Behind her eyes, he thought he could see the same anger he felt. But there was something else there as well. Sadness mixed with a fear that reached down into her soul. He handed his coffee back to the old woman.

"I'm sorry for what they did to you."

As she turned back to the fire, the expression on her face was one of sadness. He walked away more upset than angry, passing the group of six at the central fire. He locked stares with Rob again, this time returning the malice.

Dark clouds moved in from the north, bringing with them an early night. Thunder rolled across the sky, long slow rumbles that seemed like they would never end. A cold dinner was quickly thrown together and eaten before the rain mixed with snow came. He hoped the storm would pass them by quickly and went into his tent.

Even though he watched the Threads around his tent, the same way he had when they were traveling back to San Diego, he barely got any sleep. Dreams of Rob plagued him in the scant few minutes he did get, waking him almost immediately. In one, Rob heated a knife over a small candle before roughly grabbing Darwin's tongue, reaching back, and slicing it off in one savage stroke while Teresa laughed silently behind him.

He finally gave up on getting any more sleep and crawled out of his tent into the cold pre-dawn light, shivering in his clothes, and wandered over to the central fire where Carlos sat alone.

"You're up early," Carlos said.

"So are you." He paused. "I couldn't sleep. Bad dreams."

"We'll do everything we can to get her out. You know that."

"Do I? You said yourself it wasn't your primary goal."

"Yeah . . . I've been thinking about that. I'm sorry. I let my anger, my hatred, toward the Qabal—what they did to Enton and SafeHaven—take over." He pointed his chin at the Salem side of the camp. "Trading with Salem, keeping everything at arm's length, made it easier to ignore what they were doing. All Enton and I wanted to do was feed our people, and we made choices I'm not proud of.

"Enton always said SafeHaven was about the people, the individuals that made the society. That's what mattered. He was right. I wish we didn't have Rob with us at all, I wish we could do this without him, but we just don't have the time." Carlos paused. "We have two days to get to the Qabal ahead of Wally. We'll do whatever we can to get Teresa out. You have my word."

Darwin sat silently staring into the flickering flames of the fire. He pulled himself upright, deciding to tell Carlos of his plans, to sneak in while the main battle was going on.

"I think a small group sneaking in while everyone else is fighting out front works."

"That's what I would have done," Carlos said. "And I think it still works. A small crew can get in and get out quick. You've been inside that place. You have an idea where they may be holding her. With some luck, once we are inside their perimeter, maybe we can hole straight in."

"I don't know how to hole."

"Well, that's on your list for today. If you pick it up as quickly as you did defense and offense, you'll be able to master it before dinner. You've covered in two days what we usually take half a year to teach. If we had the time, your control would be phenomenal." Carlos stood and stretched. "Come on, let's get the other fires started and wake everyone. We've got enough people we can hole twice this morning. I want to be in Erie, Pennsylvania today and New Jersey tomorrow."

They both grabbed sticks from the central fire and began to light the smaller ones outside the tents, waking people as they went. Darwin did the SafeHaven ones and Carlos did Salem's. It was better that way.

After breakfast with the new Forsyth recruits, extra holers went through first, creating the next link. Darwin stepped through into the Wisconsin Dells, took two more steps to the next hole, and came out onto the cold concrete path of Liberty Park. A frigid wind blew over Lake Erie, chilling any heat put out by the sun. He pulled his parka tighter around him and moved out of the way.

When everyone was through and the hole collapsed, the Skends attacked.

FAMILY IS MORE THAN BLOOD

THE SALEM CREW was hit first. A hole formed south of them, and the Skends poured out, blocking the exit from the park. There were ten of the monstrosities, and they were followed by three Qabal before the hole closed. Red Threads the color of blood formed in the air and arced across the opening between the two groups as the Skends surged forward.

Carlos grabbed Darwin's arm, stopping him from running forward with the others. "You hang back here and let us deal with this."

"But I know how—"

"I know you do, but you're our surprise card. I don't know if someone in this group told the Qabal we would be here, or if this is just a fluke. If someone told them, I don't want them to know that you're here, or what you can do. Stay." With that, he rushed off to join the fight.

Darwin hung back with the slaves and the healers. What Carlos said made sense, but watching them fight while he stood back and did nothing cut him to the core, and he realized he had changed. Before he came here, he would have stood by meekly, not wanting to be part of the crowd or of the damage. When he was alone, he was in control. The number of variables here was almost too much for him, but now that he was being asked to stand back he found it almost impossible to do. These were his friends.

The Skends rushed into the front lines, and the screams began. Smoke rose into the cold air and was pushed back by the wind. The lines separated and more red Threads filled the space in between.

A Thread arced from the Qabal, landing in the middle of the group. A circle of red exploded, and a couple of people fell to the ground before blue Threads built a defensive wall. Another Thread, this time from the SafeHaven group, retaliated and two Skends collapsed.

Dale rushed past him and he grabbed her, pulling her back.

"No. You healers should stay here. The rest of us will bring back the injured for you to look at."

"And if you get hurt? Who'll be left to find Teresa?"

The thought made him hesitate for only a second. Teresa was his priority, but he couldn't stand around while the others fought. "Carlos and Mellisa will. I can't stand here and let others do all the work." He ran into the fight, following the Salem slaves, and left Dale to manage the healers. On his ninth trip, the line of Skends had thinned considerably and he couldn't see two of the Qabal. The battle raged on.

He stepped into the mass of moving bodies, dodging a Skend's outstretched hand before a Forsyth Threader sliced it off with a bright red Thread. Darwin crouched over another fallen body, a young Salem woman—too young to be here, he thought—with burns over most of her torso. A hand grabbed his shoulder and spun him around. He fell on the burned woman and her scream echoed over the sounds of the fighting.

Rob towered over him, his face flushed and contorted into a parody of a human. "It *is* you!" Spit flew from his lips. "You damn near got us killed in Salem, and now you're doing it here. I'm not giving you another chance." He lunged forward.

Darwin rolled to the right, down the woman's legs. She flailed at him, delirious with pain, landing a heel on the back of his head. Stars flew across his vision as he rolled into the legs of someone else.

He looked up, squinting through the pain, and recognized another Salem Threader towering over him. Rob stood on the other side of the woman, grinning.

"No one here to save you now," Rob snarled.

Darwin looked around. Every person in view was from Salem. There was no one he knew. Each one had their back to Rob and Darwin, blocking the view of anyone outside the circle. Rob stepped on the woman's burns, grinning wider at her screams.

"Let's see if you scream like a girl," he said.

Rob drove forward again, landing a boot in Darwin's gut. He bent down and whispered in Darwin's ear. "Feel familiar? Bring you back to Salem, does it? Well, this will feel new." He lifted a blade to Darwin's chin and placed his other hand on the pommel, pushing it slightly into Darwin's neck. "It's a shame I gotta make this quick. Can't be caught, ya know?"

Darwin lashed out without thinking. A bright blue Thread wrapped around the knife and Rob's hands while a crimson one shot into his chest like a closed fist, stopping short of coming out the other side. Darwin chose the image of the fist opening up, fingers spreading wide. He jerked out of the knife's path and let the Threads go.

"You. That was you . . . I knew it. You bast—" Rob fell forward, his glassy eyes staring at Darwin.

One of the Salem people in Rob's protective circle turned, his too-young face filled with shock. His stare flicked between Rob's still form and Darwin, looking unsure of what had just happened and what to do.

Threaders from Forsyth backed into the group, their attention on the fight in front of them. Two Skends ran toward them and Rob's group turned as one to fight, leaving Darwin in the muddy grass beside the burned woman and Rob's body. The woman's breathing was shallow; she was unconscious, but still alive. A boot print pressed into the raw burn marks.

He went on autopilot, grabbing her arms and dragging her away from the fighting and halfway to the healers before the realization of what he had done sank in. *I've killed someone.* The impact felt like a physical blow. He still saw the dead stare of Rob on him, and shuddered as he kneeled beside the Salem Threader at the edge of the battle.

The rest of the fight was a blur that seemed to go on forever. Slaves and healers—people—came to collect the wounded and dead he dragged out. When it ended, he wasn't sure, but he found himself beside the patients, sitting with his head in his hands and covered in blood. Too tired to even notice or care.

At some point Carlos came by, sitting beside him and talking about what had just happened. That they'd gotten lucky, most of the wounded would be healed and ready to travel in the morning. Darwin reciprocated by telling him about Rob. Carlos simply smiled, a sad smile, and left him to rest, limping from a nasty gash in his leg.

That night, his sleep was restless. His dreams, instead of being filled with images of Rob, were consumed by pictures of death and blood and fire. In the morning he woke still gutted by what he had done. He knew he'd had no choice, that it was either him or Rob who walked away, but it didn't help. He had killed another human being.

It had actually been easy, and that was what bothered him the most. *With great power*, he thought.

He drifted through the camp in a daze. They had lost eleven Threaders. The losses seemed to be spread fairly evenly amongst the three groups, and the number was surprisingly low, considering what they had been up against.

The dead lay in an uneven row by the water, a solemn line of ghosts in the morning mist. Almost everyone was already up. Some, like him, not sure what to do. Others getting ready for the day ahead. As he walked, he realized something had changed. It took him a while to figure out what it was.

Everyone mingled and spoke quietly amongst themselves. Even the Salem slaves were included as they tended to the wounded with the healers, or were helped as the camp was dismantled. The three disparate groups had become one, working together. A whole.

In the back of his brain, Darwin wondered if that would have happened if Rob was still alive.

Carlos's travel plans took some doing, but they had expert holers with them. They ended up in New Jersey that day, pooling in the street before being led to the last place Darwin thought he would be. Home. His home, but not quite.

They walked in through the front door. He scanned the familiar room. Gone was the dark blue couch his mother had bought just before the accident, replaced with a black La-Z-Boy recliner covered in dirt and dust. There was a stack of old vinyl records in the corner beside the stereo. His mom had always preferred the sound of records over CDs. Darwin didn't think she'd have liked using her phone for music either.

He wandered to the pictures on the wall in a daze. It was strange to see the younger version of himself with his mom and dad in them. He knew this wasn't his home, he never grew up here, never talked with his mom here, but there was so much that was the same.

The clock on the wall was huge, with the minute hand almost seven inches long and the number four printed wrong. The china cabinet in the corner held trinkets from some of their family trips over the years. This one was packed to almost overflowing, making his at home seem empty.

He stopped at a larger picture on the wall. In it, he was standing between his mom and dad, dressed in his high school graduation robe. On the other side of his mother was a girl. She looked to be around ten years old, and an almost spitting image of his mother. All four of them were smiling, as if life was simple and carefree. It was a picture that could never have existed in his world. He traced his finger over the glass, clearing the clinging dust from his Mom's face and the sister he had never had. His mother looked older, but still how he remembered her. The picture portrayed the perfect family. He almost broke thinking of what they had lost, plugging the hole that yawned open in his chest before the guilt of living could pour out. He'd done enough of feeling guilty. He lifted the picture off the wall, leaving a clean square in its place, and sat down at the dining room table.

The young girl looked familiar. Not just because she resembled his mother. It was as if he had seen her before . . . seen her recently. He closed his eyes and tried to remember. It didn't take long for the memory to bubble to the surface. The teenager who had brought in his meal the first day he'd come over, when he was still locked in the office on the second floor of the Quantum Labs building. He remembered thinking she was his mother, until she'd gotten closer. It had to have been her. It had probably been her every time he thought he'd seen his mother there as well. Did she know who he was? How couldn't she? And if she was his sister . . .

He stopped that train of thought before it went much further. She wasn't *his* sister at all. She was the sister of this world's Darwin.

He focused on the dining room table, trying to get the family he'd never had out of his head.

This is where it had all started. The Coke cans, the searing pain, the Threads. And here he sat again, looking at a picture that, in his world, could never have been. Was his mom still alive here, working, breathing in some small community, holding out against the Qabal like he was? He removed the picture from its frame and folded it, making sure not to crease his mother's face, and put it in his back pocket beside Teresa's note.

Carlos walked up to him, limping slightly. The healers had been able to repair most of the damage, but part of the bone was too deeply sliced.

"How are you doing?" Carlos asked.

"I'll be okay. Why this place, why here?"

Carlos shuffled his feet and a hint of color touched his cheeks. "It was the closest place I could think of without being right on the Qabal's doorstep. I think I mentioned that I'd been here before."

Darwin turned back to look at the pictures on the wall.

"Is it Rob, or this place, that has got you down?" Carlos asked.

Darwin thought about it for a while. "Both, I think. I'm not sure what I could have done differently with Rob. I . . ." He looked at the clean square of wall. "I just saw a picture of my mother. In my world, she died before it would have been taken. I was just thinking about her."

"Enton taught me that family, and not just related family—not just blood—is something to be cherished. This is my family," Carlos said, looking around at the people in the room. "And yours, now. You may never meet the woman in that picture, but if you do, you'll know right away if she is still family as well." Carlos stood, silent until Darwin couldn't take it anymore, before he spoke again. "Now, enough moping. We still need to teach you how to hole. Come on."

"Wait! How . . . how did my dad die?" The words tumbled out in a mad rush. He didn't know where they had come from, only that the answer was the most important thing right now. He had to know.

Carlos paused, focusing on the bright square where the picture had been. "You both died that day, trying to turn off the QPS. The story is that you tried to pry off the side. Your dad grabbed a fire extinguisher and started smashing at it. Something sparked. Maybe the metal of the extinguisher connected two points it shouldn't have. The story says the room lit up like the Fourth of July. By the time things settled down, there wasn't much left of either of you. Mainly just shards of metal from the fire extinguisher and a machine that kept on running as if nothing had happened."

"And my mom?"

"No one seems to know. The world descended into chaos, you know? There's no record of what happened after. We lost track of your sister as well." Carlos nodded at the clean spot on the wall.

"What was her name?" The question popped out of Darwin's mouth before he'd thought it.

"Ada," Carlos said. "Ada Katherine Lloyd. Your dad said he named her after Ada Lovelace and Katherine Johnson, two women who helped shape the world. She was only eleven when the world changed. Sometimes I think that may have been a good thing. The younger ones adapted so much quicker than the rest of us." He turned toward the stairs. "Come on, let's get on with it."

Darwin followed Carlos upstairs, lost in thought. No matter

what the similarities between his world and this one, things were different. Enough to drive home the point that he didn't belong here, that this wasn't his home.

They walked into the first bedroom, his dad's, and sat on the floor. This room had the same furniture as the one in his world, except here, his mother's vanity was still in its spot, and some of her things lay scattered across the surface covered in a thick layer of dust and cobwebs. He ignored it as best he could.

He had his back to the bed, and Carlos had his to the closed door. Carlos created a tiny hole between them and tossed a rock through it, explaining everything along the way.

"Now you try."

Darwin closed his eyes, pulling on the Threads until he duplicated what Carlos had done. When he opened them, a hole had formed between them. He could See it was the wrong color, moving more toward amber than yellow corn. He threw the stone back through it anyway. Carlos was sprayed with a fine dust, and the hole collapsed.

"A good first try, Darwin. I've never seen anyone get it on the first try, so don't worry. Do it again, but this time . . ."

The training went on for hours, leaving both of them drained. In the end, Carlos created a large hole from one side of the room to the other and stepped through. "Your turn again."

Darwin concentrated, watching the hole form. The bigger version was just an upscaling of the small ones he'd been creating. He tweaked the Threads, ignoring the far end of the hole as he had been taught. The perfect looking yellow Threads coalesced into images, and he focused on those, building a door that opened to where he wanted to go, drawing on what he now knew as his strength. When he was done, he opened his eyes and prepared to walk through. Carlos stopped him.

"You don't have it, Darwin, look again."

Darwin searched, finding small variances in his work that made what he saw better, more stable. Complete. Listening to Carlos, he made it look closer to the one he had seen just a moment before. To his eyes, it still looked good, but not perfect anymore. Putting it down to exhaustion and lack of sleep, he stepped through, feeling the biting cold and ending up exactly where he had wanted to be.

Carlos forced the hole to collapse. "We're both tired. Why don't we get a bit of rest, and maybe try again later."

"That wasn't right either?" he asked.

"Not quite. Good enough to get you through in one piece, otherwise I wouldn't have let you do it. It was better than most of Wally's." He grinned, some of his old humor showing through.

"Don't be disappointed. You've made some fantastic progress. We've really pushed you over the last few days. Now it's time to rest. We'll start again later." Carlos shook out the dusty bed cover, making Darwin cough in the cloud he threw into the air. "Now go to bed." He lay down and closed his eyes as Darwin left the room.

His feet automatically took him to his—to the bedroom he— Darwin gave up trying to figure it out and swung the door open. The feeling of something being not quite right hit him again. He ignored it and moved to the bed.

He would have liked to have looked around the room of his counterpart here, but exhaustion took over as he sat on the edge of the bed. He didn't even shake off the dust before lying down and falling asleep.

He dreamed of glassy eyes staring at him in the dark, watching him as they transformed into the face of his mother.

"Wake up, Darwin. Come on, wake up."

A hand shook him, slowly at first, and then rougher. He swam to the surface, pushing aside the dreams and memories that crowded his sleep. He sat bolt upright on the bed, images of the family life he'd never had still imprinted on his retinas.

"Come on, it's time to go," Mellisa said.

"Go?" he mumbled.

"Yup. There's been a change of plans."

Darwin pushed sleep further away. "But I'm not ready."

"Carlos says you are. It's something we need to risk. If the Qabal we met last night were there because they knew we were coming, we need to attack before they expect us to. We changed the plan and surprised everyone with it. If we have a leak, hopefully they won't have time to tell the Qabal."

"Yeah, okay. Give me a minute. I need to wake up."

Mellisa walked from the room, leaving the door open. He heard voices and bangs from downstairs, the sounds of people getting ready.

When he reached the bottom of the stairs, the voices were muted. Everyone moved with a silent efficiency, preparing physically and emotionally for what lay ahead. They knew some of them wouldn't make it back.

Carlos stood in the corner talking quietly to Dale and Mellisa. Darwin walked over.

"—situated far back. If there's any wounded, we'll bring them to you," Carlos said.

"That's simply not going to work," Dale said. "By the time you have a chance to bring people back, it may be too late. Thread damage needs to be looked at immediately. We need to be there."

"She's right, Carlos," Mellisa said. "You know she is. The healers knew what they were getting into when they signed up."

"But the Qabal won't discriminate between healers and the others. They'll Thread down anyone and everyone. We can't lose our healers."

To Darwin, Carlos's plan sounded like what he had come up with when the Skends attacked in Liberty Park. Dale didn't seem to think that would work here, and he trusted her. He spoke up. "Why don't we bring three healers for instant triage and assign one or two Threaders to protect them? You'll need a couple of people to haul the injured back to the rest of the healers as well. The Salem non-Threaders can do that if they want. They might not have had the choice to be here, but I think they want to help. Let Dale handle the details, and you supply the Threaders."

Carlos looked at Darwin as though seeing him for the first time. He nodded at Dale, and she turned to gather up the healers. "If I didn't know it was you," said Carlos, "I'd have sworn Enton was standing there. He had a way of seeing the answers as well."

Darwin watched Dale walk away before turning back. "And what about me?"

"You'll stay behind with Mellisa and a couple of others. She'll be there just to keep an eye on your back and make sure you create the hole right. Once you and the rest of the team hole into the Qabal building, we'll need her back here. The rest of you will be on your own."

Darwin was used to that.

"You know the building," Carlos continued. "You know Rebecca. Use that knowledge to find Teresa and hole back out. Like we agreed, a small group will be easier to keep hidden once you're inside."

Darwin nodded. "Agreed. If we're not out by morning, don't come to get us. Just worry about the Qabal."

"We're not giving you that long before we try a rescue." Carlos reached out his hand and Darwin shook it firmly. "You're an incredible man, Darwin. I'll see you when this is over." He left to join the Forsyth leader and talk to the other groups milling inside the house.

Mellisa came back. "Are you ready for this?" she asked.

"Yes." He shook his head. "No, but I guess I'm as ready as I'll ever be."

She studied his face and the look of doubt in her eyes vanished. "Okay, it looks like they're starting the holes, let's move."

He walked into the backyard with her. The holes were ready, three of them this time, and the first line had already moved through. They stood behind Dale, waiting their turn. Dale turned around.

"Thank you," she said.

Darwin shook his head. "No," he said, "thank you. Help bring back as many as you can."

"And you bring back Teresa."

"I will."

Dale walked through the hole. Darwin turned and saw Mellisa watching him again. "What?"

"I thought Teresa was a secret."

"Yeah, well . . . Dale had the right to know. She helped us both." He stepped into the hole before Mellisa could respond, and the cold bit into his skin.

They ended up in the shade behind a short office building. Darwin remembered the place. They were just across the expressway from the Qabal. This close, if the Qabal were alert, they should know what was happening. The healers were already setting up a triage tent, preparing for the wounded who were sure to come.

He stopped Mellisa as she walked past. "Isn't this too close? They should have Seen the holes."

"We moved obscurers in this morning. If they did their job, we're still good."

"And if they didn't?"

"Then we'll both know. You find me, and we get you inside. Okay?"

Darwin nodded. "Okay."

She moved off to the healers' tent.

Half an hour later, the teams were lined up and there had been no sign of the Qabal. The obscurers had done their job. The plan was that two lines would attack directly from the front, while a third would get in from the rear. If they could split the Qabal defenses, it would be easier for Darwin to slip inside unnoticed. Or so they hoped.

With a single command from Carlos, all three teams holed to their positions and began work on dismantling the blue Threaded wall around the parking lot.

Mellisa and Darwin and the small team of three waited a minute before holing to the office building beside the Qabal headquarters. They advanced around the building, crouching in the tall grass to stay out of sight. From their position, they could see the Skends stream into the parking lot.

"That's our cue. Let's go." Mellisa, staying crouched low, ran to the edge of the grass, watching the fighting only thirty yards away. "Where you holing to?"

"I figured I'd try the room they kept me in. It's far enough away from the QPS room that it hopefully won't be watched. I doubt any-one will be on the mezzanine level, unless Rebecca is directing the fight from her office."

Mellisa looked at him, a concerned expression on her face. "Are you sure?"

He wasn't, but it was the only plan he had.

She created a small hole in the wall and held it open for him.

"Why isn't everyone getting past the wall?" he asked.

"It's just too many people. This isn't as easy as I make it look, you know. Now move."

As he crawled through, he could see her trembling with the

effort of what she was doing. He moved faster, and she let the others through before following them.

Darwin had already started the hole, making sure to stay below the top of the tall grass. He ignored everything else going on around them and concentrated on the task at hand. When the hole was finished, Mellisa nodded and he stepped through. He'd become used to the cold, and simply shook it off as he exited the other side. The QPS with its blue glowing *QL* stood before him.

Mellisa followed him through, took a quick look around to make sure he wasn't under attack while the others followed. "I thought we were going to your room?"

"I did as well, but when I started the hole it felt wrong. This was the next place that popped into my head."

She nodded once, not questioning him. Her gaze lingered on the QPS, the source of her—of all Threaders'—abilities, before returning through the hole and closing it behind her.

They were alone.

As soon as the hole closed, Darwin felt exposed. He joined the rest of the team at the wall between the QPS room and the lab, kneeling under the empty window frame where they wouldn't be seen, and planned the next move. His initial hope was that Teresa and Rebecca would be here, despite what he had told Mellisa. He had planned on grabbing Teresa and returning before Rebecca even knew what was happening.

A stupid idea, but it was what had gotten him this far. Now he felt lost and crippled by uncertainty. The three Threaders looked at him for directions, as if he knew what he was doing.

The first thing was to get out of here. There was only one exit from the lab, and it would get them to the hall, and then up into the foyer under Rebecca's office. His best guess now was that Teresa was being kept on the mezzanine level, like he had been. Maybe even in the same room he had been in. He should have stuck with his original plan. He was an idiot.

The rest of the team still watched him, and he sighed. Teresa wasn't here, so it was time to move. He whispered quick instructions and the Threaders moved as one into the other room.

He crept to the door of the QPS room and looked into the lab. Except for the presence of the SafeHaven Threaders, it was basically the way he had last seen it. Broken equipment pushed to the far wall to make room for the Qabal, and a single door into the hallway. He ran, still ducking low, to join the team by the door and pressed his ear against it.

A low raspy sound came from the other side. It could have been his own breathing or someone standing there, guarding the QPS room. He forced himself to calm down and listened again, holding his breath. He thought he heard a shoe slide across the floor. Someone was out there. He was sure of it. The only woman Threader nodded when he looked at her.

Thinking of Rob's sensitivity to the Threads, about how he knew they were there just because Darwin had followed a Thread, he was cautious about following any in the room. In the end, he decided it was the only way to know what, if anything, was on the other side.

He lightly landed on a Thread that passed through the door. It slid through the wood, leaving a bitter scent of sawdust and old glue in his mouth.

Almost immediately he smelled coarseness and tasted blue. Filth crawled over his skin. Definitely a lab coat. He pulled back, hoping he hadn't been detected. He waited for the door to open, his whole

body vibrating, his heart thudding so loudly he was surprised everyone in the building didn't know he was there.

Nothing happened.

Feeling more confident, he chose another Thread and followed
it through, feeling the wood grain of the door on his tongue before
the coat enveloped his senses once again. He hopped Threads, trying
to find one that would tell him which direction the figure was facing.

The Threads swirled around the hallway. He couldn't seem to
find one that helped. He jumped from one to another, and although
he could definitely tell someone was out there, he couldn't figure out
anything else. He pulled back, waiting again to see if he had been
detected. After a few minutes, he knew he would have to risk it.
They were no good to Teresa in here.

He turned the knob, cringing at the scraping noise made by the
bolt. At every small turn, he paused and waited before starting again.
When the bolt released from the strike plate, the door popped
slightly from its frame and a whoosh of air brushed against his face.
He couldn't detect any changes from the hallway, no new Threads
moved into the room, and the blue smock didn't move. He stood and
rested his hand on the door. It was now or never. He tensed his muscles, ready to spring into the hall.

The woman Threader pushed past him. He heard a soft thud
before he stood and followed her. A young kid, no more than sixteen,
lay on the floor. His neck was bent at a bad angle. Darwin looked at
the woman and she shrugged in return.

"Best not to use Threads until we need them. It might keep our
presence here a secret a little bit longer."

The only thing he could do was nod. Another life gone, taken
before its time. He shoved the thought away and followed the team
down the hall as they disappeared up the stairs. He was just about

to follow them when voices came from the first floor. He froze mid-stride as the voices rose to a shout. Deep red Threads cut through the air like a knife, and the woman from SafeHaven fell backward down the stairs, her chest a mass of blood and bone.

The two men stumbled back down into the hall, throwing a shimmering blue wall between them and the Qabal. It was ripped away even before it was completed. One of the men pivoted and pushed Darwin back toward the lab. Darwin turned and ran.

He stepped over the body of the young man and pushed open the door, expecting the two men to be right behind him. Instead, they'd stayed near the bottom of the stairs and fought. He took a step back to join them just as they both fell, and he changed direction back into the lab. He let the door swing shut behind him and looked around the room, panic pulsing through him. There was no place to hide. Given time, maybe he could have shifted the old equipment and ducked behind the pile. He didn't have any time.

He ran back into the QPS room, ducking behind the machine itself just as the door swung open, the blue *QL* reflecting sharply into his eyes. He willed his heart to slow down and placed his hands on the machine, feeling it pulse under his fingertips. There was something else there as well. A familiarity that took his breath away.

"Get this body out of the way." Rebecca's voice, shrill in the enclosed space, cut through him worse than the cold at Lake Erie had. Bill hadn't killed her that day on the street. Too bad.

The door slammed shut and Darwin heard footsteps approach the QPS room.

"It seems your boyfriend has sent an army to try to get you out of here, while he sits still a day away," Rebecca said. "He is as weak as I always thought he was. I have no idea what I saw in him. So he could See. It changed nothing."

"You will lose."

Teresa! Darwin almost jumped to his feet, fighting against the urge until Rebecca was closer to where he hid. His leg started vibrating, and he longed to release the energy building up inside of him.

"I doubt it, girl. But if I do, you won't be around to see it. Once your usefulness is gone, once we have him, you won't be needed anymore. Until then, you will never leave my side. I don't want any surprises."

The voices got closer, entering the QPS room. Darwin heard the door open again. He barely dared to breathe, never mind follow the Threads to See how many people were out there.

"Revered Mother, we are ready to begin."

"Good. Check the bindings on the girl. We'll be too busy to keep an eye on her."

"Bitch!" Teresa yelled.

Darwin heard feet running, followed by the sharp sound of a slap and someone falling down. He peeked around the QPS and saw Teresa lying on the floor covering her face.

"Gag her as well."

Darwin stood, his hand on the QPS. "No!"

DON'T MAKE ME DO IT FOR YOU AGAIN

*T*HE SCENE IN front of Darwin unfolded in slow motion. Teresa looked up from the floor, the look of dismay on her face
matched by the intensity of her scream. "Get out!"

Red Threads appeared in the air, arcing toward him, reaching
over the QPS, planning to envelop him in pain. He reacted, blocking
the multitude of Threads with barely a thought. The QPS beneath
his hand pulsed in time with his heartbeat, picking up the pace as
the realization of what he had just done hit him.

A Thread raced toward Teresa, hitting her in the leg, and she
screamed in pain as the muscle spasmed and the skin broke. Darwin
imagined a solid shell, sending navy blue Threads over her body,
completely encasing her, barely stopping another barrage. It wasn't a
prison, but a shield made to keep out any more attacks.

The Threads stopped, and Rebecca stood looking at him, making no attempt to cover the hatred etched into her face. Her voice was cool and collected, the sound of someone who knew they had won.

"Welcome back, Darwin."

He remained silent, staring at her, watching every Thread in the room with a clarity he had never Seen before. The increase in his perceptions made all of his training seem sophomoric.

"There are four of us here, and soon we'll have all thirteen of us. You don't stand a chance."

"Teresa. Can you come over to me? Is the leg bad?" Darwin asked.

Teresa lay on the floor, her leg useless. She raised herself on her arms and moved toward him. As soon as her leg straightened, she screamed again and fell back to the concrete floor.

He moved to reach her. The moment his hand left the QPS, half of the Threads in the room disappeared. He barely saw the powerful crimson Thread surging across the floor toward him, only deflecting it at the last possible moment. He put his hand back on the QPS and the room jumped back into sharp focus. He'd known the QPS was the source of the Threads, but he'd had no idea how direct contact affected his abilities.

The familiarity hit him again, and this time he recognized it, felt his mom's arms around him holding him tight. *What the hell?* Teresa cried out in pain and he was back where he needed to be. Where he could help her.

"I can't come to get you, Teresa. I'm not strong enough to keep us both safe if I leave the QPS. You have to come to me."

Teresa raised herself up again and moved another few inches, the blue mesh moving with her.

"You can do—"

"Darwin," Rebecca interrupted, "the rest are coming. You don't have a chance. If you come over here, we'll let the girl go."

He barely had the time to give Rebecca's offer a thought before the rest of the disciples walked into the QPS room, forming a semi-circle behind Rebecca. A fourteenth person followed them. One more than he had seen last time Rebecca and her disciples had gathered around the QPS. The disciples parted and the fourteenth figure picked its way through the gap.

"Elizabeth, your son is here with us," Rebecca said.

The figure gasped and stumbled to a stop. Rebecca strode over, roughly pulling the figure forward.

Darwin's mom stood before him, Rebecca's hand still clutching the back of her jacket. It felt as though time stood still, and the room narrowed into a tunnel. Threads ripped through the space, hazy and out of control. The years of therapy he'd had after her death fell away in a rush, leaving him scared and raw.

She was just like he remembered her, just like the photo on the wall in his house—the house—earlier today. He breathed deeply and could almost smell the apple blossom and vanilla over the stench of the unwashed bodies.

"M . . . Mom?"

"Darwin? I thought—"

"Yeah, great reunion, isn't it?" Rebecca asked, her voice dry and sarcastic. "You walk over here right now, and they both live. You don't, and they die right before your eyes."

Darwin's palms rose off of the QPS, leaving only his fingertips brushing the cool metal of its casing. A scream slashed into his brain, shattering the tunnel and bringing the room back into focus.

"No!" Teresa screamed again.

"Now, Darwin. Come here now."

His world spun and tears fell freely down his cheeks. "Mom?"

"Darwin, my baby. Please, do as she says. She'll kill us both if you don't."

"I . . ."

"Oh god, please, Darwin. I don't want to die," his mom cried.

A scene popped into Darwin's head—one that he had recreated over and over again, trying to change the outcome of his actions. His mother's car swerving on the dry concrete road, the steering wheel slick in his hands as they impacted the railing and spun across the highway, flipping end over end down the concrete.

His knees almost buckled and he moved to the side of the QPS, his fingers still resting on its surface.

Teresa screamed again. A red Thread had crept through Darwin's watch and jabbed itself into her already damaged leg, ripping the wound wider. Blood welled up from the exposed meat.

He jerked back behind the QPS. The Threads in the room shifted at his command, and the protection around Teresa reasserted itself, doubling the number of deep blue Threads, killing the red one. At the same time, a barely visible pink Thread wrapped itself around the material grasped in Rebecca's hand. The blue smock tore at the seam. His mother, leaning against Rebecca's pull, lurched forward, leaving Rebecca with the ripped jacket in her hand, and his mother free. Without hesitation, she ran toward him, passing Teresa without a second look.

Keeping one hand on the QPS, he moved again, holding an arm out to catch his mother. She fell into him and he gave her a fierce hug. He barely noticed the lack of apple blossom and vanilla.

Pain pierced his side and he stumbled, letting go of his mother and falling against the QPS. He reached down and felt warmth and wet. His hand came away bloody. Darwin slid to his knees and fell sideways onto the floor.

"Mom?"

Blood covered her hand as she knelt down beside him. He registered the knife she gripped, still at the ready.

The look on her face was one of sadness and pain. "I'm sorry.

They—" She raised the knife again, ready to plunge it into Darwin's chest.

Instinctively, he pulled Threads toward him, forcing them to change from the wispy gray of normal Threads to the blue of protective ones, visualizing a suit of armor. The knife plunged down, stopping at his armor, and rose again. Somewhere in the distance, he heard another scream from Teresa.

Threads moved off to his right, the pattern different from what was around him. It looked vaguely familiar, but he was drawn back to his mother. He saw the pain in her eyes, and loss, as the knife came down again and again, each time bouncing off the shield he'd created.

A red Thread pushed her hand away, slicing into her palm, and the knife clattered to the floor uselessly. Someone grabbed Darwin's shirt, dragging him away from the QPS, before he was plunged into bitter cold.

The cold ended, and he was next to Mellisa on the back lawn of his house.

The world came back into focus, shifting levels of gray dissipating in waves. Darwin watched as soft white Threads pulled away from him. It took him a few minutes to remember where he was as the fog lifted from his brain.

Reality came back in a sudden, painful rush.

He pushed himself upright, a wave of nausea pulsing through his body. Two hands reached gently for his shoulders and pushed him back down.

"Nice and slow, Darwin. You've just been through major surgery. Everything is healed, but your body needs to rest. This isn't magic, you know."

It was Dale's voice. Firm in its commands, yet soft and caring.

"Rest for a bit longer, sleep if you can. It will take a couple of hours for the pain blockers we used to fully release. Until then, stay put. We don't want you to trip and reopen the wound."

Darwin lay his head back on the pillow and stared at the wall. He recognized the posters. His old clock, the LEDs dark and lifeless, sat on the dust-covered nightstand. This was his bedroom, his house. He shook his head, bringing another wave of nausea, and closed his eyes.

No. No, it wasn't.

Sleep took hold before he realized it. His last thought was of Teresa, her cries echoing in his head. When he woke up, the sun shone low in his window, resting in between a layer of dark clouds and the horizon. The red glow coming through the curtains made the walls look like they were running with blood. He blinked, bringing everything back into focus.

He reached a hand under the sheets, gently probing where the knife blade had entered. The skin just around the wound felt smooth before it puckered into a tight scar. It didn't hurt. He struggled to sit up.

The scar was barely visible, whether due to the dim light in the room or Dale's skill, he didn't know. He shook his head slowly, then more rapidly, waiting to see if dizziness swept over him. When nothing happened, he pushed his legs over the edge of the bed and stood up.

The house was quiet. He could make out some soft talking from downstairs, but nothing else. Were the others still fighting it out at the Qabal headquarters? He grabbed a Thread and rode it down the stairs, not trying to be subtle. There were three people in the living room, and from what he could tell, no one else.

The conversation stopped, and Carlos's voice echoed up the stairs.

"You may as well come down."

Darwin found his clothes on the foot of his bed, a new t-shirt replacing the one with the hole in it. His jeans still had blood clinging to the deep seams of the material, making the waistband coarse and hard. He opened the door and headed down the stairs.

Carlos and Mellisa sat on the couch with Dale on the loveseat across from them. Moving to the armchair, he lowered himself into it and stared at the faces around him.

Dale watched him, and he could See white Threads move toward him and start prodding at his scar. Carlos and Mellisa looked on, concern written clearly on their faces.

"How are you feeling?" Dale asked.

Darwin stared at Mellisa, allowing his anger to build before he spoke. "Why did you do that?" His voice was quiet with the harsh edge of fury behind it.

"Do what?" Mellisa asked.

"Pull me out of there."

Carlos cleared his throat and responded. "Darwin, with Rebecca concentrating on you, we managed to punch a hole through the shield. As soon as we did, Mellisa tried to find you. She realized you had been hurt."

"They were going to let them go."

"Them?" Carlos and Mellisa responded in unison.

"Teresa and . . . and my mom."

"Your mother was there? I only saw the Qabal and Teresa."

"She was right beside me; she was forced to—"

Mellisa leaned back on the couch, shock on her face. "The one with the knife? She *stabbed* you, Darwin. She tried to kill you. She's part of Rebecca's inner circle."

"She's not! Mom was just following them. She just happened to be there. Rebecca was controlling her." Darwin's voice rose to a feverish pitch.

"Darwin, think about it. Did you See any Threads controlling her? Did Rebecca attack her or threaten her in any way?"

"You weren't there! You don't know!" Darwin pushed himself to his feet and strode to the back door, only stopping at the fence to stare into the deepening shadows. His gut still ached where the knife—where his mom had stabbed him.

Had she been under Rebecca's control? He thought back to the QPS room. The look of shock on her face when she saw him, how Rebecca had grabbed her jacket to hold her back. He remembered those things, could still see them vividly in his memories. But he couldn't remember the Threads. Was she being controlled? Darwin couldn't—didn't want to—think of any other possibility.

The house door opened and closed behind him. He followed the Threads and knew Dale was walking toward him before she laid a hand on his shoulder.

"Come back in, Darwin. You lost a lot of blood today. Your body still needs to rest."

Everything left him in a sudden rush, the anger, the hope, the tears, leaving him hollow and lifeless. He slumped against the fence, suddenly too exhausted to stand.

He let her lead him back to the house and up the stairs, his mind a mess of contradictions. On the way up, he removed the picture of his mom from his back pocket. He unfolded it as he lay on the bed, staring at the face he knew, noticing how age had changed it, until the picture blurred and his body finally took the rest it needed.

Darwin woke with a start, sitting bolt upright in his bed. The harsh remnants of his nightmares pushing at the edge of his senses. *His mom sitting in the passenger seat of her car, sliding across the highway divider. Her face morphing into a mask of terror, and from there, into a creature from hell, with horns that blew fire and eyes that were pits of lava.* He rubbed his eyes, trying to force the images out of his mind. It didn't work.

The house was quiet, and through the window Darwin saw stars in the night sky. He followed the Threads through the dark hallways and rooms, finding Carlos and Mellisa asleep in his dad's bed, their deep breaths disturbing the quiet of the room.

He roamed further, coming to the perimeter of the property, jumping Threads to remain in the confines of the men and women assigned to protect the house. Their main job was to disguise the house's use and make it appear empty to anyone who might have been looking for them. In case that failed, they could protect in other ways as well.

He pushed the blankets aside and stood, bending over to grab his shoes. He would put them on once he was outside. Creeping through the house in his socks, he stepped over the parts of the floor that creaked, using his years of living there—no, he corrected himself— living in a house just like this one, for years. The two universes were similar in most ways, but not where it counted. His mom was alive here. He paused in mid-stride. His dad wasn't. The thought almost took over, threatening to pull him back into the deep dark pit.

As he moved, he duplicated the Threads of the people standing outside, mixing turquoise and pale green into a bubble around him, hoping they'd obscure him from Carlos and Mellisa the way theirs hid them from the Qabal.

He opened the back door and stepped out to the patio, sitting on the stairs to tie up his shoes. Three more had died because of him. They had gone into the lion's den with him, and he didn't even know their names. He'd been too scared to ask. Maybe scared wasn't the right word, but it didn't matter. He'd shown them the way in, and they'd paid the price for that.

And he knew he had to do it again.

He couldn't beat Rebecca alone, that much he knew, but with the QPS's help he'd be more than capable. All he had to do was touch the machine and he would have already won. If the Threaders could get him close enough, he'd be able to take it from there.

He sat in silence, the only sound outside made by the animals that thrived at night. The Milky Way slashed across the night sky, brilliant in its color and detail, reminding Darwin how much the world had changed.

Threads drifted through the empty spaces and his thoughts shifted to the QPS. Even now, he could feel it, creating and sending out its Threads for the world to use. He knew it was the source of his and everyone else's abilities. He hadn't been able to See Threads until his dad had turned the damn thing on. Distance didn't seem to matter; he didn't feel or See the Threads any stronger now that he was closer to the source, even though he could feel the machine itself. He saw things differently, but that was mainly due to the training he'd received while they were traveling.

But when he'd touched the QPS, everything was different. He could remember feeling the machine pulse under his fingertips, and it was as if the Threads were a part of him—his slightest whim could change them, make them do whatever he wanted them to. There was something familiar when he'd made contact with the machine, a comforting blanket that lay over his shoulders, carrying the faint scent of apple blossom and vanilla. What was it about the machine that made him think of his mom?

Did Rebecca have the same connection? Maybe with someone else who had died, someone close to her? If so, it was obviously the reason the Qabal stayed in the building. Away from direct contact with the QPS, she would be no stronger, and no weaker, than anyone else who knew Threads.

It was as if touching the QPS pushed the limits away, opened the person's mind to all the possibilities. Did it protect them from the insanity that threatened Thread users? Rebecca sure as hell wasn't right. Her creation of the Skends, how she wanted to rule over everyone. Her grab for power. And now that she knew there were other worlds, controlling her own wasn't enough. She wanted it all. That was why she wanted him, wanted to peel back his mind layer by layer until she found what she thought was there. Those weren't the actions of someone in their right mind.

He pushed himself off the fence, the decision that had been nibbling at the back of his brain solidifying. He would do everything he could to get his mom and Teresa out of the Qabal's—out of *her*—clutches. Once they were safe, he would worry about Rebecca and himself. He doubted she would willingly let him get close enough to the QPS to touch it again. She couldn't risk the advantage it would give him. Yet it was obvious she still feared him and what he could do. He had no idea why. What he did know was that he would do whatever he had to do to stop Rebecca and the Qabal. And if he was lucky, if he survived, maybe he could move back to San Diego with Teresa and his mom.

If he was lucky.

The plan was to convince Carlos to send in another team. This time, he'd follow his first instinct. They would hole into his old room and find Teresa, hole her out and then follow her through.

It made sense—at least to him—that they would keep her there. It was close to Rebecca and had already been used as a prison. At least he hoped it made sense.

Finding his mom would be tougher.

He patrolled the border of the property, making sure to stay inside the protective boundary. Watching the Threads, he knew the obscurers were aware of him, compensating for his moving around.

He knew they had compensated while everyone had holed to the Qabal, and his movement would cause them no trouble.

As he walked to the far corner of the yard, the Threads shifted. He felt more than saw the work of the Threaders obscuring the house and yard pass over him. Without warning, he was outside the protective barrier.

Darwin heard a muffled shout from the house and felt Threads weaving their way toward him. Threads moved in front of him as well, quickly forming into a small tunnel that continued to grow. He concentrated on destroying the still-forming hole, only to have his own Threads torn apart.

Carlos sprinted onto the patio a little out of breath from dashing down the stairs. Darwin saw him move closer and let go of the Threads. A steel blue mesh grew between them, stopping Carlos in his tracks.

"Darwin? Wha—"

"It's not me," Darwin interrupted. "Someone moved the shield."

"Darwin—" Carlos raised his voice, a hint of desperation coming into it.

Threads pulled around Carlos and headed for the hole. A dull red Thread flew from behind Darwin, breaking his concentration and knocking Carlos to the ground.

Mellisa stepped from the back door and ran to the fallen figure just as Darwin felt a hand grab his arm. As he was yanked backward, he recognized the Threaders protecting the house. Salem.

He fell through the other side, ice crystals falling from his body as he hit the ground. His breath rushed out and he struggled to inhale.

The mesh that stretched into the sky over his head pulsed, and he was dragged through. The gap between the individual Threads was wider than before. He could have put a fist through it without being stopped. SafeHaven's work had weakened it.

They were halfway across the parking lot before he was able to breathe again.

He reached for the Threads, wrapping red ones around the hands of the person pulling him. They let go with a sharp gasp. Darwin struggled to his feet.

He didn't have much time to think about what to do next—an attack came first. Red Threads shot from a broken window on the third floor and raced toward him. He responded by blocking them, almost feeling the QPS inside the basement responding to his wishes as though he were touching it. He knew that couldn't be true.

The attack continued and he broke into a sweat in the cold night air fending them off. Eventually they stopped, and he stood, waiting. There was no point in trying to get back through the blue wall. He'd be too busy protecting himself to even make an attempt.

He didn't have to wait long before a large contingent stepped from the building. He followed the Threads and recognized Rebecca in the mix.

"I didn't think that plan would work as well as it did. It's amazing what a couple of turncoats can do."

He didn't respond.

"Not talking?" She smiled and the flickering light cast her face into a mask of bitterness. "We can change that."

"I want a trade. Me for my mom and Teresa."

"You think it's a fair trade?"

"It's the deal I'm willing to make. You want me, here I am. Send them out and let them go."

"We already have you."

"If you thought that, we wouldn't be talking."

Rebecca stood staring at him, her lips pursed. "Come with me."

"Send them out first."

She turned and walked back toward the building. The Threader who had dragged him here from the house pushed him on his shoulder and he took a halting step forward.

"Send them out," Darwin shouted. He watched as Rebecca's group crossed the parking lot, filled with uncertainty. She wasn't going to give them up, and he was on his own now. Not seeing any other way in, he pushed the doubt and fear aside and followed her.

Darwin walked cautiously across the asphalt, watching the Threads and the group just ahead of him. The black rock around the entrance resembled a beast even more now as it swallowed them and the Threads. He hesitated before taking a deep breath, and stepped inside, still not sure he had made the right choice, wishing he had time to think things through better.

Nothing had changed. He wasn't sure why he was expecting it to have, but the drab and dirty carpet was still the same. The stairs still went up to the overhanging balcony where Rebecca had her office. She wasn't going there, though. Instead, she went through the door to the basement lab.

Now that Darwin was inside, his pace picked up. It wasn't that he was more confident, it was simply that he finally realized there was nothing more he could do in here than he could have done outside, or less. He pulled his shoulders back and forced a look of what he hoped was bravery on his face. The man who had taken him split off, heading toward the offices. Rebecca and the group that had come outside with her continued on. Disciples. And they were heading straight for the place they were the strongest, the QPS room.

Inside, he was trembling, and his eye twitched uncontrollably.

He kept a constant watch on the Threads, waiting for anything that could be an attack of some sort. He remembered when he had first come here and Rebecca had forced him to sit in a chair. What were her words? *Don't make me do it for you again.* There was still so much about the Threads he didn't know. What the hell had made him think he had a chance? Simply that the people he loved needed his help. It had to be enough.

It was too late to do anything about it now.

They were halfway down the stairs when he opened the door off the foyer. He followed them, and the door clicked closed behind him.

There were only thirteen in the QPS room, Rebecca and her disciples. They stood in the circle around the machine, facing inward, ignoring him completely. He watched as the Threads around the machine thickened.

"Where's my mother and Teresa?" He hoped they couldn't hear the panic that filled him, that threatened to consume him until there was nothing left but a quivering lump of flesh on the floor. He rubbed his eye, trying to stop the twitch. What the hell had he done? He couldn't beat the entire Qabal if they didn't do what he asked. He should have stayed outside, though he didn't know what that would have gained him.

Rebecca turned to face him, leaving her disciples where they were. "Of course, Darwin, as we agreed. I'll send for Teresa now." A disciple turned and walked past Darwin, through the door.

"And my mother."

"Ahh, of course. Your mother. You poor, sweet dear." Rebecca's voice practically dripped with sarcasm. She raised her voice. "Your son would like to see you."

The disciple standing beside Rebecca, one who hadn't been outside with her a few minutes ago, turned away from the QPS.

"Mom?" The word had barely left his mouth when he stumbled

back as though physically hit. His mother stood beside Rebecca. A disciple. She took a step forward, bowing her head slightly toward Rebecca, and stared at him. He looked into her eyes and saw nothing but hatred and contempt. "Mom?"

"I am not *your* mother. My son died years ago, trying to turn off the Source. You," she almost spat, "are nothing but a cheap imitation."

"I came back to get you out."

"*My* son would never have been caught so easily. *My* son was smarter than that. *My* son would have been standing at my side, at our side," she said, bowing her head again to Rebecca.

Anger overrode the fear of being trapped with Rebecca and the realization that his mother *was* one of them. "Your son would never have let you join this cult."

A Thread slammed into his chest faster than he could respond and he stumbled back, hitting the window ledge between the QPS and the lab.

He barely heard Rebecca laugh.

THE JOURNEY HOME

DARWIN DIDN'T HEAR the lab door open. He sat on the QPS room floor, staring at his mother's face, hoping for a sign that she was just waiting for the right time to turn on Rebecca. That her loathing for him was just a ruse.

It never came.

He remembered the knife in her hand, only yesterday, and how she'd slid it into his side, crying that she had no choice. Did she mean any of it? Watching her now, he knew he couldn't believe her, but part of his brain refused to give up, refused to let her go.

"Mom?"

A red Thread shot toward him. Rebecca placed a hand on his mother's arm and the Thread disappeared.

"Not yet," she said. "Not yet."

The look on his mother's face changed, a small smile that didn't reach her eyes. He saw the anticipation and sagged lower on the floor.

He had missed her so much. He had spent every night for months crying into his pillow, trying to hide his grief from his dad. Trying to figure out why she had died in the crash and he hadn't. He had made it through the pain then, both physical and emotional, but suddenly it all came crashing back, hitting him with the force of a physical blow, coupling with the guilt that had never left. He gasped for air, the walls crushing in on him, pressing the oxygen out of his lungs.

Rebecca looked up, out the door to the lab, and smirked. "Your girlfriend is here."

Teresa was thrown into the room, landing in a heap between him and his mother. Her pants were still torn where the Threads had cut into her, and the wound below it throbbed red, the blood dried and crusted. They hadn't healed her or let her heal herself. Her hands were tied behind her back, and a gag had been bound roughly over her mouth.

"Do you think we could turn her against him?" Rebecca asked. "Do you think she would willingly hurt him in order to save herself?"

His mother grinned. "Why don't we see?" Threads formed above Teresa, turning pink and then red as they wove themselves into a mesh like the one outside the building.

Teresa turned her head, looking at him, the tears in her eyes drying as she watched him. He tried to send her all of his strength through their small contact. He reached for the Threads to help her, but Rebecca tore them away from him.

The mesh lowered, settling on Teresa like a blanket, sinking underneath her clothes. He barely registered the difference in how the

Threads worked. He looked up as Teresa whimpered. Ugly red welts appeared on her exposed skin and she cried out. The Threads sank into her, and she tried to screamed through the gag. He could still See them, barely below the skin, wriggling and twitching, each movement wrenching a new cry from her.

He used the wall to push himself into a sitting position and forced out a strangled shout. "Stop it!"

His mother laughed, a strange, screeching, maniacal sound that made him feel like he was in an old cartoon.

His voice turned hard. "I said stop it."

She shifted her focus from Teresa to Darwin, releasing her hold on the Threads. Teresa lay still on the cold concrete floor.

"You have some fight in you, Darwin, but nothing to back it up." A Thread lashed out, barely missing Darwin as he redirected it into the wall beside him. The drywall split, covering him with a fine layer of white powder.

He coughed, clearing some of the dust from his throat. "It's me you want, not her. Let her go."

Rebecca responded. "Why? What do we gain by letting her go?"

"You get me!"

"We already have you." Blue Threads formed in the air around him, tying his arms to his sides. She turned to Darwin's mother. "Just kill her."

Threads appeared around Teresa again, forming the same net created earlier. This time, the color shifted to deep red, and he could feel the animosity used to create them. It radiated from his mother in waves.

Fear and anger—not for himself, but for Teresa—enveloped Darwin, and he drew on the emotons, finally getting a grasp on the Threads he'd been denied. He pushed back.

. . .

Darwin's blue Threads wrapped around Teresa, embedding into the floor to create a complete cocoon. She stirred and opened her eyes, trying to move. His Threads held her in place.

His mother's Threads wrapped his, and he could feel them pushing against his shield. He pushed back again, tasting the pain harnessed in her red Threads. He slowly expanded the cocoon. Somewhere in the back of his head, he could feel a slow pulsing.

"Quit playing with her, we have a war to win."

He felt more pressure, fighting against it. From the corner of his eye he saw a thin Thread form between his mother and the QPS, and with the feeling of a balloon popping, his Threads gave way. He wasn't strong enough. His mother smiled, pushing her net slowly in toward Teresa.

"No . . ." The sound that came from him was more of a whimper than a word.

The background pulsing turned into a steady beat, and he finally recognized what it was. It was the same pulse he had felt through his fingers when he had touched the QPS. It was a soft voice, calling out to him, reaching into his brain and caressing him. With it came the familiar touch he had lost twice—once when the accident happened and again just today.

Pain shot through his head, forming behind his right eye and temple, and the pulsing got stronger.

He opened his eyes and stared at Teresa and the red net. It lowered itself, creeping up to her, as though the world had suddenly slowed. The pulsing threatened to split the back of his skull open, and he groaned, falling sideways onto the floor. With Rebecca's Threads binding his arms, his head hit the concrete and stars swam in front of his eyes. He found himself lifting his head and lowering it again, banging it against the floor in time with the pulsing.

His mother's red Threads lowered some more.

Darwin lay his head on the floor, letting it rest, and opened himself to the pulsing completely, giving in to the siren's call of the QPS. The room filled with Threads, wrapping themselves around the people and equipment, spilling through the boundaries of the walls and expanding outward to the rest of the world. He let them flow through and around him, becoming part of who he was, before following them back to the QPS.

His head exploded in pain until he couldn't take anymore, but he couldn't pull back. His heart beat in sync with the QPS, each push of blood creating new Threads, new possibilities. New probabilities. His eyes closed, but the room remained in sharp focus, then the building, then the grounds around it, spreading himself thinner and thinner. He forced himself back into the QPS room, struggling to remember who he was and why he was here.

His mother's Threads had sunk into Teresa's clothes, hovering just above her skin. He could already see small tears appear on her arms as the Threads moved closer.

He whisked them away without a thought, replacing them again with the navy blue of protection, a shield so solid it barely let air through. Inside the blue, he worked with the soft white, and Teresa's wounds began to disappear. It barely occurred to him that he hadn't been taught how to do that.

Rebecca's face slowly changed from a look of determination to one of surprise or horror and then an anger so deeply rooted, it showed her as she truly was.

Thick bundles of crimson Threads formed around the disciples and Rebecca, moving toward where he lay. He glanced at them.

They were moving as though they were underwater, slowly forming and slithering nearer. He ignored them as he healed Teresa.

When he was done, the Threads had moved only a few feet closer. He nudged them aside, turning them into ordinary Threads of gray with barely a thought.

As one, the disciples reached for the QPS. Rebecca, standing further away, lunged for it, leaving his mother alone beside Teresa. His mother moved in the opposite direction, jumping closer to where he lay. The room threatened to split into multiple possibilities. He focused on only one, sharpening the image until all the others disappeared.

He laughed.

The disciple's fingers touched the QPS, and he felt a sudden drain. The pounding in his head weakened, and without thinking, he reached out for more. A thick trunk of Threads arced out of the QPS and into his brain. The world shattered into thousands of pieces.

From a distance, he heard Teresa scream, yet he knew she was still safe in the protective net he had thrown around her. Threads formed from the disciples and moved toward him. He couldn't See their color. Color no longer mattered. He tasted the hostility behind them, saw the death they contained, and pushed them from the room.

Rebecca's hand touched the QPS.

He halted the new Threads she created, holding them in place, feeling the anger and hate in them. And something else. Fear. He doubled her Threads' strength, then doubled it again. He did it one more time for good measure, felt them trembling against his hold.

And let them go.

The room filled with a chaotic mass of Threads whipping through the walls and equipment, through the people who stood around the machine, and he knew the destruction those Threads carried. A single thick fiber split the air, weaving toward the QPS. In it, he heard his mother's laugh, felt her hand on his arm, smelled the apple blossom and vanilla in her hair. The fiber touched the surface of the QPS and a complete sense of family and belonging soaked through his skin and into his bones.

The DNA his dad had planted into the source code of the machine, which had yanked Darwin from his world, strengthened. For a brief moment, he felt Ada's presence as if she were standing beside him. He could sense her shock, and the realization of what had just happened and who had done it. In return, he knew without a doubt where she was . . . in Salem. The connection broke.

In the space of a single heartbeat, the fiber split into hundreds of strands and leaped into the air, disappearing into tiny holes that led to other worlds. Each running QPS was linked, and each demanded a piece of the others.

Stillness cascaded around him, settling like a blanket over the room. The QPS continued to pulse in his head, and the thick bundle connecting him to it strobed in sync. Darwin didn't know how much time had passed before a soft whimpering pushed through and he opened his eyes.

Teresa lay on the floor where she had been thrown. She stared at Darwin, fear plain in her eyes, unable to move under his protective shield. Beside her lay the body of his mother. He struggled to his knees and crawled over to it.

What was left was almost unrecognizable. The soft features of his mother's face had been cut deeply by the Threads he had released. The rest of her body hadn't fared any better. He looked inside her for a pulse, a trace of life, and found nothing. He realized, without knowing how, that the QPS had taken her essence—the silver strand, her DNA—into itself, doubling its potential link to him. Making it more of what she had been than before.

Moving a strand of hair back behind her ear, something she had always done, he let out a soft moan.

"Darwin?"

He stirred from his memories.

"Darwin, she wasn't your mother."

He looked at Teresa. Some of the fear in her eyes had left, replaced by concern.

"Your mom died in a car accident. Remember, Darwin? This . . . this woman just looked like her. Would your mom have done what this woman did? Would she have tried to kill you? Would she have joined Rebecca and her hatred?"

He pushed himself to his feet. His slightest movement changed the pattern of the Threads. He shoved them away, trying to ignore them. It was impossible.

"I don't know."

"You do, Darwin. You know. Your mom loved you, Darwin. She cared for you. She would never have done any of . . ." She paused, looking around the room as best she could. "Any of *this*."

"I did this."

"You were defending yourself. You were protecting me."

The Threads pressed in on Darwin, pulsing with sound and light and pressure and taste and smell—the sense of his mother. He shook his head, trying to clear them away. A single thought took shape, his sister . . . this world's . . . He pushed the thought away. He hadn't seen her, hadn't sensed her in the room. She, at least, had been spared from his insanity.

"Darwin. Darwin!"

He focused back on Teresa.

"Darwin, let me go." She pushed against the blue mesh. It disappeared with less than a thought and she stood, staying a few paces away from him. "Let me help, Darwin."

He shook his head. "You can't. I've—I've *Seen* so much." He waved his hand around the room. "I've *done* so much." Tears rolled down his cheeks. The pulsing continued to push into his head. His tears fell on his mother's tortured body. He had killed her again.

"Please, Darwin, let me help."

"I don't think you can." He held his hands up to his ears, squeezing the sound, the pounding, from his head. He felt Teresa's warm touch.

"I'm here, Darwin. We're okay. Let's just go home."

Light exploded behind his eyes, and the QPS gave an audible hum.

"Darwin, let's go now."

He let his hands drop and took a step back from Teresa. "I can't. The QPS . . . it . . . it's calling me. It wants me for something. I—" The bundle of Threads thickened and he lurched closer to the QPS. He took two more steps and lay his hand on the cold machine.

Threads flooded into him. His body twitched, but his feet remained rooted to the floor. Threads, instead of leaving the room, rushed in from outside, weaving into his body with the rest. He went down to his knees, laying his forehead against the blue *QL* logo.

Somewhere in the Pacific, off the coast of Hawaii, a fisherman fell off his boat into the shark-infested waters.

In what was left of Russia, a gang hid behind a burnt-out shell of a building, waiting.

In Berlin, an old lady stepped onto the cracked concrete, carrying a bag of stale bread.

Thunder rolled down the mountains in New Zealand, loosening the mud and scree on their slopes.

A baby took its first breath, still covered in its mother's blood.

More images rushed in. Copies of what he had Seen, all with different outcomes. The worlds pushed themselves into Darwin's too-small frame. He vibrated with the energy and the knowledge.

A small Thread from the QPS found its way in. The heart of the machine, beating in time with Darwin's. Pounding out a steady staccato. He followed it back, watching as Threads formed in the beast's heart. This was the way to turn it off. With a sudden certainty, he knew why he was here. And yet, in that pulsing heart, he found his mother again.

This was how *it* wanted it all to end.

"Darwin!" Teresa screamed, piercing through the layers of Threads wrapping him.

He pulled his sight from the machine, just in time to See a red Thread shoot over the top of the QPS. It hit him dead center, cutting through the Threads swirling around him. He felt his skin split where it touched him and closed the wound, pulling the Thread deeper into his body, powerless and impotent. He raised himself to his feet, facing Teresa to make sure she was okay. He couldn't see her. Instead, his view was made up of the Threads. Through them, he saw what she was truly made of. She emanated empathy and love and concern. Concern for him, for what he was becoming, for what the machine had made of him. Love for him as well.

Though his Sight filled the room and beyond, he still knew that Rebecca stood behind him, on the far side of the QPS. He turned and faced her. The Threads where she stood were black and red, writhing in the air like an angry beast. As he watched, he could feel the QPS responding to her requests for more. More power, more control. More.

It responded the only way a machine could. It supplied what was requested. Deep inside it, he could feel a sense of revulsion. It echoed in and through him.

A mass of black and red separated from Rebecca and flew toward him. He watched as it approached, let it touch him, absorbed it into what the machine had made of him. All living creatures were good and bad. Some tipped the scales so far in one direction it was almost impossible to see anything else.

Rebecca had tipped the scales until there was no going back.

She threw more Threads his way, and he found himself laughing again, absorbing everything she gave him, balancing it back to his normal with what the world had to offer.

Her connection to the QPS faltered as she threw everything she had at him. He noticed and decided to give her what she wanted.

He grabbed hold of her connection and increased it. Her eyes flew open wide, revealing the whites around her irises. Her pupils dilated to pinpoints as her pipe to the QPS surged in size.

He allowed himself to follow her bundle of Threads. Entering her mind was as easy as reading a book. All he saw was anger and pain. He drove past her recent memories, drove past when the QPS came online. Drove past her defenses and saw who she had been.

A physicist with a master's degree at a mid-sized company, lonely and alone. Hoping that the work environment of a smaller firm would be less toxic than at the bigger places she'd interned. Some-place where her opinion mattered, where her contributions weren't just tossed aside as a fluke or the credit given to a male member of the team. Someone she had most likely had to handhold through the process just so they could meet the tight deadlines and heavy work-load. Years of being treated as less intelligent, less capable, just be-cause of her gender had built into an anger so deep it had become part of who she was.

And then the QPS came and changed her world.

Suddenly, instead of being one of the ignored working women of the world, she became one of the powerful. She'd tried to help, tried to ease those who couldn't See into the new world. And for a while, she believed she was succeeding. Believed she was making the world a better place.

Then it all crashed down.

Others came and tried to take her power, and when that failed, tried to take her life or to make her their property. To not give her her due. She wasn't going to take it anymore. She'd gained the strength and the knowledge to not only protect herself, but to fight back. To destroy those who tried to hurt her, to subjugate those who tried to control her.

And she'd enjoyed it.

Darwin began to withdraw. Embarrassment at the violation he had just been a part of raced through him, followed by disgust at what he had done. He hadn't meant to . . . he didn't know . . .

No person, no woman or man or child, deserved to be treated the way she had been. His intrusion without permission was her last straw. He watched as the Threads overpowered her mind, as insanity crept in from the edges, crushing what was left of her. He tried to help her fight it, tried to stop the collapse of who she was, but he didn't know how.

Her last action before she was gone, before he had left her mind, was to forgive him for what he had done, and to ask for forgiveness in return.

He gave her what she wanted without a moment's hesitation. The last part of Rebecca, the single Thread left of her before she disappeared, thanked him and felt remorse.

Darwin, fully back in his own mind, watched as Rebecca crumpled to the floor, drool running from her open mouth, her eyes glazed over in a madman's glare.

And he felt truly sorry. Society had helped make her, and she had forced that society to pay. Neither action was right, but he understood. In the end.

. . .

Darwin saw the hole before it began to form, following the beginning Threads back to the source. Mellisa. He could hear her spirit
in the Threads.

She was back at the house, trying to get through the maelstrom
of Threads created by the QPS. By him. He breathed, letting the
Threads tell him what was there, trying to push the noise of the
world farther into the background. He succeeded, slightly. Carlos
stood near her, watching her push herself to the limits trying to get
the hole open.

He helped her, reaching out to her and strengthening the
Threads. He felt her react, backing off from the creation, letting her
mind rest. The hole appeared in the QPS room, and Carlos stepped
through first.

He moved to the side, an automatic action after holing, and
stood stock-still. Darwin could See him probe the room, could See
him balk at the number of Threads coursing through it. He stopped
at Darwin, gaping open-mouthed at the connection to the QPS.

Mellisa followed, and he let the hole collapse behind her. She
became a mirror of Carlos, standing open-mouthed at the sight before her.

Carlos took a step toward him, and Darwin threw up a wall of
steel blue. The wall stopped Carlos short, and stopped half the
Threads from entering that part of the room. Carlos backed off and
grabbed Mellisa's hand.

Darwin felt Teresa move behind him, reading the eddies in the
Threads as though he was born with the ability. The QPS continued
to hammer at him, feeding more Threads down the conduit that
joined them. Information poured into him, past any defenses he
could throw in its way, and he crumpled to his knees.

In a place called Winnipeg, a farmer fell from his horse.

In Beijing, a small child slipped and tumbled into a rice paddy.

In Accra, a young man kissed the girl he loved for the first time.

Darwin clamped down on the Threads again. He could feel—could See—his brain fighting—and losing—to maintain control. Soon, he would be just like Rebecca. Soon.

A warm hand touched his arm, soft white Threads wrapping them in a snug blanket.

"Let me help."

Darwin struggled to speak. "You can't help. I can't stop it."

"You—*we* have to try."

"I can't!" Tears pushed through his defenses as he felt himself losing control. "I. Can't. Control. It." He panted as he struggled. His heart picked up its pace, pushing the QPS to stay in sync.

The fisherman grabbed at a rope trailing over the edge of his boat and pulled himself back on board.

An old lady carrying groceries went home with fresh vegetables and meat.

Two teens hunting in the mountains ran to safety, narrowly missed by rocks and mud.

A mother held her newborn daughter to her chest, crying with the pain of pure love.

He helped it all happen.

He turned to Carlos, his voice barely above a whisper in the quiet room. "Get her out."

Carlos nodded.

"I'm not leaving you."

Darwin stood, leaning against the QPS for support, and turned back to her. There were tears in her eyes, running down her cheeks. He wanted to take her pain away, wanted to erase himself from her memories. But he couldn't enter another person's mind again. Not without permission. Not Teresa. Not anyone.

A skittering horse kicked a rock with its hoof, just before the man's head landed in the same spot.

A passerby rescued a small child from near drowning.

A kiss was returned.

Hands grabbed at his shirt, pulling him roughly away from the QPS. "You can't let this happen."

"I can't stop it." He wasn't sure if he had said it, or just thought it.

"Fight it, damn you. I'm not going to lose you. Not again." Her voice had risen to a scream.

"Teresa?"

"I'm here, Darwin. I'm here. Come back to me."

"I . . . I . . ."

The bundle of Threads connecting him to the QPS collapsed, and with it, Darwin.

The Threads. They surrounded him, embraced him, held him with the strength of a mother's grip, squeezed him with the force of the entire universe, caressed him with the touch of a lover, then let him go. Darwin opened his eyes and looked into Teresa's. Had he ever noticed how the deep brown was flecked with gold? He reached up a hand and wiped away her tears. It only made her cry more.

She helped him back to his feet, and he rested his hand on the QPS. It pulsed under his fingers, still beating in time with his heart, but it wasn't pounding into his brain like before. Through the contact, he smelled apple blossom and vanilla. He pushed himself upright, opening his Sight. The room filled with Threads, more than he had ever Seen. But they were simply . . . there. He could follow them, he could manipulate them, but they didn't pull at him like they had before.

The Threads had tried to turn his brain into mush, tried to conquer him with too much power, and then stopped.

His heart beat once.

He pushed his Sight farther, expanding to the building, the perimeter, past the collapsing mesh, farther out to the house, to the city limits. He observed but wasn't bombarded with each Thread calling out to him. He had control.

His heart beat again.

He dropped the wall holding back Carlos and Mellisa at the same time he destroyed what was left of the perimeter mesh. Two forces clashed outside and he clamped down on their Threads, leaving them to fight it out with their fists. He found the memories of the Skends in the group, followed the Threads that created them and reversed the process.

Another beat.

Mellisa rushed around the QPS, giving it a wide distance. She pulled Teresa and Darwin farther away, back to the empty window frame, and looked at them.

He could see the concern in her eyes. With barely a thought, he probed the Threads around her and read the hope and despair. He stopped before going further. He would never do that again.

"Are you okay?" Mellisa asked. Darwin simply nodded, still not sure if he wanted to speak. There was so much to say.

Instead, he looked at Carlos. The words came to him then. "I'm sorry." It ended up being all he had.

Carlos moved closer and pulled him into a tight hug. "You scared the hell out of us."

I still might, Darwin thought.

Teresa grabbed his hand in hers, squeezing tightly, refusing to let go when he pulled back. He smiled and tugged again, slipping from her grip with gentle help from the Threads. No one seemed to notice. He looked past the QPS, at the empty area behind it, and started to create two holes at the same time. The one on the right was different. He'd Seen it only once before, a crisp lemony yellow that was almost blinding to look at, not knowing what it was. Not remembering . . . until now.

Carlos whistled and muttered to Mellisa. "Wow."

When he was done, he turned back to his friends. "The one on the left will take you back to the house. The one on the right goes back to my home."

"I can't even See what you did," said Carlos. "The complexity of maintaining two holes, one of them stretching across the universes. I . . ."

Darwin moved to the left hole and waited for Carlos and Mellisa. He stopped them before they stepped through. "I have one more thing." He closed his eyes and reached for the QPS. Carlos gasped and grabbed his shoulder. Darwin shrugged him off.

The QPS pulsed out Threads, still in time with Darwin's heartbeat. He reached in, following the Threads to their source. The heart of the machine. He pulled Threads with him, enclosing the heart in a tight blue mesh. He weaved Threads through the mesh, pushing them inside the heart. Then he turned them black, granting the machine its wish. Giving it what it could not give itself.

A final Thread pulsed out of the QPS. Pure gold in color, bright beyond imagination. The Thread entered Darwin and he felt his mother's touch. The QPS had given him a gift. Its final breath. He didn't know what it was.

When Darwin pulled out of the machine, he saw the room had dimmed. The continuous blue light from the *QL* logo was out, and the system lay quiet in the darkened room. Threads still moved around, the holes he had created still held their form, but the QPS was dead. No more power would come from it.

Carlos had his arm around Mellisa, pulling her tightly to him. "Is that it, then?"

He shrugged. "I don't know. The Threads may have needed the QPS running to stay, to give us the ability to See them. Or maybe we'll always have the ability, the QPS just won't be pumping any new Threads out. I wish I could say."

"Is this what Enton wanted?" Carlos asked.

He shrugged again. "It's what the QPS wanted. Go home. Wait, watch. Live. Things may change, or they may stay the same. All I know is without the QPS, there will never be another Qabal."

Mellisa pulled away from Carlos and gave Darwin a quick hug. She grabbed Carlos's hand and stepped into the hole.

He heard footsteps behind him. Teresa's arms wrapped around his waist and she pressed herself into his back. He hugged her arms and whispered, "I could stay. Or . . . or you could come with me."

"I want to, so much. To have you stay, or to join you. But I don't think that's possible."

He twisted in her grip, facing her. "Everything is possible. I can See that, now. I love you, Teresa. I can't leave you."

Teresa pulled from his hug and held his face in her hands, examining it. "What about your dad? The whole time we've been together, that has been your goal. It's what kept you going, through the good times and the bad."

"I know, but that was before I knew . . . before I understood how I felt about you."

She stood on the tips of her toes and leaned forward.

Her lips were warm. Her mouth opened and her tongue caressed his lips. Heat rushed through his body, and he followed her example.

"I love you too, Darwin Lloyd."

He could see the tears forming in her eyes.

"But you need to go home," she whispered. "You need to shut down your QPS. My place—my family—is here, and yours is there." She stepped back, her hands on his chest. She pushed as hard as she could, the tears tumbling down her cheeks.

Darwin tripped, falling over his own feet. Before he could regain his balance, he slipped into the hole. His last view was of Teresa, her back turned to him, shoulders shaking.

The cold gripped his insides, freezing his eyelids, slowing the blood in his veins. He popped out the other side and watched the hole disappear.

THE MEASURE OF A MAN

"**D**ARWIN? DARWIN. COME on, wake up."

He felt a light slap on his cheek, followed by another one. He opened his eyes to the bright cold flicker of fluorescent tubes.

"He's coming around. You, bring me the first aid kit." The blurry shape of a blue anti-static smock swung into his view. "I'll bandage the cut on his head."

He blinked slowly, willing the noise to stop, just for a second. He felt the Threads respond, though they were slow and sluggish. He stopped them before they listened to his wishes.

Someone slapped him again. This one stung and he jerked away. "Come on, Darwin. Stay awake. Stay focused."

"Where . . . Dad?"

"Your father's pretty busy. He'll come and see you when things are—"

"Dad!" He pushed off the back wall, ignoring the throbbing in his head. He reached behind him, yanking on the window frame, and got to his feet. Shattered glass shook from his clothing as he rose. The woman beside him tucked herself under his shoulder and pulled his hand off the broken glass still stuck in the frame, sinking a little as his weight transferred to her. He didn't even notice the pain of the fresh cut on his palm.

His dad stood at a desk only a few feet away, hunched over a control panel beside Garth. The schematics from his office lay scattered over the surface. He ignored Darwin's call.

"Come on, sit here." The woman led him to a chair near the door. "Let's get a bandage on your head and hand, then I'll get your father, okay?" She didn't wait for an answer. "Now, sit."

Looking around the lab, he saw people huddled around computers. A few of them just stared at the overhead monitors, slowly shaking their heads. All of them seemed to be talking at once, and the air felt thick with tension. Two people lay on the floor, fellow workers helping them to their feet or tucking lab coats and sweaters under their heads. He didn't see any major injuries, but most of them looked groggy and out of it.

He was back home at the exact same time he had left. He hadn't Seen any green in the hole.

He leaned back in the chair as the woman worked, watching the Threads move around the room. Over her shoulder, he could barely see the top of the QPS. The Threads coming out of it were fresh, young. He pulled at them, and they responded again.

When the woman had finished patching him up, she did as she had promised, and pulled his dad over. Darwin didn't know what she said to him, but he dropped everything he was doing and jogged to where Darwin sat.

Darwin stood, faltering on shaky legs and almost falling, to meet his dad halfway. He wrapped him in a hug, gripping so tight his dad had to pull away.

"Slow down there, buddy. You're okay." His dad grabbed his shoulders and pushed him an arm's length away. He looked at Darwin, his gaze lingering on the bandage. "Come on, let's get you sitting down again. I'd never forgive myself if something happened to you."

If that was true, then why was he by the computers when Darwin came to? Darwin shook his head. That wasn't him talking, it was what was left of Rebecca's attack. It would take time to get rid of the remnants of that.

"What happened?" Darwin asked.

His dad sighed. "We're not sure. We went to a hundred percent and people started falling, you included. You hit your head on the window ledge. Are you feeling all right? Dizzy? Sick?"

"No. I'm fine. It was just a little bang." He paused, taking a deep breath before continuing. "You need to shut it down."

"I know. We're trying. It seems to have a mind of its own, though. Nothing we're doing is working."

"I can do it."

His dad scoffed. "I know you worked on almost every part of the project, but we have some of the best minds, the actual developers, working on it, and they've been unsuccessful. What do you know about shutting it off when it's gone rogue?"

"I've done it before." Darwin reached for the QPS, trying to create a Thread that would carry him into the heart of the machine. The Threads were still too weak, too scattered to be of much use. He'd have to touch the QPS.

He left his dad and walked to the door. It was closed and locked when he tried to turn the knob. Returning back to the window, he scraped glass from the empty frame using a keyboard lying on the floor, put his hands on the frame, and jumped through the opening.

"No! Darwin, wait!"

Walking over to the QPS, he placed his hands on top of the blue logo. The machine's pulse pumped through his fingers. It was different than the other QPS, but somehow the same. It felt young. New. Fresh. He felt his mother touch his cheek. He pushed Threads into the machine, reaching for its core. The heart lay open. Smaller than he had Seen before, but the pattern of its death was the same. What was missing was the will to die.

When he pumped the black Threads into its heart, and the blue glow died from its logo, a cheer rose from behind him. Silently, he tried to create a hole back to Teresa, using every Thread he could find, pulling them into him and spinning them back out. A hole tried to form, but the Threads dispersed before he could finish. There was no going back.

Exhausted, he slumped against the QPS. Teresa was gone forever. There just wasn't enough power in this world to recreate the hole.

When the noise behind him started to quiet, he turned. His dad stood in the now open doorway, staring at the cold QPS.

"What did you . . . *How* did you . . .?"

Darwin smiled. "Later, Dad. Let's just go home."

His dad looked around. "I can't. I need to figure out—"

Darwin strode up to his dad and grabbed him by the shoulder. "Dad!"

His dad refocused on Darwin. "I . . ."

"Dad, let's go home." He pulled his dad from the lab. Rebecca stood near the door, a glazed look to her eyes. Darwin nodded at her as they passed. "You really should trust Rebecca's work, Dad. She knows her stuff." All he got in return was a puzzled look.

At home, Darwin made a small dinner for both of them. As they sat down, he leaned forward.

"Dad, there's some things I need to tell you."

He started with the Qabal, how they'd used the power of the QPS for their own purposes, how they corrupted it to become stronger. He didn't mention Rebecca, there was no point. He talked about SafeHaven, about the Skends, and about Teresa. He didn't get into all the details, but by his dad's response, he knew. When he talked about the final battle, he left out how he'd violated Rebecca by entering her mind. The shame of it still washed through him.

He didn't—couldn't—mention his mother. What he had done was something he could never talk about, but it was something he would have to live with for the rest of his life. It was something he'd learned to do once before.

The gold Thread the other QPS had given him remained a secret as well.

As the hours had passed, it dawned on him how he'd gotten to the other world in the first place. It wasn't any connection between the machines.

It was his mother's DNA.

"The DNA sequence I saw in your office, that was in the QPS, wasn't it?" he asked.

His dad nodded. "Your mother had some tests done when she was pregnant with you. We kept a copy of those records."

"You hoped the QPS would link multiple universes, didn't you? You used Mom's DNA to try to target it, try to get it to create a hole to a universe with Mom in it."

Another nod.

"Then you believe me?"

His dad didn't answer the question. "Did . . . did you see her?"

Darwin just nodded his head. "She was different. She wasn't Mom. She looked like her, but it wasn't her."

His dad had questions, more than Darwin could handle all at once. It was past midnight before they were done. He crawled into his own bed, crying himself to sleep, a gaping wound where his heart used to be, and dreamed of Teresa.

For the first time in months, Darwin woke in his own bed, in his own house, in his own world. The grass was still green outside, and winter had not yet dropped its first layer of snow. He wasn't quite sure how he'd managed to travel back to the same point in time that he'd left. He hadn't Seen a time component in the hole he'd created, hadn't even known it was possible. Maybe that was the problem.

Memories of Teresa threatened to overwhelm him again, and he fought to push them aside, to forget her kiss, the way she'd pushed him into the hole and turned her back on him.

He felt his dad move in the kitchen downstairs, and with that thought came the realization that the only reason he knew was because the Threads had told him. But the QPS hadn't been running long enough to create the quantity of Threads needed for monitoring.

He lay his head back on the pillow and closed his eyes, opening himself to the Threads the same way he had on Teresa's world. The room shimmered with life. But how? He expanded his sight to the rest of the house and saw more Threads, saw his dad moving from the stove to the fridge.

The Threads stopped just outside the walls of the house, hugging the structure as though held there by an invisible hand. Further out, there was nothing. If any of the Threads the QPS had created still existed, they had either dispersed themselves around the world, or . . . or followed him back to his house.

As soon as the thought formed, he knew it was wrong. It *felt* wrong. He had learned to trust many things while he was gone, and one of those was his feelings.

If only he had done that with Teresa.

He pulled back into the house and followed the Threads backward, ending up in his bedroom. Of course he'd be there, he was the one monitoring everything. But again, it felt wrong. Where—

The QPS, back in the room with Teresa and Carlos and Mellisa, just before he'd—for lack of a better word—killed it. The machine had sent a gold Thread into him. What if the gift had been the Source itself, what if *he* was generating the Threads?

He leaped out of bed, the Threads responding to his touch, and ran to his bathroom. The mirror showed what it always had, a young man who was unsure of his place in the world, though he thought he might have seen a flicker of inner strength that hadn't been there before. In the past, he'd always stopped there, too scared or too hurt to look any deeper. New was the white scar on the back of his wrist and one just below his ribs.

Today, this morning, he went deeper. And what he saw scared him more than Rebecca had, more than the Skends had. More than the rage and hatred on his mother's face had. Today, he saw what the gift had made of him.

He stumbled back into the shower, tripping over the threshold and sliding down the wall. He looked in deeper and felt the pulse of the power given to him, matching his racing heart. He smelled apple blossom and vanilla.

This wasn't a gift; it was a curse.

He didn't know how long he sat on the shower floor, lost in a misery he couldn't even share. No one would believe him. Maybe his dad, but look what he had already done trying to get his wife back from the dead. What else would he do when he found out his son was a walking QPS? Where would he stop? Even thinking those thoughts about his dad scared him. His mind would never have gone there before all this happened, before he saw what people could become given the right circumstances.

Walking back to his bed, he made a choice the machine couldn't, despite its near sentience in wanting it all to end. He chose to not create the Threads, to not become what the QPS had—a thing to be coveted, hoarded by a few to give them more power.

He reached in and created his last Threads, wrapping the source inside him in a prison of blue, and went downstairs to have breakfast with his dad.

ACKNOWLEDGMENTS

This one was a long time in the making. I think if I look back at the very first draft, I'd find it was about eight years ago the germ of this story formed into a rough draft of 75,000 words or so. Even then, when I was still unpublished, I knew I had something in those words. Over the intervening time, it's been through multiple revisions and several sets of eyes. Between then and now, a few other books have been written and published. I'll do my best to remember everyone, but some days I forget what I had for breakfast.

I wrote the first drafts of this using Google Maps to get the feel of certain locations. Later, I attended When Words Collide—a great writer's convention in Calgary, Alberta, Canada—followed by World-Con in San Jose. I took that opportunity to drive through the majority of the West Coast of the United States to visit some of the locations in person. Gaston, Oregon is a beautiful small town. I ended up there later in the evening, and slept in my Jeep beside a small sports field. The sprinklers going off in the morning woke me up. When I reached Salem, I parked and walked parts of the same route Darwin and Teresa did, getting the feel of where Rob saw them, and where the camp was set up. Alpine, California was the complete opposite of the lush green around Gaston, and visiting there really helped me figure out how SafeHaven would operate. The border crossing from Oregon into California is a real place, pirates and all. Those pirates got some comments from my editor, but I managed to keep them. I wish I could travel for every book.

I'll start with my beta readers, as is usual. These are the fine folk that catch the stupid mistakes that creep in and gleefully point them out while laughing (with me, or so I've been told). They also catch the subtle little things that a writer no longer sees after working on a book for a long time. Some only see typos or the odd character getting a sudden name change. All of them are helpful in their own way, and so greatly appreciated: Evan Braun, Sherry Peters, Bev Geddes, and Julie Czerneda were the only ones that saw those early meanderings. Sharon Bass, Marnie Kacher, Bev, and Sherry looked at some of the later iterations.

The cover artwork was done by the Penguin Random House in-house art department, and the starting point they gave me to look at was absolutely stunning. The final product you see on this book is so close to that original art. Thank you so much!

There are so many great people at DAW that have their finger-prints all over this final product. Sheila Gilbert, my wonderful (two-time Hugo Award-winning) editor. I always look forward to our editing phone calls with joy and a little trepidation. Her insight is a wonder to behold, and always makes me look like a better writer than I really am. Joshua Starr makes sure everything is on schedule and is my interface to the copy editor and production staff. I'll tell you, this guy knows how to keep things going. I don't get to know who my copy editor is on any book or series . . . although I've never tried asking either. To the wonderful soul who copy edited this book, thank you so much! Being Canadian, I sometimes get things wrong when setting things in the US, and (among many other things) they caught all of those mistakes and assumptions. And to all the others I only see at conventions or via infrequent emails . . . thanks for all you do!

Even further behind the scenes, but no less important, is the work my agents do. Sara Megibow of KT Literary handles the book side of the business, and without her, I'd be lost in the world that is publishing. Jerry Kalajian at IPG deals with the even more convoluted world of Hollywood. Thank you both for all you do.

I did a reading of a very small section of *Threader Origins* in 2019 at Minicon in Minneapolis, and I'd like to throw out a huge thank you to everyone who attended, and then got mad at me when I told them the book wouldn't be out until 2021. Well, here it is. I hope the rest of the book holds up to what you heard that day.

I'll finish where everything starts, with my family. You helped me with this book every day, whether you realized it or not. I am, and will be, forever grateful to have you in my life.

Gerald
2020-04-30